1174

Leaving
Van Gogh

Leaving Van Gogh

A NOVEL

∞

CAROL WALLACE

SPIEGEL & GRAU

NEW YORK

2011

Leaving Van Gogh is a work of historical fiction. Apart from the well-known actual people, events, and locales that figure in the narrative, all names, characters, places, and incidents are the products of the author's imagination or are used fictitiously. Any resemblance to current events or locales, or to living persons, is entirely coincidental.

Copyright © 2011 by Carol Wallace

Published in the United States by Spiegel & Grau, an imprint of The Random House Publishing Group, a division of Random House, Inc., New York.

SPIEGEL & GRAU and Design is a registered trademark of Random House, Inc.

Library of Congress Cataloging-in-Publication Data
Wallace, Carol
Leaving Van Gogh: a novel/Carol Wallace.
p. cm.
ISBN 978-1-4000-6879-1
eBook ISBN 978-1-58836-943-7
1. Gachet, Paul-Ferdinand, 1828–1909—Fiction. 2. Gogh, Vincent van, 1853–1890—
Last years—Fiction. 3. Gogh, Vincent van, 1853–1890—Mental health—Fiction.
4. Gogh, Vincent van, 1853–1890—Relations with physicians—Fiction.
5. Psychological fiction. I. Title.
PS3573.A42563L43 2011
813'.54—dc22   2010015082

Printed in the United States of America on acid-free paper

www.spiegelandgrau.com

2 4 6 8 9 7 5 3 1

First Edition

Book design by Caroline Cunningham

For Rick, as always

It is my constant hope that I am not working

for myself alone.

—VINCENT VAN GOGH TO THEO VAN GOGH, MARCH 1888

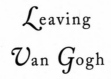

Leaving
Van Gogh

$\mathcal{P}$rologue

1905

∞

I HELD VINCENT'S SKULL in my hands yesterday. It was a strange and melancholy moment. As I examined the yellowed cranium, my imagination clothed it with flesh; I could see the strong ridge over his eyebrows and the steep ledges of his cheekbones, which were the foundations of his face.

The doctor in me could not help looking for something else as well. Phrenology is out of fashion now, but I am an old man. When I began my medical training, there were doctors who believed the shape of a skull betrayed or predicted a man's mental state. What should this skull have told me then? Should I have detected from it that Vincent was mad? Or that he was a genius? Perhaps that he was both?

I had been hoping . . . Well, it was foolish. I suppose I had been hoping that Vincent would speak to me again. Nonsense, of course. I did not really imagine that a voice would issue from between his few, ruined teeth, but I thought the sight of his skull might prompt a new memory, something I had forgotten—a phrase, a glance, a gesture that would provide me with new insight into his mental predicament.

Of course I could not wait as long as I would have liked for some ghostly trace. We were reinterring the man. It was no time for investigation.

The ceremony was moving but peculiar. At nearly eighty, I often feel that I have done everything in life, but until yesterday I had never reburied anyone. We would not have had to disturb Vincent's grave if there had been an empty plot alongside it for Theo's remains. Now, in a new plot, the modest headstones rise side by side, each engraved plainly with one of the brothers' names. Theo's body still lies in Utrecht, but his widow promises to bring it to Auvers when she can, because she feels their fraternal bond should be honored, even in death. Not many widows—certainly not those who had remarried, as Madame van Gogh Grosschalk did—are so self-effacing. I am certain, though, that she is right.

The new grave site is better. It lies on the north side of the cemetery, against the wall. Vincent would have liked this spot, surrounded as it is by the wheat fields he painted with such bravura and devotion. I transplanted some sunflowers from his first grave; they gave poor Theo pleasure and consolation back then. I am glad to think that something I did might have been a source of comfort to that poor man.

We all waited until the gravedigger had shoveled the last handful of earth onto the coffin. It was a warm afternoon; not as hot as that searing July day fifteen years ago when we last buried Vincent, but hot enough for the gravedigger's task to seem interminable. Yet we stood there, Van Gogh's survivors if you like, watching the casket vanish beneath the crumbly soil and thinking about him. He told his brother that I was sicker than he, yet there he is, a pile of bones, and here I am, still trying to grasp what he was to me and I to him.

I have known many artists. Vincent was something different. Everyone who knew him well understood this, so I have not been surprised at Theo's wife's unremitting efforts to foster his reputation. Of course she does so because she possesses most of his paintings. That is natural. But she must also feel, as I do, that her life was briefly illuminated by the presence of a remarkable person. I have children, but I will have no grandchildren. Marguerite is most emphatically an old maid, and Paul is no family man. If anyone knows my name a hundred years from now, it will be in connection with Vincent van Gogh. His portrait may make me immortal. If it does, I will also be known as the doctor who let him die. Vincent wrote once in a letter that a man who commits suicide turns his friends into murderers. What does that make me?

Many rumors have grown up about his death. So much could not be explained: where the gun had come from, where the gun vanished to, why he shot himself so clumsily. It has been said that the gun was for shooting crows, and that Vincent had borrowed it from Ravoux. It was a rifle, some said, or it was a shotgun, and he tripped over it while trying to shoot rabbits. There is even a tale—rather more durable than the rabbit nonsense—that Vincent was murdered. He was killed, it is said, by the farmer whose wife he had painted. Some say they had been caught together beneath a haystack. The Parisian version (for some of these stories had even reached as far as the city) mentions an unnamed painter whom Vincent had insulted in a brothel. I don't imagine anyone believed that for very long.

I never respond to the gossip, of course. Why should I tell what I know? It was a secret I shared with Vincent alone. And he took it to the grave.

One

When Theo van Gogh first approached me about caring for his brother, I was in my sixties and I had been practicing medicine for thirty-one years. I was well established. My patients were a varied group, but for years I had specialized in diseases of the nerves and mental maladies. A handful of other men in Paris had similar qualifications, but it was my connection to the art world that brought Theo van Gogh to me in the spring of 1890. In fact, it was Camille Pissarro who sent him.

As a boy in Lille, I had studied painting, and through those lessons I came to know Amand Gautier. He was a little younger than I and significantly more talented, so it was no surprise to me that he was accepted to the École des Beaux-Arts in Paris. I had already spent two years at the Faculté de Médecine when he arrived in Paris in 1852, and my life was much livelier from that day. Gautier was an open, affable man, handsome and eager to make friends. What's more, his fellow painting students were far more entertaining than my fellow medical students. I cared deeply about medical problems, but what I wanted to talk about was art, so I often went with Gautier to the artists' cafés. And thus over the years I came to know them all—Courbet and Manet, Pissarro and Cézanne, Monet and Renoir, Sisley and Guillaumin.

In 1855 I was accepted as an extern under Dr. Jean-Pierre Falret at what was officially called the Hospice de la Vieillesse-Femmes at the Salpêtrière. Most of the patients were elderly, as the institution's name would suggest, but Falret was famous for his innovative treatment of women of all ages who had lost their minds. My wife, Blanche, used to tease me, in the gentlest possible way, that the first women I ever knew were mad, pretending that this was why I found her so delightful. She may have been right. When we finally met, in 1868, I had known plenty of sane ladies, but none seemed to see the world in such a clear light as the woman who became my wife. I always relied on her generous but sensible perception of people and their emotions. It is precisely those points that the mad get wrong. You could even say that the definition of madness is a flawed understanding of the world around you. By that standard, Blanche was the sanest person I ever knew. Perhaps my years working in the asylum had made me especially grateful for her soundness.

Despite its reputation for modernity, the Salpêtrière, which had been built largely in the seventeenth century, looked like an old provincial town. The entire hospital was surrounded by a wall and formally laid out around the domed chapel. Parts of the grounds were beautiful: there were old trees, long, symmetrical walkways, and buildings constructed from the golden stone typical of Paris. But its history came with drawbacks. A warehouse for saltpeter, erected on a damp and isolated tract of riverbank, cannot easily be transformed into a rational, modern hospital building. Nor, when many of its patients are mentally fragile, can it be helpful that one of its most prominent wards is housed in what was once known as La Force, France's most notorious women's prison. Fear and grief still lingered in those walls.

Only sixty years before I arrived, the great Dr. Philippe Pinel had released the patients from their chains. This was a revolutionary action,

for until that point the mad had been thought to be possessed by malev-
olent spirits. They could not be treated, it was supposed, but must be restrained. Pinel and others believed that madness was rather a kind of
alienation from the true self (which is why we used to refer to the mentally ill as *"aliénés"*). The new "moral treatment," by appealing to what
was left of the patients' reason, could bring them back to themselves. As
a young doctor, I found Dr. Pinel's theories thrilling. The merciful and
humane attempt to guide a mad person back to his or her senses is not
a simple task, and it is not always successful. Even now, in a new century, we do not know what keeps some of us tethered to reality while
others go astray. We still do not know exactly how to diagnose the various forms of madness, and we certainly do not know how to cure them.
This I have learned to my cost. But in those days, I still believed we
could. I thought that kindness and regular hours, good, plain meals,
fresh air, and moderate distraction—even work for the most capable—
could relieve the mad.

Once I finished my medical training, I began to build an indepen-
dent practice. I am not a man for committees and meetings. I could
never have run a division of a hospital the way Falret did. Instead I
worked in the city's clinics, offered free consultations to the poor, and
served as the medical officer of a spa for a few summers. I was even, for
a spell, the doctor for a comic theater, soothing sore throats and wrapping twisted ankles so that actors could go back onstage. It was a hand-
to-mouth existence, but I was a rich man compared to my artist friends.
At least everyone recognizes the need for doctors.

Those were the days, in the 1850s and '60s, when academic art was
slowly giving way to something more individual. Courbet and Cézanne
and their friends painted not flattering, fashionable portraits or gigan-
tic mythology paintings but rather their own responses to the life that
we all lived. These revolutionary canvases were not well received at first,
so my friends were often in desperate straits. I owe several of my loveliest paintings to the fact that I helped them from time to time. I loaned
Monet money, I took care of one of Renoir's favorite models. They gave
me canvases as payment. It was a satisfactory arrangement for everyone.

Though Cézanne and I became quite friendly, it was Camille Pissarro I knew best. At times he could barely feed his wife and their children. Of course I helped when the little ones became ill, when Madame Pissarro grew exhausted, when the painter's eyes began giving him trouble. When he was living north of Paris, in Pontoise, and I bought a house for my family in the neighboring village of Auvers, we saw each other a great deal. Once Cézanne, Pissarro, and I made etchings together, using the little press I had in my attic studio. Pissarro, too, gave me paintings in exchange for medical care.

Over the years, some of these attachments faded, as the bonds of young men do. Cézanne moved to the South and rarely visited Paris. Gautier and I had a falling-out over money he owed me, Monet became rich and grand, and Pissarro bought a house south of Paris where he could live cheaply. Or perhaps it was my own fault—it was true that after Blanche died I became somewhat withdrawn. Yet I kept up with the art world through the 1870s and '80s. I went to the Salons and other exhibitions, I visited dealers, I read the art criticism in the newspapers. I knew from Pissarro that his dealer was a Dutchman named Theo van Gogh, who worked for Boussod and Valadon. I had occasionally visited their premises on Boulevard Montmartre, but most of what I saw there was dull and conventional. Yet Pissarro claimed that this Van Gogh worked hard for him, trying to sell his beautiful landscapes. Over the years I had heard snippets of gossip about Theo van Gogh's painter brother. He had lived with Theo for a year or two in Paris in the late 1880s, but our paths did not cross and I had no clear idea of what his pictures looked like.

In his letter proposing that I meet Theo van Gogh, Pissarro explained further. Apparently this brother, Vincent, had a history of mental troubles. He had spent a year in an asylum in Provence, having committed himself voluntarily. He felt that he was better now, but that the company of his fellow patients was hindering any further progress. He wanted to come north to be near Theo, but he did not want to live in Paris. The city, he felt, would be too busy, too jarring to his nervous state. He also felt it important that he be under the care of a doctor. At first Theo van Gogh had hoped that his brother could board with the Pissarro family, but Madame Pissarro did not care to receive a recovering mental patient into a home full of small children.

Pissarro then thought of me, his former neighbor. I practiced medicine in Paris, seeing patients four days a week. On Sunday, Monday, and Tuesday, I was a rural family man in Auvers, where Pissarro thought Vincent could find inexpensive lodgings and paint in the country. I had a great deal of experience with nervous ailments, I knew painters, and voilà—I was the solution to Theo van Gogh's difficulty. I replied to Pissarro, saying that I would be happy to meet with Theo.

But I heard no more from Pissarro for several months. I had put the matter out of my mind when, one day in March of 1890, an extremely courteous young man arrived at my Paris premises on the rue du Faubourg St. Denis, a busy street between the Gare de l'Est and the Gare du Nord. My consulting room was dark and formal, with tobacco-colored velvet curtains and many framed prints on the wall. I had long since grown accustomed to the noise from the street—carriages, wagons, hawkers, even the omnibus—but new patients were sometimes distracted by it.

At first I thought this was the case with my new visitor, Theo van Gogh. He was well dressed and well groomed, in a frock coat and silk hat, a conventional bourgeois like thousands of others you would pass in the street. He was no taller than I, and pale-skinned, with short russet hair and a sandy mustache. He spoke flawless but faintly accented French and exhibited the highly attentive air of a man who sold things for a living. Yet he seemed to lose the thread of his tale from time to time. Now, as I think back, I realize that he may simply have been selecting what to tell me—and what, strategically, to leave out.

Vincent, Theo told me, was his elder brother by four years, not the firstborn but the first surviving son of a Protestant pastor in the Netherlands. Several uncles of the family were art dealers like Theo, and Vincent himself had originally worked in the Hague branch of Goupil, a gallery with Parisian roots. It was a kind of apprenticeship, I gathered. He did well, Theo said, and was transferred to another branch.

"And did he always demonstrate interest in painting?" I asked. "Painting, for himself?" I had been sitting near Theo in an armchair, but now I stood and moved to my desk. I began taking notes as Theo spoke.

"Not until about ten years ago, when he was twenty-seven," Theo answered. "He had made a few drawings at home, but that was all."

"Was he gifted?" I asked.

Theo hesitated. He was evidently torn between honesty and affection. He shrugged slightly, indicating to me that Vincent's talent had not been visibly overwhelming but that Theo's fraternal loyalty forbade him to say so.

Vincent's career as an art dealer came to an end when the young man took it into his head to be a teacher instead, but after a brief spell at a small boarding school in England, he abandoned that career. "He decided to become a minister," Theo said. "Mind, I am telling you everything. It would be very painful for him to talk about these things, but you should know them. Earlier there had been a situation with a young woman, a cousin of ours. Vincent . . ." He fell silent again, eyes on a rather gloomy etching of a Dutch landscape. Apparently there was no way to tell the tale that reflected well on his brother. "Vincent could not believe she did not have feelings for him. He, his fervor—it alarmed her. Then there was another young woman in England, and another unhappy outcome. So, the church."

"Like his father. A familiar way of life, perhaps," I suggested, trying to make the decision seem rational.

But Theo could not quite accept my reasoning. "Yes and no. He went to the Borinage as a missionary to the coal miners. I don't know if you know anything about that part of the country—perhaps you've read Zola's *Germinal*?" I nodded, recalling the bleak account of unremitting labor, poverty, and violence. "Zola spares nothing. It is as he portrays it, a terribly harsh way of life. Vincent became ill. He gave away all of his food, all of his furniture."

I thought of the women at the Salpêtrière. The wards had been full of monomaniacs, patients fixed on one dominating fantasy. Many of them refused food for one reason or another. "Yes. I see," I said. "Did he know who he was? Was he emulating Christ? Or did he believe he *was* Christ?" Such a delusion was common among the mad.

"He knew at all times who he was," Theo answered. "He had by then lost his faith. I brought him to our parents' house to recover. That was when he decided to be an artist." There was another pause. "You must understand, Dr. Gachet, that Vincent's goal is to help people. He thinks that somehow, with his art, he can express important truths about the nature of life. He believes that it is his absolute duty to do so. At any cost."

We were silent for a moment. Theo's last words seemed to echo in the suddenly hushed room. One had to wonder, then: was it the art itself that had attracted Van Gogh? Or was it the chance for self-sacrifice? Monomaniacs are capable of harming themselves in the most preposterous ways. When you question them, however, their thinking— you could not call it reasoning—has a certain coherence. Apparently this Vincent saw himself as some kind of savior. Theo did not appear to grasp how grandiose the delusion was.

"And why was he in the asylum?"

Theo did not answer right away. He looked down at his knees. I waited.

"It was a complex incident." He paused again, then raised his head and made as if to rise. "I realize that these are your consulting hours, Monsieur le docteur, and I don't want to trespass on them."

I gestured to the empty chairs. "Do you see any other patients?" I asked. "I am at your disposal. And if I am to be of any help to your brother, I really must know his whole history. Surely you understand."

"Yes, of course," Theo said and folded his hands somewhat formally in his lap. He looked unseeing at the wall for a moment, clearly seeking to frame his tale. "Vincent lived at home in the Netherlands for a while, teaching himself how to paint. It was difficult for our parents. In a big city like Paris, it might not matter so much if the pastor's son roams around bareheaded in near rags. But in a Dutch village, I assure you, such behavior prompts talk. My mother loves Vincent very much, but the neighbors were cruel." He stopped, apparently lost in the painful memory for a moment, before flapping his hand dismissively. "In any event—I need not go into detail. Vincent came to Paris. He lived with me. He made great strides in his painting, great strides. But he is . . . a very difficult person to live with. His energy is frightening. He needs little sleep. He can be very argumentative. Intense. And he paints so quickly! The paintings, Doctor—they piled up. It's not a large flat I live in. There are paintings everywhere: under beds, rolled into wardrobes. My wife is remarkably tolerant." He took a deep breath, as if to calm himself. "We were not yet married when Vincent lived with me, and she has not yet met him, but she lives with his work."

He abruptly changed the subject. "Do you know Gauguin?" I wanted to ask more about this ferocious energy. I saw that, too, sometimes in the hospital wards. We call it "mania," and it is sometimes found in combination with another form of derangement. Yet I decided to follow Theo's lead for the moment.

"I've heard the name. Somewhat *farouche*, I understand? Bold, swashbuckling?"

"Yes. Enormously talented. As impossible as—no, actually more impossible than my brother. Vincent, at least, is full of gentleness and loving-kindness. His intentions are pure. Gauguin is ambitious and guileful. I think he's quite capable of malice, but Vincent admires him very much. My brother conceived an idea that he wanted to go paint in the South. Paris was too crowded, too busy. He felt he could live cheaply and simply somewhere in Provence, and he found a house in Arles. He was going to form a 'Studio of the South,' and he wanted Gauguin to join him." Theo fell silent again, now staring at his thumbs. Then he looked up at me.

"Before he went to the asylum, I made Vincent an allowance of 150 francs a month, and I have always supplied him with painting materials. I expect to do the same once he leaves St.-Rémy, where he is now. It's not much, but I can't afford more; my wife will have a baby soon. I agreed to send money to Gauguin as well if he joined Vincent in Arles. Gauguin was there for only two months. I did not hear this directly from either of them, but the visit was not a success. Their temperaments . . . Vincent gets so set on an idea, but nothing lives up to his visions." He took a deep breath and smiled at me. "You are very patient, Doctor, I am almost at the end."

"Not at all. In fact, you have mentioned . . ." I looked down at what I had written: *Mania? Argumentative. "Studio of the South"—delusions? Delusions about women.* "You have mentioned several characteristics that are familiar to me from other patients. Do go on."

"Well, Gauguin and Vincent quarreled. To this day I do not know exactly what happened. Gauguin says Vincent threatened him with a knife. After their argument, my brother appeared at the local brothel, covered in blood. He gave one of the whores . . ." Theo visibly gathered himself for the effort. "He gave her a section of his ear." His left hand flew to his own ear and touched the lobe, as if to ensure that it was still there. "He had cut it off."

"So he was put under a doctor's care?" I interjected. This was familiar territory, unfortunately. A patient's family could often tolerate delusions or melancholy without calling upon a physician's expertise. Self-mutilation, however, was going too far.

"Yes. Taken to the asylum in Arles. And then released back to his little house. But the townsfolk had turned against him. Vincent is, I must tell you, a spectacle. The boys of the town took to chasing after him. He threatened them. He was considered a menace to public safety. They put him in the asylum again." He stopped again and took a deep breath. "And then, because he did not feel safe alone, he went to the asylum at St.-Rémy. His doctor in Arles recommended it. They have been good to him there. He paints. They allow him to leave with an attendant. He says it is quite beautiful. From what his letters say, they are fond of him."

"Yet he wishes to leave," I prompted.

"Yes. He is finding it more and more difficult to be around the other patients. He feels they make him worse."

"This is a good sign," I pointed out. "It is not unlike the fever patient who becomes contentious and difficult once he is on the mend. If Vincent chafes at his surroundings, that is progress."

It is a strange kind of comfort to offer. In fact, I suppose it is a paradox of sorts: that those patients who are sufficiently in command of themselves to be unhappy are better off than those whose minds have simply taken flight from the world. Theo stood up, apparently unaware of what he was doing, and went to the window. He peered out, unseeing. "Vincent is afraid that staying at St.-Rémy will have a bad effect on him. He is insistent about this."

"Does he say what it is that he fears?" I asked. "Has he ever mentioned visions or hallucinations? Many patients find these terrifying."

"I think he feels he cannot paint as he would like," Theo answered, still looking out the window. "With Vincent, that is always the concern."

"And he is at the asylum voluntarily? He was not committed?"

"No," Theo confirmed, turning back to face me. "I believe he signed something to that effect."

"Then there will be no problem with his leaving," I stated.

"But—he cannot be completely alone," Theo said. "This is what I have come to ask, Doctor. Pissarro indicated that you were open to the idea. Would you be willing to supervise Vincent? He knows that he is too fragile to live in complete independence. If you were willing to meet with him, keep track of him, warn him . . ." He was now looking at me directly. "He is a difficult man, Doctor, but a good man. He is kind. He wants so much to be of some service to the world. His art is everything to him." He gestured at the walls of the salon. "I can see that you are sensitive to artists, Doctor. You have known all of the Impressionists. Pissarro cannot praise you enough, as a doctor and as a connoisseur—"

I cut him off. "Monsieur van Gogh, there is no need to go on. I would be happy to supervise your brother, as you put it. I think Auvers would be a very good place for him. I have a great deal of experience with mental maladies. I will know what to watch for, and how to help your brother. Very often, a patient's circumstances contribute significantly to his illness. Auvers is a peaceful village. We will find your brother an inexpensive inn, where he can have a room and his meals. As you may know, I myself paint and etch. There is a studio in the house, and I am always delighted to have company. I have a son and daughter, and we share a quiet family existence, regular and modest. Does your brother neglect his meals?"

Theo nodded. "I'm afraid so. Ever since the terrible episode in the Borinage, he has seen food as an interruption. Even when I tell him that he must eat to keep his strength up, he gobbles a few mouthfuls and then forgets." He seemed to have finished but drew a breath and spoke again. "I should mention that in Arles he drank a great deal of absinthe. He used it as a way to . . . I think he said 'stun' himself. To quiet his agitation. But since he has been at St.-Rémy, he has not been drinking. He even says he feels better for it."

"You see, he is already on the path to better health," I answered. "If we can persuade Monsieur Vincent to lead a wholesome life, with plenty of work to distract him from his troubles, I think he will do very well. And I would certainly be glad to help him, in any way I can. You do understand, I hope, that I am not the doctor for the town of Auvers. I practice here in Paris, so I will not be able to offer him official medical care."

"But what kind of medical care is there for cases like my brother's?" Theo asked, standing again. There was bitterness in his voice. He slipped his watch from his pocket and frowned at it. "I am sorry, Doctor, to have taken up so much of your time. I must get back to the gallery." He stepped forward and held out his hand. "I am very grateful. I will write to Vincent immediately. We will let you know when to expect him."

I had no doubt at all that I could help this Vincent van Gogh. I could not—and to this day I cannot—imagine who would be better suited to the task. There were not so many physicians in those days who had studied and practiced mental medicine. Of those, the "mad doctors," how many were acquainted with the new painting and those who produced it? I knew all too well that artists put a great strain on their nerves. Their perception of the world is as important as their touch with a brush or their color sense, and it is very easy to overtax this faculty. At the same time, many of them live in terrible conditions, as Vincent had evidently done. Vincent van Gogh felt he could help the world with his painting. That seemed unlikely. It was probably this very conviction that was driving him mad. I had written my doctoral thesis on the topic of melancholy, and I knew how closely linked it was with the artistic temperament.

If you are a doctor—indeed, if you are a man of science—another man's suffering may become your project. I cannot deny that, as Theo van Gogh trotted down my stairs, I felt a surge of excitement. This Vincent, this mad artist, sounded fascinating, like a case study of my keenest interests. It was a fortunate thing for both of us that Pissarro had sent Theo van Gogh to me. I still believe that. I do.

Two

I THOUGHT OCCASIONALLY about Vincent van Gogh in the subsequent weeks. Theo's visit had piqued my curiosity. I was convinced that Vincent's state would improve once he was settled in Auvers. We are all affected by our surroundings—surely a painter, with his artist's sensitivity, would be especially susceptible to the peace and beauty of our village.

And then, before I knew it, spring came. As I get older, I find myself more astonished every year when the gray tones of winter give way to the gentle tide of green that creeps across our landscape. That spring, it seems to me, I was already anticipating Vincent's presence, seeing the village with the eyes of an artist seeking subjects to paint.

Auvers nestles along the bank of the Oise, northwest of Paris. The town fits into a narrow band between the river and a high chalk plateau. Although the railroad came out from Paris before 1850, it brought very little change: there are neither factories nor suburban villas in Auvers. It is still farming country. The plateau is planted with wheat, and the fields along the river are a patchwork of peas, asparagus, and grapevines. Old chestnut trees line the main street, known simply as la grande Rue, which runs east to west through the village.

It was the beauty of this landscape that brought Daubigny here in the 1850s. Daumier came too, though of course orchards and peasants made quite a contrast to his usual urban subjects. Then Pissarro moved to neighboring Pontoise. This was in the late 1860s, just before the years when many of the other painters—Monet and Caillebotte, for instance—were working in the industrialized suburb Argenteuil, with its strange and alluring contrasts. But while Argenteuil offered smoke-stacks and laundry boats alongside the Seine, Auvers and Pontoise had an old-fashioned charm that Pissarro preferred. Its highlights were simply the everyday sights of trees and fields and the weather that acted on them.

In the early 1870s, before I had moved to Auvers, I frequently came out from Paris to visit the Pissarro family as a doctor and as a friend. The train ride took only an hour from the Gare du Nord, but one might have been traveling back through time as well, so great was the contrast between the bustle of Paris and the deep peace of the countryside. Cézanne was staying nearby, and he and Pissarro sometimes painted side by side—such beautiful pictures! I still have a number of them. I cannot say I care for the direction Cézanne's work took after that period; I find his canvases from the South harsh and sometimes unpleasant. But he painted my house several times, and I never fail to wonder at the solidity he managed to convey in those pictures. The house is a white cube, perched on a rock, surrounded by trees, approached by the curving road. In Cézanne's paintings, it appears quite monumental.

My house had once been a boarding school. It is on the upper side of the rue Rémy, situated slightly above the town. I must have thought, when I bought it, that higher ground would be better for my wife, Blanche. It was for her sake that we moved from Paris. She needed better air. There were other reasons, of course: we were living in the apartment on the rue du Faubourg St. Denis, which was and still is my office. It was not always easy to see patients there while Blanche and the baby,

Marguerite, and our housekeeper were just steps away. Sometimes I administered electrical treatments that startled or pained my patients (temporarily only, I must add). Sometimes the baby cried, which I found distracting. The streets outside were noisy and crowded and dirty.

But in truth, I hoped the move would improve Blanche's health. I knew she had consumption. She must have known as well; her mother had died of the disease, and Blanche surely recognized the symptoms. I could not bear to think of her breathing the dirty air of Paris. There was nothing I would not have done for her, or so I thought. And indeed, she loved Auvers. Our tall white house very soon shed any trace of the *pensionnat*. We planted gardens, in front of the house and behind. Our housekeeper, Madame Chevalier, who was the willing slave of the baby, Marguerite, sat for hours on the grass outside, watching the child explore her new surroundings. One of my prized mementos from that period is an etching I made of the two of them sitting on the grass side by side. They had their backs to me, and they were shaped exactly the same, the stout little woman and the sturdy toddler.

To our human household we added animals. I have never been able to resist the plight of a wounded beast, and sometimes villagers would bring me their injured creatures. Blanche never minded that the animals rarely returned to their original owners. She was even patient about the peacocks, which Madame Chevalier despised. It was true that the male's showy plumes never did grow back after his encounter with a herding dog, and nobody could love the sound a peacock makes. Madame Chevalier often threatened to bake them into a pie.

Having come to us first in Paris as housekeeping help for Blanche, Madame Chevalier soon revealed her true nature as a benevolent despot. She took over the housekeeping, working with an efficiency that made Blanche's efforts unnecessary. ("Go play the piano, Madame," she would say when my wife picked up a duster. "The work will go so quickly if I can listen to you.") Then when Marguerite was born, she ruled the nursery as well. She was pleased with our move to Auvers, sure that all children should be raised in the country, though she herself was Parisian born and bred.

And then we had Paul, as lovely a baby as Marguerite had been, and curiously elegant for an infant. To this day he has long, slender hands, an inheritance from his piano-playing mother.

Blanche's symptoms went into remission while she was pregnant: tuberculosis often retreats that way. So we were a happy family of four in our tall white house on the hillside. Briefly. Then Blanche died. It was a terrible time.

Blanche had been gone for fifteen years when Vincent came to Auvers. The children were almost grown by then. That summer Paul was still in the lycée in Paris, coming home on weekends until the term ended in June. He was tall, fair-skinned, blue-eyed—a very handsome boy. He had a fastidious quality unusual in a youth of seventeen. Yet he was a feckless student, given to secrecy and a kind of mute stubbornness. Now that we are both grown men, he is something of a confidant and colleague. But in that summer of 1890, I was anxious about him; I could not imagine his course in life. I know that Madame Chevalier shared my concern. She adored the boy, but she wanted to be proud of him. He did not always make that possible.

While Paul went to no trouble to please his elders, Marguerite never ceased doing so. She was a sober, earnest girl, quick to understand what we expected. She learned to keep house at Madame Chevalier's side, wearing her own miniature apron, pushing around a tiny broom with grave self-importance. Paul's fluent chatter may have heightened Marguerite's tendency to reticence. But she was a musician, as Blanche had been. I often thought that Marguerite did not need words because she had the piano. Sometimes when I heard her playing, I would think for a heart-catching instant that she was her mother, though Blanche had seldom played the piano in this house. She was generally too ill, too weak to do very much at all. Still, Marguerite found a folder of her sheet music some years ago—well before that summer Vincent was with us. She learned to play those Chopin pieces as quickly as she could. Blanche had marked the music with fingerings and dynamic notations, which Marguerite found difficult to read. Seeing my wife's handwriting gave me a little shock when Marguerite brought it to me to decipher.

Yet for me, these memories of Blanche gave a special sweetness to our comfortable, peaceful way of life. I hoped it would bring solace to Theo van Gogh's brother, if he came to Auvers. I thought about him from time to time as April passed. I had expected to meet the two brothers in Paris, once Vincent had made the voyage north, but that was not what happened.

On a sunny morning late in May, I was in the scullery at home in Auvers, sorting some herbs to dry. This was a matter of some contention in my house. As a homeopath, I sometimes brewed remedies from ingredients grown in my own garden. But Madame Chevalier (who, I might add, benefited substantially from my tonics and tinctures) had more than once voiced her displeasure at the preparations taking place in what she called, quite incorrectly, *her* kitchen. We reached a truce when I conceded to use only the scullery for my practices, and only at certain very limited hours. That afternoon I had just begun to hear Madame Chevalier muttering in my vicinity (I discerned the words *sorrel* and *luncheon* and possibly *soup*) when the bell for the street door rang. Her muttering crescendoed into a complaint about visitors who had so little sense that they arrived while she was supposed to be preparing the midday meal. As the house is above the road, it is reached by a long flight of stone steps that descend through our terraced garden to a gate. Visitors ring the bell there, and Madame Chevalier must trot down, grumbling, to let them in. The grumbling is something of a performance; she begrudges nothing she does for us.

I listened very carefully to the footsteps when Madame Chevalier returned—I heard a man's heavier tread as well as the housekeeper's own pattering. Our house is not large, so I could hear her somewhat shrill voice insisting that the visitor stay where he was while she got the doctor. She spoke to him as if he might be hard of hearing.

"A man to see you, Doctor," she told me, coming back to the scullery. "Says he has a letter for you. He brought a whole load of . . ." She shook her head. "Sticks. And things. A bundle. Very untidy." It certainly did not occur to me that this could be Vincent. I had expected to hear from Theo before he appeared.

I took off my smock and heard our pug, Pekin, begin to howl. He was the only animal allowed in the house, and he took his responsibilities as a watchdog very seriously. I was imagining a woodcutter of some sort— though why would he have come to the front rather than the back door?—being assaulted by the small, determined dog as I opened the door to the little room where Madame Chevalier had put my visitor. But of course, it was no woodcutter.

Theo's warning had not prepared me for the physical state of his brother. The two looked alike, enough so that I recognized Vincent right away from his blue eyes, fair skin, and reddish hair. But Theo's features were smooth, refined into conventionality. Vincent's cheekbones, in contrast, were more pronounced, and he had a heavy ridge of bone above his very blue eyes. His skin was rough and uneven, as though it had been ruined by sun or by poor nutrition, and he had not shaved in recent days. More than that, he wore workman's clothes: sturdy boots and heavy canvas trousers and a blue shirt with an open collar. And he smelled. A strong tang of turpentine, tobacco, oil paint, and unwashed man filled the room.

"Dr. Gachet, I apologize for coming to you with no warning," he said, holding out a letter. "Here is a note from my brother Theo. It explains everything. I am Vincent van Gogh." His voice had a cracked, rusty quality, like a hinge that was rarely used and never oiled.

"Of course," I answered, nodding at him and shaking his hand. His grip was firm and the skin of his palm as hard as a laborer's. "Won't you come sit in my salon? This is not a terribly comfortable room."

The dog was now frantic, in the manner of pugs. He jumped repeatedly on the legs of the painter, howling a challenge. I picked Pekin up and showed Vincent into the salon across the hall. "Please sit down, make yourself comfortable. I must dispose of this animal. Can I offer you some coffee?"

"No, thank you," he answered, looking around the room. His eyes went immediately to the prints and paintings on the walls, an eclectic group. There were, among others, several eighteenth-century portraits, a copy of Titian's *Salome*, two strange figures created from fruits by an Italian artist called Arcimboldo, and a group of Dutch flower paintings from the seventeenth century. I wondered what Vincent would make of them. I left him in order to toss the dog outside and ask Madame Chevalier to bring us coffee and some rolls. Vincent was desperately thin, all hollows and sinews beneath his loose shirt.

When I returned to the salon, Vincent turned and said, "My brother said you are very much interested in painting."

"I am," I answered. "I try to keep up with the way art has changed, I go to the galleries and the exhibitions. And I'm lucky enough to possess some paintings that I think very highly of. I don't hang them down here." I gestured around the room. "These are more . . ."

"Conventional," he finished the sentence for me.

"Yes," I agreed. "Some of the others are somewhat . . . demanding, perhaps. They are all upstairs. Perhaps you'd like to see them later?"

"Very much," he answered.

Madame Chevalier came in with the tray and set it with some emphasis on the table between us, making it clear that she had better things to do than treat peddlers as honored guests.

I sat on the small sofa and gestured to the armchair. Vincent sat down. He might have looked like a laborer, but I could tell from the way he moved in my salon that he had once been used to surroundings like these. Some of my patients in Paris—the ones I treated without charge—were overwhelmed by my parquet floors and very ordinary brocade upholstery. They would sit rigidly on a chair, unconscious of their fingers tracing the patterns in the fabric. But these things were not new to Vincent van Gogh. More, they did not matter to him. They were simply not worth noticing.

Once I had taken in his shabbiness and his general air of poor health—he looked ten years older than Theo—I was struck by Vincent's alertness. And indeed, over the next months, each time we met I marveled again at how I could see him *looking*. It was as if his eyes had a special sensitivity. You could almost feel him scanning everything around him and accepting or rejecting objects as interesting, or not. Sometimes this created a strange tension as people became aware that, sooner or later, he would look at *them*. One would want to be worth looking at.

He didn't care for my furniture, that was clear. The salon was furnished with a few antique pieces I had bought years before—a big Renaissance buffet, a Louis XIII armchair—and Vincent's eyes passed over them without hesitation. The stained glass I had installed in the north window might as well have been invisible. But I could sense his curiosity when he spotted the portfolios of prints next to the large table I used as a desk.

I poured a cup of coffee and handed it to him. "Would you care for milk? I would recommend it," I said. "In fact, I suggest you drink milk every day. Preferably goat's milk. We have a goat here who keeps us well supplied, and there would be plenty for you."

"No, thank you, Doctor," he said, politely enough.

"Take a roll, then," I urged him, "for you must have made a very early start. I will read the letter from your brother." As I bent my head to Theo's clear handwriting, I noticed that Vincent seemed to chew with some discomfort. False teeth, I thought. That might explain his thinness, if it hurt him to eat.

"Can you tell me," I asked him, "about your stay in Paris? Monsieur Theo said you found it tiring?"

He gulped the last of his coffee and set the cup neatly in the saucer. "The noise." He shook his head. "I had forgotten . . . Or I was so unused to it . . ." He looked up at me, and again I saw his brother's gaze, but with greater concentration. "Do you know the South, Doctor?" I nodded. "Then you know how the nights are. The enormous stars, the crickets, that warm air like a current of water, the sense of all the tiny creatures of the night moving around you. Or the days, the afternoons when nothing moves that isn't tossed by the wind? When the train pulled into the station in Paris, I felt like a little moth, or a tamarisk leaf. Buffeted. So much movement, so much noise, and all of it human! I was completely overwhelmed."

I poured more coffee into his cup, but he was so caught up in his description that he didn't notice. "And then at Theo's— Well, Doctor, you know what an asylum is like. You do, don't you?"

"I do. All those separate people, in their own worlds. It can be terrible, because you cannot make a connection."

"True, but at the same time, you owe them nothing. If you feel like howling, you howl. Now imagine going from that to a lovely little bourgeois apartment with a wife who was meeting me for the first time. What kind of impression could I make on her? And then there is the new baby. Everything must be so soft, so controlled!" He shook his head. "I cannot do that, Doctor. At least, not now. I have forgotten how. Theo and Jo live in such a way that, if one draws a breath, the other notices. I am not . . ." He paused, picking at a bit of rough skin on his thumb. "I am not sufficiently master of myself for that."

"Yes," I answered, careful to sound as if his concerns were ordinary. "I have often noticed what a large task that is. Those of us who manage it completely tend to underestimate the effort involved. Tell me about how you felt in St.-Rémy. Monsieur Theo mentioned that the other patients were a problem?"

"Not at first," he answered, picking up a roll. He tore into it, looked at it, and put it down on the tray. "I was very poorly myself, you understand. Did Theo explain?"

I nodded. "Yes, but it would be helpful to hear how it felt to you at the time."

"It's difficult to explain," he answered. "There were periods that I don't remember at all. When I did terrible things." He gestured to his ear. "This, for instance. I have no memory of that. But more generally, I would say . . ." His voice trailed off. "Unhappy, of course. I was unhappy. And afraid." He brightened a bit. "Perhaps you will be able to see from the pictures. The last paintings I did at St.-Rémy were not dry when I left. I am having them sent here. Theo has others, some of the paintings from Arles, and the early ones from St.-Rémy. They may help you to understand." He paused again, then went on. "There is one that, I think, captures the mental effect of life there. It is a view down the central hall—it is long in real life, but I made it look interminable. Arches and arches receding, and a tiny figure scurrying into a doorway."

"Did you sleep in wards?" I asked, thinking about the long rows of beds at the Salpêtrière. It is necessary in an asylum to be able to watch the patients lest they harm themselves or someone else. Yet for a man with Vincent's sensibility, this enforced togetherness must have been a constant irritant.

"No, there were private chambers," he answered. "They were quite large, and since many rooms were empty, they gave me one as a studio."

"And can you describe it further for me?" I wondered if he would be able to talk about this period of his life with calm and detachment.

"Oh, gladly," he replied. "It was once, I believe, a monastery, St. Paul-de-Mausole. Some of the buildings are very, very old, and it is not in good repair. The asylum is in a long, low building, yellow, with green shutters. There are beautiful gardens, full of flowers and trees, with benches and fountains. I suppose this is where the monks used to walk and pray. I painted the gardens a good deal."

"I look forward to seeing your paintings," I said. I agreed with his premise; surely they would permit me some insight into his mental state at the time. "And the treatment?"

"Oh, no, Doctor, there was very little treatment in this place. Dr. Peyron had no expertise in mental maladies. There were baths, of course. They often calmed us down."

"And how often did the doctor see you?"

"He lived there, so he saw us all the time."

"But examinations?"

"When we arrived."

"Then how did you spend your days?"

"That was the difficulty, you see. Aside from painting, I read a great deal when I felt well enough. I see that we share some of the same tastes," he added, looking at the bookshelf. There were several novels on the corner of my desk, and he turned his head to read the titles on their spines. "Ah! *Bel-Ami!* I did a still life in Paris—a little figure of Venus, a vase of roses, and this novel. Do you like Maupassant? Have you read *A Life?* Theo loaned it to me just before I came here. I would be happy to bring it to you when I am finished with it."

"I would like that very much," I answered, pleased. I was not accustomed to discussing literature with my patients, but of course Vincent was not, strictly speaking, a patient. Perhaps he might even become something of a companion. I found his enthusiasm appealing. "So your days in the asylum—there was no structure, no schedule?"

"No, Doctor. For the most part, the patients just sat."

I was startled, but I should not have been. The doctrines of moral treatment—kindliness, tolerance, distraction, and a firm effort to make the patient aware of his delusions—that I had absorbed in Paris thirty-some years earlier had not been accepted everywhere. And of course they required a great deal of effort from the medical staff, not to mention training. The asylum at St.-Rémy was probably one of the more benign institutions, even if the patients received little care.

"But you were able to work?"

"Yes," Vincent answered. "Dr. Peyron felt it would not harm me. He was right about that. It would have been a great deal worse for me if I had not been able to paint. As it was, I was able to turn out some things I am not ashamed of."

The coffeepot was empty, and so was the basket of rolls.

"Monsieur van Gogh, this has been very helpful. I told your brother that I could not officially be your medical practitioner; I work in Paris, and the doctor here is Dr. Mazery. If you were to become ill here, he would care for you, but he will certainly consult with me. I would be able to suggest treatments if they were required; a sleeping draft, for instance, or a homeopathic cordial to reduce agitation. As you may know, I have considerable experience with maladies of the nerves and the mind. I have often been able to help patients regain their mental equilibrium."

"I am glad to hear you say so, Doctor, for it is a terrible thing to misplace," Vincent said with a wry little smile.

I smiled back at him. "If I am to be of any help in your mental troubles, I must examine you physically. It is somewhat awkward to do this here, where I do not have a proper examination room. But we could go up to the studio, where the light is good. It won't take long. Would you mind?"

"No, Doctor," he answered, getting up. "If it must be done, let us not delay."

I preceded Vincent up the stairs, feeling somewhat self-conscious.

I was usually delighted to show off my collection of paintings. But I found myself especially eager to please this man. It was peculiar. I was older than he by a generation. I was the expert, the doctor, about to examine him. Yet I was almost apprehensive. I wanted him to like my pictures. I had found myself disappointed that he did not compliment the atmosphere of the salon; visitors usually admired my antiques and decorative objects. I considered myself a man of taste, yet apparently Vincent van Gogh did not.

I saw my familiar studio as if with new eyes when I stepped through the door that day. I noticed how small and stuffy the room was, how low the ceiling, how much space was taken up by the dusty printing press. The plaster walls were stained in many places, something I had ignored until now. Still, I thought, the paintings were beautiful, and I hoped Vincent would agree.

Some of the pictures were too fragile to hang on the walls; Cézanne had left a few studies on cardboard that I didn't care to expose to sunlight. I could not afford to frame all of them, either, so many were simply stacked against each other on the floor, stretcher resting on stretcher. But I remember clearly that I had Pissarro's painting of the red house in wintertime on one wall, for Vincent made his way instantly to stand before it. While I cleared various paint boxes and rolls of paper from the little divan and pulled it into the light, he stood before the picture.

"May I take this down?" he asked, his hands poised to lift the canvas from its hook.

"Of course," I replied. "Take it to the window."

He did so, turning the canvas this way and that to examine the paint in the raking light. It is a small picture, a simple scene of chestnut trees in front of the house, with a woman and child standing on the snow and a winter sky behind. When Pissarro painted it, I was astounded at its freshness, the way it captured the instant with the blue shadows on the snow, the lively, interlocking branches of the trees, and the peaceful charm of the house right in the center. I heard Vincent sigh a little bit, and turned around as he gently placed it back on its hook.

"It is very fine," he said. He glanced around at the other paintings: a

Sisley of the Canal St.-Martin in Paris, my tiny Renoir portrait of a woman in profile, a Guillaumin of some smokestacks outlined between a setting sun and the blue-gold surface of the Seine. "I can see that you have some beautiful things here."

"They give me great pleasure," I told him, grateful that he approved of my taste. "And you are welcome to come and look at them whenever you like. I normally spend four days a week in Paris, but Madame Chevalier will be glad to let you in. For that matter, I hope you will visit often when I am here, from Saturday evening to Tuesday morning. Now, if you could take off your shirt and sit down here. I will be back in a moment."

I went downstairs to get my stethoscope, and when I returned, slightly breathless, Vincent was on his knees in front of a row of paintings, flicking through them. "I hope you don't mind, Doctor," he addressed me without turning around. "I was overcome by curiosity."

"Not at all," I answered. "But now, if you could sit down here." I patted the faded wine-colored plush of the divan, and a tiny cloud of dust billowed into the shaft of light coming through the window. Vincent had simply dropped his shirt on the floor, and as he crossed the room I picked it up. There was no hook or hanger for it, so I draped it on the back of my easel, which I moved toward the wall. I was grateful that there was no unfinished canvas on it. I would not have liked to watch Vincent's blue eyes pass over my work and move on without comment.

The little couch was so low that Vincent's head was not much higher than my waist when I stood over him. I looked down on the top of his head, the tops of his ears, his shoulders.

There was a little stool in the corner, spattered with paint. I stepped forward to seize it and brought it back to the divan. Vincent sat, waiting, his forearms resting on his thighs and his hands dangling. Compliant, enduring. He had undergone, I supposed, many examinations. I sat on the stool. Now my eyes were level with my patient's. I set my hands beside his neck, turning his head back and forth, pressing down on his skin. I was sitting on his left side, nearest the ear he had slashed. Gently, I folded it forward, feeling the scar tissue along the cartilage where he had cut the lobe. A disturbing idea came to me.

"Did you hear voices? Do you think that is why you cut your ear? To stop them?" If that was the case, he was more troubled than he seemed. Now that I thought of it, I had asked Theo this question, and he had not answered it directly.

"I don't know if I did," he answered. "My memory is so addled . . ." He said no more.

For all my experience as a man and as a doctor, I knew I could not quite imagine his predicament. I am a sympathetic man. I have known melancholy and a kind of panic-stricken grief when it seemed that to exist for a moment longer was beyond what a man could endure. One of the reasons I was so drawn to Blanche was that she seemed able to push back those dark tides of feeling. She had a temperament of sunny certitude that I grew to rely on. When she died, I was left in a terrible state, nearly paralyzed by my emotions. But I have always managed to retain control of myself. What must it be like, to know yourself untrustworthy, to have something take over your free will? Was it like being possessed? It is difficult enough to live, knowing one's strengths and limitations. But most of us stumbling through life do not bear the burden of knowing that we may turn into monsters. Vincent seemed to have put this particular threat behind him, but the memory of it must, I thought, influence his nervous state.

"Has your hearing been affected?" I asked, releasing the ear.

"No," he answered. "I don't believe that was ever a concern. I was very ill afterward, and I remember none of it. Theo says he came to Arles, but apparently I did not recognize him. I was raving in the hospital. I suppose they had restrained me by that point."

I was certain that they had. Even though Dr. Pinel and his followers had gradually done away with the use of chains on the mad, there were still times when a patient was so disturbed that he or she had to be subdued. The solution was the *gilet de force*, a heavy canvas jacket that fastened up the back. The sleeves were extraordinarily long; crossed over at the waist in front and tied in the back, they immobilized an unruly patient's hands. It was always shocking to see a patient controlled in that way, but it was frequently a necessary measure.

I stood up and moved the stool around to place myself directly in front of Vincent. "Were you often restrained at St.-Rémy?" I looked into his eyes as he answered. The whites were perhaps a touch yellowed. The irises were a clear, deep blue, each with a dark ring; the pupils small black dots in the flood of light from the windows. He had stiff reddish lashes, bleached by the sun, and faint scars from bad sunburns on his brow and cheekbones. It was a workman's skin, the skin of a man who spends his days outside in all weathers.

"They sometimes put patients in straitjackets, so I expect I was restrained, too."

"Would you mind opening your mouth?" I asked.

He did so, stretching his jaws wide. As I'd thought, some of his teeth were false. His gums were inflamed, bleeding in places. His breath smelled of coffee.

"When did you lose those teeth?" I asked.

"Ten years ago, perhaps? I was very ill when I came back from the Borinage. I hadn't been eating."

"Do the false ones hurt you?"

"Not especially," he said. "My own teeth, the ones they pulled out, hurt a great deal by the end."

I sat back on the stool. "I have said this before, but it bears repeating. You must eat. Simple meals. Food gives you the strength to work." I put a hand on his right shoulder, and stretched his arm out. Blood vessels, muscle, and sinew ran beneath the pale skin. He looked almost like an *écorché*, one of those flayed figures used to teach art students about anatomy. His hands, as ravaged by the sun as his face, were dingy with paint. It looked as if he applied his pigments with his fingers.

It was warm in the studio, so I stood to open the window. The fly that had been buzzing against the pane flew out, and a current of fresh air drifted in. In the garden below, the goat's bell jingled and one of the larger dogs barked.

I went back to my patient and asked him, "Could you turn around? I would like to listen to your lungs." He shifted his legs to offer me his bare back. The knobs of his spine were clearly visible, as vulnerable as a small boy's. I applied the stethoscope and adjusted the earpieces. "Breathe in, please. Out. In again." The air rushed in and out smoothly, without catches or gurgles or rasps. "Thank you. Now lie down."

He lay back and hung his legs over the edge of the divan. Once again, I could see every muscle, every bone. The hollow of his belly made the outline of his ribs as dramatic as a skeleton. I palpated his abdomen, pressing down firmly to feel the shapes of his organs. "Now your heart," I said, applying the stethoscope to his chest. As I bent down to listen, the double beat came, firm and regular. His heart was not the problem any more than his eyes, lungs, or hands were. I closed my eyes for a moment, listening to Vincent slowly breathing. He sounded peaceful, at ease.

I straightened, and folded my stethoscope back into its case. "You may sit up," I told him. When he rose, his eyes met mine. There was no question in them. "Am I well? Will I be ill again?" You can always read that anxiety in a patient's face. Not with Vincent. His body did not interest him unless it failed him.

"I see nothing wrong," I said cheerfully, as though to a child. "Your body is strong, though you are thinner than I would like. I am slightly concerned about your liver."

I lifted his shirt from the easel and handed it to him. Normally, as with disrobing, patients would retire behind a screen for this moment, the resumption of the public face. Vincent merely slipped his arms into the sleeves and fastened the crude buttons. He looked down at the last of them, then looked up at me. This time there *was* a question in his eyes, and I felt I must answer it. I have thought about this moment so often. Was there something else I could have said? A warning I could have delivered that would have changed the outcome? I will never know. He did not seem particularly mad. The episode of the ear had occurred about eighteen months earlier and was not repeated by further injury or aggression. I did not doubt that Vincent drove himself hard or that he fitted uneasily into society, as Theo had warned me. But there had been considerable wisdom in his decision to stay in the asylum until he felt steadier.

"As for your mind," I told him, "I am confident. You have been through a difficult ordeal, but you have recovered. You traveled here on your own without incident. Paris was too noisy, and you had the good sense to leave. This is an excellent sign. You must, you *must* come to me if you feel any change. A new sense of difficulty, perhaps. Melancholy. Despair. Trouble sleeping." He was buttoning his cuffs, head down. "I do not rule these things out, but they would surprise me. You are perfectly lucid, your reasoning is intact, your senses are undisturbed. Still, I can help you if you require it."

"And you believe I should continue to work?" he asked.

"Oh, yes," I said, "you must! I have seen many alienated patients improve by working, though it was usually labor of a routine kind, repetitive. Your work is—" I paused and caught his eye again. I tried to make my voice as impressive as possible. "If I understand you at all, Monsieur van Gogh, your painting is the reason you continue to live, is it not?"

He nodded, his eyes still on mine, his hands hanging at his sides.

"Then paint," I added quietly. "Paint and live. And come to me if you feel disturbed." I put my hand on his shoulder and turned him to face the stairs. "Now let us find you a place to stay."

Three

∾

I WALKED VINCENT down the steps to the gate and watched him trudge along the street, back toward the train station. He did, I had to admit, make a conspicuous figure. In Auvers we have always been accustomed to painters with their rucksacks and collapsible easels and stools, often settled where you least expect them, at a turn in the road or in the hollow of a meadow. I like to think that, in painting our landscape, they become part of it. But even from behind, Vincent's shambling gait, his battered boots, and his coarse straw hat made him an unusual and unmistakable figure in Auvers.

I later learned that Vincent had chosen to lodge at the Auberge Ravoux, across from the *mairie*. It was the cheapest inn the town offered; Vincent was very careful with the money that Theo sent him. He had made the right choice, for Ravoux's customers were working men, unlikely to be disturbed by a painter's eccentricities.

The same was not true of Madame Chevalier, who was waiting for me at the front door when I had seen Vincent on his way. The force of her opinions did not match her small size.

"And who was that?" she demanded. Without waiting for an answer, she went on, "If he is to come back, you must tell him to come to the back door with his bundles. We can't have word getting around the village that peddlers come to the front like guests."

"But he is a guest," I said mildly. "He is a painter, named Vincent van Gogh, and I hope we will see him often. I asked him to stay for luncheon today, but he could not."

I said this only to tease her. Madame Chevalier was a wonderful cook, but she hated being surprised by guests.

"Vincent van what?" she retorted. "Van Goog? Dreadful name! I'll never be able to say it. And if he's going to paint here, you must tell him that I don't want his oil paints all over the place. Outside, that's where they stay, or in your studio, Doctor. Now come and sit down, Marguerite and Paul have been waiting for you. They want to know all about him." I obeyed her, of course.

It had been some time since an artist had visited us. Pissarro's move away from Pontoise in 1882 had limited my country contacts with artists. I saw them in Paris, at galleries and cafés, but I realized that Vincent's presence in Auvers could be stimulating for all of us. I imagined lively conversations with him about art and literature. I might even paint with him, as I had with Cézanne and Pissarro. For many years now Auvers had been a kind of refuge for me. But the cultural life there was limited.

I began to wonder very much what Vincent van Gogh's painting looked like. The man had struck me so positively, with his stoical approach to his illness and his quick enthusiasm for my treasured paintings. I hoped the artist would be one I could admire. I was eager to see Vincent's work for another reason as well: though I had conducted a physical examination, I felt that my knowledge of the man and his mental state would be incomplete until I had seen how he viewed and depicted his world. I did not want to wait until his canvases arrived from the South, so I hoped that Theo could show me examples of Vincent's paintings while I was working in Paris.

∞

I made my way to the Boulevard Montmartre on the Friday evening after Vincent had first knocked at my door. "Dr. Gachet," Theo said, coming forward with his hand out to greet me as I walked through the polished glass door of the gallery. Just as I had seen him in his brother's rougher features, now I saw Vincent's heavy brow and bold cheekbones superimposed on Theo's more delicate face. "I am so happy to see you. I have heard from Vincent." He clasped my hand warmly. "Doctor, I can hardly tell you . . ." He looked away for a moment, and I could see that he was struggling with emotion. "I am so relieved."

Naturally he was relieved, poor man. He must have worried desperately about his brother. I had understood that before, but now that I had met Vincent, I could guess how his circumstances must weigh on Theo.

"He is terribly high-strung, of course," I said, hoping to give Theo some time to recover himself. "But I thought he showed good sense in leaving Paris when he did. That is a wonderful sign, along with the fact that he was able to travel by himself from the South, without incident. I believe he is much better."

Theo had turned back to me, after a swift glance at a man in a black coat examining a painting of a volcano in a heavy gilt frame. We had moved no farther than the entrance of the gallery, but now he drew me away from the door, to a long red leather bench in the middle of the back room. It was a pleasing space, with gleaming floors and luxuriant potted palms in the corners. He sat down, glancing again at the man, who appeared to be the only customer. "Please, sit down, Doctor. I am delighted to hear you say this. Can you tell me what you think was wrong with him?"

"Do you need to attend to the gentleman over there? I realize this may not be a convenient time for a visit."

Theo shook his head. "He visits us frequently," he said in a low voice. "He is very partial to our traditional landscapes, and I believe he is in no hurry to get home. In any event, I will be closing the gallery shortly. If you would like to wait, perhaps we could take a glass of something together. I have a new Pissarro upstairs. Would you like to see it? Are you

acquainted with his most recent work?" The smooth gallery employee
had quickly replaced the distraught brother, but I felt that his politeness
was automatic. I could sense that he was still preoccupied with Vincent.

"I would be happy to see what my old friend has been painting some
other time. I cannot say I like these pointillist canvases of the last few
years, and I keep hoping he will abandon that style. But for now, I
would like more than anything to see your brother's work. Have you
anything here?"

He smiled wearily. "Unfortunately, I do not. Vincent's paintings are
magnificent, but . . . startling. Very strong. He has been invited to show
with a group in Brussels, but I can't think of a gallery in France that
would hang his work now. Of course, I believe all of this will change.
You read Aurier's piece?"

"Albert Aurier?" I shook my head. "No. He wrote about Vincent?"

"Yes, in the *Mercure de France*. In January. It was a long article about
various artists whose work does not seem related to any of the contem-
porary movements. He called it 'The Isolated Ones.' He said wonderful
things about Vincent's painting. Unfortunately, Vincent is also isolated
personally."

The jingle of the doorbell announced that the devotee of traditional
landscapes had departed, and Theo stood up. "I don't believe I'll be for-
feiting any sales if I close now. I could take you to see some of Vincent's
paintings, if you like. You will forgive me for not taking you to my
home—we have many of them there—but we have a new baby, and to
be honest, Vincent left the place as if a whirlwind had gone through it."
Now the anxiety of the new father peered through the polish of the art
dealer; Theo had so many sources of worry for a young man.

"Of course," I told him, putting as much sympathy into my voice as I
could. "I have two children myself. They're older now, but when Marguerite was small we lived in Paris like you. I know how difficult it is."
Actually, I did not. I could not really know how life was for Theo van
Gogh, who had to take care of a wife, a new baby, and a brother who
was prone to nervous difficulties.

He moved around the gallery, extinguishing the lights, then closed
and locked the steel shutters. He led me out the back door, through a

courtyard. "We bring the canvases through here," he said. "Most of the big Salon-style productions go to the main branch of the gallery, on rue Chaptal, of course. Few of my clients have room for that kind of enormous painting. I think, and so does Vincent, that art buyers are looking for something completely different now, anyway."

"You mean easel pictures?" I asked, as we emerged onto the street and he locked the outer door.

"Oh, of course. But more than that. Vincent believes that colors, certain combinations of colors, can prompt or express emotion. You will see," he added, heading up the street. "I am taking you to Père Tanguy, the paint seller. Vincent left some canvases with him. We'll go up by Notre-Dame-de-Lorette. Do you mind walking? It is a lovely evening."

"Not at all," I answered. "I will be delighted to go to Tanguy's. I have met him several times, but I've never visited his shop. Tell me, did your brother have any formal training?"

"He spent some weeks at the academy in Antwerp but could not submit to the discipline. Here in Paris he took lessons at Cormon's studio, but in truth he is more or less self-taught. You will see, his paintings have none of the technical expertise taught at the École des Beaux-Arts. With Vincent, it is more a matter of . . ." He hesitated for a moment. "I can only say that he sees the world as no one else does. Naturally this makes his paintings difficult to sell. But . . . Well, you will see."

Tanguy's tiny store was wedged into a small building on the rue Clauzel, off the rue des Martyrs. If Boussod and Valadon represented the official face of Parisian art, with its chandeliers and crimson carpets, chez Tanguy was its other face, all charcoal dust and pungent fluids and shiny lead tubes. I had been in shops like this before. There were always poorly groomed men standing around arguing about the shape of a brush or the flexibility of a palette knife, the grain of a canvas or the luster of a glaze. Even at this late hour, the shop was open, though there was only one customer, choosing between a pair of palettes that the bearded, burly Tanguy held out for him. I glanced around, pleased by the familiar clutter of stacks of paper, jugs of brushes, and the wall of tiny drawers to store the pigments for oil paint.

But then I caught sight of the portrait. Instinctively I knew that Vincent had painted it. I had spent only an hour in his company, but the picture obviously came from that vigorous, discerning sensibility. The subject, Tanguy himself, in a blue jacket and wide-brimmed hat, sat in the center of the canvas, looking out, not directly at the viewer but somewhat down. He seemed to focus on the body of the viewer—possibly on the heart? Behind him was a patchwork of Japanese prints painted in brilliant colors; a glowing blue, saffron, emerald green. Directly to the right of Tanguy's hat floated the pink cloud of a blossoming cherry tree set in a landscape of beauty and peace, with a stream leading the viewer's eye through green fields to a series of low hills beneath a sky stippled with white clouds.

I had never seen brushwork like this. I owned at that point a Monet, several Pissarros, many Cézannes. I was and still am fascinated by the technique, inaugurated by the Impressionists, of breaking up the application of color. Those painters drew attention to their method of placing paint on the canvas while still constructing a complete image. But Van Gogh, if it were possible, took this tendency further. His paint lived. It seemed to flicker or dance on the canvas—yet the image held together. I have seen canvases rendered in this manner that do not, somehow, engage your eye. You are so distracted by the brushwork that you cannot see the picture. This portrait, though, seized my gaze and my emotions. Moments earlier Theo had told me that Vincent believed he could elicit certain feelings through his juxtapositions of color. I was struck to the core by the beauty, the peacefulness, and the intricacy of what he had created.

Above all I was astonished at his mastery. Composing a canvas is harder than it looks. Painters like Amand Gautier, trained at the École des Beaux-Arts, go through an extensive series of preparations. They draw components of their painting in charcoal. They try out different angles, different combinations of elements. They make oil sketches, to see how their colors work together. Then they build the painting slowly, first drawing on the canvas, then filling in areas of dark and light, gradually thinning their pigments and using smaller brushes until they have created their picture. It seemed as though Vincent had omitted those steps, somehow creating an immensely complicated image in a single burst of energy, using large quantities of bright, unmixed colors. He had depicted Tanguy—a former radical, a man of the people—in his blue workman's jacket and brown trousers. But the jacket was grooved with vertical strokes of paint, lighter and darker blue, yellow for highlights, curving with the collar, rumpled at the elbow, heavy and thick. His beard and eyebrows—white and brown mixed—were laid in with a finer brush and bristled off the canvas. Vincent had painted the background prints with thinner pigments, emulating the flat quality of Japanese woodcuts. Somehow a harmony of colors and shapes reigned among them. Yet if one brushstroke had been in the wrong place—one flicker of blue highlight on the brown trousers, one fleck of greenish shadow on the backs of the hands—the painting would have dissolved into a wreck. I was awestruck. How could this be the work of the high-strung man with the damaged ear whom I had examined days earlier? I felt there should have been some physical sign that he was a genius.

I looked down and found my hands locked together like those of Tanguy in the painting.

"Everyone does that," Theo said, nodding at my hands. "You don't even know you're doing it." He looked back up at the portrait and shrugged. "So you see, my brother is brilliant. There is no one like him."

He did not say it with excitement or pride. There was no sense of anticipation, no vision of a future in which Vincent's paintings would be prized and Vincent himself— Well, what would one hope for Vincent? Even based only on my short acquaintance, I could not imagine a glowing future for him. He was not a man made for success, I thought. He could never tolerate having a busy studio, multiple commissions, an assistant to run errands, and a dealer to broker sales. He was like a monk. He belonged in a different setting, somehow withdrawn from the world.

Tanguy closed the drawer of the massive cash register, and the sole customer edged past us with both of the palettes beneath his arm. "Monsieur van Gogh," Tanguy greeted Theo. "And I believe it is Dr. Gachet?" We shook hands, and he gestured up at his portrait. "A thing of beauty. Monsieur van Gogh, your brother is a giant. They will see."

"It is the doctor who would like to see now," Theo said. "Vincent is staying in Auvers, where the doctor lives."

"This is the first time I have seen his work," I added. "The portrait is magnificent. I would be very proud to be painted by him."

"I am proud," Tanguy responded. "Monsieur van Gogh feels as no one else does. He puts his heart on the canvas every time he lifts a brush. And if you sit for him, you will find that he puts your heart on the canvas as well."

A harsh female voice called from the doorway at the back of the shop. "Julien! If you want to eat your supper, you must come now!" He rolled his eyes at us in the age-old gesture of the husband harassed by a shrewish wife, and held back the dark green curtains behind the counter.

"The stairs are there." He pointed. He lifted two small lanterns from hooks on the wall. "You can light them?" he asked Theo, who nodded. "I'd best join my wife," he added in a low voice and slipped through the doorway into the room beyond, where the aroma of long-stewed onions vanquished the chemical tang of the shop.

We stood awkwardly at the bottom of the stairs while Theo found a match safe in his pocket. "If you could open the doors," he murmured to me, once we had light. "Now that I think of it, I should not have brought you here. What can we possibly see in this dim light?"

"Oh, but this is an adventure," I said, my eagerness apparent in my voice. "We could be characters in a Dumas novel, hunting for hidden treasure."

Theo smiled gratefully and led the way up the stairs, his lantern swinging gently, making the pool of light before him rock in response. Two flights up, he opened a door into an attic, even more pungent than the shop downstairs. As Theo looked for a place to hang the lantern, I tried to identify the different odors—turpentine was very strong, but so was the unmistakable scent of dead rodent.

"Here," Theo's voice said, as he reached a shelf where he deposited his lantern, which provided only a moderate glow. Even doubled by the light from my lantern, the area of visibility was narrow, dim, and wavering.

"This really is like a Dumas novel," I remarked. "Or Aladdin's cave. I feel there should be massive jars."

"We never heard those tales growing up in Holland. Not in a preacher's house." Theo was busying himself with a pile of stretched canvases. "I doubt Vincent knows them to this day, though he is very well read. Oh, here we are. Most of these he painted in Paris a few years ago. Some were sent from the South. This, for instance."

He pulled forward a picture of a coach resting against a brilliant yellow wall. Even in the shadowy room, the canvas crackled with heat. Green and red and black sizzled against each other, respectively the body, trim, and wheels of the carriage. I could almost hear the thrumming cicadas and the crunch of the dusty roadway beneath my feet.

"I begin to see what Tanguy meant about 'feeling,' " I said.

Theo nodded. "This he painted here while he was living with me in Paris. An entirely different mood."

"Ah, how lovely!" I exclaimed. It was a still life, a copper vase of fritillaries—their bell-shaped, golden blossoms and needles of leaves glimmered on the surface of the canvas. "What a color sense he has. Could the background have been anything besides that blue?"

"In a better light you'll be able to see all the colors that make up the blue; it's mixed with lavender, green, pink. . . . One doesn't want to say it's like a Monet—Vincent's work is not like anyone else's—but there was a moment when he was fascinated by Impressionist techniques." As he continued to sort through the disorderly rows of canvases, I saw colors flicker past: ultramarine, scarlet, a surprisingly soft green, and that searing yellow. "Ah. This is what I was looking for." He held up a horizontal rectangular canvas. At first I could only make out the simplest forms: round tables with crude chairs, clumsy ceiling lamps, a billiards table, awkward, blocky figures. Theo lifted the canvas to take it closer to the lantern on the wall. The colors became more distinct, but I almost wished they had not—the walls of the room were a throbbing red, trimmed with a green so vivid the eye bounced off it. The perspective was distorted so that the floorboards rushed upward while the chairs tilted, ready to eject anyone unfortunate enough to sit on them.

I could not look away from it, but I hated what it made me feel—despair, dislocation, and agitation. Melancholy seemed peaceful compared to this jangling, buzzing, lopsided room peopled with the vacant and desolate. As a window into Vincent's mental state, it was startling. Could this be the same artist who had painted the fritillaries, or the lovely portrait of Tanguy? "I see," I told Theo. "This is very disturbing."

Theo craned around to see the image more clearly. "He calls it *The Night Café*. He intentionally put all those colors together, to make it harsh. I think he said 'like a devil's furnace.' I hate to think that this was what his life was like in Arles, where he painted it. Do you see that figure standing in the center?"

"Yes, the waiter? With his hands hanging down?"

"Yes. He looks so helpless to me. As if he were trapped in this infernal place. Look at how much paint he used for the lamps." I reached out and touched one of them gently, a small ridged dome on the canvas. I remembered how the skin of Vincent's hands was seamed with paint. It was as though he sculpted with his pigments.

Theo lowered the painting, as if to set it down at the front of a row of canvases, facing the room. But he changed his mind and slipped it in behind, no doubt to conceal the alarming image. "The worst of his illness dates from Arles," he said, dusting off his hands. "The doctor in the asylum told us that when he was very ill he did not know who he was. At times he could describe his feelings, but in just a few hours, he would turn morose. He suspected everyone around him of seeking to do him harm."

"That is very common with melancholiacs," I said, watching Theo as he idly flipped through more pictures. "They feel they must be perpetually on guard. It is very difficult to win their trust." He pulled one out and put it at the front of the stack. A golden pottery vase of sunflowers stood against a cream background. Even in the dim light, the blossoms appeared to be so thick they were almost three-dimensional. Aside from the green stems and a narrow blue line dividing the lemon surface on which the vase stood from the pale background, the entire painting was yellow: primrose and mustard and egg yolk, ocher and daffodil and straw. It should never have worked. Yet it was a tour de force. Stepping closer, I could see the signature, "Vincent," in blue on the side of the vase. He must have been proud of it.

"Vincent painted a series of these sunflowers to decorate his little house in Arles for Gauguin," Theo said, straightening up. "His expectations were so high that his disappointment must have been dreadfully painful. Do you think he suffers from melancholy? Is that what ails him?" He stood, I couldn't help noticing, as stiffly as the waiter in *The Night Café*, hands empty at his sides.

"Not at the moment," I told him. "Patients afflicted by melancholy are always on the verge of fading away. You feel they would like to vanish if they could. But Vincent has such force. You can feel his eyes always moving, seeking motifs and rejecting them. He seems to think of nothing but painting."

"That is almost true," Theo agreed and turned to lift his lantern from the shelf. "To the extent that he thinks of anything else, it is almost always related to painting. Even when he reads, he thinks about how the writer's thoughts could be expressed in color. When he meets someone new, he wonders whether their face would be interesting to paint. He sees the whole world as if there were a palette always in his hand. Shall we go? I must get back to my wife and baby. We called my son Vincent, you know," he added, looking back from the door. "After my brother, of course, although Vincent thought we should have called the child after our father."

"Yet he must be pleased," I said, following Theo's lantern down the narrow staircase.

"Yes, of course." Theo's voice came from below. "In his own way. He painted the most beautiful canvas when he heard that our son had been born. He was in the asylum then. The painting is a branch of blossoming almond against a blue sky, the most limpid, serene blue. A picture of immense tenderness." By now we were back in Tanguy's shop. Theo carefully snuffed the lanterns and hung them back on the hook.

"Thank you so much, Monsieur Tanguy," he called through the door to the back room. "Please do not disturb your dinner. Good evening,

Madame Tanguy. I left the lanterns on the stair. We will see ourselves out."

I was almost startled to find myself on a busy Parisian street on a warm May evening, with light and noise coming from the little square at the end of the block. I turned to Theo and held out my hand. "I am most grateful, Monsieur van Gogh, that you took the time to show me these paintings. Of course I will see more of Monsieur Vincent's work in Auvers—I believe it is vital for his health that he continue to work— but I am glad you could show me some of his paintings from recent years." I took a deep breath, trying to control the emotion that I knew was in my voice. "Please believe that I will do everything I can to preserve the welfare of a man with such a gift."

I knew I might seem overwrought, but I was not embarrassed. Let Theo think what he pleased. If he was taken aback, he had enough command of his features to hide it. "One could ask for no more," he answered.

$\mathcal{F}$our

AFTER THAT EVENING, the image of *The Night Café* rose before me each time Vincent entered my mind. I wished that I had been able to see the painting of almond branches in bloom that Theo had described. It would have given me something to set against the desolation of the red and green café. But what was more significant, I found that I was now thinking of Vincent van Gogh as an artist rather than as a patient. Before I saw his work, he was for me a troubled man whom I might be able to help as I had helped others. Now I was glad that I had not seen his work before I examined him. As a patient, I had found him intriguing; as an artist, he was formidable.

My mind was full of the beautiful and terrifying paintings stacked up in Tanguy's attic when Vincent came to visit on the last Sunday in May. I was a little bit startled when Madame Chevalier, with an air of faint reluctance, showed him into the salon. He seemed so small compared to the image of him that his work had built up in my mind. The man who painted those canvases should, I thought, be a titanic physical presence, a man whose courage could be read in his features, not a slight figure in an ill-fitting coat.

We skirmished over coffee and rolls—I was always trying to feed him. But Vincent had come ready to paint, and he would not be distracted. He roamed about the gardens a bit, considering, hesitating, then finally set up his easel before the house, where the terraces step down to the street. I left him, not wanting to hover as he worked. Curiosity, however, drove me to my studio on the third floor several times in the course of that morning. From its window, I could watch his progress. I saw him set a small oblong canvas on the easel and start squeezing colors onto his palette, tossing the mangled tubes back into his box in no order at all. Less than an hour later, the canvas was half-covered. I could not see the details, but Vincent's brush darted at the painting like a hummingbird.

The time for luncheon approached. I had suggested that Madame Chevalier make a soufflé because of Vincent's ill-fitting teeth, but that also meant we could not be late to the table, lest the soufflé deflate. While our housekeeper was very fierce in protecting our interests, she had a soft spot for the vulnerable. I was playing on this when I told her about Vincent's pain while eating and his great need to become stronger; his life in Auvers would be more comfortable if Madame Chevalier was one of his allies. Promptness at meals was essential to winning her over, but I was reluctant to interrupt Vincent. He was painting in a furor, and I feared that, if I disrupted it, the picture could not be finished. I expected him to be possessed, in a way. I could not imagine that the spirit that allowed him to slash paint onto the canvas at such a rate could coexist with the mundanities of a soufflé and the necessity to clean the paint off his hands. He was perfectly affable, however. He finished a twirling orange knot of blossom—I was proud of my dahlias, and delighted to see them painted—and willingly put his brush down.

The painting is before me now, as I write. Vincent gave it to me later that week, when it had dried somewhat. I think he meant the gift as an exchange of sorts, a kind of payment for my care of him, like my paintings from Renoir and Monet. I am still startled by the life and vigor bursting off the canvas. I am lucky enough to own some two dozen of his paintings, many of which are more important than this, which he thought of as merely a "sketch." But I cannot see this one without being reminded of the first time I watched Vincent van Gogh paint.

I will confess to some initial confusion. I had thought I was abreast of the times, accustomed to the new techniques that involved painting spontaneously to capture fleeting visual conditions. By definition, this goal required swift execution. But Vincent van Gogh did not even appear to think about this composition, let alone plan it. It looked as if he merely tossed paint at the canvas. I could not help contrasting his slapdash approach with my own much more painstaking process: sketching, underpainting, blending pigments. I understood the principle of what he was doing; the eye would do the blending. And of course, as I now knew, he was immoderately gifted. That, no doubt, was why I had to work so much harder for results that pleased me much less.

Vincent became a familiar presence in our house over the next few weeks. On the days when I was in Auvers, he would ring the bell at the gate whenever he passed by. He came to the house one morning and made a beautiful painting of Marguerite watering the roses in the garden. Sometimes he came in just to drink something cool, or to drop off a book he had mentioned to me. We would sit in the shade behind the house and talk about what he had seen or painted that day. He never stayed very long, though; Vincent was industrious, and his next project always called out to him.

Once, I persuaded him to go fishing with me. It was a dull day, one of the few that summer, with low clouds that periodically released showers as if they could no longer be bothered to restrain them. For some reason I don't remember, Paul was not with us. Perhaps it was so early in June that he was still at the lycée in Paris. Marguerite and Madame Chevalier had embarked on some ambitious and noisy housekeeping task. It was one of those days when I was out of sorts and nothing pleased me, so I barked my displeasure when the women came to the door of the salon with their aprons and feather dusters. Marguerite

quailed, as she always did when I raised my voice, but Madame Chevalier, a creature of stronger fiber, thumped down her infernal tools, advanced on me, and suggested forcefully that I remove myself to the
riverbank. "If it's dirt and mess you want, you'll find it aplenty there.
We'll be finished by sunset, but you'll have to find yourself a meal elsewhere. I did tell you this, you know."

I was grateful at that moment that I did not have a wife. There is occasionally something intolerable in women's obsession with order. I put
on my oldest jacket and tore off a good third of a baguette I found in the
kitchen, seized my fishing rod, and headed to the river as Madame
Chevalier had suggested. It even bothered me that I was obeying her—
but fish do come to the surface on damp days like that.

I encountered Vincent near the train station, walking slowly with his
shoulders hunched against the rain. He was carrying his painting kit,
but a discouraged look on his face suggested that the weather had
forced him to change his plans. He had hoped to paint the cottages in
the rain, but the humidity interfered with the application of pigment to
the canvas. "It so rarely rains in the South," he told me. "I feel very foolish as well as disappointed."

I, on the other hand, was delighted to see him. A solitary afternoon
beneath the willows would not have been terrible, but Vincent's company in a rowboat—that would be quite charming.

It was not easy to persuade him to join me. I had to walk back to
Ravoux's with him and beg the loan of a large umbrella so that Vincent
could still sketch on the boat in the rain. He refused to have anything to
do with a fishing rod. Then at the landing stage, where I rented a boat
for a paltry sum—there was certainly no one else out that day—Vincent
balked at stepping into the craft. One does not want to laugh in such a
situation, for he was masking genuine fear, but his almost childish apprehension was comical. Once we were launched, he seemed consoled
by my obvious competence at the oars—at least he could be sure I
would not overturn the boat—and before long he was intrigued by the
entirely new vantage point provided by the little craft. For my part, I
was pleased for once to be the expert, showing him how to sit in the
center of the boat, pointing out little landmarks like the river otters'

den. Paul had long since seen everything and sometimes attempted to snub me in similar circumstances, but Vincent was much more receptive. Bit by bit, his apprehension diminished. Then he confessed: "I cannot swim, you know."

"The river is shallow. And I would have thought you Dutchmen were all at home on the water."

He laughed. "You know, even fishermen often can't swim. Imagine what a predicament! Spending your time on the open water, every day, in every weather, always aware that it can kill you."

"The Oise cannot kill you," I remember saying, not entirely truthfully. A hip bath can kill you, if you want it to. I shipped the oars and prepared to bait my hook. Vincent watched intently. Then I dropped the hook overboard and let it drift in the current.

"Is that all you do?" he asked.

I was surprised. "Yes."

"I was expecting nets, I think," Vincent said. Then he began to laugh. "But that would be ridiculous! I was thinking of ocean fishing, where men go out to sea and put their lives at risk!"

I had to laugh with him. "That being the case, you were very brave to get into this boat with me."

"That was certainly my opinion!"

This short exchange put us on a new footing. We were companions rather than doctor and patient. Vincent refused to bait the hook, claiming that he could not bear to be cruel to the earthworm, but he took his turn with the rod and reeled in a fairly respectable perch, which he then sketched, lying on the flat seat between us. I wish I knew what had become of that drawing. I suppose those notebooks went back to Holland with Johanna.

"Do you ever paint still lifes?" I asked Vincent, as he admired his catch. I had seen flower paintings at Tanguy's in Paris, but I wondered about other subjects. "When Cézanne was here, he painted apples over and over again."

"Because he could find nothing better to paint?" Vincent asked.

"No, we put bouquets together and painted those, and he went out into the village as well. He was experimenting with rendering volume, I believe."

"That seems to be all he ever does. I understand that this is his primary concern, and I can imagine that he must find it interesting, but the results are quite dull. The colors are always the same, have you noticed?"

"Not always. You've seen my flower pieces—he uses clearer tones there."

"True, but the landscapes are most monotonous. Always the same dreary green." He pointed at his fish. "Now, you see, if I had my paints, I could make something beautiful with that gleaming skin, something Cézanne would never think of. I would have liked to do that. A kind of silvery olive, shaded with pink. Can I take him with me?"

"Of course," I said, "but you'd better give him to Ravoux to cook for your dinner. The skin will dull very quickly, and then he will start to smell."

"Yes, that's true," Vincent said with a frown and returned to his sketch. "I painted some sardines once, but even though I work quickly, I could not tolerate their smell for very long. It was a while before I could eat sardines again after that."

He ended up not painting that fish but eating it, which made me even happier. He came back to the house with me, and Madame Chevalier sautéed his catch and mine with almonds and fresh parsley. I saw him eyeing the skeleton on his plate when he had finished, as if he would have liked to draw it, but he let Madame Chevalier remove the plate without any protest.

If Vincent came to the house on the way to Ravoux's at the end of the day, he liked to show me what he had painted. Soon we were accustomed to his speed, to the élan with which he covered even large canvases with paint. Once Paul finished his school term, and returned home for the summer, he would often clean up after our new friend; you could always tell where in Auvers Vincent had been working, and often what colors he had used. Paul sometimes came home from his wanderings around the village with one of Vincent's paint tubes or abandoned brushes, tossed aside when the bristles failed. As I knew, Theo kept him supplied with materials; the shipments from Paris must have been prodigious.

It was the first sign Paul showed of having any artistic inclination, despite my numerous previous attempts to share my interests with him. I told myself that this was because Vincent was a younger man, closer to Paul in age than I was. Certainly Vincent made no attempt to win Paul over, though my son followed him around like a puppy. Paul sometimes tried to strike up a conversation, but Vincent rarely responded beyond mere courtesy. This did not seem to discourage Paul, though. He was always persistent when he wanted something. To this day I wonder what he hoped for from Vincent. Some kind of approval or acknowledgment, I suppose.

The paintings accumulated quickly. I was slightly concerned about Vincent's almost feverish pace, lest he wear himself out. Yet he seemed to be delighted rather than anxious. This ardor was one of his most compelling traits. Each time I returned from my customary four-day stint in Paris, he was eager to show me what he had done in my absence. It was as if he were discovering the world I lived in with eyes that unveiled a new splendor. It appeared that he could not be deterred by discomfort or fatigue or discouragement. When a painting did not please him, he thought of another way to approach the subject. He was always thinking about the next thing he wanted to paint. His speed reflected a kind of hunger to make the beauty all around him his own. I found this both fascinating and inspiring. ✔

Vincent was using a kind of shed at Ravoux's as storage, and by early June, it was beginning to fill with images of Auvers, then with shipments of paintings Vincent had made in the South, then with more Auvers paintings. He loved the crooked little thatched cottages and the fields patchworked with their different shades of green. I never tired of examining the way he applied the paint—in waves or dashes or thick, swirling rosettes. Sometimes he would cover a background with a kind of woven effect, painstakingly applied.

He did not mind at all when I watched him, I discovered. In fact, he said he concentrated better with someone to talk to.

I thought that was why he wanted to paint my portrait—that he might as well make use of my constant presence. He was surprisingly modest in his request, asking if I might be able to spare him the time for a sitting. Of course I was flattered and intrigued. I had by then seen his exquisite self-portrait, the one with the swirling blue background that I am fortunate enough to own now. There was a rigor to it that I admired immensely. It was not a portrait in the old-fashioned sense, a painting that demonstrated a sitter's position in life and permitted him to think well of himself. Van Gogh's self-portrait with the blue flames is an examination. In fact, I thought, that afternoon, as Vincent arranged his easel, that it was now his turn to examine me. I had peered at his body and attempted to diagnose the state of his mind, and he would now do likewise to me.

When my old friend Amand Gautier painted me as a young man, we discussed the format, the pose, even which one of my two coats I should wear. He sketched a few different poses, drew my figure three or four times to work out his lighting scheme. That portrait was finished in three weeks, and we thought his swiftness astounding. (I might add that it was a great success in the Salon of 1861, and that I gained a degree of renown from the painting and the lithograph reproduction of it.) Now here I was, sitting at the red table in the garden behind the house, without any obvious preparation. But of course Vincent van Gogh never did anything conventionally. I would have liked to change into something more elegant, but Vincent would not permit this.

"No, Doctor, just as you are," he said. "We'll do very well with your old jacket." I made to take off my hat, but he would not permit that, either, though it was only a stained sailor's cap with a narrow leather brim. Vincent stood a few feet away, squeezing blue and red and yellow paint onto his palette.

"And how would you like me to pose?" I asked, feeling somewhat at a loss. "Perhaps I could be writing something?"

"No, no," he answered, scrutinizing the bristles on a brush and discarding it. "Just lean your head on your hand and look at me." I obeyed. I already knew better than to suggest an alternative.

He stepped back and gazed at me. "We need another note," he muttered, almost to himself. "Yellow." He glanced around, as if the desired color would appear before him.

"Have you any yellow blooms, Doctor?" he asked. "I don't know your northern plants very well. I want something strong, like the yolk of an egg."

"There are the orange dahlias you painted the other day," I suggested.

"No, I must have yellow, the primary color. You see the red of the table and the blue of your coat require it, a strong, true yellow like the cover of a novel. Actually, a book would do nicely."

"Yes, of course," I said. "Shall I get one?"

"Yes," he said. "But I will paint your figure first. I like this pose. It shows that you have been long acquainted with grief."

So he was indeed examining me, and he had managed to discern a truth about me that I did not often acknowledge. Blanche had been gone for many years already; perhaps I should have been able to put the pain and guilt of her death behind me. Yet I often felt that I carried it with me like a heavy stone, a burden I could never put down. Many a man has been widowed young, but there is a special anguish in being a doctor who cannot cure his wife. Vincent watched me as if waiting for a response. "I lost my wife to illness fifteen years ago," I confessed. "It is a long time, yet the sadness persists." I looked around the garden and gestured to the trees and shrubs. "It was at this time of year. Sometimes the way the sunlight falls, or a certain scent on the breeze, brings back a rush of memories."

"And you did not marry again," Vincent observed. He had begun to paint, but I hardly noticed his hand moving swiftly from palette to canvas and back.

"No, I did not," I confirmed. "I never met another woman . . ."

"Another woman like Madame Gachet?" Vincent prompted.

"No," I agreed. I fell silent again. It was the truth. Yet there was a freedom, too, in being unmarried, which brought me occasional solace.

Sometimes bachelors like Vincent imagine marriage as a blissful union, but there is a constraint. A married man must live up to his wife. Or perhaps I felt this only because of how Blanche had died. The last days of a consumptive's life are wretched and painful, yet Blanche showed only courage and kindness as she left us. For me she had forgiveness and more. There is a terrible rebuke in pity from a woman you have failed. I felt that, in contrast to her steadfastness, I had discovered only cowardice in myself. That discovery has haunted me ever since. In any event, I did not expect Vincent to understand.

Looking at one of his canvases, you can imagine how he moved constantly while he painted. The pigment seems to have been applied with his whole body. As I sat still on that early summer afternoon, he danced around me, stepping back and forth to the canvas, bending his knees, shifting his weight. And talking all the while. I value intensely some of the things he told me that afternoon. He was fascinated by portraits, and loathed photographs; he despised their slavish recording of physical features.

"I believe that, with color, I can capture a more enduring truth," he said. "Something more in the nature of a dream, that has a truth of its own that may be different from what we experience every day. For example, I will paint your face in brick red." (Naturally I found this notion somewhat alarming.) "Next to the blue background, it will appear much paler. Your face will look rosy, healthy—but I will be able to show also how the distress of time has played on your features." He hoped, he told me, that his portraits might still be valued a hundred years hence, allowing the people of that distant era to better understand the conditions of life as we ended the nineteenth century. He seemed not to think it at all unlikely that people would still know his paintings in 1990. It was a strange kind of confidence for a man whose work had been seen primarily in cafés, a paint shop, and his brother's apartment, and bought by precisely one collector.

When he was satisfied with a rough outline of my figure, he allowed me to stand up and move about. "Would you find me that novel, Doctor?" he asked. "Two volumes would be best. I don't mind what they are, but they must be yellow."

I returned to the garden with a pair of volumes that he placed carefully in front of me. "Have you read any of the Goncourts' novels, Doctor?" he asked.

"No," I answered. "I have heard of them, naturally."

"I will give these books two of their titles. One of them, *Germinie Lacerteux,* concerns a remarkable case of mental degeneration. I understand it was the authors' maid who inspired it. When she became ill and died, they discovered that she had led a secret existence of complete debauchery. She drank and went with men—she had even had a child, I believe. Yet they never guessed it."

"What a tale!" I answered. "Of course I have seen women subject to these compulsions, but they normally become apparent. It seems those brothers must not have been terribly observant."

"Perhaps not." Vincent knelt on the ground, his head hidden by the canvas. The palette rested on one of his bent legs, and, a brush laden with cadmium yellow darted between canvas and palette. "Yet because it is about the woman's disastrous mental state, it will allude to your work with ailments of the mind. And the other title is *Manette Salomon.* You don't know it either?" He peered out from the side of the canvas as he asked this.

"No," I said.

"A marvelous book. Not unlike Zola's *L'Oeuvre.* Which you certainly know," he went on and withdrew behind the canvas again.

"That one, yes," I answered. "I was especially interested in it because of my connection with Cézanne." Zola's novel had created quite a furor in the circles I frequented. It was an unsparing portrait of an unsuccessful artist who was so obviously based on Cézanne that after it was published the artist and author had parted ways, despite a lifelong friendship.

"Well, *Manette Salomon* is quite similar, only there are also echoes of Manet's career. In any event, it concerns the harsh life of the artist who tries to create something new. And it will refer to your interest in art and artists."

Vincent got to his feet and stepped back. "Yes, that is what I wanted. The yellow heightens the blue and the red. It locks the whole composition into place. Yet we are still missing a note. You wouldn't have any lavender, or mauve? Surely somewhere in your garden?" He came around to my side of the canvas to look over the flower beds. There was a spot of vermilion on his sleeve.

I pointed to the bells of the foxglove just a few meters away. "Would that do?" I asked. "Shall I cut it for you?"

"No, Doctor, I can get it. Do you mind if I break off a stalk?" He didn't wait for permission. "What a pretty blossom. What is it called?"

"Foxglove," I told him. "Also known as digitalis. We doctors use the extract of the leaves to control some heart disorders."

"Oh, wonderful," he answered. "For we could also say, Doctor, that you take care of your patients' hearts, couldn't we?" It was the kind of allusion that made him happy.

It is easy to forget, in light of what happened to him, that Vincent had a playful side, but the evidence of his humor is right there in my portrait. We had been discussing my career and some of the more striking incidents that had earned me nomination to the Order of the Legion of Honor. For instance, when I was still a medical student, I traveled to the Jura to help care for the patients in a cholera epidemic. Upon my return, one of the doctors sent my nomination to the minister of health, but nothing came of it. Other episodes resulted in subsequent nominations: my activity during a train wreck on the Chemin de Fer du Nord, for example, or my medical services during the siege of Paris. When I related these to Vincent—I had been nominated, without success, six times by 1890—he laughed and took up a narrow brush, dashing it through a streak of scarlet on his palette, and slashed a thread through my lapel on the canvas—the red ribbon of the Legion of Honor. "Never mind, Doctor," he said, "you'll get your ribbon yet. Perhaps for your services to the arts!" he crowed, taking the joke a step further. "Doctor to all the renegade painters in Paris, the *refusés* and *intransigeants* and Impressionists and every kind of rebel. The Ministry of Arts will reward you for keeping us all alive and making masterpieces!" He paused in the midst of laughing and frowned, scrutinizing the canvas. "In any event, that streak of red intensifies the blue of your coat. I like the effect." Still, he did not include the "ribbon" in the duplicate portrait he made for me at my request. I suppose I am glad, since

I still have not received the award. It might have been difficult to explain to viewers that this was a little painterly joke.

When Vincent allowed me to stand up and stretch, I could see that it was indeed my face appearing on the canvas. I looked despondent. My eyes gazed out beyond the viewer to something—or nothing. You could say I was lost in an unhappy reverie. The skin of my cheek was pushed up and wrinkled by the fist it rested on. There, identifiably, were my red hair, my mustache, the tiny bit of beard I wore in those days. The features were mine.

Yet in a way it was also not me. There I was, a haunted man, with the gay yellow books and the bells of the foxglove pressed up to the front of the picture. The angle of the flowers echoed the way my body leaned to the side of the canvas, so that the yellow books somehow held us steady. But for all the physical resemblance, what makes this portrait a marvel is not the way it captures anything specific to me. It is more than that: Vincent used my features to create a portrait of world-weariness. He later told me that he had described it to Gauguin in a letter as having "the despairing expression of our times."

I have thought of every conversation I had with Vincent so often that I could repeat them all exactly. Vincent asked questions. He solicited opinions. However, looking back, I wonder if these conversations were ever true exchanges or just Vincent's attempts to seek confirmation for what he already believed. And I have wondered, in the years since then, whether Vincent perceived the people he knew as individuals. He had a great love for humankind—he spoke often about the suffering in the world, and I do believe that he felt it deeply. What he did not seem to feel was the suffering of the particular human beings around him. Or, for that matter, their anxiety, their impatience, their satisfaction, their longing. Certainly this inability affected his relations with Theo. It also explained the unfortunate episodes of his attachments to women, as Theo had described them to me. It was a mark of the extent of his mental alienation, but, alas, I did not recognize it until much later.

When I arrived at this conclusion, I felt somewhat disillusioned, I must confess. I had become accustomed to thinking of him as a man of wisdom. I preferred not to see his limitation: he had compassion for mankind but not for individual men. I felt that, in sitting for a portrait, I had trusted him to plumb my soul, much the way he had trusted me when he first arrived in Auvers. And indeed, he had done that in a way, by seeing the grief that I carried around as an invisible burden. He saw it, and he used it in my portrait as an emblem. He did not, I realized, understand it. He knew what my grief looked like, but not what it was to suffer it.

But there was no reason why he should, I had to remind myself. I was the doctor, he the patient, and one does not anticipate that the patient shall turn and diagnose the one who is supposed to cure him. Further, I had been painted before and was painted again afterward without expecting such profound revelations. It was just that Vincent was so extraordinary that one tended to expect marvels from him. Disappointment was inevitable.

Five

∞

VINCENT WORKED almost exclusively in oils when he was with us. He made some pencil drawings while he was in Auvers, but he was first and foremost a colorist. Yet he was always curious about other ways of making images. One day, not long after he painted my portrait, we were in my studio looking at the etchings Cézanne had made back in 1873. Among them was a little sketch, very precious to me, of Cézanne preparing the copper plate for an etching while I look on. Pissarro had drawn it on a scrap of black-edged letter paper he'd found in my drawer, left over, I suppose, from the period of mourning after Blanche's death. The black border lends a strange emphasis to an informal record of a collaboration.

"So the three of you made etchings together?" Vincent asked.

"On several occasions," I confirmed. "You can imagine what a challenge it was for Cézanne to think about line instead of color. He was painting almost entirely with the palette knife in those days, in blocks of color, so he had to proceed very differently." I leafed through the little prints in the folder, and pulled out one of the painter Armand Guillaumin, seated somewhat awkwardly on the ground. It had a certain freshness but was undeniably clumsy.

"Yes," Vincent agreed. "You can see here, on the shoulder, that the line is quite tentative."

"Mind you, it's not a simple process. First you have to remember that your image is going to be reversed. Then you also have to pull the needle through the varnish on the plate. If it's been correctly prepared, the resistance is consistent, but when the three of us were working together back then, Cézanne was a novice. He might have been using a plate that he'd covered himself, as you see in the drawing. Then the needle would have moved slower or faster depending on how evenly the varnish had been applied."

Vincent glanced at the small press that took up rather too much of the space in the studio. I had not used it in some time, and there were stacks of paper and boxes of charcoal piled on it.

"Could we try it?" he asked. "Perhaps I could make a series of etchings after my own works, for sale."

"Of course we could." I moved to lift the clutter from the bed of the press. "In the cabinet near the window you will find some copper plates," I told him, pointing. "I think there are several sizes. We'll start with something small." He followed my instructions and brought out a clean copper plate. I had a moment's qualm; the waxy varnish would require heating before we could paint it onto the plate. The fastest way to heat it would be on the stove, but Madame Chevalier would not be pleased to see us entering her kitchen.

Vincent evidently shared my trepidation, for as we went down the stairs, burdened with the etcher's equipment, he said to me in a low voice, "I would not want to be in your housekeeper's way. Perhaps we can work in the garden?"

"Absolutely. But we must melt the varnish on the stove. Here." I handed him the needles, the rags, and the sealed vial of acid. "The acid is terribly strong, so be careful with it."

Madame Chevalier was sitting at the table peeling a large pile of potatoes when I pushed through the door into the kitchen. "May I help you, Doctor?"

"I don't want to disturb you," I said, "but Monsieur Vincent asked if I could show him how to etch, and I must warm the varnish for the plate. May I just put it on the stove?"

She stood, as I had known she would, and pushed the metal bowl a few centimeters back from where I had placed it on the stove's surface. Over the years she had become a master at communicating without resorting to words. This little gesture demonstrated to me that she was mistress of the stove top, not I. "What were you planning to use to stir this with, Doctor?"

I looked into the bowl, where the black substance was turning liquid around the edges. "Not one of my spoons!" she warned me as I lifted a hand toward the jug of implements next to the stove. I sighed and went back up the stairs to my studio, to find an appropriate brush.

Later, while Vincent was carefully stroking the black varnish onto the plate, Madame Chevalier surprised me by coming out the kitchen door with a pitcher and glasses on a tray. She set it down on the nearby bench, saying, "Here is some mint syrup, gentlemen. I thought you might be feeling the heat." She straightened up and looked at the two of us. "Monsieur Vincent, would you like to wear one of the doctor's hats? The sun is very strong."

"You are very kind, Madame Chevalier," he answered, "but after my time in the South, I barely feel your northern sun. Thank you anyway."

She nodded sharply and stumped back into the house.

"Madame Chevalier does not usually coddle my guests," I commented to Vincent. "She must have taken a liking to you."

"She terrified me the first day I visited here. When she opened the gate, she looked so fierce that I almost ran off down the street."

"She is inclined to be protective of us. Apparently she now considers you one of the family. I am afraid that means she will nag you to eat."

"Do you think she would pose for me, Doctor? I love to paint those older ladies with their determined faces. And her coloring is so interesting."

I had never noticed Madame Chevalier's coloring before. Now that it was pointed out to me, I realized that her ruddy face and bright blue eyes were, indeed, striking. I wondered how Vincent would render them. "I expect she will tell you that she does not have enough time to sit for a portrait," I answered, "but you may ask her, of course. Now what will be the subject of your first etching?"

"I thought perhaps you would pose," Vincent answered. "As I have already painted you, I have worked out some of the fundamental questions of tone, what needs to be darker or lighter, and how pronounced those variations should be. This way I can concentrate on using the needle. Do I handle it as if it were a pen?"

"Almost," I answered. "You have no control over the width of the line, of course. And you should try to keep it perpendicular to the plate. You will also need a light touch. You are just removing the varnish; the acid will make the mark in the plate."

"Would you sit at the table?" he asked me. "In that chair, leaning on the table? Just like the painted portrait. And for dark areas, I assume I should make some kind of hatching pattern?"

"Yes, like an ink drawing. The closer the lines, the darker the tone."

He went to work quickly, showing no hesitation. The copper plate lay on the table between us, and Vincent's eyes moved back and forth between it and me. "I think I would like to include your pipe, Doctor, do you have it nearby?"

I almost cautioned him against making the composition too complex. Etching is disconcerting. Most artists new to the technique would have experimented with something simple, like a vase of flowers or a few apples on a plate. But Vincent grasped the process with remarkable speed. No doubt he was helped by the fact that, as he said, he had already analyzed the patterns of dark and light made by my face. Yet he managed, in his first and only etching, to communicate not only what I looked like, what I was wearing, and my expression, but the texture of my hair and coat. He even sketched in some of the garden behind me, somehow indicating the distance between me and the nearest rosebush.

I had already acknowledged to myself that Vincent van Gogh was enormously talented. I knew that my experience as an artist helped me to understand how exceptional his paintings were. But for years I had thought of myself as primarily an etcher. If I, a doctor, had an artistic medium, it was this one, the elaborate and messy process of etching, biting in acid, wiping the plate, inking it, and finally printing an impression on dampened paper. When Vincent had asked to try his hand at it, I was pleased to think that I could be the expert. His portrait of me, *L'Homme à la pipe*, showed me definitively that this was not so. His first attempt at a notoriously difficult medium demonstrated once again the magnitude of his artistic gift.

When I began my externship at the Salpêtrière, in 1855, I was twenty-six and advanced in my medical studies. By then I had already trained with a surgeon and with a general physician. I had seen the human heart laid bare and had taken a saw to living bone. Yet our mad patients drew my interest as no others had. There seemed to be so little, sometimes, between us. Who has not felt the shroud of melancholy, that pall of listlessness that devalues any effort and washes all color to gray? Who has not become attached to a notion and blindly refused to see reason? Who has not chosen to see himself as something entirely other than what he is?

They seized my imagination, these madwomen. I spent more and more time at the hospital and neglected my other studies. But the lectures in the vast amphitheater of the Faculté de Médecine, delivered by gray-haired professors in academic robes, seemed to have very little to do with helping human beings in pain. I thought we could do better.

One of Dr. Pinel's innovations was to distinguish among the different kinds of mental disturbance. Until his direction of the asylum, the epileptic and the idiotic, the violent and the meekly melancholy were all housed together. Pinel established the first classifications of madness—differentiating among melancholia, mania, dementia, and idiocy—and attempted to relieve them. Yet some patients improved, while others did not. It seemed clear that we could not successfully cure madness until we knew what caused it, which was one of the great debates of the day. Many patients who died were autopsied. Their brains and nerves were searched for lesions or anomalies so that connections could be made between anatomy and behavior. Perhaps there were other physical causes so far undiagnosed. So we studied the madwomen with intensity, taking notes and consulting each other. I began to carry a pocket journal, in which I took down fleeting impressions. "Kindness is not drowned in madness," I wrote one day. "Ursule and Marie-Ange often walk in the courtyard with Yvonne. She does not appear to recognize them." And "Certain sounds are especially disturbing to the women. I hate to see them flinching when the bells chime the hours."

Most of our patients were poor and came from the dark, damp, congested, disease-ridden parts of Paris. This was before the famous transformation of our city under Baron Haussmann. The broad boulevards and grandiose monuments like the new Opéra did not yet exist. Instead there were large areas, like the entire Île de la Cité, where medieval buildings leaned together across moist alleys, where chunks of fetid plaster dropped from walls, where families of eight crowded into a single room, a single bed. The Salpêtrière, with its rows of beds and refectory tables, its regular meals and tall windows, its sympathetic treatment of inmates and measured, predictable periods of work and leisure, provided many patients with a level of health and comfort they had not previously known. Sometimes their mental states improved swiftly.

Many earnest efforts were made to counter the tedium inherent in an establishment like the Salpêtrière, whose buildings and courtyards, though spacious, tended toward gloom. The notion of moral treatment included extensive recreation for the patients. They spent time in the courtyards each day and went to services in the chapel if they chose. There were performances and social events, like the annual *bal des folles*, a costume ball that traditionally took place a few Sundays before Easter. The patients spent hours beforehand planning their costumes and hours afterward discussing the party. At first I found the idea of the costume ball bizarre—when you are already mad, a stranger to yourself, why dress up as someone else?—but I realized after witnessing it myself how important it was in breaking up the monotony of life in an institution.

A few weeks after the ball, I unintentionally provided another distraction for some of the women in my division. My superior Dr. Falret was in charge of two hundred women, mostly victims of melancholia or manias. The madwomen seemed to like me, though I suspected they did not take me as seriously as I would have hoped. I often spent my free time with them during their recreation sessions, which grew livelier as the weather warmed. Some of the enclosures had grass or flowers, which were highly valued by the patients. Woe to the woman who stepped off the slate path onto the tender green blades and jeopardized their growth! She would be shrilly scolded by her fellow patients. In the graveled courts, the patients had more freedom to move. Some skipped aimlessly like children and loved to play with a ball. Some drifted around as if hearing private music, raising their arms, swaying, bowing. When I could, I would sit on a bench and watch, or talk to the women who approached me. They were like all of us in this: they loved attention.

Of course not everything they told you was true. They gossiped eagerly about each other, but with even greater zeal about us, the doctors. According to them, we were always madly in love with our patients.

I was sitting on a stone bench in a patch of sun one day when this amorous fantasy was brought up. Next to me was Laure, a patient—and a former nurse—a little older than I who had actually grown up in the Salpêtrière. Her case was not especially unusual. What could be more normal in this enclosed world than a marriage between a gardener, her father, and a nurse, her mother? And what more normal than that the daughter of such a marriage should take up her mother's occupation? It had struck me as strange at first that she should have gone mad. Could madness be contagious, then? Or was she feigning illness? Trading the authority of a staff member for the fecklessness of the patient? I could not decide, but I always listened carefully to Laure.

"There is a strange young man here today," she told me on a warm day in April. "He goes everywhere, I hear, even the dormitories. He has a pad of paper, and he is drawing us! What do you think about this, Doctor?" she asked.

"It seems harmless," I told her. "He is my friend, you know. I have known him for many years. He is called Monsieur Gautier."

"But why is he here?"

"He came for the ball, a few weeks ago, with the art students. He was the Roman soldier. Were you there?"

Over the years, the *bal des folles* had also, oddly enough, become an informal tradition for the students of the École des Beaux-Arts. Every year a group of them dressed in elaborate costumes and arrived at the asylum to enliven the party. Gautier had borrowed the costume of a Roman soldier from the studio of his teacher, Cogniet. With its breastplate and red-plumed helmet, he would have been conspicuous in any group. But the costume also included a kind of short, pleated skirt covered with strips of leather. My friend's strong, bare legs had been much admired.

"Oh, yes, I remember him, Doctor. We all do. But nobody knows why he has come back."

"He is an artist, so he wants to draw the women here. He thinks he might like to do a painting of some of you. I asked Dr. Falret if he might visit. After the doctor spoke to him, he agreed to it."

Laure's eyes narrowed. "I don't understand. We aren't beautiful."

"Perhaps you are beautiful in his eyes," I suggested.

"He is certainly beautiful in ours!" She sniggered. "Don't you remember that he was the king of the ball? The women loved seeing his legs! Now they will want to show him theirs!" She rocked with laughter, slapping her thigh. The coarse humor of a nurse? The lack of control of a madwoman? The former, I thought.

"Then no one will mind his presence here?"

"Oh, far from it, Doctor!" She chortled. "The more young men, the merrier." She stood up to leave me. "They're already calling him Jules César," she said and walked away.

"Apparently they refer to you as Jules César," I informed Gautier when he strolled into the courtyard a few minutes later. "Because of your costume for the ball. They voted you king for your legs."

The remark would have made me blush, but Gautier was always difficult to embarrass. "So I've been told," he said, sitting down next to me. "The patients see my legs as more of an advantage than Dr. Falret did."

"Did he tell you that?"

"Not in so many words. Just warned me about the general standards for behavior around here. He impressed upon me that these are women without inhibitions, not aware of what they're saying. I didn't really understand what he meant until one of them walked right up and kissed me. The doctor is wrong, they know exactly what they're saying," he protested. "I've been propositioned very explicitly twice, and I've only been here since noon."

"Oh, yes, that's the other thing. I was informed last week that this group of externs is disappointing. Not handsome enough. So you shouldn't be proud, it's only that they're desperate."

He looked me up and down theatrically. "Well, of course they are. Look at you!" He was quicker-witted than I was.

We sat silently for a few minutes, watching the women. There was a quality to their voices that I was trying to analyze, a kind of high timbre that made them sound more like children than grown women. I took out my notebook to write down some of the phrases I could make out: "Take it, take it!" called one woman, while another sang a bit of plainsong, perfectly.

Gautier had his portfolio on his knee, with a sheet of paper clipped to it. As if without thinking, he drew a few lines, and the space of the courtyard was suddenly defined on his page. A light vertical, the tree in the center. Two more lines, the path. I had seen him do this over and over again since he arrived in Paris three years earlier. Out of nothing, he conjured something. Though you knew it was just charcoal on paper, your eye accepted the illusion. A tree, a wall, a hat, a man, a bowl of fruit. He complained endlessly about the École des Beaux-Arts and the ceaseless repetitive drawing exercises that he considered useless, but I had known his work as a student back in Lille. He had improved immensely since then. ,

Now he began to rough in the figures. Laure and a friend were strolling up the walkway. An old woman, one of the "restantes"—a permanent patient who would live out her days at the Salpêtrière—was standing still in the sunlight, gabbling up at the sky and gesticulating with her hands raised. "Can you tell, by looking at them, the nature of their illness?" he asked, his eyes swinging between the patients and the paper.

"Sometimes," I answered, watching his charcoal. My own notebook felt clumsy in my hands. "The one in the cloak," I went on, "sitting on the ground, is a melancholiac. Always sad, lacking spirit, lacking energy. They turn in upon themselves. You often see them curled up like this," I said, folding my arms to my chest and lifting my knees. "That one, over there, is another." I pointed. "The woman with her face to the wall. She will remain there, immobile, until the wardress brings her inside."

"Will she get better?"

"She won't get worse."

"And why does that woman have to wear a straitjacket?"

"She is what we call a *furieuse*. Normally they are housed in their own ward, but her madness has just recently become violent, so she is still with her usual companions. She may yet calm down, and we don't like to move patients to different divisions unless it's necessary. The *furieuses* have manic spells when they hit and scratch and shriek. They become dangerous to themselves and to others, so they must be restrained in the jackets."

"And the one flouncing around with the imaginary fan?"

"What we call a monomaniac. She believes she is the Duchesse de Berry, and when she has delivered the heir to the throne, she will move to the Tuileries."

"Don't tell the emperor," Gautier joked. "Does she know about any of it? About 1848?"

"We tell her. She doesn't hear. She awaits her confinement stead-fastly. She sometimes even begins labor. And here is the remarkable thing, Gautier—she has not had her monthly courses in years, and when her imaginary labor begins, her heartbeat rises and her stomach muscles actually contract. Look at the way she walks," I added. She took slow steps, almost waddling, the hand without the fan at the small of her back.

"And don't tell me, she'll get better when there's a Bourbon back on the throne?"

"We do our best," I said sharply, turning to face Gautier. "There is much we don't know. If you're here to mock, you're no better than the barbarians who used to jeer at the lunatics in chains."

"No, no," he said, in a soothing tone of voice, shading the melancholiac's cloak. "You're such a hothead, Gachet. I mean no disrespect. But you have to admit it's funny. Walking around thinking she's pregnant with the heir to the throne, two regimes ago."

"I don't agree," I answered shortly.

"It's not even funny that the regimes changed so quickly?"

"Least of all that. Listen, I cannot laugh at these women. There is so little separating them from us."

He turned and looked me full in the face. "You always were very sensitive. I mean no disrespect."

"But you find madness amusing," I insisted, refusing to let it go.

He didn't respond right away. Instead he sketched the old woman with the raised hands. It would have been easy to exaggerate her pose in order to mock her. A grimace here, a clenched hand there, and the women would look like hags, somehow less than human. But Gautier's drawing did not put a distance between the observer and the observed. From the sketches he made at the hospital, he later created a painting called *The Madwomen of the Salpêtrière*, which was exhibited to great acclaim at the Salon of 1857. People found his portrayal of my patients remarkably sympathetic.

"I don't find madness amusing," he finally said, "and I don't find any of these individuals amusing. But I'm not trying to save them. That may be the difference between us."

"No," I admitted, "I can see that you aren't laughing at them." I gestured to his drawing. "It would show."

"Well, then," he said, teasing the page out from beneath the clip and sliding it into the portfolio. "You can stop protecting them from me, can't you?" He got up quickly and was gone before I could formulate a response.

I sat there for a while longer, thinking about what he had said. Perhaps I did feel protective of the women, but that did not seem inappropriate. They were vulnerable. With Gautier, I was not worried about their physical welfare. Since he lived next door to me, I knew that he was currently occupied with both a hatter's apprentice and a barmaid.

Surely the two of them (each ignorant of the other) satisfied his lust and delight in intrigue.

I perceived a different kind of vulnerability in the madwomen. Gautier had come close to it when he mentioned the women's propositions to him. "They know exactly what they're saying," he'd insisted, contradicting Dr. Falret's assertion. Perhaps both men were right, or neither was. Perhaps the madwomen expressed their truest thoughts, regardless of the audience. They had lost sight of what was expected or forbidden and obeyed impulses as they occurred. That, then, was the source of the madwomen's frailty: They were missing the cloak of convention. Their emotions were laid bare.

I surveyed the women in the courtyard, wondering if this notion applied to them. To the melancholiac sitting on the ground, most certainly. This woman felt her very existence as a burden too heavy to bear. The woman talking gibberish to the sky was also so lost in her own world that she seemed oblivious to the world in which she lived, the way a feverish patient may kick off all coverings and expose his body, unaware of his immodesty.

Was that why I was so uncomfortable with Gautier drawing them? Did it seem like an exposure? Somehow the idea made me cringe, the idea of drawing the mad. It had been done often before, I knew, usually with satiric intent. But I had acquitted Gautier of that. Whence my anxiety?

I turned the page of my notebook and looked at the women. I drew a line on the page: the cloak of the woman standing still by the wall. A simple, U-shaped line. Now what? I looked again. I tried to force myself to draw only what my eye saw, not what I knew was there. Not the body in the round, the shoulders or the bowed head, but the patterns of dark and light. Drawing the mad. To see why I felt it was wrong, I would try it.

The pen was a terrible instrument. Every mistake was permanent. It was too black, too coarse. I could make only lines, not shadows, and the lines I made were ugly. The memory of Gautier's deftness annoyed me. It was so simple for him to draw. He scarcely thought about it, barely considered where the charcoal should next touch the page or how to shape a stroke. I made a few sad, vertical lines to indicate folds on the woman's cloak. The hem rippled. I drew a wavy line. I hated it.

Hands are difficult. Even gifted artists shy away from hands. I blew the ink dry on the page and turned it over. At the center, toward the top, I made two clusters of tiny lines—one, two, three, four, five. I drew another line down from them, and another—arms, raised overhead. I glanced at the woman talking to the sky, who was now singing and gently swaying, reaching upward. I drew in an oval between the lines, for her head. It was the most rudimentary, clumsy sketching. I had taken lessons in Lille; I knew better ways to do these things. But something drove me to continue. I wanted to finish what I had begun. Features in the oval; dashes for eyes, an open O for the mouth. Hair; straight lines with no hint of the limpness of the real thing.

It was impossible. I had no idea how to render what I saw into marks on the page. The woman turned, bent at the waist, turned again. I drew a line that gave her a torso, hips, a skirt. The line sagged. I persisted. The shoulders were nonexistent. The nib of the pen sputtered and skipped as I drew, leaving ragged outlines. I didn't know what to do about feet. I tried, remembering the words of my teacher, to lay down a shadow with a few parallel lines.

I was working faster now, driven by frustration but also a kind of hunger. I didn't like what I was producing; it made me despise my incapacity. But as I drew, something strange happened. I could not translate what I saw into lines on the page. But I could, by trying to draw the women, share their physical state. I could sense the strange internal rhythm that prompted one to dance, the black weight that surrounded and stifled the melancholiac.

One of the *furieuses* had come into the courtyard wearing her straitjacket. Like some of her fellow patients, she had very short hair. Sometimes the wardresses cut patients' hair to keep them from pulling it out. Her head looked strangely large and her neck slender, like a child's. She walked carefully, very upright, as if barely keeping her balance with every step. I flipped a page and made a quick, narrow triangle—her skirt as she walked. I didn't know how to continue. For her upper body I drew nothing more than a kind of block, with angles indicated to signal the bent elbows. Her head was not round, but I had made a circle anyway, then corrected it. I was pressing too hard with the pen now, dragging threads of paper with the nib, almost tearing the page. My hands were shaking with my rage and frustration. I could not draw. I could not draw these women. And yet I felt a kind of compulsion to do it. I was sure I knew now how to walk in a *gilet de force*.

The chapel bell began to ring, and I knew it was time for me to go. My absence at the Faculté de Médecine had been remarked on with disapproval. I screwed the cap onto my pen and slipped it into my pocket, but I carried my notebook by the cover, to let the pages flutter themselves dry in the air. Later that day I returned to the hospital and coaxed a wardress to button me into one of the straitjackets. She must have thought I looked comical, pacing up and down the empty dormitory with my hands trapped in the endless sleeves and tied behind my back.

That night, at home, I tore the sheets from my notebook and spread them out on my table. What I saw made me flinch, yet it also held my attention. The drawings were raw, even ugly. But they had a vivid quality that surprised me. They were direct and urgent. I had somehow managed to capture some of the emotional force of my mad patients. And though I never said so directly to Gautier, his big Salon painting *The Women of the Salpêtrière*—an achievement, a success, an example of everything painting aspired to in 1857—remained for me a beautiful but somehow tepid canvas.

I understand this now, years later, having known Vincent's work, and having drawn Vincent myself. He was able to create haunting images that reached the heart of the viewer. That was his astounding gift to the world. I achieved only that a handful of times. Was it because my subjects, in all of these cases, were mad? Did my lack of technique correspond to their mental anomalies? Or was it that my sympathy for them, in their alienated state, allowed me to reach beyond the conventional in my art?

Then I sometimes wonder, would I have been a better artist if I had not retained my sanity? And, would Vincent have been a genius if he had not been mad? Was his madness the price of his talent? I don't believe that it was. And yet the doubt lingers.

Six

ANYONE WHO BECAME a friend of Vincent's learned very quickly what an important part Theo played in his life. Vincent referred to his brother constantly, quoting him with admiration and respect. He also made it clear that he did not consider himself the only artist in the family. "I may be the one who holds the paintbrush," he told me, "but Theo is in every way a partner in this enterprise. You have met him, so you know his ideas about painting."

"I have to confess that we have spent most of our time together discussing you."

Vincent laughed. "Well, now that I am so pleasantly settled, you can discuss art instead." He was intent that Theo and his family should spend a day with him in Auvers, and on the second Sunday in June, they finally did.

It was one of Vincent's chief desires that everything in his life be connected. He felt that the people he liked must know and like each other. We should all have read the books he admired, and agree with him about them. Likewise with painters. He even told me several times that he felt at ease with me because I was just like him and his brother: a redhead of a nervous temperament. When I told him that I had grown up in Lille, on the Belgian border, I became for him a Man of the North, yet another bond I shared with him and Theo.

Theo had promised to come on Sunday regardless of the weather. Johanna and the baby would join him if the day was fine. It rained on Saturday night, and when I woke on Sunday there were puddles in the garden, but the sky had begun to clear. The street bell rang while I was behind the house sweeping water off the red table. It was Vincent, come to see that all was prepared.

He was more garrulous than I had seen him, talking rapidly and gesturing. In his right hand he held a bird's nest that he had found, which he intended to give to the baby. He was terribly early; the train would not arrive at the nearby station of Chaponval (closer to my house than the bigger station of Auvers-sur-Oise) for another hour. I handed him my broom.

"I hope that we will be able to have our meal outdoors," I said. "I think that if we brush the water off the table and disperse the puddles, they will be dry by the time Theo gets here." I took the bird's nest, which Vincent was in danger of breaking with his nervous fidgeting. "I will put this on the table by the front door," I said. "We'll make sure you remember it when you leave for the station."

Madame Chevalier was unhappy at having "that nasty thing" in her house, but I found a box for it. Then I raided her scullery for some rags to wipe the red chairs. When I went back outside, Vincent had cleared off the table and was thrashing with my broom at an especially deep puddle, watching the drops fly in arcs through the sky. Each time he hit the water, the dog Nero barked and tried to catch the drops in his mouth. It was hard to say which was more agitated, the man or the beast.

"I do believe the sky is brighter now, Doctor," Vincent said, dropping the broom to the brick terrace. "Will there be cushions for the ladies to sit on?"

"We can bring cushions from the house if you think we should," I said. "In the meantime, let us dry the chairs."

"I hope Johanna and Mademoiselle Gachet will be friends," he said, tipping a chair so that the water ran all over his feet. "I think they have a great deal in common. Music, for instance."

"I know Marguerite is looking forward to meeting Madame van Gogh," I said, though there was no telling what Marguerite might think about anything.

"I am sure Theo will love Auvers," he went on. "I have hung some of my paintings around my room at Ravoux's so that he can see what I have been doing. I painted the church this week, Doctor. And the replica of your portrait. I'll bring that up as soon as it's dry."

"Have you ever done your brother's portrait?" I asked. I would have loved to see what Vincent made of Theo in a painting.

"No. Even though I paint quickly, I have never been able to persuade him to take time to sit for me. He works such long hours, as you know. And now, with the baby, his responsibilities are even greater. Still, I would like very much to paint him and Johanna and little Vincent. Perhaps if he does come here for his vacation, we might find time for that."

"Is he thinking of coming to Auvers? How pleasant that would be. I am sure Madame Chevalier would love to help Madame van Gogh with the baby."

"I hope to be able to convince him," Vincent answered. "Do you think I should go to the station now?"

I did not. He was as impatient as a child awaiting a treat. He would have had to wait on the platform for nearly an hour for his brother to arrive. I cast my eyes around the garden, trying to find a task he could do that would be time-consuming but require no skill. Brilliant as he was with a brush in his hand, Vincent was careless and distractible at almost any other manual activity. I told him to continue dispersing the puddles; he could do no harm that way—beyond further soaking his trousers. When I finally sent him to retrieve Theo from Chaponval, the sky was blue and the garden looked as if every leaf had been individually washed. The ducks and chickens had come out to begin their incessant pecking for grubs and insects, and even I felt a little bit of Vincent's excitement.

When the street bell clanged upon his return, Vincent led a merry little procession up the steps to the house, carrying the infant in his arms. (Theo had taken possession of the bird's nest, which Vincent had carried to the station, and which went back to Paris with them, secure in its box.) There was the usual confusion of introductions, the tour of the house, admiration of my paintings, all very congenial. Madame van Gogh—whom I think of as Jo, since Vincent referred to her that way— was older than I had expected, not a young girl but a settled matron. I liked her right away. She was quiet but cheerful, and she did not need to be the center of attention. I saw her talking to Paul and Marguerite, looking around the house and the garden, smiling at everything. Only when Vincent took the baby to introduce him to the animals in the courtyard did she look faintly anxious and whisper something to Marguerite, who was by her side.

Vincent had showed no previous interest in our beasts. I don't expect everyone to share my pleasure in them, but I would not have thought that Vincent was even aware of my domestic menagerie until that morning. (At that time we had, in addition to the goat, six cats, three dogs, a dozen hens, one rooster, and four ducks.) He began a little game. Carrying the baby, Vincent would rush at two or three ducks pecking in the grass. They bustled away from him squawking, ruffling their feathers, and the baby laughed.

There is no success in life as sweet as making a baby laugh, and one is instantly compelled to try to do it again. Vincent dashed at a group of chickens this time. They were even more gratifying, for several of them lifted off the ground momentarily with a great flapping of wings. Even Paul, who had little patience for children, found this entertaining. I glanced at Theo, who was watching this performance. He, like the rest of us, was laughing, primarily at the deep chuckle that emerged from the child. But I observed that he put a hand out for a chair and sank into it as if he could not have stood upright for much longer. I noticed also that he was squinting in the sunlight and shading his eyes with his hands. It occurred to me that I had previously met him in the evening and in my office, which was rather gloomy. Now that we were in my sunny garden, I thought I detected something wrong with the way his eyes reacted to light. I felt a jolt of alarm. Sometimes we doctors reach an intuitive diagnosis. I knew nothing about Theo's physical state, yet these two symptoms combined—weakness and a visual disturbance—often had a dreadful significance.

Just as my thoughts strayed in this unwelcome direction, Vincent met his match in the animal kingdom. Among the flock of chickens pecking at seeds near the coop was our rooster, a vain and proud creature. Vincent ran toward the flock, holding the baby, and they scattered with the flapping and squawking that entertained the child. But the rooster stood firm. More, he flew up to the roof of the coop and crowed.

The adults all laughed at this tiny drama, but the poor infant was startled, and in an instant he was making as much noise as the rooster. Johanna, laughing, scooped the poor child from his uncle's arms and cradled him closely to her.

"Well! The cock went 'cock-a-doodle-do!' " Vincent said, and we all laughed again. Despite the baby's wailing, the episode had created a sense of camaraderie, and when Madame Chevalier brought out the tablecloth and silver, we all did our bit to set the table.

It was a jolly meal. Theo and Johanna asked all kinds of questions about Auvers, its history, and the painters who had worked there. There was a little bit of friction over Cézanne, whom Theo admired but Vincent did not. Johanna, however, quickly intervened to ask about the train service to Paris, and Cézanne was forgotten before anyone could get upset.

We lingered outside after the meal. Johanna put the baby onto a blanket, and Marguerite sat down next to him to shoo away the cats or chickens who came too close. He fell asleep quickly. Theo pushed his chair into the shade, and I placed another one near him, suggesting he put his feet up. "We are in the country, after all, and practically family. No need to stand on formalities." He smiled and thanked me. Though he was in the shadows, his pupils had not expanded, and he had to lift his legs onto the chair using his hands. Theo was younger than Vincent, and no man of less than thirty-five should be so weak. My concern for him grew.

Vincent did not require a special invitation to sprawl on the grass, and Paul introduced him to a new game. They would lie still, faceup, eyes closed. Sooner or later a cat would slink over to investigate. As soon as the cat's whiskers touched his face, Paul would open his eyes and blow a puff of air at the cat. Paul always enjoyed insulting the cats' dignity, and of course it was entertaining to see them skitter away, then energetically begin washing as if they had never, ever made a hasty move.

It was this inconsequential amusement that caused the one uncomfortable moment in the whole day. I confess my hasty temper was the cause.

We had a cat named Chopin, an elegant black creature with bold white markings. He was normally fastidious, preferring to have nothing to do with humans unless it would result in being fed, and he was very quick with his claws. After watching Vincent and Paul for some time, Chopin sauntered over to them, and, with no provocation at all, scratched Paul's face.

Paul sat up with a yelp, clutching his eye. The cat streaked away, invisible in a moment. The baby awoke with a start and began to roar.

So, I am sorry to say, did I. "Paul, control yourself!" I shouted. I was ashamed of him, embarrassed that a nearly full-grown man should be making such a fuss over a little scratch. "Look what you've done, you've wakened the baby! You're not hurt at all, let me see." I got out of my chair and tried to pull his hand away from his face, but he was too strong for me. He turned away, facing the shrubbery, and I heard him sniff. "Ridiculous," I hissed at him. "Go into the house and have Madame Chevalier look at it."

Without turning toward me, Paul sidled away and climbed the steps to the back door.

"Is he all right?" Vincent asked, looking up from the grass where he still sat.

"Yes, of course," I said. "Just making a childish fuss."

"He was probably just startled, like poor little Vincent here," suggested Johanna.

"But unlike little Vincent, he is old enough to control himself," I muttered.

"Well, in any event, we must all go down to the inn, to see what I've done since I've been here," announced the elder Vincent, scrambling to his feet. I was grateful for the distraction. I had not put myself in a favorable light by being so harsh to my son.

It was a perfectly beautiful afternoon, with a touch of freshness in the shade, which provided respite from the glitter of the summer sun. Vincent chose our route, and it was touching to see how considerate he was of Jo's strength. She seemed robust, but I think he had the bachelor's romantic sense of woman's fragility, combined with an almost mystical respect for her maternity. He would say, for example, "I have painted a scene of the fields down in that direction, but that would be too long a walk for Johanna." I thought privately that, given this disturbing weakness of Theo's, it was as well that Johanna was with us to limit the itinerary. Theo could never have managed to walk down to the fields. Vincent was so excited, though, that he did not notice his brother's apparent infirmity. Nor, to be fair, did Johanna—I did not see her watching him, as a worried wife surely would.

Vincent was so accustomed to the heat and dryness of the South that the cool freshness of our village was a revelation. He kept talking about the greens and blues that he saw everywhere, and his paintings were full of this wonder. In fact, one of the profound effects Vincent van Gogh had on my life was that he changed the way I saw the world. To this day, I look at the shadow beneath a bank of willows and see the brown, the green, the purple tones together, contrasting with the yellow, green, and even orange of the leaves. I notice patterns in the windows of city buildings or the ties of a railroad track, and I am always aware of the relations between colors, like the way a brick wall heightens the intensity of a green vine. I have seen much more beauty in my surroundings since that summer Vincent spent with us. And though I cannot capture it myself, I sometimes think I know how Vincent would have done so. He loved

to talk about painting, and that day with Theo, he was especially elo-
quent. As we strolled through the village, he kept up a commentary, explaining what he had already painted, how he had handled it, whether
he was pleased with the results.

I have explained that Theo made Vincent an allowance, but their
arrangement was a little bit more complicated than that, at least in Vincent's view. He saw his brother's subsidy as an investment, and Theo as
part owner of every painting or drawing that he made. More, he saw
Theo as part creator. Thus his brother's opinion was of the utmost importance to Vincent. Theo was fundamentally his partner in the creative enterprise, so it was essential that he be kept abreast of Vincent's
progress.

It is not a long walk from my house to the Place de la Mairie, opposite which lies Ravoux's café and inn. The route passes several rows of
cottages, whose mossy, thatched roofs Vincent found fascinating, and
runs beneath the giant chestnuts that Vincent had painted when he first
arrived. We were ambling slowly, passing the baby among us, pointing
out this or that sight—a geranium blazing in a window or the twisted
angle of a branch. Theo, however, was falling behind. I paused beside
the largest chestnut tree in the village, an old giant that has since been
cut down.

"Is this the tree," I called out to Vincent, "whose blossoms you
painted in that big canvas?" I own the painting now, a strikingly beautiful picture almost a meter wide. It portrays nothing but branches of
chestnut blooms and leaves, with no horizon, no spatial orientation at
all, almost like wallpaper. The brushwork is especially remarkable. The
background is mostly blue, with darker pigment stroked over a lighter
tone in a series of nervous-looking dashes that echoed the way Vincent
rendered the leaves, with their strong diagonal veining. He must have
used six or seven different shades of green for those leaves. But it is the
blossoms themselves, an explosive mass of pink and white, that took my
breath away when I first saw them. Twists of cream and ivory paint, they
cluster along the branches in loose cones. Some are dotted with pink,
the kind of precise detail that seems incompatible with Vincent's swift
production but that he never overlooked. Toward the left is one branch

from a tree with pink flowers, more loosely brushed, lending the entire composition just the variety it requires. It is a magnificent canvas. But at that moment, on our walk to Ravoux's, I did not care which tree inspired the painting. I wanted to give Theo time to catch up to us without drawing attention to him. When he did so, I stayed with him, asking about business at the gallery. I also observed him. It is something we doctors are good at. When a practitioner looks at you, he is not merely exhibiting good manners. He cannot help noticing your puffy face, your brittle hair, the strange way you hold your left arm.

Theo dragged his left foot. The medical term for this symptom is "locomotor ataxia." The medical term for what seemed to be his eye condition is "Argyll Robertson pupils," a syndrome defined by a Scottish doctor some years earlier. The name refers to pupils that contract to facilitate examination of something near at hand but that do not respond to light. The syndrome had not been named when I was an intern, but it had been observed informally. At the Salpêtrière and the men's asylum of Bicêtre, experienced physicians had linked these unusual visual symptoms with muscular degeneration similar to what Theo displayed. The patients thus affected suffered an illness we saw all too often—syphilis.

I knew that Theo's health was delicate: Vincent had alluded to episodes of coughing or fever. I would not have been surprised to learn that Theo had consumption. In fact, as we strolled, I realized that I had unwittingly been assessing him for the familiar symptoms that had marked Blanche: the flushed cheeks, the distinctive wet-sounding cough. I never encounter them in a patient without a dreadful sense of recognition. But this time I was certain, as we sauntered along on our Sunday outing behind his brother and his wife and his baby, that Theo van Gogh had what was crudely known as the pox. The symptoms were still subtle, and I doubted that anyone had noticed them, but to me the diagnosis was conclusive. Furthermore, his illness was advanced. If he had been my patient, I would have begun looking around for a private *maison de santé* where he could end his days. It is a frightening and degrading death, for the patient may become paralyzed or mad. Was it possible that this lovely little family, so fond of each other, so happy with their baby, would soon be wrenched apart, as my family had been when Blanche died?

I wondered if Theo knew of his own condition. So much shame attaches to this ailment that patients and their families are often desperate to avoid acknowledging it. It was possible that Theo could have overlooked his symptoms, or told himself that his legs were weak because of rheumatism. Johanna, preoccupied with the baby, might not have noticed anything. And Vincent? Could he have an inkling that his brother was ill?

I had no time just then to reflect on how Theo's possible illness might affect Vincent; we were drawing near Ravoux's inn. It is a pleasant place, with a café facing the Place de la Mairie and very modest bedrooms above. Vincent insisted we climb the two flights to his spartan chamber. There was no window other than the skylight, and the room was hot and stuffy, smelling of oil paint and tobacco and unwashed clothes. But he was proud of how tidy it was, with his spare boots tucked under the cot and his battered straw hat hung on a nail in the mottled plaster wall. I found it cheerless, despite the three landscapes mounted on the wall. Their brilliant colors only exaggerated the shabby discomfort of the room. But Theo praised it: "You've made it very homelike," he said, touching the comb on what served as a dressing table. Vincent had placed a bright blue linen cloth beneath the pottery basin, the kind of cloth Madame Chevalier uses to dry glassware. I was surprised that the man whose paint box was always such a jumble had made an effort to create domestic order.

"It's not as pleasant as the house in Arles," Vincent said, "but it is much better than at St.-Rémy. At least my neighbors here are only other painters, not madmen. This is one of the fields where they grow peas." He showed Theo one of the smaller canvases. "And here are the chestnut trees we just walked beneath. I was so struck by that green! But come down and see what else I've done," he went on, seizing his brother by the elbow. "Ravoux lets me use the shed in the back."

We trooped back down the steep stairs and went out to the shed. I had seen most of Vincent's pictures, of course, so I hung back and listened as he showed them to Theo. Johanna, weighed down by the baby, sat on a low stool, her eyes traveling around the walls from one canvas to another. Marguerite stood next to them, smiling at the baby.

Here the contrast between the space and the pictures was even more dramatic than it had been in Vincent's bedchamber. It was barely a room, more a lean-to that had been closed off with flimsy walls. Fortunately for Vincent, there were several windows, which meant that the light would permit him to work indoors in case of rain. It also meant that, on that sunny Sunday, his pictures blazed from the walls like windows punched into another world.

I had not seen the painting of the church that he had mentioned and was curious to know how he had portrayed it. The Auversois worship in a sturdy Gothic building with a square tower, perched halfway up the hill on the way to the cemetery. Its chief characteristic is its air of permanence. As ever, Vincent had seen something new in his subject. Rather than portraying the severe front with its heavy door, he had set up his easel facing the apse, perhaps finding the repeating pattern of the arched windows more interesting. The sky he painted in several shades of blue, the darkest of which almost matched the color of the stained glass. The result was that the building seemed to be a mere façade, as if we were looking through the apse to empty blue air beyond. And this was not all: the stonework of the church, so rigid in life, became flexible under Vincent's brush. The rooflines wavered, the tower tilted. The space of the apse seemed swollen. Gray stone was touched with dashes of blue and green, as if the surrounding grass were beginning to swallow the dissolving structure. A small female figure in a white hat scurried along a path that Vincent had depicted in a rushing river of brown and yellow dashes. The two most durable-looking elements on the canvas were the sky and the shadow cast by the building.

"This is the church I was telling you about," Vincent said to Theo. "Perhaps we'll have time to walk there before the train, if you like."

"Magnificent," Theo said, peering closely at the canvas. He stepped to one side, letting the light rake over the brushwork. "Cobalt for the sky?"

"Yes," Vincent said. "And ultramarine in the windows." He looked at it for a moment more. "You don't suppose—"

"No," Theo cut him off. "It could not be improved upon."

"No, but listen," Vincent insisted. "There is no yellow, I wonder—"

"But for what?" Theo asked. "This is right. This is so—monumental."

"Maybe more orange in the roof," Vincent went on, as if he were not listening at all. "On the other side. But then, too symmetrical, blotchy even . . ." He was by now talking to himself. Theo had moved on and was admiring the painting Vincent had made of Marguerite in our garden.

"This is just lovely," he said to all of us. "It might have been today. So fresh. Mademoiselle Marguerite looks like a flower herself." We all turned toward Marguerite, who blushed.

"No, but Theo," Vincent said, still absorbed by the church painting. "Do you think perhaps a touch more yellow in the path? The color balance doesn't seem right."

I happened to be watching Theo at that moment, for I was fascinated by the way the brothers behaved together. There was a rapport between them that you rarely see between men. It was as if, rather than living apart for the previous years, they had been in the same room. They spoke as if they knew the same things, had had the same experiences.

Theo's face revealed only a flash of impatience or anger, quickly mastered, and his voice was calm. "No, my friend, it is wonderful. You always doubt what you have done, but I assure you that it is splendid. Now come and tell me about this lovely painting."

Vincent proceeded to do so, only casting an uncertain glance back at the canvas of the church. "Well, of course, it is Dr. Gachet's garden. And I would like to give the doctor this painting, Theo, if you approve."

"But of course," Theo said, with a genuine smile. "You know you should do what you like with your canvases."

"Oh, I usually do," Vincent answered. "But I needed to be sure you didn't want to keep this one."

"Lovely as it is, I think it should stay with the doctor, if he will accept it. Your paintings will be in fine company in his collection."

I stammered my pleasure and mumbled something about generosity, which Theo dismissed. For a man so much younger than I, he had a remarkable way of assuming authority. This seemed to be how he kept

Vincent on an even keel, and I admired it, even as he turned it on me. "Doctor, we are all so grateful to you. To see Vincent so well settled—" He gestured around at the pictures. "Ah!" he said, glancing at the portrait of me. "You see! You have even been coerced into sitting for him! The least he can do is give you a canvas or two!"

We all laughed and moved over to the portrait. It is a strange situation, examining a portrait of yourself in the presence of the artist and a third person. So much is on display: the artist's skill, the sitter's face, the artist's idea of the sitter, the sitter's idea of himself all jostle, as it were, for acknowledgment. None of us would have expected a conventional likeness from Vincent, but it was still my face there on the canvas. He had not yet delivered the second version I had asked him to make, so I had not had the chance to get used to this haggard man clothed in my features. There was a strange moment when I hovered between recognition and surprise, when I could see the picture as an image of a stranger who gazed at me wearily.

Theo did not speak for a moment. He gazed at the painting with his hands clasped behind his back. Vincent stood next to him, frowning slightly. He reached out to touch, very lightly, the edge of the canvas, to check that it was drying as he wanted. Theo put his arm on his brother's shoulder and said, "This is magnificent. You have become a portrait painter like no other."

Vincent turned his head to smile at Theo. I never saw that expression again on his face. It was pure happiness and affection. I wish that some of the many, many portraits Vincent had made of himself had showed that side of him to the world, but the mood was fleeting. It was as if, from the shell of the stoical man I was getting to know, peered for an instant the tenderest creature, full of hope and delight. I supposed only Theo saw that side of him with any frequency. I must admit, I envied him.

Seven

WE ALL FELT LET DOWN after the excitement of the Van Goghs' visit. Paul was especially sulky. That evening I tried to put some antiseptic lotion on his scratches, but he kept flinching and I finally left Marguerite to minister to him. It was at times like this that I missed Blanche the most. Seeing the accord between Theo and Johanna reminded me of what marriage had been like. Vincent had described the bond between Theo and Jo vividly: "If one draws a breath, the other notices." I remembered those days, but sadly. There were so few of them.

Blanche found me dashing, brilliant, gifted. She came from a somewhat modest family of Gascon origin, and though she had lived her entire life in Paris, it had been a sheltered existence. She was dazzled by the breadth and depth of my interests. Naturally I flourished in the atmosphere of womanly warmth and admiration that she created. I never doubted myself in Blanche's presence—until the last days of her illness, when I doubted everything. Man of medicine that I was, I could not even relieve her pain. Worse still, I refused her the one thing she asked of me.

I had thought, when I was drawing the madwomen at the Salpêtrière, that I was entering their madness in a way. After Blanche's death, though, I truly knew their despair. In my bones, to my core, I knew what it was to fall into melancholy. I knew the bleakness, the withdrawal, the lassitude. I would sit for hours at a time, watching slices of dust-filled sunlight creep across a room. My dark mood frightened the children, which made me ashamed. Madame Chevalier grew impatient, then angry, and lectured me. She said that, for the children's sake, I must at least feign an interest in life.

There is a saying I have always loathed: *"L'appétit vient en mangeant."* My father used it often when I objected to working in his fabric mills. "You say you are not interested, Paul, but you will be! You will see how the business works, and soon you will be hungry to know more: *L'appétit vient en mangeant."* As much as I hate the old proverb, I must ruefully confess that I did find this to be true when it came to my mourning for Blanche. Bit by bit, I forced myself to take up the threads of my former life. I discovered that Marguerite was learning to read. I visited Pissarro, whom I had neglected in the last months of my wife's illness. Blanche had written a pretty piece of piano music that I had privately printed, giving it the title "Espérance." I did not exactly feel hope, but I began to think that hope might exist, somewhere, if only for other people.

Still, the sadness remains. In some ways I am a solitary man, even though I am surrounded by my family. There is no one who shares all of my concerns, my doubts, my fears. Paul is the closest I have to a confidant these days, but in that summer Vincent was with us, Paul was only seventeen. I could not tell him—I could not tell anyone—that Johanna van Gogh's affection for her husband made me feel lonely. I could not tell him that I feared for Theo's health.

Besides, it was Vincent who was my primary concern, and, as the days went by, he did seem to be benefiting from the calm, wholesome atmosphere I had established in our home on the rue Rémy. He had gained some weight, I thought, and claimed to be sleeping better than he had slept in years. I guessed from Theo's stories that Vincent had spent a great deal of time among people who did not have his best interests at heart. For all his stoicism, Vincent was desperate for honest friendship and concern, which I was happy to extend to him. And though he did not fit comfortably into a domestic setting, I sensed that he relished it deeply while he was with us.

However, in the summer of 1890 I was beginning to recognize a certain disruption of our tranquillity. Perhaps Vincent's presence among us cast a brighter light on the issue, but the fact was, Marguerite was growing up. Paul reminded me of this when we were feeding the chickens one afternoon. He and Marguerite shared a birthday. He was turning seventeen, she twenty-one, and Paul was eager to know how the day would be celebrated. Could we, he wanted to know, invite Vincent for a birthday luncheon?

Nothing could have been easier, and so it came about. Yet I realized, that day when we were sitting around the red table in the garden, that it was a very quiet way to mark Marguerite's birthday. At twenty-one, she might reasonably have expected something more exciting. I thought of her as a girl of good sense, practical, honest, and modest. But even sensible girls think about young men—and there were none in her life. At lunch, Marguerite looked pretty, in a pale pink dress with a few roses in her hair. She was quiet—she is always quiet—but I did catch her glancing at Vincent more than once with a somewhat speculative look in her eye.

The thought was laughable. I dismissed it. Vincent could be nothing to Marguerite Gachet, a gently reared girl of twenty-one. Vincent, with his false teeth, his constant odor of tobacco, and his impatient, single-minded temperament. Nor could Marguerite be anything to him. Theo had told me of his younger brother's unfortunate relations with respectable women. Vincent and Marguerite were as ill-matched as a bear and a lapdog.

I wondered whether Marguerite thought about marriage. Many girls were wed by her age, yet I knew almost nothing about how *jeunes filles à marier* were courted. Blanche was not young when we married, and I had met her, strangely enough, in the park in front of the Church of the

Trinity. I had always thought it was remarkable good luck, for a sudden gust of wind blew her umbrella inside out just as I was passing. Of course a well-bred girl would not ordinarily speak to a passing man, but Blanche's struggle with the broken umbrella in the storm compelled her to accept my help. I walked her home, and received her father's permission to call on her. Until that time I had had very little contact with young ladies in Paris. I was never one of the youths with gloves at evening parties, assessing the relative charms of Mademoiselle this or that.

Who would assess Marguerite's charms? There were no gentlemen in Auvers. There were farmers, of course. The man who punched my ticket to Paris every Tuesday was pleasant, and just a few years older than Marguerite, but he probably had a wife and three babies already. Who would give Marguerite babies? And how could she meet him? I had overlooked one of the principal responsibilities of a parent: to find his daughter a husband. Just like that, I had overlooked it.

My daughter did not seem aware of my concern. She sat in the dappled shade, smiling at her brother's teasing and Madame Chevalier's affectionate praise. She was presentable. She played the piano. She could run a house. I had made sure she had a dowry. But what could be her future? Not the red-haired man across from her, lighting his pipe, thinking of something else entirely. She glanced at him again. No, there was nothing but curiosity in her gaze. But I resolved to talk to some of my friends in Paris about her. Some of them had wives, and mentioned first communions and daughters who went to dances. Perhaps Marguerite could go to Paris to stay with one of them and see the wider world.

"Marguerite, would you play for us?" I asked, as she stood up to help Madame Chevalier clear the table. I knew that she took her music quite seriously, but she normally did her practicing on the days when I was in Paris, so as not to disturb me.

"Oh, how dull!" Paul cried. "It's my birthday, too!"

"Yes, and do you have an accomplishment you would like to share with us?" I asked. "Have you been working at something special? Perhaps you would like to recite? Some lines of Racine? Plutarch?" Paul blushed; he was not a brilliant scholar.

"Possibly you and I may rent a skiff to fish later this afternoon," I told him. This was a treat, since I preferred to fish on the quieter weekdays. I did not care for the loudness and roughhousing of the day-trippers from Paris. They shrieked and splashed each other and scared away the fish—but Paul adored the bustle, especially on a summer Sunday.

He turned scarlet and said, "Thank you, Papa." Then he murmured to his sister, "I will clear away the coffee cups while you decide what to play."

We moved the little piano to the window facing the garden so we could enjoy an alfresco recital. Vincent and I puffed away on our pipes while my daughter made a reasonable job of playing a pair of Chopin waltzes. Paul lay in the grass at our feet, messing about with a sketch pad and some charcoal.

Marguerite made an appealing picture with her hands moving over the keyboard, unaware of her audience. She was a self-contained young lady, but her concentration on the notes seemed to dissolve a layer of her personal decorum. She did not sway and pant over the music, of course, but a little smile lit up her face, and her feet worked the pedals with a kind of emphasis.

We all applauded when she finished, which appeared to please and disconcert her. Vincent, gripping his pipe between his teeth, said, "Doctor, with your permission, I would like very much to paint Mademoiselle Gachet at her piano. I think she would be a splendid subject." He had barely glanced at her during her little recital: I had thought he was dozing. But of course nothing ever really escaped Vincent's eye. I was delighted, and we agreed that the following weekend, when I returned from Paris, he would begin the portrait. He thanked us for the party and walked with Paul and me down to the landing stage, where we were able to secure a gaudily painted rowboat for a few hours, but he refused to come fishing with us, despite Paul's urging. As Paul carefully maneuvered us through the confusion of craft on the river (many being rowed with notable lack of skill), I caught sight of Vincent, walking slowly past the cheerful café tables set out along the riverbank. He trudged along, hands in pockets, puffing his pipe, his eyes devouring it all. He had said he planned to head up to a nearby vineyard and paint it in the afternoon light. He seemed to feel obligated to do so. "I must . . ." was how he had put it. But I thought that, as he walked past all the merry-makers, couples, and families on a Sunday outing, he seemed forlorn.

At dinner that evening I asked Marguerite if she looked forward to being painted by Vincent. She glanced at me with a furrowed brow, and lowered her gaze to her empty plate. "Will it be difficult?" she asked. "I don't know if I can do it right."

Paul crowed with laughter. "You'll just sit there, silly," he said. "And pretend to play the piano. Anybody could do it."

"Not at all," I corrected him. "It is precisely your sister that he wants to paint. Not 'anybody.'"

"But he's already painted you," Paul retorted. A sister less gentle than Marguerite might have pointed out that Vincent had not asked to paint her brother—who was, to be fair, a lively, handsome youth who would have made a wonderful model.

"Yes, and now he thinks that Marguerite will make a beautiful paint-ing, and I have no doubt she will." I turned to her. "Vincent will not ask anything of you that you cannot do," I told her. "I am sure of that."

Though I rarely feel bound by society's conventions of propriety, I was relieved that Vincent had asked to paint Marguerite's portrait when I would be in Auvers. I felt it would have been inappropriate for the sit-tings to take place in my absence. Vincent understood that both my permission and my presence were necessary for him to paint my daugh-ter. As he set up his easel on the following Sunday morning, he gleefully recounted what he had painted that week: young women. "The daugh-ter of Monsieur Ravoux, all in blue with a blue background, in profile. You will see the way her hair and her skin stand out. And then a peas-ant woman, sitting in the corn, wearing a beautiful straw hat with a big blue bow. The clothes of these women are such a delight." He turned around to look at me. "You see, Doctor, we men wear dark things on the whole. Look at poor Theo, buttoned into a black frock coat every day. But the women in their pinks and greens and reds are like bouquets of flowers." He straightened up, assessing the distance to the piano. Mar-guerite was still upstairs, no doubt readying herself for the sitting. "Could we perhaps pull the piano this way? I would like to have Mademoiselle Marguerite in full figure, you see, against that wall," he pointed.

I called for Paul to come and help. He appeared instantly; apparently he had been just outside the window, drawing in the garden. The three of us pushed the piano on its tiny wheels while Vincent continued his monologue. "I could not find anyone to pose at St.-Rémy. Well, you can't blame them, they were all crazy. Aside from one or two, I could never get anyone to sit still for more than a few minutes. But even in Arles, it wasn't easy with the women. I suppose I didn't know any, except prostitutes." I glanced at Paul, who turned bright red but pretended not to have heard.

"But here in Auvers, I have been so fortunate," Vincent continued. "It is a great thing for me to be able to paint a young lady like Mademoiselle Marguerite." He turned to me and asked, "Is she wearing the pink dress?"

"Oh, yes," Paul said, with the weary tones of a man among men, discussing women's vanity. "She knows you're here, Monsieur Vincent. But she had to do her hair. She said she would be down in a moment."

"Never mind," Vincent said, "I can set up my palette." He set to work, squeezing colors from tubes in what seemed like fantastic amounts, glossy coils of crimson lake and lead white and yellow ocher and emerald green. Finally Marguerite's skirt rustled down the stairs, and she entered the room with as much self-effacement as is possible in a woman three men have waited for. She avoided looking us in the eye and cast her gaze to the floor, murmuring an apology for the delay. Without any direction, she sat on the piano stool.

"Excellent!" Vincent exclaimed, looking at her. "Mademoiselle, this will be a beautiful painting." He screwed the cap on his tube of Prussian blue and tossed it back into his box, then gently set the loaded palette onto the stool I'd brought down from the studio.

"Now, as for the pose." Marguerite looked up at him, blushing. My children were keyed up this morning, it seemed. Vincent moved over to Marguerite and opened the lid of the keyboard. "Could you sit just as you did on Sunday, when you so kindly played for us? Perhaps play a chord or two?"

She complied, resting her fingers on the keys. I was struck by what a pleasing sight she made, silhouetted against the wall as Vincent wanted, her slender figure all gentle curves against the black-lacquered angles of the little piano. Her small foot tapped the pedal, her fingers lifted from the keys, and Vincent said, "Lovely. Do you think you can stay in this position, mademoiselle? Will you be comfortable?"

Until then Marguerite had not addressed a word to him. She turned and said, "Yes, monsieur, thank you," in her quiet voice. I noticed for the first time how very blue her eyes were. She was really quite attractive. It was one of those strange moments when you see a familiar person with new eyes; in this case, with Vincent's eyes. I felt a rush of affection for my daughter.

Vincent had placed a tall rectangular canvas on his easel, and he stood hesitating for a moment, glancing back and forth between Marguerite and the canvas. He usually painted with apparent fearlessness and spontaneity, but today he first took a small notebook from his jacket pocket and roughly sketched his subject, establishing the positions of the piano, Marguerite, the wall, and the floor. Once he had done this, however, I did not see him refer back to it.

He stepped back, took up a brush, began to blend the red and the white paint, then put down his palette. He stepped over to Marguerite and placed a hand under each elbow. "Like so, mademoiselle, if you can," he said, moving them forward. "Will this tire you?"

"No, not at all," Marguerite whispered to the keyboard. Her face was flaming. I knew why, or thought I did. Vincent's hands on her elbows, his voice in her ear, the heat of his body against her back—all of these sensations were utterly new to her. No man besides me had ever touched my daughter. I was not sure what I thought about this.

Clearly Vincent thought nothing of it. Moving back to his palette, he took up the brush and began to outline her figure swiftly, laying down a thick layer of pigment that he would then shape with his brush, stroking brighter or darker colors into the pale pink. To him, Marguerite was a set of shapes and textures to be rendered in his own re- markable combination of colors. When he had his painter's eye on me, I found it to be both searching and impersonal. Now I looked at him as he frowned at my daughter. No. There was nothing in his gaze beyond the calculation of the artist, considering, selecting, eliminating. A streak of gray-blue defined the billow of Marguerite's sleeve. Lightened, it slid down her bust. Another touch marked the cuff. There was nothing to worry about.

Vincent normally enjoyed having someone to talk to while he painted, but he was so quiet as he painted Marguerite that I went into my study to take care of the mail that always accumulated during the days when I was in Paris. During the course of the morning, I went about my business, cutting some verbena from the garden to dry, discussing household accounts with Madame Chevalier. Once as I walked by the open window, I saw that Marguerite was sitting in an armchair while Vincent said, "Lean back and rest, mademoiselle, you have been a remarkable model." At one point I heard the opening bars of a waltz coming from the music room. By the time we gathered for luncheon, the whole figure had been laid out and a few lines of dark violet paint indicated the piano. Paul had been attempting to draw his sister, too, but so badly that I sent him up to the studio after luncheon to get a pair of vases out of the cupboard for us to draw together. If he was so intent on sketching, I thought, I could at least share with him some of the fundamental principles that I had learned so long ago in Lille.

Marguerite must indeed have been a patient model, for by the time Vincent had finished working that evening, he had all but completed her figure. Once again, I was awestruck by his skill as a portraitist. But this time his painting exhibited an adaptability that was new to me. On his canvas Marguerite's dress was a beautiful arrangement of the most delicate hues, ranging from the deep rose of her sash to cream to slate in the folds. Vincent had painted the gown with vertical strokes that curved around the hem of the skirt. It was true that the paint did not look in the least like the crisp folds of muslin or batiste or whatever it was that Marguerite was wearing. Yet at the same time, Vincent had created an image of delicate femininity with the sculpted application of oil paint on canvas.

Vincent stayed for dinner that night. Marguerite went upstairs to rest for a while and eventually came down in her everyday brown calico to help Madame Chevalier in the kitchen. Once I had showed Paul the rudiments of using light and dark to model volume, he was fascinated, so he prowled around the house looking for simple shapes to draw. Every now and then he would show me the result. When I saw what he'd made of a cylindrical jug, I resolved that perspective would be the next lesson.

Vincent told us that he would not need Marguerite for most of the next day, so she was in the yard when he arrived on Monday morning. When the bell for the street door clanged, Paul's light footsteps sounded on the gravel as he dashed to the gate to let Vincent in. I came to the door of the salon to greet the painter, who entered the house carrying a loose bunch of flowers that I assumed he had gathered to paint.

"Shall we put those in a vase?" I asked, gesturing toward the poppies and daisies in his hand.

"Perhaps, but they are actually for Mademoiselle Marguerite," he answered. "To thank her for posing so generously yesterday. She was a wonderful model, so patient and still. I hope it did not tire her. I cut these in the fields this morning."

First a portrait, now flowers! Marguerite would not know what to think of this. Still, it was a kind gesture, and I could not reasonably prevent Vincent from giving my daughter the nosegay. "She is in the courtyard gathering eggs," I said. "The flowers will please her." Vincent went out the back door to find her, and I returned to my desk, slightly disturbed. It struck me as significant that the blossoms did not appear on the luncheon table. Evidently Marguerite had taken the little bouquet up to her bedroom.

The portrait progressed. Although the wall behind Marguerite was, in real life, hung with numerous paintings, Vincent chose to paint it in a vivid apple green, covered with tiny orange dots. This, he explained, would emphasize the pink of Marguerite's dress. Also contrary to fact, he painted the carpet crimson stippled with vertical green dashes, which made for a strange recession that surged upward to meet the wall. Our mahogany piano stool was also painted apple green. The dots and the dashes took Vincent well into the afternoon.

"Doctor, might I request Mademoiselle Marguerite's presence again?"

he said, standing at the door of the studio. I was making a list of supplies to bring back from Paris, so the cupboard doors were all open. Even the paintings were in disarray, since I had used many of them to demonstrate the lessons of modeling and perspective to Paul. My pretty Guillaumin nude was lying flat on the floor, and Vincent picked it up. "This should have a frame, don't you think?" he said, examining it closely. "Look, the stretcher is none too sturdy."

"You are quite right, I will order one this week. Here," I said, passing over a folding ruler. "Would you mind telling me the measurements?"

"Forty-nine centimeters by . . ." He paused, measuring the width. "Sixty-five. I admire the way the curtains frame her, and the delicacy of her skin."

I agreed with him. The model in the painting had that kind of skin that is often described as "pearly," with blue and pink lights swimming beneath the pale surface. Vincent went on, "If Mademoiselle Marguerite can spare me another hour or so, I believe I can finish the picture."

"Of course," I said. "Let me call her. You would like her in the pink dress again?"

"Yes, Doctor, that would be best. Just to retouch the color a little if it's needed."

So Marguerite was summoned, and she resumed her pose with her hands on the keys. I stood behind Vincent, admiring the painting. "Yes, excellent. The arms are perfect," he said. "But the angle of your head— could you look down a little bit more?" Vincent stepped to her and corrected her position. He put a hand on the top of my daughter's head, and gently tipped her chin with two fingers of the other hand. Marguerite barely breathed. He came back to the canvas, concentrating this time on the knot of hair. He picked up a brush to add a few flecks of citron. Then he moved back to her and said, "If I may—your hair is not exactly as it was yesterday. May I . . . ?" Marguerite only nodded. She must have felt too shy to speak at that moment. Vincent loosened a few locks at the back of her neck, then pulled forward the little curl that, in the painting, hangs above her forehead. It seemed to me to be an immensely intimate moment. I imagined Marguerite must have felt that as well. Of course he was simply adjusting the pose of the model. Marguerite as a person—whom he had acknowledged that morning with the little nosegay—was again merely a subject. I only hoped that my daughter would grasp this.

An hour later, Paul knocked on the door of the salon where I worked. "He's finished, Papa. Come and see."

In the music room Vincent was crouched by his paint box, attempting to tidy up. His palette lay next to him, having been wiped in a cursory fashion with a rag that left tiny smears of orange and green on our floor. They are there to this day. He glanced from time to time at the easel, where Marguerite in her pink dress played the piano. Captured. Just like that, a twenty-one-year-old girl in all the freshness of her youth, sharing her accomplishments. The girl herself stood to one side, barely able to look fully at the painting. She would cast a glance at it, then her eyes would dart away. Madame Chevalier was planted before the picture with her feet apart, arms folded, beaming.

"Congratulations, Van Gogh," I said. "It is very beautiful."

He stood up. "Thank you. I am very happy with it. Perhaps someday soon we could do a companion piece with Mademoiselle at the parlor organ; a kind of musical diptych. You can see how the vertical canvas would lend itself to such a format—two of them side by side?"

"Indeed," I agreed. "But for now I am content to admire this painting."

"With your permission, Doctor, I would like to give the canvas to Mademoiselle Gachet," Van Gogh said.

Marguerite gasped, and her hands flew to her face. Her blue eyes met mine.

"That would be more than kind, if you think Monsieur Theo would agree," I said. "More than generous. I certainly cannot stand between Marguerite and such a kind gesture."

Then Vincent gingerly lifted the canvas from the easel, hooking his fingers beneath the stretcher at the top. "Here it is," he addressed my daughter. *Mademoiselle Gachet au piano.*" He turned to me. "Shall I take it up to the studio to dry?"

"Could it not dry in my bedroom?" Marguerite asked, as loudly as I had ever heard her speak.

"It could," Vincent conceded. "But the odor of the paint may trouble you."

She shook her head, eyes shining.

"Is there a hook in the wall?" Vincent asked.

"I'll go check," Paul offered and was out of the room in a moment.

"Doctor, you have wire upstairs? And the eyes to thread it through?"

"Of course," I said, feeling that the situation had somehow moved beyond my control.

He replaced the canvas on the easel. "Might I find them in the studio?"

I could only nod. "In the drawer nearest the window. The wire cutters are there as well." I wondered what the drawer would look like when I saw it next.

It was a delicate operation, and foolhardy. If the face of the canvas touched anything, it would smear disastrously. Paul held it, with his arms rigid, while Vincent screwed the hooks into the stretcher and strung wire through them. Then, strangest of all, we all trooped up into Marguerite's bedroom.

Perhaps some fathers frequent their daughters' bedrooms. That was not our way. Marguerite was always a reserved child, and her bedroom somehow seemed to be protected by her natural requirement for privacy. Yet here we were, Paul and Madame Chevalier and Marguerite and I and Vincent van Gogh. We crowded into the small, austere chamber on the second floor. Marguerite, who always closed the door of the room as she left it, did not seem at all perturbed. In fact, there was no reason why she should be. The room was orderly and immaculate.

Paul and Vincent argued a little bit about where the painting should go. The hook was here, the picture should hang there, could we hammer in another hook, could the wire be tightened, did Mademoiselle like the arrangement? Marguerite was speechless, hands clasped at her chest, alight with excitement. At last the painting was hung on the wall opposite her bed, displacing an admittedly banal engraving after Fragonard.

As I had seen so often with Vincent's pictures, it brought air and light into the small room, making everything else look faded or shabby. Except, perhaps, for Vincent's bright nosegay, carefully placed in the center of Marguerite's dressing table.

"Now you must be very, very careful, mademoiselle," Vincent said, standing in the doorway. "The surface will not be dry for several weeks. Even the lightest touch will disturb it. And after that, the impasto, in the skirt for instance, will be malleable for months. Eventually the doctor should have it framed."

"I will be careful," Marguerite promised. In time I did have it framed, and the picture hangs there to this day.

$\mathcal{E}$ight

THEO MIGHT HAVE THOUGHT I would be doing a good deed by watching over Vincent, but instead I felt grateful to Theo for sending Vincent to me. I had at first been drawn to the idea of Vincent as a patient. I had looked forward to observing him, to tracing the links—for I was certain they existed—between his genius and his melancholy. The melancholy had not yet declared itself, but the genius thrilled me.

Vincent's presence seemed to be affecting my children as well. Paul had taken to drawing with an enthusiasm that was utterly unlike his usual aimlessness. I often found the studio littered with sketches of every pot or flask in the house. One might have wished for a somewhat steadier figure for Paul to emulate than Vincent, yet I was happy that my son, who had always seemed rather idle, should be inspired to take up an interest in art. But what about Marguerite? Was it possible that, in her innocence, she could mistake the attention of a painter for the attention of a man? I feared so.

∞

It was with great relief that I stepped onto the platform at the Auvers station on Saturday evening. In late June the sun lingers on the horizon, casting its long amber rays on field and hedge and cottage. It was a good deal cooler than in Paris, and I listened with pleasure to the sounds of a summer evening in the country: the leisurely clop of one tired horse's hooves, the shrieks of children playing out of sight, kitchen clatter drifting through an open window. I ambled along the street, watching the dust film my city boots. The week had been dry. The wheat up on the plateau would be ripening, I thought—a fine subject for Vincent.

As I passed the sturdy little town hall, made grandiose by the square and the pollarded trees before it, I remembered that Madame Chevalier had asked me to order some wine. Ravoux sold wines from a little counter in the front of the café facing the *mairie,* so I crossed the street and went in.

The room was quite a bit darker than the street, so at first I did not quite grasp what I was seeing, only that there was a female figure just steps from the door, clad in a light-colored dress and hastily moving backward. But the confusion was momentary—the girl in front of me carrying a market basket was Marguerite!

While Marguerite routinely ran errands for Madame Chevalier, there were some tasks that were inappropriate for a young lady. We did not send her to a certain farmer's barn to buy grain for our band of poultry and the goat, nor of course to the blacksmith's to buy nails or hooks or tools. There were too many coarse men in those places who had nothing better to do than lean on a counter and make remarks about young ladies. What was true of the ironmonger was even more true of Ravoux's café. It was not a place where a young lady would go alone.

My daughter knew this. When I stepped into the dim space, she gasped, and tried to vanish between her basket and the tiny wine counter.

"Ah! Marguerite!" I said, thinking quickly. Auvers, like all villages, is full of gossip, and I did not want to provide a delightful scene for the pleasure of those watching. "Madame Chevalier has sent us on the same errand!"

She was scarlet with embarrassment and could not speak. I took the basket from her arm. "Is your business here finished? Shall we walk home together?" I turned to Ravoux, who was standing behind the counter with an impassively pleasant smile. "Has my daughter managed to let you know what we need? I am surprised Madame Chevalier sent her—affairs must be in a terrible state in the kitchen!"

He laughed, showing all of his big white teeth. "We were having a little bit of difficulty, Doctor. Mademoiselle did not seem to know what you would like to drink with dinner."

"My dear, what are we eating?"

"I don't know," she whispered to my shoes. I hastily asked for a bottle of the local *ginglet,* put it in the basket, and shepherded my daughter out of the café with an elbow under her arm.

We walked for a few minutes. I was aware that Marguerite kept darting glances at me.

"My dear," I finally began. She did not answer. "Paul goes for the wine. Was he not at home?"

"No. Madame Chevalier could not find him."

"All the same," I went on. "You should not be going to Ravoux's. It is not a suitable place for you."

"No." The answer was so quiet that I barely heard her.

What else could I do? What more could I say? She was all but cowering at my side. I did not have the heart to show my displeasure. My puzzlement about her behavior was even greater.

I shared my concern with Madame Chevalier, when I asked her to join me for coffee in the salon. For a moment I allowed myself to imagine discussing my worries with Blanche instead. A mother and a daughter shared a kind of sympathy, I thought. Blanche would have known how Marguerite felt, and I—well, I would not have needed to intervene.

After Madame Chevalier stirred her coffee, she set her spoon on her saucer and looked expectantly at me.

"As I was coming home from the train this evening," I said quietly, "I stopped in at Ravoux's for some wine. Marguerite was there."

"At Ravoux's! Inside?"

I nodded. "The pretext appeared to be buying wine for dinner. She did not know what you were cooking, though."

She shook her head. "Were there many people there? No one made any comments?"

I thought back to the figures I'd seen at the tables. "No. Ravoux was there, and his daughter was serving at the tables. I think he keeps order while she is there."

"He is a father, after all," she observed. "Not so different from you." Then she sighed. "Marguerite has been very strange this week, Doctor."

I got up and brought the decanter of brandy over to my desk, where we were sitting. "How so?" I asked, gesturing toward her coffee cup with the decanter.

She nodded. "Dreamy, absentminded." She took a sip of the brandy-laced coffee and smiled up at me. "You know Marguerite is like my own daughter, Doctor. I love her. She has never wanted anything other than to please me, and to please you. Now there is something new," she concluded, shrugging her shoulders.

"Vincent," I said, a statement rather than a question.

"I believe so," she answered. "You remember he brought her those flowers on Monday." I nodded. "Well, poppies, daisies, how long do they last once cut? So on Wednesday I went into her room to take them away, and besides I wanted the little jug to keep some béchamel cool in the larder. The flowers weren't faded, Doctor. She must have put new ones in."

This did not seem conclusive to me. "Perhaps she just liked having the flowers in her room?"

"Yes, but she must have gone up to the wheat fields where Vincent paints to cut new poppies. I can't think where any grow down here."

"Or perhaps she just wanted to replicate the bouquet, or she wanted a long walk. I am not so worried by that. This evening, when she went to Ravoux's—the only reason to do that was to see Vincent." Once again, she nodded, to confirm my notion. "Has there been another time this week when she might have been . . . out wandering?"

"Marguerite, no," she said firmly. "Paul, very possibly."

"But Paul wanders anyway. There is no place in Auvers where Paul should not go."

"No, Doctor. Not so much that. But I suspect he may be following Monsieur van Gogh."

"Why would he do that?" I asked, baffled.

"He's done nothing but draw all week. I doubt there's any paper left in the studio. I think he hoped Monsieur van Gogh would help him. But I don't know if he ever actually spoke to him."

"What makes you think he'd been trying to find him?"

"You know how Monsieur van Gogh is not very neat," she began, replacing her coffee cup on the saucer. "And how when he first came, Paul would bring home those paint tubes he'd found that Monsieur van Gogh had discarded, and show them to us. Well, he stopped after a few days. Lost interest. But he's begun again, only he keeps them in his room."

I looked at her for a moment, trying to imagine the four days that had just passed while I was in Paris, with my children apparently roaming around Auvers, hoping to catch a glimpse of Vincent. Or, more likely, to attract his attention in some way.

"Let me ask you this, Madame Chevalier. You have seen how Vincent is with Marguerite. Do you think there is . . ." I did not know how to phrase it. "Is he, has he shown any signs of special interest in her?"

"None at all," she stated. "He barely knows she's alive."

I laughed. "But he painted her!"

"Oh, of course. But he paints flowers, too," she pointed out. "And thinks no more of them when he's finished."

"True," I conceded, relieved. "But the little bouquet of poppies?"

"A gesture," she said, waving her hand. "Kindly meant, soon forgotten. Mind you, Doctor," she went on, leaning forward, "you can see how a girl as innocent as she is might take it amiss."

"But what can I do?" I asked. "Do you think I should send her away? I've been thinking that she ought to get to know some young men. Maybe a visit to Blanche's family?"

"Not now," she answered with confidence. "Doctor, look at Monsieur van Gogh. He is not so very different from the woodcutter I thought he was at first. Uncouth. Let her come to realize that on her own. The business of the flowers, and her going to Ravoux's, is odd. But when you think about what other girls have gotten up to, Doctor, we've nothing to be concerned about. Nothing." With that she got up, putting my empty cup on the tray. "Anyway, with you here this weekend, Doctor, Monsieur van Gogh will be around and both Paul and Marguerite can get their fill of him. That may be enough. Open their eyes."

Vincent came to lunch the next day. I found myself watching my children very carefully. I thought Marguerite had made a special effort in her dress: there was a brooch of Blanche's pinned to her collar, an unusual bit of coquetry for her. Paul was somewhat bumptious, eager to insert himself into the conversation even when we were discussing topics he could know nothing of, like Gauguin's current misery in Brittany, or a portrait by Puvis de Chavannes of which Vincent thought very highly. Even Vincent seemed more peculiar. There was a quality to his conversation that I had not noticed before. He spoke just a little bit too loud, just a little bit too fast, and appeared unable to let an idea go until he had brought everyone around to his view of the thing. He had been painting a peasant woman's portrait that week, and was exalted with the triumph of it. The modern portrait, he informed us, would not be a mere visual record but rather an evocation of a certain grief and tension that was our lot in the nineteenth century. A hundred years hence, when we were all forgotten as individuals, he hoped his canvases would still be seen, and felt, and understood. He had told me almost exactly the same thing while painting my portrait.

Aside from the improbability of the scenario he described, he was lecturing us. Marguerite was content simply to look at him, Paul hung on his words, and Madame Chevalier's mind was clearly elsewhere. I began to understand what Theo had endured while living with his brother. Theo had told me that sometimes he would go to bed to try to evade Vincent's monologues, but his brother would simply pull up a chair next to the bed and keep talking, hectoring Theo for a reaction, but growing furious if he disagreed. I had once found this difficult to imagine, but on that Sunday, I detected the first hint of Vincent's mind in an unbalanced state.

I feel ashamed of this now, but it must be remembered that I was, I am, a doctor. As his friend, I wanted only a quiet, easy life for him, but as a medical man, I was keenly interested in this hint of manic behavior.

When luncheon was finished, Vincent and I went up to the studio because he wanted to look again at my Cézanne flower paintings. He had been contemplating his own canvases that had been sent from St.-Rémy, among them a magnificent vase of irises set against a yellow wall. Though he did not care for most of Cézanne's paintings, he thought the flower pictures the best of them, and I believe he wanted to measure his own against that standard.

He was in a fault-finding mood. I had not seen this irritable quality in him before now. Cézanne's palette, with its grayed colors, struck him as murky and unpleasant. He also took exception to the older artist's brushwork, which he called "timid." Of course, in comparison with his own bold treatment of paint, it would have been difficult to find brushwork that was not "timid." There was no pleasing him that day, though.

I had just found one of my favorite Cézannes, a painting of my house under heavy gray winter skies, when I heard Vincent exclaim. I think it was a Dutch oath; I could not understand what he had said.

I turned around to see what was amiss. He was standing facing me, with my Guillaumin nude dangling from his hand. "Doctor!" he snapped. "You were going to frame this!"

I was taken aback. I had ordered the frame from Levert, the town carpenter, but he had not yet finished it. The delay did not seem to merit Vincent's fury. "Yes," I said. "I am going to. The frame is not yet ready."

He stepped forward, coming very close to me in the small space. He was quivering with rage, the knuckles of his free hand clenched white, his skin flushed. "Is this the way you treat the work of painters who have *bled* for these paintings?" he spat at me. "You think you are a patron of artists! But look!" He gestured to the paintings stacked on the floor. "You are hoarding these things, stuffing them in an attic, pretending to appreciate them. You are the ruin of these artists!"

He raised the Guillaumin over his head with two hands, as if to bring it down with a crash, his eyes darting around to find the most satisfying object to hit. I could hear him panting, and there was an odor coming from him, a kind of rankness in his sweat. Suddenly I was alert, my mind racing. Until that moment, I would have said that Vincent was much the same as any other man. But in that instant when I glanced at his face, it was as if I saw what I had been waiting to see all along. Finally, I could imagine Vincent slashing his ear or requiring a straitjacket. It was true, then: he could be dangerous.

But I knew what to do. I even, I must confess it, felt a surge of pride. How many times had I confronted a raving patient at the Salpêtrière and brought her back to her senses? This was not a common skill; if my Auvers colleague, Dr. Mazery, were confronted by Vincent on the verge of a violent act, he would not have been capable of calming him. I was glad to think that I could take care of this man.

Moving slowly, I placed the canvas I was holding on the cabinet behind me, keeping my eyes on Vincent's. I then positioned myself in front of him with my hands hanging at my sides. When you are attempting to pacify the deranged, you must call them back to the actual world from their alienated state. This requires a combination of force and composure. I took a deep breath.

"The frame is being made. Give me the painting," I said, with the sternest voice I could muster. His blue eyes were boring into mine, but I did everything I could to project the power of my will. The doctor must determine the reality—he cannot allow the patient's view of things to prevail. That is his duty to the patient. I stood still for an instant longer, then raised a hand, imperious. The gesture repeated my command: "Give me the painting." My breath was now coming as fast as his.

There is a game they play in the cafés, when two men clasp hands and each tries to push the other's arm to the table. It is a test of strength, and you can see one man's force gradually overcoming the other man's. I felt that happening, that afternoon: Vincent resisted, the madness in him tried to overcome my sanity, but I stood firm. "The painting," I repeated.

Then he put it into my hand. A look of puzzlement came over his face. He glanced around, as if to confirm where he was. The surroundings seemed to reassure him. "I'm sorry, Doctor, what were you saying?" he asked. The rage was gone. It was as if a beast had peered through his eyes and then retreated somewhere deep within. Now in front of me stood my friend, the painter Vincent van Gogh, chastened, alarmed. I confess to a brief, private surge of triumph.

"I was saying that Levert is making the frame for this painting and it should be ready next week." I scrutinized him. "Come, sit down," I said, drawing him toward the divan where I had first examined him. "You seemed somewhat unwell just then. Sit and rest for a moment."

He allowed himself to be guided to the dusty old divan and collapsed. He was now quite pale. "Stay here for a moment," I told him. "I am going to get you some cordial. If you feel faint, lie down."

"Why would I feel faint?" he said as I went down the stairs.

In a moment I was back before him, with a glass of water into which I had poured a special calming cordial I had developed. It has an unfortunately unpleasant flavor, being derived from the lavender plant. I try to mask the bitterness with a syrup of elderberry, but I must admit, my patients dislike it. Vincent made no comment, however, drinking it down obediently.

"Does your head ache?" I asked, laying my palm across his brow. It seemed cool enough.

"Perhaps a little bit."

"Can you hear me properly?" He just nodded. "And only me? Nothing else?" This time he shook his head very slightly, as if unwilling to jar his brain.

"Vincent, has anything like this happened before? Theo did not mention spells or attacks." Actually, I remembered, I had asked Theo about attacks, but he did not answer me directly. A sense of unease crept over me.

"I wish I could answer you properly, Doctor. I have no memory of the time when I injured myself, and there were days afterward that I do not remember, either. I suppose that could be considered an attack of sorts."

"You do not know how you behaved?"

"Aside from taking a knife to my own body, Doctor, I do not."

I sat back on the floor, looking up at him. "Has anyone ever suggested that you were epileptic? In the asylum perhaps?" But surely Theo would have mentioned that to me.

"Yes." He seemed terribly weary.

"It's not exactly the same as madness, you know."

"What does that matter?" he asked. "It's not the same as being sane. Can you stop it? Prevent it?"

"We can certainly give you potassium bromide. It is usually very effective against seizures."

"Yes, I suppose I have taken it. I believe it made me drowsy."

"I have none here in the house, but I can send Paul to Mazery to get some," I offered, still watching him carefully. Was he epileptic? Or had he almost slipped into a kind of manic delusion? It was difficult to tell, but I thought it was the latter.

He dropped his head into his hands. "I should be all right for a while now," he said. After a long moment of silence, he slapped his hands on his knees and pushed himself to standing. He looked exhausted and haggard. "I am fortunate—we are both fortunate, Doctor—that it was insignificant. Or perhaps"—he brightened—"you were able to stave it off?"

"I believe so," I said. "I wish you would stay here and rest a little longer. Would you like a proper bed downstairs? Sometimes it helps to sleep after a disturbance."

"No, Doctor, I am going to cure myself in my own way," he said, turning away from me to the stairs. "I'm going to paint. It will quiet the noise in my head."

I argued, I remonstrated, I mentioned what Theo would have wanted, but there was no swaying him. The authority I'd used on the madman did not work on the sane man. Maybe I didn't dare exert it to the same extent. For though he was lucid again, it was clear that Vincent was fragile.

The mistake I made, I know now, was to let him go that afternoon. In a way it set a pattern; I believe that, for the rest of the summer, Vincent used painting as a way to soothe himself. It was the only way he knew of to escape his trouble. Yet there might have been another way, if I had come to a better understanding of his illness.

An alienated patient's ailment is not visible; there is no rash, no wound, no fever. Doctors must rely on the patient's perceptions in order to judge the malady. However, this is by definition a faulty method because the patient's perceptions are damaged. We used to say at the Salpêtrière that it was only the patients who acknowledged being mad who did not belong there. The others, furiously proclaiming their sanity, were clearly far from sane. Sometimes a patient can be believed, and sometimes not. Only experience helps a doctor distinguish the well from the ill.

I learned this lesson in a dramatic fashion at the Salpêtrière. It was summer, a terrible, hot day in August. There was a dreadful reek coming from the river, an odor of rot and muck, while the damp corners of the hospital buildings sent out a kind of olfactory echo, a whiff of mildew and drains. I was confined to a dank ground-floor cubicle, examining reports on our patients. This is one of the reasons I did not pursue one of the grand medical careers in Paris; I am not at home in the world of rules and files and committees. I believed fifty years ago, as I believe now, that a doctor's business is with his patients rather than with other doctors.

Thus I had a patient with me, even though I was away from the ward. We had some freedom in this regard: though the women's days were very strictly regimented, a doctor could request that an individual be released from her normal routine. Marie-Claude was unusual in that she could read and write. She had been raised by an uncle who was a priest, and upon his death she secured a job as a governess, but a subsequent series of misfortunes brought her to us, a victim of mania. On more than one occasion she had attacked fellow patients, wardresses, even, once, an unfortunate gardener. Yet between these episodes she was calm and highly intelligent. I had borrowed her from the workroom to help me with my current task alphabetizing three months' worth of intake reports and checking them for completeness.

Marie-Claude was in her early thirties, and what distinguished her from her fellow patients was her expression. I thought it was something about her eyes: They moved in conventional fashion. She looked at things, examined them perhaps, then looked away once she had gleaned the information she wanted. She met my gaze but did not stare. She might frown over a page that she had trouble reading, and hold it closer to the lamp—it was so dark in that wretched room that we had to light a lamp in the middle of the August afternoon. She never looked too long or too closely at anything though, and her eyes did not evade you.

We talked as we worked. This was not the first time I had asked for her help, and I wanted to be sure that she did not resent my appropriating her time.

"Will you still be paid, even though you are not in the workroom?" I asked, as we settled down to our task. I had had to go to the atelier to pick her up: even the patients considered closest to recovery were never permitted to wander around alone.

"I'll be sure of that, Doctor," she said, with a smile. "I'm quite sharp with numbers, and I always check my pay packet."

"Would you like to do work like this when you leave here?" I asked, sitting at the desk and pulling the folder of reports toward me.

"Who says I'm to be leaving here?" she asked, startled.

"No one. But you are doing so well."

She shrugged. "That's as may be, Doctor. Well today does not mean well tomorrow."

I opened the folder and took out a sheaf of reports, each of which described a patient's first examination. We were thorough; we could not dismiss the possibility that mental ailments might have their origin in physical causes, so each woman was examined minutely and the results recorded. I spread the sheaf out on the desk, and Marie-Claude, reading the patients' names from the other side of the desk, began to pluck them from the pile.

"Do you not think you are cured?" I asked. "There is not another woman in this hospital who could do what you are doing at the moment."

She paused for a moment, and looked at me. "Doctor, I would not want to be disrespectful," she began. "I am grateful for your interest." Her hands were still on the documents.

"And? But?" I prodded.

There was a long pause. She seemed to be formulating her response. After drawing a deep breath, she said, "I was going to tell you that you should not rely on a patient's opinion. Yet there are times when we can judge our own condition. The difficulty is that we cannot tell the difference, we do not know when we are right and when we are wrong. And you, Doctor, can't, either."

I sat up, excited. Marie-Claude was the patient we all looked for, the patient who was sufficiently lucid and educated to describe her state. Perhaps she could help me understand what it was like to be mad. I had my ideas, I thought I might know, certainly I was sympathetic. However, she was the one who could not walk from one building to another without a wardress, the one who slept in a row of a dozen beds and was watched even as she bathed.

"But what does it feel like?" I asked, leaning toward her. "Can you remember? Do you recognize it?"

She shook her head regretfully. "No. I cannot say that I do." She looked back down at the papers, and plucked four more from the sheaf, placing them facedown in what I knew would be the correct order.

"I'm sorry," I said, suddenly overcome by a convulsion of conventional manners. One should not pursue a topic that made anyone uncomfortable. Marie-Claude seemed unwilling to discuss this matter further. But it was such a chance for me! "You have no way to describe the state? Or is it different each time?"

"I don't even know," she answered, and went back to her work.

I had pressed her too hard, it was clear. The next time I tried to borrow her from the workshop, the supervisor told me she could not be spared. She kept her eyes lowered the whole time I was in the room. I was terribly downcast.

Yet that was not the great lesson I learned from Marie-Claude, if indeed I could glean anything from this puzzling encounter. It was a few weeks later that I saw her again. We externs were required to be on duty several nights a month. The senior medical staff went home at night, naturally, but a doctor had to be available in case of a crisis. We slept in a kind of annex not far from the women's dormitories, and the nights were normally uneventful. On this occasion, however, I was roused well after midnight by an orderly with a lantern that looked as if it had been left behind some time before the Revolution.

"Doctor," he whispered, though we were alone in the room. "You're needed."

I sat up and ran a hand through my hair. It took me a long minute to understand where I was. "Yes, I'm coming," I said, feeling beneath my cot for my boots. I thought about leaving my coat hanging on the chair where I had left it: It was still a hot night. Reluctantly, I shrugged it on. If I were to be the doctor, I must look like the doctor. I picked up my medical bag as well, having no idea what I might do with it.

I was apprehensive, I will admit. This was my first midnight call, and I did not know what to expect. As the orderly led me to the ward, I listened for disturbance, but there was none—merely our footsteps, treading quickly down the long stone corridors. "Here we are," he said, finally, turning a corner.

I was surprised. There was no crisis. We were at the door of the principal dormitory of Falret's division, where the most capable women were assigned. The two women at the door were the wardress, a capable woman known as Madame Boguet, and Marie-Claude. They stood side by side, apparently awaiting my intervention. They were not speaking. I looked for recognition in Marie-Claude's expression, thinking that my presence might reassure her. There was none.

The orderly turned and took his ancient lantern down another corridor, while Madame Boguet began to explain the situation in a whisper. That must have been why the orderly did not speak aloud to me; he had carried his whispered instructions the length of the building and delivered them as he received them.

"Marie-Claude is unwell," she said. She glanced at our patient in an unfriendly way. "She claims she needs to be confined in a *gilet de force*. You know that I need the approval of a doctor for this, and she insisted that you be roused. So here we are. In the middle of the night. With two dozen women awake on the other side of this door, and a fine time we'll have settling them down!"

I glanced around. It seemed to me that my first step should be to separate Marie-Claude from this forceful and angry woman. I would have liked to find a little room where we could speak calmly. The corridor, of course, was dark as pitch, and Madame Boguet had the only lantern. There was a window a few meters away, a deep indentation in the thick walls, through which the hazy moonlight seeped.

"May I speak to Marie-Claude?" I asked Madame Boguet. "I would like to step over to that window, so that we might not further disturb your patients."

She looked at the window, at me, at Marie-Claude, then nodded. "I must check on them. I will come out in a few moments," she said and whisked herself through the heavy oak door to the dormitory. I took Marie-Claude by the elbow and led her to the window, positioning her so that the light fell on her face. It was not much help. Her expression was closed.

"Can you tell me, Marie-Claude, why you want the *gilet*?" I asked. I hated to see the women bundled into those coarse strappings of canvas, shuffling along with their balance impaired, lost without the use of their hands. I saw it as a punishment, and a return to the old days of chains. Surely we had made progress beyond this.

She took a deep breath, but it was not steady, and she closed her eyes. Then she shook her head.

"Are you hearing voices?"

Another shake of the head. I stood still for a moment. I could not think what to do. "May I take your pulse?" I finally asked, thinking that I might receive some information in that way. She did not answer but did not object when I took hold of her wrist. Her pulse was fast, but not alarming. I considered taking out my stethoscope—I was grasping at straws—but Madame Boguet came shuffling out of the dormitory, closing the door behind her.

"Well, Doctor," she hissed, approaching us. "Will you put Marie-Claude in the jacket?"

"Can you tell me something more of the circumstances?" I asked. "Has Marie-Claude felt unwell before today? Is there . . . has she been weak, or had headaches?"

Madame Boguet looked at me with manifest impatience. "Marie-Claude is a lunatic, Doctor, like the rest of the women here. There is no telling, ever, what any of them will do. When we find a patient sensible enough to ask for constraint, normally we put her in the jacket. I don't hold with the doctors interfering, we do very well on our own and we know what's what. Marie-Claude is a good girl, but she's done some harm in her bad moments." Here she put a reassuring hand on the patient's arm. I found this confusing.

Who was right? I was the doctor. I was the one with the training, the seven years of medical school. I was the one wearing the black coat and carrying the bag full of diagnostic tools. The wardress, it seemed to me, was harsh. She could know nothing of what we doctors were trying to achieve. Yet her comforting touch told me she had Marie-Claude's well-being at heart.

Clearly, there would be no help from Marie-Claude herself. If anything, she seemed to have withdrawn further.

It seemed so wrong. The *gilet* was humiliating. Nevertheless, the patient had requested it. I had regarded her as practically sane, even ready for freedom, but now she wanted to be confined. She had warned me of precisely this turn of events; that even she could not judge her own condition.

And yet where was the harm in granting her wishes? I could feel my mind changing. If I granted Marie-Claude's request, threaded her arms through the long sleeves, tied the knots up her back—what then? She would sleep poorly, perhaps. If I denied the request, the risk was much greater—Marie-Claude might rise from her bed and attack one of the other patients. Her records proved the potential for violence; she had once come close to throttling a woman much larger than she.

So I gave in. I agreed that Marie-Claude should spend the night confined, and further ordered a series of cold baths over the next few days. Many women found that these restored them to normalcy. I returned to my cot and lay down with my boots on, running over the sequence of events in my mind. I should have stood firm, I thought. I had submitted to the authority of a madwoman and an uneducated wardress who, for all I knew, had done her own time as a patient. Could they possibly know more than I, the physician?

Nine

THE NEXT DAY BEGAN peacefully enough. My daughter was under the housekeeper's eye: Madame Chevalier set Marguerite to the task of checking over all the fruit preserves and washing the empty jars, in preparation for the next batch. I proposed that Paul help me organize the studio; I had recently brought a substantial order of paints and supplies down from Paris, and the space is so small that everything must be carefully stowed, as on a boat. I thought if Paul's enthusiasm for art persisted, we might need to store the paintings on the second floor to give us more space to work.

But Paul was surly that morning, careless and inattentive. He took little interest in my suggestions. He picked things up and put them down aimlessly, he tossed brushes into a drawer, all jumbled. I asked him to show me what he had done that week, and he told me he had destroyed all of his drawings.

"They were useless," he said, looking out the window.

"Nothing is useless if you learn from it," I told him. "Would you like to sketch in the garden after luncheon?"

"What use is sketching, anyway? Vincent never sketches."

"Drawing is the foundation of painting," I instructed. "If you do not draw . . ." I had to pause to consider my argument. Paul was right, in a way: Vincent rarely used drawing to prepare a canvas. "Drawing helps you understand what things really look like," I said slowly, as I attempted to make my thoughts clear. "Vincent draws all the time, you've seen his notebook. There is a difference between the way we know things to be and the way they appear to the eye. And of course," I added, on surer ground, "artists make sketches to plan canvases. You remember that Vincent did that for his portrait of Marguerite."

"But usually he just heaps paint onto the canvas," Paul countered. "And you think he is brilliant."

I looked at Paul's slightly rigid back. He had found something on the windowsill to occupy his hands, a leaf blown in from the garden perhaps. "Yes," I said. "The way Vincent paints is unusual, but he *is* brilliant." There was silence. I turned back to the box of paints I was transferring to drawers.

"Anyway I don't want to draw today, Papa," Paul said. "I'm going to fish."

"Now?" I replied, surprised. It was a bright, hot morning, the kind of weather that drives fish deep into the cool, silty depths of the Oise.

Paul only shrugged and left the studio. My thoughts that morning were not pleasant. I had a heavy feeling, a sense of something ominous but unnamed. The house in Auvers had always been a refuge for me, but now it seemed full of worry.

We were very quiet at the luncheon table that day, each occupied by his or her own thoughts. I half-expected to hear the bell ring, and Vincent to appear with a blank canvas and his portable easel, but he did not come, which added to my unease. Even the dogs, whose behavior at mealtimes could be intrusive, had dispersed to shady corners. Only

Nero barked from time to time, in a hoarse series of cries, then left off. Finally, as she got up to clear the salad plates, Marguerite broke the silence to say, "Paul, what is the matter with Nero?"

"Nothing," Paul said, looking down at his plate. "He got wet down at the river, and I tied him up so he wouldn't disturb us at the table."

"Well, he must have dried off by now, it's so hot," said Madame Chevalier. "Why don't you go untie him? The noise is unpleasant."

"No, he got some slime on him," Paul said. "He smells terrible. I was going to wash him after we finished."

At that moment, though, the dog revealed him to be a liar. Nero had somehow slipped free from his tether and came galloping up to the table, barking with joy at every bound. We all turned to look at him and, as one, stood up, ready to escape. Nero was of an indeterminate breed, though I always thought Newfoundland predominated. He was large and black, shaggy and irrepressible. I found his boundless affection endearing, but the women complained about his size, his exuberance, and the impossibility of controlling him. Paul, who was fifteen the summer Nero joined us, worked hard to civilize him and was the only member of the family who could exert any influence on his behavior.

But Paul's influence had evidently failed in the recent past, for Nero's coat was matted with paint. It was mostly yellow, with areas of dark blue and green and flecks of white clumped in streaks and blobs on his side. There were smears on his muzzle, as if he had made an attempt to lick off the colors. The tip of his joyously wagging tail was frosted with orange. On top of it all, he was wet and smelled of turpentine.

In a flash I understood the reasons for both Vincent's absence and Paul's strange behavior that morning. I could imagine it now: Paul, importunate, tracking Vincent around Auvers. Vincent, unhappy at the interruption, the dog creating havoc. How could Paul have been so stupid?

Paul froze for a moment, but before Nero could reach us, he leapt from the table and planted himself a few feet away. "Sit!" he commanded. Nero obeyed, tail thumping the ground. "Stay," Paul added. "Marguerite," he said, using the same tone of command, "go get the rope, would you? It's tied near Henriette."

Marguerite, leaving a wide berth around the dog, trotted off toward the far end of the garden, where the goat's bell clanked behind the trees. The rest of us stood still, unwilling to attract Nero's attention and an affectionate, paint-streaked canine embrace. In a minute Marguerite returned, rope in hand. She flung it to Paul, who fashioned a kind of collar that he slipped over the dog's head. The tail wagging instantly ceased, and Nero lowered his forequarters to the ground. Paul looked at him and sighed. He did not even glance toward me, but seemed quite frozen, as if braced for a flurry of blows or a tirade. His shame and fear cooled my anger.

"Paul and I will chance drinking our coffee out here," I told Madame Chevalier. "If you and Marguerite wish to protect your dresses, you should stay indoors."

"I should think so," Madame Chevalier agreed, picking up the wine carafe and the water pitcher. "We'll just be a moment, Doctor. Shall I get you an old blanket? Your smock?"

"Yes, what a good idea." I turned to my daughter. "Marguerite, would you go up to the studio to see what you can find to protect Paul and me from Nero's paint?"

When the women had gone inside, I asked, "Would I be correct in thinking that the two of you had an encounter with Monsieur van Gogh?"

Paul merely nodded, looking down at Nero. The dog gazed back at him.

"I hope all that paint came off a palette?"

Paul winced. "No. A finished canvas."

"A finished painting!" I exclaimed, hands to my head in agitation. "This horrid creature destroyed a painting? I have a mind to drown him!" I shouted, glaring down at the dog.

"I should not have brought him," Paul said in the dog's defense. "How could he know? Monsieur van Gogh was shouting, and Nero tried to get away from him. It was awful! Nero knocked over the easel, and then I think he fell on the picture, and Monsieur van Gogh was *terrifying*, Papa, he was screaming and ranting . . ." He turned away from me and dashed his hand across his face, trying to hide his tears.

It is a terrible thing for a young man of seventeen to cry before his father. My outrage diminished. I bent down, quite awkwardly, and held out a hand to Nero's bright-spotted head. He nuzzled me, and I took his soft ears into both hands, gently twisting them in the way he loved. He rolled onto his side, all worries forgotten.

"When did this happen?" I asked Paul, without looking up. There were bits of gravel stuck in the clots of paint on Nero's fur.

"Yesterday, late in the afternoon."

"Where has Nero been?"

"I closed him in a shed up on the plateau." His voice was becoming steadier. "Nobody uses it. I took him some food and water. This morning I tried to get the paint off with turpentine and a rag. That was where I went. And it didn't work, so I tried the river."

"Oil paint is not water-soluble," I commented, unthinking.

"No. And there was too much for the turpentine."

Madame Chevalier appeared on the steps with the tray of coffee cups. Marguerite followed her, carrying an ancient blanket and my studio coat. "This will only cover you to your knees, Papa," she said, "but I could not find anything else."

"Thank you," I said to both of them. "Marguerite, do you have a very large pair of scissors? Perhaps for cutting fabric?"

"I do," said Madame Chevalier. "I'll bring them." She set down the tray. "You'll pour?"

"I'll pour," I agreed, taking the blanket from Marguerite. "Paul, my boy, perhaps if you put this on like some kind of toga, you may yet salvage your trousers. We are going to give Nero a dramatic clipping."

It took us most of the afternoon, and we did not entirely escape being smirched, but our appearances at the end were less alarming than Nero's. He looked like a newly shorn military recruit. At first we just removed the fur that was matted with paint, but he was so piebald that we had to clip the rest of his coat simply to restore his natural symmetry. Paul seemed relieved when we finished our task.

"I am very sorry, Papa. I should have kept Nero under control." It was a handsome apology.

"Yes," I said mildly. "But it's Monsieur van Gogh you need to speak to."

"Must I?" he asked, stepping back in alarm. "He was so frightening!"

"Yes, you must," I insisted, annoyed. "He has nothing to live for, Paul, except his painting. Do you understand that? Think of how he exists, how lonely he is, among strangers."

"But he has us," Paul protested. "He seems to like us; to like you, at least."

"All the more reason why we should not destroy his work, don't you think?"

"Yes, all right," Paul conceded, scuffing the gravel with one foot.

I looked at the sorry pile of black hair at our feet. "We need to replace the paint that Nero wasted. That, at least, we can do. The finished canvas is beyond restitution. Why don't you go get tubes of cobalt, malachite green, lead white, and yellow ocher. A large tube of the ocher, if we have one. Make them into a package. If you take them to the inn after dinner, he'll be there."

Paul looked at me with an appeal: "You wouldn't come with me?"

I considered. Going with Paul could give the boy courage as well as provide me with an opportunity to check on Vincent. "Yes, I will," I told him. He flushed, and tears again started in his eyes.

Paul was silent as we walked to the inn after dinner. We carried lanterns, though the last rays of the sun still diluted the dusk. Our steps were silent on the dusty road, and we heard only the sounds of a summer night: rustling and peeping in the trees, a far-off dog's bark. The lights from Ravoux's glowed at some distance, and the tables set out in front of the *mairie* were occupied with drinkers. We crossed in front of them, and I nodded to those I knew—the carpenter, the stationmaster, and the eldest son of the town's biggest farmer. We turned down the alley beyond the inn, going directly to the back door, for Vincent would most likely be found in the shed where his paintings were stored. But he was neither there nor in the stuffy garret where he slept. Trying to quell my alarm, I turned to Paul. "I think you may know more of Vincent's movements than I do," I said. "Can you imagine where he might be?"

"We can try inside the café," he said. "I can't think what else to do."

"He's not drinking too much, is he?"

"Why do you think I would know these things, Papa?" Paul asked, annoyed.

I sighed and opened the back door to the café. "Never mind," I told him.

Ravoux had had gas put in, so the room was bright with that pitiless, cold glow that I have never liked. I suppose it was more cheerful than the dim yellow halo from a solitary oil lamp—certainly the marble tabletops and the mirrors gleamed. But gaslight casts harsh shadows, and Vincent's face, when he looked up at us, had the hollow-eyed look of a skull. He was sitting in front of a small glass of brandy and an empty coffee cup, elbows on the table, shoulders hunched. When he recognized us, he merely lifted one of his hands a few inches from the marble, to acknowledge our presence. "May we sit down?" I asked, and he nodded, gazing into his cup.

Paul set the brown-paper parcel of paint tubes on the table and pulled a chair from the next table to sit. I caught Ravoux's eye and gestured to Vincent's brandy. We would join him. Before the glasses arrived, Paul nudged the package toward Vincent with his fingertips. "I am very, very sorry about yesterday," he said hurriedly. "I regret the loss of your painting. Here are some paints, to replace those that the dog . . ." He paused. "I know they are not the same as replacing a painting. I know that is a terrible loss."

At this moment Ravoux brought our brandy and Paul gratefully seized his, burying as much of his face as he could in the small glass.

Vincent laid a hand on the paints and looked at me. "Thank you," he addressed Paul. "Thank you." He fell silent. A few moments passed, but he did not add anything. Paul looked at me, a question in his eyes. Vincent seemed to have withdrawn, retracted himself, as it were.

I tried to be bracing. "I hope you can re-create the painting. Make a second version, perhaps."

He turned to me and nodded. "No doubt, Doctor," he said. His voice was muffled. He took a breath as if to say something else, but nothing occurred to him.

"And you are feeling all right?" I asked, searching his face. "After yesterday? Any headache?"

"I'm tired," he said to his hands, which were clasped around his glass. "It is such a long battle, Doctor, I wonder if it will ever be over." He shook his head. "Yet I fight on. What else can I do?" He turned to me as if I might have an answer for him. Paul watched the exchange with his eyes as large as saucers.

"There is nothing else, I think, for any of us," I said. "Can I give you something to help you sleep?"

"No, Doctor, I'll sleep. And I'll wake up tomorrow and go back out to the fields and put paint on canvas." He looked at Paul. "I'm sorry if I frightened you yesterday. I don't remember what I said, but I hope I wasn't too . . . fierce."

"Not at all. But I will always regret the painting," Paul said, with dignity. He stood up. "Papa, shall I leave you two?"

I looked again at Vincent and saw only weariness. "No, I will come with you. We will leave Vincent and wish him a good night's rest." As I rose from the table, I touched Vincent's shoulder. "Remember, I can help you. If anything disturbs you, I beg you will come to me," I told him. He made as if to smile, but his eyes did not meet mine, and his smile was just a movement of the lips. He was very far away from us.

It was not until the second week in July that I went to visit Theo again. Vincent had not come to us the previous weekend, despite a friendly note I had left for him at the inn. I was sharply disappointed; I realized how much I had come to look forward to his company. I was also slightly alarmed, considering the mood in which I had left him. After Sunday luncheon, I sent Paul down to the inn to see if he could find out why Vincent had stayed away. Adeline Ravoux reported that he had taken the early train to Paris, so I comforted myself with the notion that he was with his brother. Yet he did not ring our bell on Monday, and Paul's query resulted in the answer that he had returned from Paris and was out painting. This was worrisome. I was sure he was driving himself too hard. Exhaustion makes it more difficult for a man to withstand mental strain.

On Wednesday, as usual, I returned to my apartment in Paris. A message to Theo resulted in the suggestion that we meet at a café on the Boulevard Malesherbes. It was there that I found him on the Thursday morning, stirring sugar into his coffee.

"I am so sorry I have not been able to talk to you, Doctor," he said, rising. "Will you have coffee?" He gestured to the waiter and sank back in his chair. He looked pale. I could not help checking his eyes to see if his pupils looked normal, but it was difficult to tell in the café's bright light. "It has been a very busy time. I am taking Jo and the baby to Holland for a few weeks, you see, and there is so much to do before we depart."

This was news. I was aware that Vincent hoped they would spend some of Theo's precious vacation time in Auvers: he had spoken to me more than once of finding holiday lodgings for the whole family.

"Vincent seems to have had his heart set on your coming to Auvers," I remarked.

Theo sighed and shrugged. He seemed resigned. "I know. He is terribly disappointed. But my mother is old, Doctor, and needs to see her grandson. Vincent so rarely understands why things cannot go as he wishes."

"I think I know what you mean," I agreed, picking up my coffee cup. "How did he seem to you on Sunday? He did not visit us last weekend."

"Vincent's visit on Sunday was a disaster," he said. "I cannot tell you how I regret it. We all got excited, worried, things were said . . ." He looked me in the eye. "If you had not come to me, I would have asked to see you." Here he paused, as if unable to go on.

"Was Vincent angry? I have seen a taste of his rage, and it was terribly alarming."

"We were all angry. It was a long day; the baby has been ill, and I have been driven to distraction by those gentlemen at the gallery who do not seem to understand that a man has a right to a respectable salary. I have been considering going out on my own as a dealer. Vincent urges this, though of course he has no comprehension of the risks. Jo is more cautious. She favors economy, on all our parts. She pointed out, quite forcefully, that Vincent's work does not bring us income, and that his paintings take up a great deal of space. To be honest, I had never seen Jo like that, either."

"They say that women can be fierce as tigers when their children are threatened," I suggested.

"She was fierce indeed. She said that if she could economize and reduce our expenses by one hundred francs a month, Vincent should be able to live on fifty francs less. She thinks that I should stop buying him paint and canvases until he sells something."

I could think of no reply. I was astounded that the apparently mild-mannered Jo could have struck out at Vincent in this way.

"Of course he ran down the stairs shouting, and then Jo and I had words. We have settled things between us, fortunately, and Jo wrote to Vincent. You say you have not seen him?"

"No, but he was back at Ravoux's by Monday, I know." I glanced out the window at the boulevard. A rain shower had just begun, accompanied by a gust of wind that riffled the awning of the café. "I came to you, monsieur, because I have been worried about Vincent myself." I told him about the episode with the unframed Guillaumin, and Paul's unfortunate encounter. It was evidently difficult for Theo to hear this. He fidgeted with his empty cup until the waiter arrived, inquiring, but shook his head when offered another cup. His eyes ranged over the café's interior, more crowded now that the customers seated outdoors had been forced inside by the rain. I saw him nod to a gentleman seated a table away, and his restlessness increased.

When I finished speaking, he turned back to me. "Doctor, would you mind coming for a walk with me? I would like to tell you more, but . . ." His eyes slid toward his acquaintance.

I glanced outside. The shower had ceased for the moment, leaving the sidewalk glazed with damp, but the clouds hung heavy and low. More rain was imminent. "Of course," I answered, wishing I had brought an umbrella.

He put down a few coins and stood, leaning on the table. I wondered if he was even aware of his own weakness. Sometimes the symptoms of syphilis arrive so gradually that the diagnosis takes the patient by surprise. And sometimes patients willfully ignore them. Our powers of self-deception are remarkable.

Once on the pavement, Theo seemed unsure where to go, looking around as if the neighborhood were strange to him. "Never mind, let us go this way," he said, linking his arm in mine. This was unusual: I had noticed that neither of the Van Gogh brothers seemed given to physical gestures of friendship. While exquisitely courteous, Theo did not even appear particularly demonstrative with his wife. I thought this hand on my elbow was a confession of sorts. He must feel utterly overwhelmed. It was actually quite pleasant, walking along linked to another human. I was reminded that my wife, Blanche, and I used to stroll this way, footsteps in unison, my hip against her skirts, along the Parisian streets.

Theo and I turned away from the bustle of the boulevard, down a street lined with apartment buildings. Ahead, an unusual structure loomed, surrounded by gravel paths and a few trees.

"I have often seen that building without knowing what it was," I said.

"The Chapelle Expiatoire," Theo answered. "This is the site where Louis the Sixteenth and Marie Antoinette were buried. The chapel was built by Louis the Eighteenth. The park is very quiet, we can stroll there." I could not see how the row of low arches leading to a domed building could possibly be a chapel, but I followed. There were iron chairs scattered beneath the dripping trees, but the brief rain had driven away any occupants. We set out on the path, our feet crunching on the gravel. The shower had brought a whiff of freshness to the spindly lindens. It was a strikingly quiet square. As we walked, I studied the white marble walls of the chapel, severe blocks sparsely ornamented by carved laurel wreaths and winged hourglasses. It occurred to me that the arcades along the sides might shelter tombs, and I marveled at this manifestation of death mere steps away from Parisian temples of commerce like the Galeries Lafayette.

"Monsieur van Gogh," I began, "would you tell me more about Vincent's illness? His recent behavior has prompted some questions. There was an episode last week when he behaved very strangely. He shouted at me over a trifle, and then seemed to regain control of himself."

"Yes, his temper can be very alarming," Theo agreed. "He becomes enraged. But then it passes off, and he often seems despondent afterward."

"That is just what I observed. It is this despondency that concerns me."

"Yes, of course," he answered, but then fell silent. He speared the damp ground with his umbrella at every stride.

"I am alarmed by the force of his despair," I went on, looking at the row of tombs to my right. "Has he ever spoken of suicide?"

"Yes," Theo's voice came quietly. "Not in personal terms, you understand. He has not knowingly attempted to do away with himself. But he has spoken of it, written of it. He said after one attack that he felt like a man who'd tried to drown himself and found the water too cold."

That startled me. "When you say 'one attack,' do you mean there were episodes besides the one when he cut his ear?"

"I think so, yes," Theo answered. "It was difficult to get information, you know. There were certainly spells of very irrational behavior while he was at the asylum, I did hear about that."

I could feel myself frowning. Surely I should have been told about this. "And did Vincent try to harm himself during any of these spells?"

The umbrella suddenly swung in front of us like a pendulum, left to right, nearly rapping my shin. "Apparently so. Signac—you know Paul Signac? The painter?" I nodded, for I knew his work. "Signac saw Vincent at Arles, a year and a half ago. That was after the episode with the ear, and Vincent was still in the hospital in Arles." He looked at me to be sure I remembered, and I nodded again. One would hardly forget the episode with the ear. "Signac was with Vincent when an attack came on. They had gotten permission to go back to the house so Vincent could retrieve some books. While they were there, he tried to drink turpentine, and Signac had to wrestle the bottle away from him."

"Had to wrestle . . . ," I repeated. "So this was an attack of some violence?"

Theo's eyes sidled toward mine, and I could feel his hand tense on my arm. "Yes, Doctor. According to Signac, Vincent was raving and throwing himself around wildly, breaking things . . . The gendarmes had to come in and restrain him, and take him back to the hospital."

So my idea that Vincent might be epileptic was not far-fetched. In fact, it seemed more likely with every word Theo spoke. I hardly knew what to think, or what to ask next. "Did you ever see behavior like that?"

"When I arrived in Arles, after the ear episode, he was tied to his bed. He didn't recognize me but kept thrashing around and shouting, things I couldn't understand. I only caught a few words here and there: Gauguin's name, Jesus."

"And is that all?"

There was a pause. "No. At the asylum, he once tried to drink lamp oil. And ate paint. Dr. Peyron, the doctor at St.-Rémy, mentioned these attempts in his letters. He also mentioned it when Vincent *stopped* talking of suicide. As if that were cause for hope." I had not heard this note of bitterness before in Theo's conversation, but it did seem justified.

The path turned a corner, wrapping now around what must be the chapel proper, a diminutive pedimented temple set upon a high terrace. There were still no visible allusions to the Christian faith or to the family that had once sat on France's throne, just the expanse of smooth white marble. The effect was cold and dismal. "And Dr. Peyron, did he share his diagnosis with you?"

"Yes," Theo answered. "He thought Vincent's attacks were caused by epilepsy. So did Dr. Rey, the young doctor who cared for him at Arles. Rey was not fully qualified, of course. What do you think, Doctor?"

I paused. This was such important information Theo had just given me—information I should have had earlier. My mind was whirling as I tried to assimilate it. I had spent the week evaluating tentative diagnoses and combinations of diagnoses. I had looked through old notebooks, searching out symptoms that matched Vincent's behavior. Mania would explain his furious energy, yet my last encounter with him, as he sat at Ravoux's over an empty coffee cup, seemed to suggest melancholy. And now there were these attacks, whether or not they were epileptic, to take into account.

In a way, the puzzle was exciting. What doctor would not be intrigued by such a patient? Could it be that Vincent's illness was a new one? Perhaps the highly strained nervous system of the artist could not tolerate the speed and stimulation of the current age. Possibly his •

"spells" were a kind of accumulated nerve strain, released in a form of convulsion. This might be the new melancholy of the coming twentieth century. Gachet's syndrome, they would name it . . .

I recalled myself to the present. "I had better describe more fully what happened in Auvers last week." I recounted Vincent's alarming behavior with me and with Paul. "So I must tell you that I am concerned about these attacks. Has he ever tried to harm anyone besides himself?"

Theo studied the point of the umbrella, and dug it so deep into the gravel that he reached the damp black dirt beneath it. Finally he sighed and spoke. "Yes. From what I understand. Vincent was out painting one day—they used to let him leave the asylum with an orderly—and he attacked the man. He didn't hurt him, and there were no hard feelings afterward. The fellow readily forgave Vincent. Dr. Peyron said they were all quite fond of him there."

"Your brother . . . your brother attacked someone physically?" I repeated. "While he was having one of these spells? Monsieur van Gogh, you did not tell me this! That he has turned against people and injured them?"

"The orderly wasn't injured," Theo began to protest.

"And how often does he have these violent spells, or episodes, or whatever you want to call them? Do they follow a pattern?"

"They seem to arrive every few months. I don't know what brings them on. He had his last attack in April."

It was now early July. "Is Vincent aware of this periodic quality?"

"Yes," Theo answered. He drew a breath and went on. "He wanted to come north and be settled shortly after the last episode, so that he did not fall ill on the voyage."

It took me a moment to grasp the significance of this statement. Our feet struck the gravel in unison, once, twice, three times. I found myself listening to their steady pace rather than focusing on what Theo had just told me. We sounded as if we were old friends, pacing along as one. But it was Theo and Vincent who were in unison. Vincent wanted to leave the asylum and be settled before he had another attack, and Theo made this possible. The perfect brother, smoothing the way for his ailing sibling.

"Do I understand you?" I asked, stopping abruptly. Theo, surprised, stumbled a little bit and I confess I was not sorry. "Is it correct that, when you approached me, you thought that Vincent was likely to have another attack? And you did not warn me?"

That fair skin flushed. "Yes, Doctor. I must apologize. I should perhaps have—"

I could not let him finish. The words were out of my mouth in a burst: "You most certainly should have warned me!" I shook his arm free and flung away from him, perhaps to allow space for my anger to blossom between us. "Leaving aside my safety, and the safety of my family, how could you expect me to treat your brother without telling me everything about him?" I felt myself standing taller, looming over Theo. "I cannot be expected to work miracles in the dark, you know! How could I help him without knowing this? And to think—I allowed him to paint Marguerite! Monsieur van Gogh, I am astonished! What if he had had a 'spell' in my daughter's presence? You have been reckless with our safety!"

Theo stood looking at me, hands folded on his umbrella handle. He had no answer. I walked away two steps, then turned on my heel, pivoting on the gravel and coming back to stand facing him. "He is practically living with my family!" I reached forward with my foot and kicked the umbrella aside, watching with satisfaction as Theo staggered, then recovered.

"What did you think you were doing? Finding him a nursemaid? Your brother is profoundly *ill*. He has attempted to kill himself. He has threatened my son. The last time I saw him, he was deeply despondent. For the final time: I cannot do anything for him if I do not have all of the details!"

I stalked away from him, to where the path turned. I rounded the corner, out of Theo's sight, and halted, breathing hard. Ahead of me, an elderly man tottered on the arm of a much younger man, while a well-dressed lady spoke in his ear. They were too near me to ignore. I nodded to the group and turned around, just another old gentleman walking in a damp Paris park. Seething with rage. I drew a deep breath, trying to settle my spirits.

Theo was standing exactly where I had left him, looking forlorn. I did not hurry as I returned to him.

"Do you think we are safe around him? What will happen if the attack—which you apparently anticipate—occurs?"

"But he is better with you, Doctor," Theo said, astonished. "Why are you so angry?"

"Because you did not tell me everything! Your mad brother is due to have another violent fit any moment. Did you not think it was necessary to warn me of this?"

"I did not dream that I needed to, Doctor," he explained. "Vincent seemed so happy, so productive, and I thought—I suppose he thought so as well—that the attacks came because he was in the asylum. Everything seemed to be going so well. You have no call to be so fierce," he added, with a kind of dignified reproof. "You were confident that he would continue to improve. We thought the worst was over. Surely you can see that."

It is a deeply human impulse, the urge to hope. I had known it myself again and again, especially during poor Blanche's illness. After a day without fever or an unbroken night's sleep, I could not help believing she would get well. Of course Theo had felt the same way about Vincent. Theo must comprehend the gravity of the situation, however. "I understand," I told him stiffly. "I apologize. Yet you should have told me about the rhythm of the attacks."

Now it was his turn to sigh. "Yes, Doctor, I should have. But you see, I was so afraid that you would not be willing to take him on. If I had said to you, here is my brother, he is subject to attacks when he is violent and tries to harm himself, we hope he will be steadier away from the asylum, but we cannot be certain, will you take care of him—" He looked at me. "You see my point."

"I do," I said. "Nevertheless, you have seen your brother in the throes of a spell. You have described to me how he was raving, and restrained. Yet you sent him to me as if he were a mild little lamb! I must tell you,

Monsieur van Gogh, that I wonder if your brother does not still belong in an asylum."

A raindrop hit my cheek, and another one my hand. Theo looked to the sky and held out his palm in the gesture that said, "Is it raining?" He put up his umbrella.

"Let us hope the trees will shelter us," he said. "Or perhaps we can take cover in the chapel, grim though it is."

We hastened to the shelter of a pair of plane trees and stood side by side, watching the raindrops. My last words echoed in my mind. It was impossible that Theo should not still be hearing them: "in an asylum . . . in an asylum . . ." It was not a heavy rain, rather a spattering that blew across the park in front of us. Even the gravel around us stayed pale as the tiny pebbles beyond the trees' shelter darkened slightly. We were very close together, shoulders touching beneath the double canopy of the leaves and the black silk dome of Theo's umbrella. We did not look at each other but gazed outward at the rain while the drops tapped fitfully above our heads.

"I can understand why you would have kept some of this information from me," I said into our silence. "But you may have made a grave mistake. You hope your brother is better, and so do I, but I must review the options for treatment. The situation is much more complicated than I understood." I fell silent for a moment, wondering if there were a way to administer water therapy to Vincent without the vast tubs and hoses of a madhouse. I had seen cold baths calm patients in the asylums, but I had not tried to use them since.

"I have great respect for your brother, Monsieur van Gogh," I resumed. "I admire him, of course: I do believe he is a genius. But I also honor his courage and his modesty and his devotion to his art, and his love of mankind. He wants so keenly to be useful, and he hopes so little for himself."

"Yes," Theo said. I felt him take a deep breath. "You have understood him."

"I understand the lucid man," I told him. "I do not understand . . ."

"The madman?" Theo proposed in a very low voice. "When he is making sense, Doctor, no one is more convincing. Yet there are other times when, although he seems to be clear-minded, his ideas are utterly impractical. To give an example, after the first attack in Arles, he insisted he should join the Foreign Legion."

I could not suppress an undignified snort of amusement. Theo smiled wryly. "Yes, I know, it is laughable. Can you imagine Vincent with a rifle and a kepi, marching across the desert? Yet he was in earnest, and it was not entirely the daydream of a naïf."

I looked out at the sky beyond the tree, which seemed to be somewhat lighter. "I think the rain may have stopped," I said, stepping forward from our shelter. Theo followed, collapsing the umbrella as he confirmed that we no longer needed it. We resumed our slow pacing around the vast marble monument to the Bourbons.

"Here is my dilemma," I suddenly addressed him. "First, I am not Vincent's doctor, as you know. Dr. Mazery, who has not met Vincent, has authority over him in Auvers. He is a good man, but limited in his experience of mental maladies. Second, I cannot be sure of a diagnosis. There is too much that I do not know. I have no records, no useful observations of your brother's vagaries. This makes it difficult for me to say conclusively what ails him. Finally, I am deeply concerned. I fear that he could be a danger to those around him. Or a danger to himself."

I drew a breath to continue, but Theo interrupted me. Ignoring my last statement, he said, "There are his letters. Vincent's letters to me. The letters in which he proposes he become a legionnaire were very alarming. He had just had an attack, quite a long one. He was terribly discouraged. He was not mad, and yet the logic is so mysterious." His hand tightened on my elbow. "I know you are busy, Doctor. I know that your other patients and your family take up your time. But if you were inclined, you could go up to Cité Pigalle. Jo could show you the letters. I can give you a note for her—"

He was pleading, so I stopped him. "Monsieur van Gogh, please. Of course I will go to call on Madame van Gogh. As it happens, I can go now, if you think that would be convenient for her." I went on, thinking aloud. "But do you think . . . Surely Monsieur Vincent wrote them for your eyes. I hesitate to intrude—"

"No," he broke in, dismissing my scruples. "If you believe they may be helpful, Doctor, you should read them. Vincent has just spent over a year in an asylum where he was watched all the time. There is no privacy for lunatics." The term sounded awkward coming from him, old-fashioned and scornful. A thought flickered through my mind: what if Theo were not entirely, selflessly loyal? The man was only human, after all. What could be more natural than some resentment of the burdens his brother imposed on him?

He stood before me now, framed by the arch of one of those marble tombs. "It may help," he said quietly, nearly whispering. "We must do anything that may help Vincent, anything we can."

I was moved. I put my arm across his shoulder, turning him away from the grim symbols behind him. I began to walk him toward the street. It must have been past the time for him to open the gallery. "I will go. I will take a note to Madame van Gogh from you, and I will go to your apartment and read some of Vincent's letters. They may help me to know what ails him. And then we will see."

I did not promise a cure because I could not, but Theo seemed content with this meager assurance. He scribbled a note to his wife on a slip of paper from his pocket book. I was relieved to see that his handwriting was quite firm.

*T*en

❧

MADAME VAN GOGH may have been surprised to see me on her doorstep, but she expressed only pleasure. The apartment was very appealing, bright and clean and cheerful, but the air of orderly Dutch housekeeping made Vincent's pictures look especially remarkable. I might even say they appeared ferocious. My hostess saw my eyes rest on a strange, dark canvas of a group of peasants in a shadowy hut, sitting around a table. A platter of potatoes lay on the table, and the oldest woman in the picture was pouring coffee. Her hands were twisted with arthritis. The colors were mostly browns and umbers, as if it had been painted with earth. I could barely recognize it as Vincent's, though in places I could see his characteristic heavy application of paint. "That was one of Vincent's first ambitious pictures," Jo told me. "He painted it in Holland, before he came here to live with Theo. Let me show you my favorite, the almond blossoms he sent after the baby was born."

She led me into the little alcove where the baby's crib was set underneath what I think might be the loveliest picture Vincent ever painted. In format it was like the painting of chestnut blossoms that I still possess, but the colors were lighter and the brushwork more serene. Theo had described it as "tender," which was right. The pink and white blossoms sprayed across a sky of an exquisite blue. "Vincent can be very difficult," his sister-in-law said, "but this is part of him, too. He can be so gentle and sweet." She guided me into the dining room and stood by a little cabinet beneath the window. "Theo's note says you would like to read some of Vincent's letters. Will that help you? Can you help him, I mean?" She opened a drawer and lifted out a loose sheaf of envelopes and folded pages. Her frank, open face seemed very hopeful.

"Madame, I do not know," I confessed, shaking my head. "Like you, I want very much to do so. I was explaining to Monsieur van Gogh that mental maladies are difficult to diagnose, especially since I do not know Monsieur Vincent very well. Your husband thought that these letters might help."

"Well, perhaps they may," she said, shrugging. "Will you sit—at the table here, perhaps? Would you be comfortable there? You could lay the letters out, and I will bring you some coffee."

"Yes, of course, thank you," I said, feeling somewhat helpless. Theo's description of his wife's quarrel with Vincent seemed less puzzling now that I saw her as mistress of her own home, with the effortless authority of the virtuous housewife.

Settled at the polished table, with a gleaming blue and white coffeepot and a platter of bread and cheese to go with the coffee, I could not help thinking of Theo. This home, so cheerful and serene, seemed like an embodiment of all that was wholesome. Yet the man of the house was suffering from a malady that was born in shame. Many of the patients at both Bicêtre and the Salpêtrière were syphilitic, so I was all too familiar with its outward signs. They were astoundingly varied: tumors and joint pains, gastric troubles and deafness, jaundice and paralysis could all be caused by syphilis. The timetable for the development of the illness was also variable. Every doctor knew that it began with a sore on the patient's genitals, and that the secondary infection, which occurred a few months later, could include rashes, fevers, and loss of hair. Then came a period of calm, which might last years, or even decades. Many patients considered themselves cured at this point. I could not believe Theo van Gogh would have married Johanna knowing that he was syphilitic, for fear of passing along the disease. But he might have thought the disease had been vanquished. Syphilis and consumption were the two secret scourges—familiar to everyone but never mentioned, advancing and retreating, deadly but mysterious. I felt a moment of deep discouragement. I had been powerless to save my wife from consumption. What made me think that I could help the Van Gogh brothers?

Yet I must make an effort. They were all counting on me. I turned my attention to the letters and was quickly absorbed. I became oblivious to the life of the apartment occurring around me. A maid was dusting in the sitting room. Madame van Gogh went out, with the baby in a carriage, and came back with a bunch of flowers. A delivery from the fishmonger was received angrily by the maid—the wrong fish, not enough fish, a bad fish.

The very first letter I read made me question what I was doing, for it was dated from Auvers. In the third paragraph Vincent described meeting me: "I have seen Dr. Gachet, who gives me the impression of being quite eccentric, though his medical experience must maintain his equilibrium while he struggles with the nervous troubles that he clearly suffers from as badly as I do." I scanned the rest of the letter quickly, stung by Vincent's assessment. On what basis could he make such a judgment? I thought back to what I had said and done on that occasion; surely nothing outside the ordinary? I found it difficult to concentrate, as my memory of our first encounter kept coming between me and the page covered with Vincent's tidy script.

But as I read I soon forgot my pique and began to notice something peculiar in the way the artist leapt from topic to topic then circled back. Money, his ability to paint, and his impression of me alternated like cards in a game of solitaire.

I put the letter aside and picked up another one. I tried to read quickly. Vincent's handwriting was quite clear and usually very controlled. Some of the letters included tiny sketches of paintings he described to his brother, like a square drawing of a cypress tree. Two small figures walked along the road next to it, followed by a horse-drawn cart. An enormous moon and a glowing star dominated the sky. Often he mentioned what he was reading as well. Evidently Theo had sent him a collected volume of Shakespeare's plays, for he commented on reading the plays about the kings: "But what I find touching . . . is that the voices of these people, which in the instance of Shakespeare reach us from a distance of several centuries, don't appear strange to us. It is so vivid that one believes one knows them." Naturally he focused on describing his work to Theo. Painters cannot always put into words what it is that they are doing, but Vincent wrote vividly and informally about his ambitions and how he meant to achieve them.

About half an hour had gone by when Madame van Gogh reappeared and touched the coffeepot to be sure it was still warm. "Do you think this is helpful?" she asked. "We have many more letters, that cabinet is just full of them. Look."

I turned, and she opened its door to show me a mass of papers, tightly packed. She laughed a little at my expression. "As with the paintings, so also with the letters, Doctor," she said. "When Vincent is not painting or reading, he is writing letters. Fortunately these take up less room than the canvases. Have you read the ones I gave you? Those were just at the top of the drawer, here."

"Yes, I have finished these," I answered, eyes fixed on the paper bursting from the cabinet. "They are in no order at all, then?"

"The most recent ones are together," she said, "but otherwise, no."

I raised my hands from the table in a gesture of helplessness.

"Do you think I could be of any help, Doctor?" she asked. "If you told me what you were looking for, could I help you find it?"

"I hardly even know what I am seeking," I answered. "Monsieur Vincent seems dejected, disillusioned. Yet at the same time, he has been volatile in recent days." I told her about the episode with the dog, and with the unframed Guillaumin. I wondered if she knew the particulars of his attacks, and the likelihood that he would soon suffer another one.

"And of course there was our argument this weekend," Madame van Gogh said, touching the corner of one of the letters. "I have written to Vincent to apologize, but I fear I said cruel things."

"He appears to have taken them to heart," I said, though I was aware that it might pain her. "Too much so. A man with better nerves would have been able to recover from your disagreement."

"Yes." She put several letters together and tapped them into a neat stack without looking at them. "That is just what Vincent does not have. So you are looking for letters that will give you a sense of that imbalance?"

I nodded.

"When I came here," she went on, "he was in the asylum at St.-Rémy. Theo shared his letters with me. They were heartbreaking, Doctor. He felt completely defeated."

"Could you find them, do you think?" I asked. "I would like to get a sense of how his mind was working then."

"Not very well, I assure you," she replied tartly. I was reminded what a difficult situation this was for her. "I think those letters are in the drawer. Let me look."

She pulled the entire drawer from the cabinet, spilling letters all over the polished surface of the table. "Here, Doctor. Why don't you put the ones you've read to one side, and we will go through these together?" I obeyed, and in a moment we were sitting side by side, surrounded by folded pages. I had to trust that Madame van Gogh knew what she was looking for. I skimmed over page after page, looking for references to madness, depression, hallucinations—I hardly knew what—but I found a great deal about paintings instead. Paintings Vincent was working on, paintings he was thinking about, paintings he had seen, paintings Theo had seen. There were requests for materials: paints, canvas, brushes. My eyes popped when I saw how much paint Vincent required, but I should not, I suppose, have been surprised, considering how thickly his canvases were covered. Most of these letters seemed to come from the asylum, and there were references to his care there: therapeutic baths, talks with the doctor, the dreadful food.

In one letter there were sketches on several pages: a path in a garden, and a magnificent drawing of a death's-head moth with Vincent's writing all around it, as if the moth had fallen onto the page and stayed there. My eye was caught by a sentence about artists who had been mentally ill: "Previously I felt some disgust for these creatures and it was distressing to me to have to think about how many men of our *métier* . . . had ended up like that." Vincent, it seemed, was beginning to classify himself among them. He was even coming to value the fellowship among his fellow patients, maniacs and hysterics among them. "If someone falls into a kind of attack the others watch over him and step in so he does himself no harm." A few pages along—it was a very, very long letter—he wrote even more clearly about the nature of his attacks, and this, I thought, might be useful to me: "I am still—speaking of my circumstances—so grateful for another thing. I notice about others that they, too, in their attacks, have heard noises and weird voices as I have, and that things seemed to change forms as well. And this reduces the terror that I still felt about the attack that I had. . . . For enduring that agony is no joke. . . . Nothing would have pleased me more than never to wake up again. At the moment this *dread of life* is already diminished, and the melancholy milder." I put the letter down quickly. There was something frightening yet familiar about the matter-of-fact way Vincent spoke of death. If you once allowed yourself to think so coolly about abandoning life, it was like crossing a border. At the next crisis, death would beckon, crooking a bony finger. Each time you saw him, he would look more familiar, less appalling.

"Here, Doctor," Madame van Gogh was saying. "Here is one of the letters where he talks about being a soldier. It is so sad! He has lost all of his confidence, you will see. Thank goodness he was able to recover from this state."

In the letter Vincent wrote that he saw himself as a burden, and he thought the army might accept him—feed him and clothe him in return for his services. It would have been a laughable notion if it had not been so pathetic: what use could an army possibly make of Vincent van Gogh? Yet even as he made his argument, he had enough sense to see that Theo might think this was another crazy idea. It was as if the tide of madness had begun to recede and currents of sanity occupied his thoughts from time to time. He found the routine in the hospital reassuring; he knew that the army was an organization that allowed its members no choice; therefore, he should be in the army. There was a certain logic to it.

Beside me, Johanna suddenly put down the letter she was reading. "But I am forgetting: we received a letter from Vincent only yesterday! It was . . ." Her eyes shifted as she tried to remember what was in the letter, and she blushed. "Oh, dear, perhaps I should not have mentioned it. I don't know if I should show it to you."

"Madame," I said quickly, "if it is a matter of Monsieur Vincent's opinion of me, you need hide nothing. I have already encountered evidence of his skepticism." I patted a pile of the letters I had read so that she would understand. "I would very much like to read his most recent letter. I have been disturbed about him. It would be helpful to know what he is thinking."

Without another word she got up and left the room, returning with a letter in its envelope. I heard the baby begin to cry in the kitchen, and with a murmur Jo excused herself.

Vincent, it appeared from the letter, was dejected. He was worried about money: would Theo continue to send him his stipend? He was worried about the baby: bringing the child up in the city was such a threat to his health. He was concerned about his brother's health, and I wondered if he suspected that Theo were seriously ill. Then my name caught my eye: "I don't think we should rely on Dr. Gachet *in any way*. First, it appears to me he is more ill than I: or let's say as ill, so there you are. Now, when a blind man leads another blind man, won't they both fall in the ditch?"

I will not deny that these words stung, and I wondered again what it was that I had said or done to convince Vincent I was "more ill" than he. He might resent me, I supposed, for failing to stabilize his mental state, but that did not mean I was mad.

I let the letter drop and looked across the room. In the alcove above the baby's crib gleamed the celestial blue of the almond-blossom painting. I wondered if Vincent could paint a canvas like that now. I thought not.

I picked up the letter and read it again. As in the first letter I'd read, he leapt from topic to topic, from my shortcomings to his artistic output back to my shortcomings and thence to the asylum at St.-Rémy, which he now termed a "prison." Compared to the earlier letters that I had just read, this one was disjointed in the extreme. There was a confusing passage in which he laid out plans to rent three small rooms—where? In Paris? In Auvers? He referred to paintings that were stored at Tanguy's, and how they were assets going to ruin. It was not the communication of a man whose mind was clear.

I thought back to the days a month earlier when Vincent had painted my portrait. It was a diagnosis of sorts. He had created an image, using my features, of a melancholy man. I could summon it in my mind, the unseeing gaze at the viewer and the skin at the temple wrinkled where the fist pressed against it, as it did now. That was how Vincent saw me.

Perhaps the difficulty was that my view of Vincent had been incomplete. For Vincent, merely seeing was enough. His eyes told him everything he needed to know about a person or, for that matter, a flower or a vineyard. His genius—part of his genius—was that he could absorb so much about the very nature of a subject from appearance alone. It seemed, then, that I was not as good a doctor as Vincent van Gogh was a painter. But perhaps I had known that all along. I heard myself sigh deeply, as if Vincent's own gloom inhabited me. I knew my shortcomings. I had no need of a painter to point them out to me. After all, I was the doctor who had not saved his wife. No one knew this. No living person knew how I had failed Blanche. Yet Vincent's uncanny eyes had discerned my grief.

Madame van Gogh emerged from the kitchen holding the baby. She moved gently, gliding to the crib and setting the child down. He stirred as she placed him in his bed, wriggling into greater comfort.

"Is the baby's health recovered?" I asked her, keeping my voice low.

"Yes, thank you, Doctor. You know how one worries when they are this small."

"I do," I said, getting up. "I fear you have a great deal to worry about, Madame van Gogh."

She did not deny it, but smiled slightly. "I do my best to take care of them. That is all I can do. Did Vincent's letter help you? I am sorry you had to read the cruel things he said about you. I am sure you realize that these are not Theo's opinions."

I smiled at her. "Thank you. I appreciate Monsieur Theo's confidence. I will not trouble you anymore, but I thank you for your hospitality. And for your company. We will do our best for Vincent, as you say." I paused. It was not really my affair, but the most recent letter somehow made it seem so. "I am glad you are taking little Vincent to Holland," I said. "It will be good for Theo to show his baby to his mother, whatever brother Vincent may say about it."

"I am pleased you see it that way," she answered, walking with me to her front door. "It is for Theo's sake that we are going." She paused with her hand on the doorknob. "What will you do, Doctor? Is there some way you can help Vincent?"

"I do not know, madame," I had to answer her. "All I can say is that I will try to find it."

I was anything but cheerful as I walked home, exchanging the quiet of the Van Goghs' secluded building for the merciless tumult of the Gare du Nord and the surrounding commercial streets. Nor was I able to raise my spirits as I met with my patients that afternoon.

Madame Duval, with her endless rheumatic aches, struck me as a spoiled and fretful creature. She had always pretended to be younger than her fifty-odd years, but she must have known that a doctor, of all men, cannot be fooled. On this afternoon I flexed her knee, feeling the unmistakable friction of bone rubbing bone. "Of course as we get on in years," I began to say. Fortunately I caught sight of her face before I could finish the sentence. I was less careful with the notary Japrisot, who had poor digestion yet insisted on eating six-course dinners. His self-satisfaction prevented him from accepting any advice, and I often wondered why he even troubled to visit me. On this afternoon I informed him that I could not help him if he did not follow my instructions. Normally, I try to offer some consolation. Sympathy has value, but I had none to spare that day.

The rain that had dampened me in the morning began to come down in earnest, and the light of the long summer evening dimmed. I had a dinner that night, a meeting of the Société des Éclectiques, a group of congenial souls from different professions who met monthly to discuss art or poetry or theater. As I pushed my cuff links into the starch-stiffened sleeves of my shirt, I stood at the window looking down at the traffic and considered staying at home. I am usually eager for company at the end of a day, but I felt so gruff and out of sorts that I could not imagine enjoying this gathering.

Directly below where I stood, the wheel had come off an omnibus. Furious passengers gathered around, some shouting, some waiting miserably under inadequate umbrellas for the repair to be finished. Everything was brown or gray, like the ugly painting of the peasants eating potatoes in the Van Goghs' apartment. All around, drivers yelled vulgarities as they passed the disabled vehicle. The noise was intolerable. I went to my dinner rather than hear the cacophony for a minute more. The first name I heard as I sat down at the table was Charcot's.

Charcot was famous, of course. His name was probably uttered at dozens of dinners every night in Paris. The man who mentioned him, a young journalist, had attended one of Charcot's famous biweekly lectures at the Salpêtrière on the previous Friday. We had all read about these by now, but none of us had ever attended one, so we let the boy talk. He described the amphitheater packed with students, the bright lights, the mounted photographs and informative placards, and the colored backdrops to set off the subjects' poses: it sounded as if medicine came very close to theater in these events. At this particular lecture Charcot had hypnotized a man, it seemed, and brought on a hysterical fit in a woman. It did not actually sound very different from the art students gathering at the *bal des folles* of so many years ago, if hundreds of spectators packed into the Salpêtrière to gape at the antics of the mad.

But though Charcot was inclined to drama, he was nevertheless an excellent physician. The popular newspapers might write about the Friday lectures, but the medical press was where Charcot and his students published their findings on illnesses of the nervous system. I found his diagnostic skills admirable. He had been an intern at the Salpêtrière

ahead of me, but as a medical doctor, treating lungs and hearts and gastric complaints rather than mental maladies. The two groups of interns
rarely mixed, but even then I had heard his name. He had published
constantly in the decades since returning to the hospital in 1862 as the
chief of a division. In fact, I realized, a collection of his informal diagnostic lectures had appeared not long before this evening, and was re-
viewed in a journal I received.

I was suddenly very anxious to be at home, and to read the article
about Charcot. I made my farewells amid much teasing, for I am rarely
the first to leave a gathering. Nothing could keep me there, however,
while I was so preoccupied.

When I got back to my apartment, a new frustration arose. I was
quite certain I had been reading the medical journal in bed. There is an
ottoman between the bed and the window where my reading material
accumulates. As I took off my cravat, I began to leaf through the pile:
newspapers, *Gazette des Beaux-Arts,* Maupassant's latest volume of stories, more newspapers, a folder of prints. That was disheartening; I try
to keep at least my engravings and etchings in portfolios. I put the
folder on the bed. Beneath the bed, by the most comfortable chair, on
the little table in the salon, I found much fascinating material but not
Le Progrès médical. When it finally came to light, I had found two more
folders of prints, a letter from a relative of Blanche's, and a solicitation
for a soldiers' charity. This is normally how things come to my attention. My life was much more orderly while my wife was alive.

The review of Charcot's book was quite long. The volume under
consideration was a compilation of clinical lessons the great doctor had
given at the Salpêtrière. He would examine patient after patient for the
benefit of his students and other interested medical personnel. Diagnoses ranged from epilepsy through paralysis and syphilis to hysteria,
with endless combinations of these and other ailments. What startled
me was the inclusion of men. Charcot had added a section of male patients to the population at the hospital, as well as an outpatient service.
These sufferers were naturally less acutely ill, giving the doctor a greater
range of subjects on whom to hone his diagnostic skills.

The conclusion seemed perfectly clear: Jean-Martin Charcot was a brilliant diagnostician. I should enlist his help in Van Gogh's case. It was said that physicians were welcomed at the informal clinical lessons held on Tuesdays, so I resolved to go to the Salpêtrière the following week. Perhaps I would be able to persuade Charcot, an art lover, to see Vincent as a private patient. If not, one of his students might help us. They might be able to make up for my own shortcomings. I felt much relieved as I prepared to go to sleep.

Eleven

ONCE AGAIN VINCENT avoided our house during the weekend, increasing my anxiety about him. That made me all the more glad that I might be able to enlist the aid of Dr. Charcot. I had written a note to him and received a very civil reply. He would be happy to discuss a patient with a former colleague, as he put it. This terminology went some small way to console me for Vincent's low estimation of my skills.

It was strange to see the changes surrounding the Salpêtrière when I arrived that Tuesday. In the thirty years since I had been there, the city had swallowed the hospital. As a student, I had often fancied that countryside lay just beyond its walls. There was a quiet, a limpid quality to the light in those days that made it easy to envision cattle grazing and rustic yokels in smocks carrying water in wooden buckets. The Gare d'Austerlitz now dominated the area. Its tracks sliced between the hospital grounds and the river, bringing whistles and coal smoke and even a kind of urgent vibration to the very earth that had once been a sodden riverbank—an inescapable reminder that times had changed.

I had to ask at the gate for directions to the new outpatient clinic where Charcot's Tuesday lessons were held. The doctor wanted to train others to see as he saw. Thus the sessions were small and informal, located in a ground-floor room holding little more than a group of chairs and a battered table. I knew I had arrived in the right place because I recognized Dr. Charcot from the famous 1887 Salon painting called *Une leçon clinique à la Salpêtrière*. The painting had been widely distributed in a lithographed version, and of course I possessed a copy. It was disconcerting at first to see the celebrated physician in person, since his image was so familiar to me; the barrel-shaped body, the hair worn brushing his collar, the solidly fleshed face. Everyone looked at me as I entered the room, so I introduced myself, adding, for the benefit of the young men, that I had been an extern myself more than thirty years earlier.

The first case was a porter at Les Halles who, several months earlier, had astounded everyone around him by falling into a fit and causing considerable damage to the stalls nearby. Worse, the fits had continued. Charcot swiftly read through a file while the man sat brooding on a plain chair before us, eyes cast to the ground. The doctor raised his eyes and addressed us. "The question, here, gentlemen, is this: epilepsy or hysteria? They are very easy to confuse. I hope we can establish a diagnosis in this man's case. I see there is some history of nervous illness in the family. Your father suffered mentally?" he asked the patient. The man looked up readily.

"Poor man went mad," he confirmed. "Thought he was St. Peter. And then sometimes it was Napoleon. When he was Napoleon, he always thought he was being poisoned. Anyway, he couldn't work. Ended up at Bicêtre."

"So you see, we have an inheritance of weakened mental processes," Charcot told us all. "We also have a situation of partial anesthesias," he read from papers in his hands. "Dr. Lagarde, perhaps you would like to demonstrate?" At this point one of the younger doctors showed us, by pricking the flesh with a long pin, how there were several areas of the patient's body that appeared to have no feeling at all. Charcot went on noting information from the chart: the attacks were sometimes preceded by warning periods with various sensory disorders. The patient heard voices; he had once seen a cabbage turn into a bleeding skull. When in the throes of a fit, he shouted and thrashed and had to be restrained, which, owing to his size and strength, was often difficult to do. Once a fit wore off, he was perfectly lucid.

Fortunately I had brought a little notebook, and I scribbled down all of these details as they were described, for this case sounded very similar to Vincent's. Charcot pointed out that the attacks differed from epilepsy in an important way: an epileptic falls in one place and does not create further disturbance. Vincent's attacks, then, sounded more like hysteria than like epilepsy. But it was the conclusion of the presentation that I found especially intriguing.

"In many cases of masculine hysteria," Charcot said, "we see changes in the patient's behavior. This is certainly true in this instance. According to the patient's wife, who accompanied him here, he has been a different man since the first episode. He is nervous, suspicious, mournful. He is withdrawn where he used to be sociable, irritable where he used to be merry. He has terrible dreams, and resists sleeping for fear of them. For all of these reasons, I believe that the patient suffers from hysteria. The standard medication for epilepsy, potassium bromide, does not appear to be efficacious in this situation, so we will keep our patient for a while." Here he put his hand on the man's shoulder. "And see what other treatments may do for him. Perhaps we shall see him again, in an improved state." He nodded, and the man was led out.

In came a tall wraith of a woman, so thin and withdrawn that her very clothes seemed to be weeping, or rather oozing around her. I followed Charcot's description of her symptoms—she had stopped eating, spoke only in monosyllables, slept around the clock—while part of my mind wandered to hysteria. I was particularly intrigued by the list of the hysterical patient's mood changes: his insomnia, his suspicions, his withdrawal. This certainly matched Vincent's behavior. If he were suffering from hysteria, would that not explain why he had avoided coming to our house? Might it even be responsible for his dark thoughts about me?

∝∞

I was first introduced to hysteria during the *bal des folles,* the annual costume ball at the Salpêtrière that took place several weeks before Easter.
I had been at the hospital for only a few months, and I found the idea
of the ball disturbing. Some of our patients, it seemed to me, were quite
fragile. I could not see how the excitement of a ball would improve their
mental states. Yet it was obviously a long-standing tradition that the
staff and patients anticipated keenly. In the weeks before the ball, little
else was discussed. The most coherent patients spent hours thinking
about their costumes, hoarding scraps of fabric, bartering and collabo-
rating. One woman with nimble fingers might twist ends of ribbon into
flowers while another folded gold paper into a halo. Even the patients
who were apparently lost in their madness sometimes responded to
the atmosphere of anticipation. The melancholy might speak; the
furieuse—confined to a straitjacket to prevent violence—might cease
her raving and smile.

I was not on duty on the night of the ball, but the junior medical staff
was expected to attend, costumed, to mingle with the patients and keep
order if necessary. Like my charges, I gave considerable thought to my
costume. I did not want to appear undignified, so I borrowed a wine-
colored velvet robe from my friend Gautier. He said the garment came
from a costume chest at the École des Beaux-Arts, which was evident—
it smelled quite strongly of turpentine and had streaks of oil paint on
the bottoms of the full sleeves. With a long gilt chain over my shoulders, I felt that I looked like a courtier in one of the larger Rubens canvases. In the interest of verisimilitude, I should not have worn my
trousers and boots, but I did not believe anyone would notice my
footwear. As it happened, I was grateful for this later.

The ball was a jolly affair. The largest sewing workroom had been
adapted ingeniously for the festivities. It seemed that every oil lamp and
every candle in the building had been brought to the atelier and set
aflame. Mirrors had appeared from somewhere and had been hung high
on the walls, reflecting the light and the heads of the dancers. The window frames and the enormous portrait of Dr. Pinel had all been deco-

rated with garlands, which I had seen prepared in the previous days: they were stitched from rags and dyed a deep pink with the peelings of beetroots, then hung to dry in the sunniest corner of a courtyard for several days.

The music was no less improvised and no less gleeful than the garlands: the chapel organist, wearing a plum velvet jacket in the style of the Restoration, with puffed shoulders and long tails, was seated at an upright piano, pounding away at a polka. He was keeping time with his head so emphatically that he almost flew off the piano bench, coattails flapping, at each downbeat. One of the groundskeepers squeezed an accordion with his eyes shut tight, while a clerk from the registrar's office sawed away on a violin. I heard, but did not see, a trumpeter and someone with a pair of cymbals.

And our patients danced. They whirled around merrily, in pairs or threesomes or alone, some keeping time and some merely moving with the crowd. The stamp and shuffle of their feet added to the din, and the heat in the room was pronounced. There were benches lined up on three sides, most of them empty, except for one that was occupied by the *furieuses*, restrained in their canvas jackets but nodding to the music. A few melancholiacs sat in the darkest corner, apparently oblivious to all the stimulation. I supposed that their wardress had wanted to see the ball and had roused them from their normal stunned state to bring them along. Perhaps she thought the music would cheer them.

I had not intended to dance, but shortly after my arrival my hands were seized by a tall dark-haired woman in the conical headdress of the Middle Ages. "Come, Doctor!" she shouted over the noise. "We'll have no hanging back. All who come to the *bal des folles* must dance!" And indeed as we whirled around the room I saw doctors, patients, gardeners, warders, even a fat laundress dressed as Marie Antoinette, complete with a white wig apparently made from a mop.

I was relieved when the music stopped with an abrupt crashing chord and the whirling circle of dancers jostled to a halt. Gathering up the hem of my robe, I hastened to what I hoped would be a quiet corner but was halted by a strong hand on my shoulder. This time it was my friend

Gautier, resplendent in the costume of a Roman centurion. I was surprised to see him there; though he had obtained my costume for me, he never hinted that he, too, planned to be present. But, he explained, attendance at the *bal des folles* was a tradition for the students of the École des Beaux-Arts.

"Where did you get that costume?" I asked.

"Borrowed it, just like yours. I wanted something showy for the parade."

"What parade?"

"There's always a parade at a costume party, Gachet, surely you've been to one?" Then a wavering note sounded from the accordion and the dancing resumed. Without another word, Gautier plunged into the crowd. I managed to avoid dancing again by standing behind the *furieuses*. More men in costume had appeared; I saw a monk, a Pierrot, and several musketeers in thigh-high boots and capes. Gautier had apparently been correct. The women gaily flocked around the men, smiling and laughing.

I did not know what to think of it. It was the animal side of their nature that caused trouble for many of our patients, since their mental state often stripped away the controls of civilization. Some women, despite every precaution, managed to get pregnant every year, and bore their babies, who were subsequently sent to an orphanage. I wondered at the wisdom of bringing these young male students into the asylum to mingle with madwomen.

But then a hubbub near the door caught my attention. All I could see over the crowd was a giraffe's head, apparently constructed of canvas and yarn. It was crude but very charming, with shiny black eyes fringed with layers of stiff bristles; numerous paintbrushes must have been sacrificed for the effect. The movement at the far side of the room suggested that the giraffe had brought quite a few friends. The door was blocked for a moment by the head of an elephant whose back end was somewhat too wide. The trunk must have been guided from the inside by wire, for it slithered through the crowd or lashed up in the air in a lifelike way. One of the musicians, watching from the dais, picked up his trumpet and made a rude blurting noise with his hand in the bell. The elephant's trunk stretched out straight in response, and all who saw it laughed.

This group of art students had all managed to dress as zoo animals; in addition to the elephant and the giraffe, there were exotic birds, a jaguar with a real animal's skin and a lion with a brown-paper mane, an enormous fish, a bear, and three mischievous monkeys. The menagerie heightened the gaiety of the evening. I was hauled back onto the dance floor by the Marie Antoinette laundress, and as she steered me capably through the crowd, I got more than one strong whiff of wine or brandy, brought no doubt by the students. Our patients were never permitted to drink spirits.

"What do you think of our ball?" the laundress shouted as we took up our position at the end of a line of couples. The chapel organist was trying to organize a quadrille, apparently.

"It seems very festive," I said, despite my growing unease. I looked up the line of women's faces across from me. There was a range of expressions on them, a much greater range than you would normally see at a dance. Yes, I saw the laughter, happiness, vague annoyance, concentration on the music that bourgeois women would display. But there were also frowns, inattention, and that expression I have only ever seen among the mad—you might call it exaltation, an exaggerated excitement in which every emotion, every perception reaches an intensity unknown to the sane.

But then I could see no more, because our two lines became a single column of pairs, and we began our grand parade around the room. We paced by the portrait of Dr. Pinel, and past the bench of the *furieuses,* who stamped their feet in approval.

Normally, the dance would have ended once we had made a circuit of the room, filed back into our original positions, and bowed to each other. But before we reached the end, the room grew much less noisy, and as the laundress and I turned the corner, we saw that there was no double line of dancers in the center of the room. Instead, one of the monkeys snatched a pair of candles from a sconce on the wall and handed one to the monkey behind him. They linked arms with their partners and disappeared through the door.

The laundress and I looked at each other in horror. This possibility had never occurred to me. I had been worried about women getting too stimulated by the dancing and the costumes and the lights, but I had never imagined that they would be taken out of the room, let alone into the darkness of the quadrangle below.

A knight and a musketeer had seized the accordion and violin from the band: they played a medley of marches at the head of the group. They were skipping up the long walkway, lit only by the flickering from candle flames or oil lamps that had been snatched from the walls. The misty evening softened the outlines of the dancers in the dark.

"Was that gate open when you came in?" the laundress asked me, pointing to the end of the enclosure.

"I didn't enter that way. I'll go check it now," I said and lifted my robe to my knees. Harm could still be averted. The Salpêtrière was like a maze. Most courtyards had two or three gates, and most buildings had two or three entrances. Of course these were all supposed to be locked—one of our primary responsibilities was quite simply to maintain custody of our charges. But what if the gates were open? I could imagine it all too clearly. Carried away by the music and the costumes and the lights, our patients could so easily get lost, become frightened and anxious. This was where madness told: these women would not be able to help themselves. They would not be able to stay calm, to scan the sky for light coming from a nearby courtyard, to listen for voices, to call for help, even to remember which way they had come—or why.

And then there were the young men, as spirited and stimulated as the women. Who knew what kinds of violations they were capable of?

I was almost at the head of the line now, a few meters from the men with the instruments, who marched triumphantly backward, facing the stream of dancing followers. A confusion of voices arose. "The wall! Mind the wall!" "Pay attention to the gate!" people called, as the leaders backed into the obstruction they could not see. As they hit the gate, they did not fall: they merely mimed the impact and pretended to stagger. Then, to my relief, they turned, following the wall, steering the crowd around the edge of the yard. Everyone changed course happily, as a procession would turn a corner in a church, following their leader, absorbed in the movement rather than the destination.

I finally reached the end of the courtyard and stood panting next to the gate. The leaders of the parade were marching gaily toward the glow of light from the tall windows of the atelier. As the stragglers paced toward me, ready to turn the corner, I leaned back against the heavy wooden panel of the gate to draw a deep breath.

But it did not support me. It shifted. I staggered as the knight with the accordion had, then fell when the gate swung open. I tumbled onto my back and rolled quickly to my knees, but not before a small group separated from the procession and followed me through the gate.

I couldn't count them in the dark. One of the art students carried something like a torch, but there was no other light. I scrambled to my feet and pushed the gate closed but met resistance. Someone was pushing against me. I set my feet in the gravel and put my shoulder to the heavy timber to push with all my strength, while behind me I heard someone shout, "Let's play hide-and-seek!"

Amid the clamor, I heard a voice calling my name. "Gachet! Gachet, it's Lemaire!" I stood up straight and pulled back the gate. One of the other young externs slipped through, then closed it behind him.

"How many are there?" he asked me.

"Perhaps a dozen."

"How many are patients?"

"Most," I answered. "And three young men, I believe. But they've split up, they're playing hide-and-seek." As I said this, one of the male voices cried out in the dark, *"Cache-cache!"*

"Are there other entrances to this yard?"

"I think so," I said. "We must be sure they are closed off. But I may know one of the men from the *École*. Let me see if they won't help us gather the women."

"Yes, you do that. Try to start them moving back inside, will you? I'll be with you in a moment. Thank God this is one of the smaller gardens," he called as he ran off.

The rest of the sounds in the courtyard had diminished. I was glad the ground was covered with stones rather than grass, so that I could at least hear my quarry. A giggle came from my far right, and ahead someone was trying to step silently but merely prolonging the quiet crunch his or her feet made on the gravel.

"My friends and patients," I called out. "This is Dr. Gachet speaking. I am an extern in training here. Some of you may know me, and the artists among you might know my friend Amand Gautier. He came tonight dressed as a Roman soldier. I would like you please to rejoin the party. I am concerned about our patients being out in the cold night air."

"Fuck the night air!" said a female voice.

"Amen to that!" said a man, and laughter echoed back and forth. I was walking toward the light of the torch, hoping that an art student still held it.

"You'll have to find us!" trilled a woman.

"It's *cache-cache,* so come seek the hidden!" answered another. "La-la-la-la-la, here I am," she sang, and her feet made rhythmic noises in the gravel.

I was trying to sound authoritative, but my breath was coming faster. The voices around me gave the scene the air of a nightmare. I kept walking steadily toward the torch.

"Are you hearing voices, Doctor?" sang out a woman. "Just like the rest of the crazies! Oh, ha, ha, ha!"

"He's one of us now!"

"Take him to Bicêtre!"

"No, keep him with the women at the Salpêtrière! We'll entertain him!"

"Who's mad anyway?" asked a female voice nearby, sounding utterly reasonable. "Not I."

"Nor I!"

"Nor I!"

They came from all around me now, a series of echoing voices. Some, I knew, were the men speaking in falsetto. The rest were the women, drawn together in uncanny unison the likes of which I had never witnessed. One of the marks of the mad was that they inhabited their own worlds and not those of others. That night, in the damp and the dark with the torch flaring straight in the sky, they were acting and thinking together. Saner than ever, one might have thought.

I reached the torch only to find that it had been tied to an old well-head with a strip of fur-trimmed leather from someone's costume. Without thinking, I untied it, then clambered up onto the wide stone lip of the well. I had hoped that the height would allow me to see better, but the circle of light around me made the darkness more profound. Across the yard, I could see the orange glow of my torch reflected from a window. I heard Lemaire's footsteps pounding toward me.

"The gates are closed. There is one doorway into a building, but it leads only to another locked door. They must all be here," he panted.

"Oh, it's the yellow-haired doctor," one of the patients said, quite near to us. "Dr. Saffron." The torch I held over my head must have made my features visible.

"Oh, I like him," someone else replied from behind me. "He's a nice one."

"Then I hope you will do as I suggest," I broke in quickly. "Why don't you all come here, toward the torch, and we will go join our friends at the ball? Dr. Lemaire, will you open the gate?"

From where I stood on the lip of the well, the workroom beckoned a hundred meters away. The rounded panels at the tops of the windows had been opened, and music escaped, this time a waltz. The light streamed through the mist in palpable-looking golden blocks. The sight was as good as a signpost: "This way to warmth and comfort and music."

"Let us go, then," I called out and jumped down from the well. "Can someone tell me if there are prizes at this ball? For the best costume, perhaps?" I started forward, walking with purpose and what I hoped looked like confidence.

I listened for a moment. There was silence. Only my footsteps crunched on the gravel, one, two, three, four . . . Then I heard a deep sigh very close to me. "Well, the doctor has a point," a woman said, stepping into the light. She was an older patient who was one of the gifted needlewomen of the curtain workroom. Once, I had walked through her atelier and seen her in charge, calmly beating a tambourine to establish the rhythm for the other women's stitches. "It's a little bit chilly for outdoor games, no?"

"Marthe, you old woman!"

"That's it, Solange," she called back. "Too old for this kind of fun, anyway." Marthe was trudging alongside me now, her arm linked in mine. I was hopeful. My authority as a doctor alone might not have been sufficient to lure the women inside, but with Marthe's help, I thought I could safely lead all of our charges back to the party.

I heard footsteps coming forward, and a few faces emerged into the torchlight. I counted six, seven women joining us. None of the men. I kept on walking.

Then someone screamed. I knew right away who it was. Odette was easy to overlook in any group. She was neither young nor old, neither tall nor short, and her behavior was such that she could pass for normal—except when she was screaming. And she did not simply scream: she threw herself to the ground and flailed and thrashed around, kicking and hitting anything nearby.

She was not vicious and had never hurt another woman, but she was often restrained. What else could one do? The power of those fists and feet posed a threat. And now, so did the power of her voice.

Once again, I had no time to plan. The evening had become a nightmare. I could only act and hope for the best. "Marthe," I said, to the woman next to me. "Will you take the torch and lead everyone inside? I need to help Odette, and I don't want the other women upset."

She nodded decisively but said, "Keep the torch. They will follow me, and you should never put fire in the hand of a madwoman, Doctor. Surely that was the first thing they taught you?" With a little smile she ran past me down the path, calling out, "Come to me, ladies, let us see who won the prize!"

I followed the sound of the screaming, which was coming from somewhere to my left. A figure brushed past me, away from Odette, with a papery rustle as I hurried to her. I remembered the lion costume with its clever brown-paper mane.

I slowed down, because I could hear that I was getting close to Odette now, and that she was on the ground. Her body was grinding against the gravel, and her boots were thudding steadily as she drummed her feet. I didn't want to be in the way of her blows, but it seemed imperative to touch her.

I had seen Odette in this kind of fit only once. It was at dinner, and the noisy order of the refectory was suddenly broken by a clatter as she threw down her mug and fell to the floor. To my surprise, the other patients just glanced at her and went on with their meals. Only the wardress came to her side and spoke to her gently, with a hand on her shoulder. It had seemed to me that Odette almost knew what she was doing. Almost. The screaming and thrashing were a way to shut out her surroundings. It did not appear that she was in control of herself, exactly, or that she had deliberately launched herself into this state, but it did seem that something had alarmed her and the fit was a form of self-protection.

As I knelt beside Odette on the damp, cold pebbles, I began to speak, though I doubted she could hear me through her screams. "Odette," I said, "Odette." Nothing more. I reached toward her thrashing body but was defeated. Her stiff arms batted away my outstretched hand. When I reached again, I touched only her chest or her breast. She was rolling on her back, becoming rigid. "Odette," I tried again. "Odette!" In a moment the flailing and screaming stopped. I wondered why, and what was happening to her. I reached out again, and made contact with her arm. It felt stiff, as if she were gripping something.

Footsteps approached, from behind me, then the gloom brightened as a soft ring of light surrounded us. Lemaire had returned with a lantern. "Dr. Theroux is the senior physician on duty tonight," he said, panting, kneeling beside me. "He will be here in a moment." He held the lantern high so that we could see Odette more clearly.

She looked dreadful. She was lying on her side, with her stiff body arched backward into a near semicircle. I couldn't imagine how she even drew breath with her body so contorted. Just a few minutes earlier, I had thought I could reach her with touch or a gentle voice, but now it seemed as if Odette was not even present. Lemaire gently pulled up one of her eyelids. Her eye was white, the pupil rolled back. Lemaire touched the back of his hand to her neck.

"So strange," he said. "It's like death, only not."

I put my hand to her wrist. I had no watch to time her pulse, but it was steady. I felt both ignorant and helpless.

More footsteps came our way, several sets this time. I turned my head. It occurred to me that Lemaire and I, kneeling side by side in front of Odette's body, looked like mourners at a corpse's bier. Dr. Theroux had brought another lantern, two porters carrying a stretcher, and a black bag. I noticed that he was in evening dress, as if he had been called from a dinner.

"Gentlemen," he acknowledged Lemaire and me as he leaned down to look at Odette. "What happened here?" he asked, straightening up. His lantern along with Lemaire's made the scene almost brilliant. I rose to my feet.

"Odette was at the ball, sir," I began, then explained about the improvised grand march, my attempt to gather our scattered patients, and Odette's screaming fit. Theroux nodded. I tried to read his expression, but the lantern light reflected off his eyeglasses and cast strange shadows down his face. "Did you do anything to help her?"

I opened my mouth to speak but closed it again. No. I hadn't done anything to help her.

Lemaire broke in. "Sir, there was no time. By the time Dr. Gachet and I found Odette, she was . . . beyond help." And, I added to myself, we did not know what to do.

Dr. Theroux looked over to the porters, who picked up the stretcher and laid it next to Odette. He bent down again, and, in a gesture that looked comforting, put his palm on her forehead. Then he straightened and nodded. "Perhaps you young men would help," he said to us. "This is a classic case of hysteria. If you have not encountered it yet in your studies, you can count this as an excellent clinical opportunity. The patient is in what we call the rainbow position. It is not possible to assume this position voluntarily. After a while the rigor wears off. The duration varies. Nothing I know of acts consistently to halt it. But we can at least get her indoors, out of the damp."

It was awkward, lifting her. She was rigid as a piece of wood, but the drastic arch of her body meant that she did not fit easily onto the stretcher. The best we could do was balance her on the poles, rather than nestle her body onto the canvas in between. It was surprising to look up at the windows of the workroom and hear cheering as we shuffled down the walkway. "I suppose they must have crowned the king and queen of the ball," Dr. Theroux commented. "They will be returning to their dormitories quite soon. We will take this patient to the infirmary."

Once we had Odette lying in the brightness of the ward, I could see how alarming she looked. Her gray uniform gown was wet and muddy. One of her cheeks was bruised, and her wrists were scratched. It was hard to know if she had done it to herself. What had set her off? What event, tiny or significant, had launched her into her flight from reality?

Remembering this episode as I sat in Charcot's classroom at the Salpêtrière, I thought of Odette with pity. Her attacks continued after the ball, and in the ever-shorter periods between them, she seemed oppressed. Before I finished my term as an extern, she had been transferred to another division, where the women were even more closely supervised, and generally restrained. It was tacitly acknowledged that there was no hope they would improve.

In the years since my encounter with Odette, I had seen many more female hysterics, and they always made me uneasy. So often the triggers for their attacks are mysterious and the attacks themselves terrifying. I tended to refer hysterical women to one of the specialist doctors who offered rest cures. I had not given much thought to hysteria in men, however. Hysteria, with noisy, thrashing attacks, hallucinations, nightmares. Hysteria that answered to no treatment.

As my mind wandered in this fashion, the melancholiac woman was led away. I had not heard the treatment plan. Charcot took out his watch and spoke in a low voice to the orderly next to him, then addressed us. "We do not have much longer, gentlemen, but I do have a case here that I would like you to see. As most of you know, many hysterics exhibit hysterogenic zones. When we stimulate these portions of their bodies, we bring on an attack. Now, I must reiterate that I do not believe hysteria to be the result of a misplaced uterus, as was the opinion of our medical ancestors. Yet . . . well, we shall see."

The next patient was a little man with pale skin and very fair hair. If he had been an animal, he would have been a white mouse. He was a clerk for the railroad. His problems dated from the moment he witnessed a fearsome accident in which an engine had severed the left leg of a track attendant. He had not himself been touched—although he was near enough to be spattered by blood—but he found, shortly after the event, that he had terrible shooting pains in his left leg.

"I cannot say how these events may be related to what I am about to demonstrate," Charcot said. "They may have no bearing at all, but merely be a coincidence. We are very far from knowing how our mental experiences affect the functioning of our bodies. I have just mentioned hysterogenic zones. This patient, we have discovered, exhibits them, and they are located precisely where a woman's ovaries would be. Would you mind standing, to show my colleagues?" The patient stood, wordlessly. The attendant lifted the white gown he was wearing and turned him around so that his back was to us. There were two ovals inked onto his lower back, on either side of the spinal cord. Charcot was now facing the patient. "May we?" he asked. The response was a slight nod. Charcot in turn nodded to one of his young colleagues, who stepped over and put the heels of his hands against the inked circles.

He leaned against the man's back. The attendant moved around to serve as a brace against the pressure. We all waited. Nothing happened. Charcot had taken out his watch again and was looking at it, keeping track of the time. Then suddenly, the patient's back went rigid, and he fell to the ground.

As an extern in this very hospital, I had grown accustomed to seeing a fellow human apparently released from all civilized controls. I'd seen patients bite warders and tear their own hair, I'd heard cries to wake the dead. But I was never as shocked as I was watching this man.

There was something cold-blooded about the situation, I thought. We all sat upright in our coats and shoes, watching a fellow human writhe on the floor. His gown was rucked up beneath his shoulders, and he was naked beneath it, no better than an animal. Two attendants knelt next to him, each holding one wrist so that he couldn't tear at his face with his nails. He bellowed: a bold, deep, blaring cry. One would never have thought such a sound could emerge from his slight frame. He beat his heels so hard so that I was afraid he would draw blood, then tried to crack his head against the floor. I could not believe that the poor man had consented to undergo this torture.

The convulsions began to subside, but as the patient's physical distress diminished, his mental distress increased. He was sitting now, cross-legged, and his garment had been restored to order. He rocked back and forth, as if in tremendous grief, and his eyes streamed tears. His mouth was open to voice an endless wail, but no sound emerged. Then a change came over him, and he leapt to his feet, crouching, fists clenched at his sides. Where before he had resembled a mouse, he was now a mouse prepared to fight to the death.

"Now we see the *attitudes passionnelles*," Charcot said quietly, as the patient glared around him fiercely. "The classic phases of the hysterical attack do not always present themselves in the cases of men. The patient has never, for example, fallen into the rainbow pose. He does not spend a long time in any of the stages, and his recovery is correspondingly brief. This makes him an excellent patient for demonstrations. Also remarkable is the clear relationship between pressure on the hysterogenic zone and the onset of the attack." Charcot glanced at the patient, who was now smiling quietly but raptly, like a mystic hearing voices. "We will leave Monsieur Bernet; he will come to himself shortly. Gentlemen, that is all for today, thank you." He nodded at us, and we stood to file out the door. Our route took us to within a foot of poor Monsieur Bernet. I looked down at the top of his head as I passed him. His scalp showed pink through the strands of his hair, dampened with sweat. He was murmuring quietly to his folded hands while the attendants crouched patiently by his side.

Dr. Charcot was answering a question from a student, so I waited by the door, watching the patient. He appeared to be discussing something with himself, taking two sides of an argument. One of the attendants leaned forward and spoke quietly in his ear, but he did not seem to hear. When Charcot introduced himself to me, he also looked at Bernet.

"What is the next phase of the attack?" I asked as we left the room.

"For Bernet, after a short fit like this, probably a deep sleep. He may feel weakened. Possibly he will have a headache for a few hours."

"And when will he come back to himself?"

"Quite soon. Probably within an hour. I must return to my office; I find that my colleagues get agitated when I am not where they expect me to be. Will you walk with me? Your note mentioned your concern for a painter, if I remember correctly. Is he someone I know of? Did he exhibit at the last Salon?"

I hastened to explain first Vincent's marginal position in the world of conventional painting and then my own concern with him. I finished with a synopsis of his medical history as I understood it. By this time we were seated in his surprisingly modest office, tucked into a corner of a new building called the Policlinique.

"My knowledge of Monsieur van Gogh's attacks is very limited," I said in summary. "But there are hysterical features, it seems. He was diagnosed as epileptic, yet during his fits he is apparently destructive and noisy. In his letters he wrote of hallucinations, both auditory and visual, though when I asked him, he had little memory of them. He is a menace to himself and others."

"Does Monsieur van Gogh's reasoning seem disturbed?"

"Without doubt," I said, describing the Foreign Legion scheme. Charcot nodded, tapping the end of a pen against his blotter. There was a moment's pause. I waited, for it seemed he was formulating a statement.

"Of course you know, Doctor, that I cannot make a diagnosis without seeing the patient." I nodded without interrupting him. "I would be very interested to meet this gentleman. There seems to be a high incidence of hysteria among men of genius; painters, musicians, authors. However, they are resistant patients. Sometimes they fear that improvement of their mental illness will adversely affect their creative abilities. I treat some of these gentlemen privately. I cannot intervene with them as strenuously as I do with my patients at the clinic. Some of the treatments, or indeed the diagnostic methods, are painful or unpleasant, like what you just witnessed. The patients who come to me reluctantly would not tolerate them."

"And, if I may ask—why does a patient like that poor Bernet willingly submit to having an attack brought on?" I asked.

"Because he is so unhappy, and he hopes we will be able to help him," Charcot answered. "With some patients who exhibit hysterogenic zones, like Bernet, an attack can be halted—as well as initiated—with pressure. We have not found this to be true yet for Bernet, but we hope that in time it will be."

I was not aware that my expression revealed my pity, but the doctor was famous for his powers of observation. "You must remember, colleague, that as doctors we are sometimes required to inflict pain in order to find out how to end it." I could only nod my acceptance. "Now, to return to your Monsieur van Gogh," he went on. "I would eagerly see him as a private patient. I have a sizable practice based at my house on Boulevard St.-Germain. Do you think Van Gogh would consent to an examination?"

"I don't know, Doctor. I believe he is very distressed. He is a great stoic, but at the moment he is in despair. If he thought his suffering could be relieved, he might see you."

Charcot now picked up his pen and held it gently between his two extended forefingers. He sighed and replaced it on the blotter, then raised his dark eyes to mine. "I cannot pretend to you that we have any way to end hysteria," he said. "I have known the attacks to become less frequent, less violent. More generally, though, they continue."

"Until?" I asked. "For the rest of life?"

He leaned back in his chair. "Our specialty is a difficult one, isn't it? I sometimes envy the men who can set a bone or stitch up a wound and be confident they have accomplished something. Despite all the progress we have made, these mental maladies are still baffling. Before you leave, Doctor, I suggest you visit the old sections of the hospital, where the *restantes* stay. The dormitories and workshops are still full. We sometimes cure patients. Usually that is when they have not been ill for long. But the truth is that we do not know exactly how we do it.

When a patient leaves here and has no more hysterical attacks, we do not know whether the baths helped her, or the separation from her family, or the nourishing food. I sometimes send my private patients to Dr. Fourgon in Passy, and the hysterics are sometimes cured, in about the same proportion as the hysterics who stay here. But, again, I don't know why."

He got to his feet. I rose, too. I am not a tall man, but he was even shorter than I. Still, there was a strong air about him, an impression of competence and assurance. Next to him I felt somehow insubstantial, as if I were not quite everything I had thought.

"Thank you for your generosity and your frankness, dear Doctor," I said, holding out my hand. "I will talk to Monsieur van Gogh. I hope I can persuade him to come and see you. His last visit to Paris was unhappy, but if I accompany him . . ." I trailed off. "I will send word if we decide to make the trip. Thank you again." He shook my hand warmly and inclined his head to acknowledge my thanks.

I visited the older wards of the hospital as Dr. Charcot had suggested. I had intended to all along: what man, returning to the site of his professional formation, would not take the time to roam around and attempt to come to terms with the intervening years? What man would not walk the paths he used to walk, hoping to see his younger self, hurrying forward toward some goal? We want to know what is the same and what is different, in us and in that old world. As I came around the corner to the *cour des agités,* I smiled slightly, and resolved to walk part of the way home, past the École des Beaux-Arts. Perhaps I would see a saffron-haired ghost peering out of a garret window on the rue de Seine.

Little seemed to have changed in this part of the great old hospital. The alterations that had brought the surrounding area into the nineteenth century—almost into the twentieth—did not penetrate the walls of the asylum, apparently. I crossed several courtyards, hearing the familiar sounds: the beating of a small drum to help seamstresses keep time in a workroom, the rhythmic scrape of a rake, a high voice wailing. In one courtyard a gardener wheeling a barrow thanked me for stepping off the path. He called me "Doctor." What else could I be, in that place?

I crossed to the archway between buildings and turned left into the long hallway without thinking. I found the door I knew was there and opened it. Three steps led down into the courtyard, and a stout wardress stood at the bottom. She looked up at me.

"Good morning," I said. "My name is Dr. Gachet. I was an extern here many years ago and I just met with Dr. Charcot. He suggested I might visit the section of the hospital where I worked. May I stay here for a moment?"

"As you like, Doctor," she said. "I doubt you'll see much difference."

I gazed around. "No," I agreed. "Nothing has changed." It was remarkable. The trees were perhaps taller. The gravel must have been renewed at some point. The patients, however, could have come from Gautier's painting *The Madwomen of the Salpêtrière*. Poor Gautier, now deep in debt—I wished he were with me now. We would have sat on the steps with our drawing pads, and I would have believed I could help these poor creatures. "Do you have any hysterics in this group?" I asked the wardress.

"No, these women are all quiet. The hysterics upset them. One minute your hysteric's strolling around calmly, next minute she's upside down and screaming. Having them in with the calm ones just upsets everybody."

"You've worked with them?" I pursued the subject.

"Of course. Some of us like it, adds some interest. I don't. I feel for these poor things." She gestured to an obvious melancholiac sitting on a bench in the shade. "Poor Gabrielle, how can you not pity her? Gentle, kind, hates to give trouble. Some of the hysterics put it on for Dr. Charcot, you know. He says they have fits, so they have fits. He says the fits look like this or that, sure enough they do. They like to get off work, go over to the studio and be photographed. Sometimes they perform in his lectures, and I do mean perform!"

This did not surprise me terribly. If the women intuited what Charcot and his students wanted to see in a "hysterical" patient, they would provide that. I had seen a few volumes of the famous *Iconographie photographique de la Salpêtrière*, published by one of Charcot's protégés, and some of the patients had appeared very knowing indeed.

"Do they ever get better?" I asked.

The wardress looked carefully at me for the first time. "You should know that if you're a doctor. Or don't you treat the mad anymore?"

I looked up at the sky, holding my hat on my head. "Sometimes I wonder if anyone gets better," I said.

She frowned, and her eyes shifted away. "Well," she said. "If you say so." She caught sight of a woman on the ground, scrabbling at the earth with her hands. "Cécile," she called out, and bustled away. "Cécile, we do not dig!" The woman, spotting her, only began to dig faster, though her busy fingers made no visible hole in the hard ground. It was a futile exercise. She was acting on compulsion, a mysterious command that told her to dig, here, now. Dig. I didn't think my compulsion to visit the madwomen had been much more productive.

$\mathcal{T}$welve

∞

I WAS NOT EAGER to have a conversation about hysteria with Vincent. It was not that I was afraid. I did not fear that he would turn on me. No, my apprehension was more complex. I was awestruck, you might say, the way a novice monk is cowed by his superior. It was as if Vincent had advanced further than I in some special devotion. He was privy to exalted mysteries in the church of mental illness, and this distinction made him fearsome.

According to Ravoux, Vincent was still leaving the inn before eight and coming home around sunset, exhausted. He was sometimes spotted up on the plateau, either sitting in front of a canvas or making his way to another site, carrying his easel and canvas like an ant with an unwieldy burden. I chose to look for him there. The sun had long since slid from the vertical, but it was still hot. The cicadas, which come late to Auvers, were buzzing in the trees, starting and stopping according to some mysterious signal.

The afternoon was quite still. Sun and shadows lapped over the wheat fields, dark gold and bright. The heads of the wheat are mobile and sensitive, bending in the slightest breeze, but there was none that afternoon. My footsteps crackled as I trudged through one of the fields. No human figure emerged from the sea of grain. Vincent must have gone in a different direction. As I traversed the long field to reach the westbound path, I thought I might as well be in one of his paintings. The golden field with its infinite tones of ocher and yellow was set off by the brilliant blue sky, provided by nature to carry out Vincent's own theory of complementary colors. Each made the other more intense. I merely crept along the seam between them, feeling very small.

I was hot, so I was very relieved when I saw a tiny figure, no more than a nick on the horizon, and recognized it as Vincent. He was perched at the top of a crest a few hundred meters away, almost swallowed by the wheat. From there he would have a magnificent view of the slope down to the Oise.

He faced away from me, but he must have heard me coming from quite a distance. I found it hard to catch my breath as I toiled up the slope. When I reached him, I could only stand behind him, panting. I looked out at what he had chosen to paint, and it was beautiful. The river, furred with willows, lay in a languorous curve. Vincent would have placed that in the bottom third of the canvas. Then, stretching toward the horizon, he would stack up the fields, those fertile lowland plots, each showing a variant green according to the crop: beans, peas, beetroot. He would use a different pattern of brushwork, too, for each. Some would be dotted, some zigzagged, some painted with a basket-weave or chevron pattern. Then he could use broader, looser strokes for the sky, whose blue softened toward the horizon.

But he had done none of these things. The canvas on his easel was perfectly white. Perhaps he had just arrived. Perhaps there was a canvas next to him, already finished.

I stepped to his side. "It is a magnificent prospect," I said. "The light at this hour is especially lovely."

"It is, Doctor," he said.

I glanced down. I saw no finished canvas. His palette lay on his lap.

The colors dotted it in slick cushions: lead white, ultramarine, chrome yellow, three different greens. His right hand clasped three brushes, but they were all clean.

"Did you just get here?" I asked.

"No," he answered. "I have been here all day."

"But," I protested, gesturing at the paint. "You just set up your palette."

He took one of the brushes and flipped it around. With the wooden end he poked the dome of white to show me that a heavy skin had formed. The paint had been drying for hours. "By now these are the wrong colors," he said. "There is too much blue. They would have been right this morning." He looked up at me. "Then after a few hours, I would have needed more yellow and ocher. A harder blue, probably cobalt. Then some darker green. Now—" He set the palette on the ground and reached into the box by his side. "Geranium lake, perhaps. The sky will show pink soon." He tossed a tube onto the ground. "I would need to mix up a purple." Another tube dropped. "And if I sit here long enough, I will need darker blues, and darker." He kept reaching into the box, scrabbling for tubes of paint and flinging them ever farther away. "No black, though, Doctor," he said, in a controlled tone. "I have painted night scenes before. I can do it without black. In fact," he went on, getting up from his folding stool, "I only have a small tube."

He crouched in front of the paint box and tipped it upside down. Out fell a small avalanche of crumpled lead shapes. He pawed through them, tossing aside one after another while saying their beautiful names like an incantation: "vermilion, viridian, Prussian blue, malachite green. Ah! Here we are. Black. You see? A small tube." He held it up to me. "I always have to ask Theo for the largest tubes of yellow." He unscrewed the top and squeezed a thin rope of darkness onto his palette. The coil grew, invading the blue, then the green. With both hands, he pressed the pigment from the bottom of the tube, carefully urging every last smear of black out of the soft metal casing. Then he hurled the tube far into the wheat, so far that I could barely hear the rustle when it landed.

He knelt on the ground now, with his palette before him. I stood just a foot away, silent, appalled. In another individual—if this had been my son, Paul, for example—I would have thought this behavior nothing more than frustration, a showy explosion of anger. Yet anger was absent in Vincent. His voice was little more than a thread, and he moved in a measured way, as if carrying out a ritual. He looked up at me. He met my gaze for a moment, then shifted his eyes to something behind me and very far away. No number of words could have said more clearly that my presence did not matter. He looked down, and put his right hand squarely onto his palette. He pressed down.

The black oozed up between his fingers. The membrane covering the half-dried pigments gave way so that streaks of white and yellow seeped into the black. He twisted his hand, sliding his splayed fingers through the knots of brighter color. Paint crawled across the tops of his fingers and crept up his wrist. Then he held his palm out to me. "You see, Doctor? This is why you have to be so careful with black, it soon overwhelms everything."

That black hand held toward me seemed like a threat. What was he going to do? Rub it on his face? On the canvas? Smear it onto his other hand, wipe it onto his clothes, suck the paint from his fingers? He sat before me on the ground, unkempt, sunburned, and streaked with paint like the maddest of madmen. Yet he was perfectly aware, completely controlled.

He lowered his hand into his lap, and his face became, if it was possible, even bleaker. "So," he said. "That is the end of that." He turned his palm down and drew it across the ground before him, dragging a shadow over the trampled stems of wheat.

"Doctor," Vincent said. "There should be a rag in the drawer of the paint box. Perhaps it might be useful." He was twisting handfuls of wheat stems into a makeshift brush and scraping at the spaces between his fingers. I stepped around him and righted the paint box, opening the drawer and finding a wad of grayish linen, crusted with orange and blue. He took it with his left hand and scrubbed his wrist where the tide of oily colors had left the shadow of a glove. Finished, he let the rag drop to the ground. Then he turned back to the magnificent scene before him, glowing more golden now. I had the sense that the episode, whatever it was, had reached its end. I lifted the blank canvas off the easel and set it down, collapsing the easel to rest beside me. I did not want that white rectangle to reproach my friend for a moment longer. Using the tips of my fingers, I maneuvered the palette out of sight. Then I sat on the stool, shoulder to shoulder with Vincent. All of my hesitation and timidity fell away.

"We have not seen you," I said. "I was worried."

"I have not been fit for company."

"Not as a guest, then," I said. "But as a patient."

He brushed away my comment with the paint-stained hand. "No," he said. "I don't think so."

"Have you been distressed?" I asked. "Do you feel there is another attack coming on?" But even as I asked my questions, I knew they were futile.

"Doctor," Vincent said, scratching his eyebrow, "I know you are a sympathetic man. I know that you would like to be able to make me feel better. I would like that myself." He turned toward me, with a dark streak now shading one of his eyes. "Do you have a potion? Or is it an electrical treatment? Little waves of current jolting through me"—here he jiggled his body slightly—"to set my brain aright?" He kept his eyes on mine, and this time I felt that he was completely engaged. This was the opportunity, I knew. He had come to a crisis of some kind and was ready to acknowledge his state.

"I saw a doctor in Paris," I began. "He studies hysteria. It sounds in many ways like what troubles you. The attacks sound very similar, with the voices, visual hallucinations, shouting and thrashing. I witnessed an attack while I was at the hospital visiting him. It was dreadful," I finished. There was a pause. "I would like to spare you from going through that again."

"But can you, Doctor?" Vincent asked. "Can this new doctor?"

The question hung there. A troop of cicadas started to thrum in the trees, then stopped. In the silence, I remembered Charcot's voice saying, "I cannot pretend to you that we have any way to end hysteria."

"He has found ways . . ." I found my voice faltering. "Sometimes he is able to reduce the intensity of the attacks, he says. Or the frequency. Or both." I met Vincent's gaze.

"I have seen doctors," he said mildly. "They did not help me."

"No, but Charcot is an expert. He has seen more cases like yours than anyone in France."

"And the patient you saw in the hospital, was he getting better?"

I had to admit it. "No."

"Was Dr. Charcot confident that he could help this man?"

I could not pretend to Vincent that Charcot had been confident. I drew breath to speak. I was going to say, "No, but perhaps he can help you." I was going to say, "He may be able to find a way. We should at least try this." I exhaled and shook my head. Charcot himself had warned me how little he could do in cases like Vincent's. I drew breath again.

"Can you imagine what it is like, Doctor?" Vincent said softly. "If anyone can, it is you. I have felt a kinship between us from the start. You have suffered, I know that. But you suffer other people's ills as well as your own. That was why I was hopeful when we met. I believe you can guess what it is like. You never know when it's going to happen. You are going about your business, perhaps in your office seeing a patient. And, suddenly, the world convulses. Your desk, your chair, your curtains writhe in front of you and groan. Or perhaps it is you groaning. Your patient—let us assume she is a lady—draws away as she sees your face. Your face is screwed up, your eyes closed, your teeth like fangs. You are drooling. You drop to the floor because you no longer control your limbs. Your bowels loosen. You flail and shout, knocking over a lamp. Your lady patient has fled the room in terror, and she brings the concierge upstairs. You are still kicking, and the concierge runs away to get help. Her husband drops the coals he is unloading and comes upstairs. He cannot hold you down. There's shit seeping out of your trousers, the carpet is ruined. You're sobbing. You've broken a chair and torn the feathers from a cushion." His speech came to a halt.

I could imagine it all. I could imagine it for myself, and for Vincent. For Vincent, this had happened again and again. He had been alone, rolling on the cold stone floor of the asylum at St.-Rémy. He had been held down by warders. He had been tied up in the *gilet de force*.

"And sometimes it goes on, you know. You come to—it's like waking up, only you're sick, your head aches, and you're bruised, of course, from thrashing around. You have a foul taste in your mouth and your arms are crossed in front of you and you can't get your hands out and that's when you know. It happened again. And maybe you are awake for an hour or a day, and then it starts again." Vincent scrambled to his feet, pushing himself clumsily off the ground. He stood for a moment, facing away from the river, back toward the wheat fields I had crossed to find him.

"And then when it's over, Doctor, you are so weak. You are terrified. Everything, *everything* is filled with menace. Especially your sleep. Oh, the nightmares! Monsters, horrors! I thought sometimes that they might be worse for me because I use my eyes, that because I see so keenly, my visions are more full of terror. But I am not sure of this. Everyone has his own terror." He took three steps away from me. His voice came a little bit more muffled. "Then it fades. The horrors diminish and it's easier to sleep. You become stronger. Pleasure comes back. The little pleasures first, the sight of a green shoot or the smell of coffee. It's like spring, in a way." The footsteps returned and circled around me. I sat slumped on the painting stool, hands dangling between my knees. I could feel tears drying on my face.

"Then you claw your way back into life," Vincent said, standing beside me. "You put one day behind another, and you try to be brave and useful. That's all I want, really. I want my life not to be a waste or a burden. So I paint. And I wonder when it is all going to come back." He sighed deeply, and gestured toward the view before us. There was a greener tinge to the sky now, and the band of shadow cast by the willows on the Oise veiled the water in places. I wondered how Vincent could have painted it without using black. "I have worked *furiously* here, Doctor. I did not think there was a moment to spare. Look, look at this. Don't you think this would make a splendid painting? A picture that could, perhaps, bring consolation to someone? The beauty of nature can do that, don't you think?"

I found my voice. "I do. Of course I do. And your paintings are beautiful."

There was a long silence between us. A hawk appeared over the trees, gliding with still wings, dipping to examine the fields with his sharp eyes. Perhaps some vole or rabbit made a move, for he planed sharply downward. But his prey had vanished, so he climbed upward again with one swift flap. I was grateful. The sound of death, even a rabbit's, would have undone me.

"Not today," said Vincent. "I couldn't paint today." I looked up at him. His eyes were fixed on the horizon, but he brought them down. "Nothing. All of this in front of me. I knew what it should look like. Knew what colors to use—well, you saw the palette. Had it planned to the last brushstroke. And I could not make my hand pick up the brush."

"You could not move your hand?" I asked. "Or was it that you didn't know how you would begin the painting?"

"Doctor," he said, "don't ask me these questions. What does it matter? I sat here all day, with my canvas before me, and the paint on my palette hardening, and the sun moving across the sky, and I was not able to paint. That is what I am saying. And I tell you this not as a doctor, for this is not a doctor's concern. Only you have shown me friendship, and I believe you understand my work. And my work seems to be done."

I stood up. This was desolation. I moved to Vincent's side to put an arm across his shoulders, but he turned away. I thought I understood. Sometimes sympathy is impossible to bear.

"It may come back tomorrow."

"It may," he said.

"We don't know why this happened."

"No, Doctor, but I no longer believe that matters." He glanced at me, then turned. In a gesture that was remarkable for him, he put both of his hands on my shoulders. Looking me in the eye, he went on, "If I am epileptic, if I suffer from hysteria, if I am simply another madman—can you make me well?"

It is one thing to doubt your métier. We all have doubts, we must. But we do not like to expose them. I am a doctor. I make people feel better, that is what I do and who I am. Yet I could not lie to Vincent. His illness was unlike any other I had ever seen. "No," I answered him, and looked down.

His hands dropped from my shoulders, but not without a gentle pressure, as if to thank me for my honesty. "Well, then, there we are," he said. He turned away from me, took a few steps, and looked up at the sky. The horizon was paler now, with a warmer cast over to the west. The surface of the Oise gleamed between the trees. "You will be late for dinner, Doctor. You should go home."

"Won't you come and dine with us?" I suggested. "You must keep your strength up."

"Do you really think so?" he asked, with an unfamiliar note of bitterness. "Why should I strengthen the vessel when the contents are so terribly scrambled? No, thank you, I will go back to the inn."

I did not know how to answer him, but I knew I could not leave him there alone. He bent down to lift his easel and fold the legs. Without another word, I crouched to pick up a handful of paint tubes. I left the empty black one where it had fallen, far away from us among the tall stalks. We walked home side by side, speechless and unhappy. Where our ways parted, I reached out to touch his shoulder.

When I arrived late for dinner, there was much exclamation. Some of Vincent's paint had gotten onto my coat and hands. Paul made a joke that I was as bad as Nero, and that my hair would have to be cut if I did not learn my lesson. I managed to smile.

It pained me to see Vincent incapable. All along, I had admired his facility, his bravura. If Vincent's brush could be stilled by madness—if he could be robbed of what made his life worth living—who was safe? He had seemed immune to the kind of doubt that always plagued me; he knew what he wanted to do and, despite immense difficulties, forged ahead. I wondered—I still do wonder—if I had ever been as confident as Vincent.

In the years since Vincent was part of our lives, I have considered this question. Few men succeed without that assurance, but where does it come from? It seems to have little connection with actual achievement. Paul is a very confident painter. In fact, he shows considerable certainty in everything he does. When he left the university with his degree in agricultural engineering, he announced to me (with none of the defer-ence that one might expect from a son to a father) that he intended to be an artist. He was willing to spend a little time selling artists' supplies in the towns near Paris, but he made it clear to me that this would be a brief episode. It was as if I had no authority over him. Indeed, I doubt that I did. He has lived in Auvers ever since, working with me in the studio, using the Paris flat more often than I do, apparently selling enough paintings to buy his own paints and canvases. He has friends in Paris, I suppose. He must also see women there, and I appreciate his discretion. I have ascertained that he will remain in this house after I die, taking care of Marguerite and painting.

And selling my pictures. He will have to sell my collection in order to live. Despite his assurance with the canvas and brushes, he does not earn his keep. Nor, it seems, does he intend to. Instead, he helps me with the catalog of my paintings. It is an important collection, worthy of documentation. The implicit bargain seems to be that he will take on my task when I die, and his compensation will be the ability to do what-ever he likes with the pictures. He has tried, several times, to persuade me to sell one or two. He informs me of the prices for Cézanne, who now exhibits with Ambroise Vollard. He urges me to put a canvas or two on the market, just to see what we might get.

As I have said, Paul is a painter of facility. He easily mimics the styles of Cézanne and Van Gogh. His own style, to the extent that it exists, is decorative. He is influenced by Art Nouveau, for instance. I readily admit that he is more talented than I am, and I would like to believe that I do not mind being outstripped by my son. Yet I am troubled by what I believe Paul intends to do with his talent.

I taught him to paint. He has never had formal lessons: I merely in-structed him, as I was instructed long ago, in the fundamentals of draw-ing, modeling, perspective. After that, he learned by copying. He spent some time in the Louvre, as artists have done for hundreds of years, but his primary sources of inspiration have been the canvases I am lucky enough to own. It is not every fledgling painter who lives with two dozen Van Goghs, two dozen Cézannes, a Sisley, a Monet, a Renoir, and so on. It was Paul who suggested that the catalog include illustrations of our canvases. We began at first by etching copies, but Vincent's work is not best represented by fine black lines. By then our neighbor's daughter Blanche Derousse was taking lessons from me, and she turned out to be dexterous with watercolor. So our volume will in all likelihood be a single precious example, perhaps to be lodged in a museum, and Vincent's luminous canvases will be represented by Blanche's watercolor copies.

Paul is also a good copyist. He is especially skilled with oils. He has made a few uncanny versions of paintings I own, using canvases of precisely the same size, practicing signatures over and over—Cézanne signed some of his things with a red scribble that Paul has made his own. I have always insisted that Paul's copies be clearly marked on the back of the canvas or even on the front. I have done the same with my copies, though, sadly, they would deceive no one.

None of this worried me until a recent episode. I had gone to Paris that day, but it was unusually warm for May. My feet began to hurt, as I was wearing new boots. I took an earlier train home than I had planned, and sat for a while in the garden with the dreadful boots by my side. Marguerite and Madame Chevalier—who is now quite stout and wheezy—were washing the landing on the second floor, making a racket with their brooms and mops and buckets, so I tiptoed past them and up to the studio. The door was open; Paul had no warning of my presence.

On the table where we set up still life subjects, he had arranged an assemblage of objects: a length of patterned fabric, a Delft vase, a small stoneware pitcher, and an ordinary table knife. These were all items that Cézanne had painted in my house, and I kept them, with some care, in a small locked cabinet. Paul knew where to find the key, and there was no reason why he should not, but these objects had taken on something of the quality of relics.

When Cézanne was in Auvers in 1872, he sometimes painted on pieces of cardboard. They were much cheaper than canvas, though of course more fragile. These were not paintings intended for collectors but Cézanne's way of working out pictorial problems. We have several such paintings, and I must admit that they are not his most accomplished, nor our most prized. Yet Paul was painting such a still life on cardboard. It was not a direct copy—it was an entirely new composition, in the style of Cézanne, using articles that Cézanne had already painted in our house.

"Paul," I said. "What are you doing?"

He whirled around, eyes wide. One rarely sees Paul at a loss for words, but on this occasion, he turned scarlet and could not speak for a moment. "Father," he finally said, transferring a loaded brush from his right hand to his left, where he held the palette. "You're back early. Where are your shoes?"

"Downstairs. They were hurting my feet." I stepped through the door to look more closely at the painting on the easel. "What is this?"

"Oh, I am just amusing myself. You don't mind, do you? That I got the Cézanne things out of the cabinet? I had found this piece of cardboard, you see, and it reminded me of some of our little paintings. Then I wondered if I could make a similar one. It's going well, don't you think?" He stepped aside slightly, to let me look more closely at his work.

I was watching him carefully. Having recovered his equanimity, he was able to meet my gaze with a candid smile. I looked at the picture. It was an unpleasant image, with murky coloring and clumsy brushwork. Yet Cézanne himself had produced several such paintings in my studio.

"What do you intend to do with this?" I asked.

"Do? Nothing. What do you mean?"

"You weren't going to . . . ," I began, then trailed to a halt. I was tired. I felt old. How could I suspect my son? Did I really suspect him? Of forging a painting? It seemed so implausible at that moment. He held my gaze, his blue eyes bright and clear and young. A challenge.

"Well, be sure to sign it with your signature," I finally finished, shaking my head. Then I tried to smile at him. "It is very like one of Cézanne's own paintings. We would not want any confusion."

"Of course I will." His brow furrowed, as if he were puzzled. "Why wouldn't I? You don't think . . ." He stepped back a bit. He showed first confusion, then comprehension, then anger. "Father! You can't possibly think I would attempt to deceive anyone! This is merely a painter's little play. A test of my skill. I'm shocked!"

Suddenly I could bear no more. My head felt light, and I grasped the edge of the doorframe. "I think I will go and rest," I said. Paul said something behind me, but I did not hear him. He helped me down the stairs. The women were alarmed, and before long I was lying on my bed with a poultice on my feet and whispers outside my door. I let them treat me like an invalid sometimes. It seems to give them pleasure.

But this is what Paul is like. He has plans he does not share with me. Perhaps this is always the way it is between fathers and sons. I feel that I am being elbowed aside, that Paul is marking time until I die. And why should I care? Dead is dead. Yet I find that I do care. I would like to be respected in the future. If my only trace is to be Vincent's portrait, well, that is more than most people leave. But if there is more, if people were to learn more about what we did in this house in Auvers, I would want them to know that I meant well. That I did my best for Vincent, that I tried to help Cézanne, that I took care of Pissarro's ailing eyes so that he could keep painting.

If Paul sells my pictures—as he will—I fear he will also sell his own, as someone else's. Among the glorious canvases by our friends that he sells will also be lesser works, paintings Paul has made that will pass at first as Vincent's or Cézanne's but that will be found out. And then what will it look like? Will we any longer be considered thoughtful men who cared deeply for our friends' art? No. We will be seen as profiteers and worse. Our artist friends will come to be seen as our victims.

Paul works to keep our name linked with that of Vincent van Gogh. He has painted, from a photograph, a portrait of Vincent's mother, in a style similar to my friend's. He is sending it to Amsterdam, hoping it will be included in the exhibition that will take place there later in the summer. He sent a bronze medallion of Vincent, his first work in that medium, to the Salon des Indépendants earlier in the spring. He called it *Homage to My Master*.

His "master"! He makes it sound as if Vincent had taught him, painstakingly correcting his brushstrokes or honing his vision, when instead he was a boy of seventeen, trailing around after Vincent and making a pest of himself! And now he catalogs my pictures and paints in Cézanne's style, and I do not trust his intentions.

I should not leap ahead. So far, every canvas that Paul has painted in Vincent's style has been signed as a copy. I do not know what plans he may have for the dingy still life I saw him painting. In any event, I am powerless. He can do whatever he likes after my death.

*T*hirteen

∞

ON THE WEDNESDAY MORNING after that incident in the wheat field, I took the earliest train back to Paris. Auvers is especially beautiful early in the morning. You could believe yourself in an idyllic rural landscape—a Corot perhaps—graced with soft hills, delicate trees, and the long shadows of dawn. When the train comes steaming into the Chaponval station, I am often startled by the noisy, insistent embodiment of the modern era. But then I sit in my accustomed seat and begin to cast my thoughts forward to my Parisian life: which patients will require which treatment, where I will dine that night, and the like.

The train moves slowly on the stretch between Auvers and Pontoise. Often one glimpses fishermen or a boy with a dog plunging through the brush. I was watching idly for such activity when I saw a figure whose presence there chilled me. I can still summon the image—a slender, red-haired man in a blue shirt, gazing into the green water of the Oise from a crumbling stone embankment. I might have been able to deceive myself and pretend it wasn't Vincent, had he not turned his head toward the train as it passed. It was undoubtedly Vincent's face. He was looking not upward at the passengers but downward, at the wheels.

Perhaps he was simply watching the train, as one does, thinking about voyages. Possibly his thoughts were of travel to Paris, to the South, even to the Netherlands—places where he had lived and where he might go to escape his current plight. Yet there was an air of tension and purpose about him. I thought I could see calculation in the way his eyes followed the engine, ton upon ton of rattling, hot steel. For a moment I imagined standing next to the track, watching the tall black machine approaching, waiting and waiting until it could stop no longer, then diving beneath it . . .

I didn't think it was possible. The train moved too slowly here. You could not, I thought, count on finishing things. If you lay on the tracks too early, the conductor might be able to stop. The chances of being hideously maimed but still living seemed too high.

I turned back to face the front of the car, feeling strangely drained. In that moment, when I had spotted Vincent, I had experienced a surge of energy. I wished to call out to him or even, somehow, to take him by the shoulders and whisk him out of danger. As the train continued to clatter toward Pontoise, my heart raced and my hands trembled.

I had not actually witnessed a suicide attempt, I told myself. I had seen a man watching a train. Maybe Vincent was planning a new painting, one that contrasted the clattering might of the engine with the delicacy of the willow trees. But Vincent had never, that I knew of, shown much interest in machines. He could certainly have been idling away the morning, perhaps waiting until the dew burned off before setting out with his easel. But Vincent was never idle. If he was not painting, he was planning a painting or retouching canvases or sketching or reading or writing letters or looking for a new motif. His every activity had a purpose. Dawdling by the bank of a river waiting for something to happen was a young man's pastime.

The train slowed further and pulled into the Pontoise station. An old acquaintance entered my compartment at that point, and I was distracted as we exchanged news. During our conversation, my thoughts occasionally strayed back to Vincent and what he might have been doing by the train tracks, but I was relieved to have a diversion.

I was so accustomed to traveling back and forth between Auvers and Paris that I automatically navigated through streets and stations at either end of the voyage without a thought for my surroundings. On this morning my eye was caught by a pair of men who happened to collide near one of the cast-iron columns in the departure hall of the Gare du Nord. It did not look as if the contact had been jarring, but one of the men fell to the floor. I was in a hurry, and they were not near me, so I intended to continue on my way, until the cluster of frock coats parted and I thought I glimpsed Theo van Gogh's face.

Instantly I drew nearer and saw that I was correct. "Excuse me, I am a doctor, and I know this man. May I be of service?" I asked in a loud voice. The gentlemen who had gathered stepped back instantly. Theo looked up at me.

"Dr. Gachet!" he exclaimed and clambered somewhat awkwardly to his feet. He bent down to pick up the flat leather case with a handle lying on the floor next to him and staggered.

I held out a hand to steady him, but he had already straightened. "Are you hurt?" I asked.

"No, not at all," he said, trying to brush at the knees of his trousers. Yet the movement set him off balance again. "I am just trying to catch a train, and I was not paying attention to where I was going." The small crowd around us was drifting away since there was clearly nothing more to be seen.

"Where are you going so early in the morning?" I asked, looking carefully at him. He seemed thinner, almost gaunt, and his face was very pale.

"I have an appointment in Brussels," he said. "But I did not allow enough time to get here, and I am afraid I have missed the train. It leaves at eight thirty-five."

We both turned to look at the huge station clock, which was showing just that time. A whistle blew, and a train slowly pulled away from a platform. "Damn!" Theo exclaimed.

"How often do they run?" I asked. "Perhaps you can catch the next one, and send a telegram to put off your appointment."

"No doubt, Doctor," he said. But he stood still.

I looked around. Living near the station, I had never entered the waiting room, but in tall letters above a double door I could see the sign: *SALLE D'ATTENTE*. "Why don't you go and sit down? I will find out when the next train leaves. And I could send the telegram for you, if you would like, though I begin to think that you should delay the trip until you feel better."

He turned to me and clutched my shoulder. "No, I must go today. But I will rest for a moment. You can just bring me the form for the telegram, I'll write it myself."

To my surprise, I was irritated. He seemed unwell, yet determined on a course of action that would worsen his health. He was as stubborn as his brother, and just as misguided.

"Monsieur van Gogh, why are you going to Brussels? It is a tiring voyage. Didn't you just take Madame van Gogh and the baby to Holland?"

"Yes, Doctor, but I have an appointment to try to sell a painting. I have no choice. I will go and sit down as you suggest, and then I will be perfectly fine. But I would be grateful if you could help me with the telegram."

He turned away from me and walked toward the waiting room. His gait was unsteady, but perhaps only a doctor would have noticed.

It took me a few minutes to find the telegraph office, but happily for Theo, the next train to Brussels left only an hour later than the one he had missed.

"That is a great relief," he told me when I returned to the waiting room. "I will not have to delay this appointment by very much." He leaned his head against the back of the bench where we were seated.

"Is it so very important that you go today? Forgive me, but you seem unwell. You need to take care of yourself. Many people depend on you."

He lifted a hand wearily. "I am trying to sell a painting, Doctor. That is my job, and those people who depend on me will be more likely to eat if I can persuade a banker in Belgium to buy this little canvas." He tapped the case at his side. "It is a Diaz, a pretty thing. I imagine you would find it insipid, compared to Vincent's work. But it is appealing." He straightened up and held out a hand. "Could you give me the form for the telegram?"

Wordlessly I handed him the square of paper. He took out a pen and flattened the form on the wood of the bench between us. I tried not to watch as he began to fill in the address at the top. There is not a great deal of room between the lines on these blank telegrams. One must write neatly. Syphilitics cannot do this. They seem unable to judge the size of their letters and often crowd the words at the end of a line.

I gazed up at the faraway ceiling, where a pigeon fluttered restlessly, searching for a place to roost. Beside me Theo muttered something. I heard the pen clattering to the floor.

I could not help looking down at the telegram form, where a large blot of ink almost hid the uneven letters.

Theo crumpled up the form. "I hope you brought more than one, Doctor," he said. "My handwriting has become erratic." His eyes met mine. It was a clear admission. I reached into my pocket and held out the spare forms I had taken from the office, just in case.

Silence fell between us.

"Are you saying . . ." I paused.

"You knew. I have seen you watching me. You recognized the signs. You brought those." He gestured to the small squares of paper in my hand.

I nodded. "I did."

Once again we were silent. When the door to the waiting room opened, the station's roar filled the room and died with the hiss of a train coming to a halt on the tracks. A couple dressed for traveling came in, with their little girl between them. They settled her on a bench and she pointed upward, to where the pigeon was still flying in circles.

"Sometimes I feel better, Doctor. I was sure for so long that I was cured. I would never have married Jo otherwise, you know. And now . . ." He raised a hand to his eyes. "Forgive me, I am overwrought. Perhaps you could write the telegram for me." He held out the pen.

"I am sure you should not go to Brussels," I said. "What will happen if you have a mishap there? You might drop that painting. You could fall in the street." I found myself torn by several emotions: pity, anxiety, and impatience. I could hardly have named which was strongest.

"Doctor, what you do not seem to grasp is that I have no choice." Theo's voice came firmly. "No choice. Put yourself in my place. What would you do?"

"You will be no good to your family if you collapse." I tried to sound reasonable. "Can you not put off this trip?"

"Until when?" He looked at me and shrugged. He glanced around the vast room, gauging if we could be overheard. "Let us be blunt, Doctor," he said in a low voice. "I have the pox. I am very ill. There are periods of respite, when I feel better, but I will never be really well again." He looked to me, as if for confirmation.

I nodded. "The muscular disturbances . . ."

"Some men recover from this. Some men live this way for months, or even years, but they require help. I may not be able to work." He spoke with a clarity and a despair that pierced my heart. I had thought of Theo as gentle, the loving brother whose patience knew no limit, the adoring husband and father. This pale, trembling man beside me was almost fierce, despite his obvious physical fragility.

"But, Monsieur van Gogh," I protested weakly. "Surely not. You're under a doctor's care, of course?"

He reached out and grasped my wrist. His palm felt hot. "Doctor, please permit me. . . ." He took a breath and glanced unseeing at the doors. "Since we have begun this conversation . . . I would not have brought this up. The shame, you understand. But you are a man of medicine. Please pay me the compliment of honesty."

What could I do? I nodded. He went on. "I may very well die." His expression tightened, and he swallowed, then looked off in the distance again, turned away from me. "I will probably die." I sensed that he was talking as much to himself as to me. "Thus I must go to Brussels and sell this painting, so that there may be something for Johanna and little Vincent and for my brother, Heaven help them all, something beyond the enormous trove of Vincent's paintings." There was a hardness to his tone of voice and a bitter twist to his mouth that startled me.

"Do I surprise you?" he asked, responding, I suppose, to my expression. "Imagine it, Doctor. I love my brother, I do. But my days, it appears, are numbered. And my concern for Vincent, my support of him, will have the terrible effect of robbing my wife. I cannot help thinking this. I have added it up, over and over again. A hundred fifty francs a month for ten years. I am not even including his paints and canvases, I could not begin to reckon that sum. I have spent well over twenty thousand francs to permit Vincent to paint. That is money that Jo will *not* have when I am gone. Instead, she will have hundreds upon hundreds of canvases that cannot be sold!" His voice was rising now, and it was my turn to glance around, but no one was paying any heed to this frail-looking man haranguing his companion.

"But perhaps, in time . . . ," I ventured. "Vincent's work is so new, so . . . so progressive, perhaps the critics will come around. There is already Aurier who recognized him."

"It is possible," Theo conceded. "I no longer think I know. Sometimes I am sure he is a genius. Sometimes I doubt my judgment. What if, after all, he is simply inept?" He crumpled the ruined telegram form. "It doesn't matter. I must go and try to sell this picture." Again he held the pen to me. This time I took it and filled out the form as Theo directed me.

As I wrote the address and the simple message, my mind was reeling. Theo believed in Vincent. Surely he did! This talk of finding his paintings "inept" was careless, something Theo said for effect, or driven by his own grief and fear. I thought back to our visit to see the canvases in Tanguy's attic. On that occasion Theo had spoken ardently about his brother's genius. I did not think his admiration had been feigned.

When I had finished, we stood up. Theo seemed a little bit stronger, and he held the case firmly under his arm. The canvas could not have been very large. I wondered what price he hoped to get for it. I held the heavy waiting-room door for him and saw him steady himself on its brass handle as he passed through. I slipped the case from under his arm, and he did not protest as I tucked it under my own.

Then something occurred to me. "You must not tell Vincent."

Theo shook his head, looking straight ahead into the crowd. "He knows."

I stopped and dropped Theo's arm. I stepped away from him slightly. "You told him?"

Theo seemed puzzled by my reaction. "Yes. I thought he should know."

"But he is *ill*." A young boy wearing a page's uniform from one of the big hotels ran past us, not even looking back as he knocked into the case at my side.

"Yes. And so am I," Theo said patiently.

"But you cannot . . . you should not have burdened him with this!" I went on, my voice shrill in my ears.

"Dr. Gachet, Vincent is my brother. I wanted him to know. This is important. We share things, Vincent and I."

"But he is . . ." I looked up at the vault of the roof, so far away. A whistle pierced the air in the distance, and a train moved off down a track. "Don't you see how this will affect him? He is so fragile! You know he cannot paint anymore?"

This was obviously news to Theo. He shook his head. Yet his face was hard.

I went on, pressing my point. "He cannot paint. He has been sitting in front of an easel for days on end, trying to will his fingers to pick up a paintbrush. Can you imagine how he feels?"

"Am I to have nothing of my own?" cried Theo, his voice rising above the din. "I am going to *die*. I am not yet thirty-five. I will leave a wife and son unprovided for. Against this you set the fact that my brother cannot paint?"

"Painting is life for him," I said quietly. "He has nothing else, *nothing*. You know that." I held out the case that contained the painting. "You may die or you may not. If Vincent cannot paint, he most certainly will. One way or another."

Theo accepted the case, which quivered a little bit as he held it against his side. "I had hoped, when I told him, that Vincent might be sympathetic," he said, looking down at the marble floor. A corner of a yellow ticket lay by his foot. He tried to guide his foot toward it. I could tell that he wanted to move it, simply slide it an inch on the polished gray stone. The foot twitched, and he gave up. He went on very quietly. I could barely hear him. "We had gone for a walk, that day he came to Paris. I don't want Jo to know yet. She is so happy with the baby." His face momentarily softened. "I cannot bring myself to spoil this happy time for her. There is nothing she can do, in any event. But Vincent should begin to think ahead and consider what he will do without me. I had to tell him as we walked along the street. Vincent has a kind heart. I know he does. He loved our mother very much." He took a breath and looked up at me. Now there was bewilderment on his face. "But he was not concerned about me at all. He did not seem to understand what I was telling him. All he could see was that, if I died, he would not have my money anymore. He did not— It did not seem to occur to him that, if I died, he would not have a brother anymore."

"What worries me," I said flatly, "is that if Vincent has his way, *you* will not have a brother anymore. This morning I saw him roaming around the train tracks. I fear he may try to do away with himself."

I saw him flinch. I felt a moment's pity. No, it would be more precise to say that for a moment my pity shifted from Vincent to Theo. I had gone too far, perhaps. But Theo had been wrong to burden Vincent with this news.

Theo's eyes met mine. I could no longer read his expression. It was as if a door had closed. "I must go send the telegram," he said. "Don't trouble to come with me." He turned and walked unsteadily through the crowd, a thin, upright figure clutching a flat leather case.

Fourteen

AFTER MY ENCOUNTER WITH THEO, I felt it was urgent to get back to Auvers. I changed as many appointments as possible and found a colleague to substitute for me at my usual clinic. I was able to take a train back late on Thursday evening.

What could Vincent's state of mind possibly be? As I sat on the train clacking through the dark to my village, I looked out the window into the darkness. My own wan reflection met me: loose skin, long face, eyes pouched by age and sorrow. Vincent discerned that sadness as no one else had done. He *recognized* me. He would lose a brother in Theo, but that did not mean he would be alone.

We had a sympathetic relationship, I thought. I could be a friend, and more than a friend. The 150 francs a month that Vincent lived on was not so very much. I could not afford it all myself, but I might find others who would help. Rich collectors, perhaps. And maybe Theo had not done everything possible to promote his brother's work. There might be eager collectors whom Theo simply had not identified.

Vincent could stay in Auvers; he seemed to like it. He could paint at my house. I could find him more models so that he could make portraits—Paul, for instance, and Madame Chevalier. Perhaps I would resume painting myself. We might paint side by side in the country, as Pissarro and Cézanne had done back in the 1870s.

I had sent word to Madame Chevalier that I would return by a late train, and she had left supper for me, roasted chicken and part of an apricot tart, which Marguerite served. Paul joined us, sitting at the table and absently devouring the end of a baguette.

"Paul," I began, trying to sound casual. "Have you seen Monsieur van Gogh this week? I am beginning to wonder how he is, since he has not visited us."

"Only from a distance."

"Yes? And how recently was that?"

"Yesterday," he said. "Up on the hillside, you know? By the wheat fields, looking down over the river."

Had Vincent gone back to the place where I had found him the previous weekend? "Yes, I think I know the spot," I said and put down my fork.

"He was there every day this week," Paul said, looking at me attentively.

"Every day?" I repeated, alarmed.

"Yes. I just happened to see him. Marguerite, is there any more of that tart?" He ate like three men in those days.

His sister rose silently and went into the kitchen, returning with a wedge of the tart on a plate that she set in front of him. I watched her, wondering what went on in her head. Was she still infatuated with Vincent? Did she spend her time in her room looking at his portrait of her?

"And Marguerite," I said, "how are your roses blooming? Did yesterday's heat fade them?"

"It was not very hot here," she replied, slipping into her chair. Then she looked up. She was blushing now. "I saw Monsieur van Gogh, Papa. I thought you would want to know."

"You saw him?" Paul asked, turning to her quickly. "You didn't tell me."

"He asked for Papa, not for you," she answered in an elder-sister tone.

"He asked for me?" I interrupted, wanting to cut off any squabbling between them. "What day was this?"

"It was yesterday. Madame Chevalier had gone to the market in Pontoise, so I answered the bell. Monsieur van Gogh was there. He asked for you. I said you were in Paris. And I told him that we could send you a message if he wanted it. He seemed somewhat . . . distracted," she finished.

"Distracted!" scoffed Paul. "What does that mean?"

"You know how Monsieur van Gogh always seems to look at things very carefully? And thoughtfully? He pays attention," Marguerite explained, appealing to me. "He hardly knew who he was talking to. I don't mean that he should know me especially," she added, in some confusion. "But he seemed . . . He seemed agitated. And his eyes did not settle on anything. They shifted around." She demonstrated, her eyes slewing right and left. It was disturbing to see my mild-mannered and sheltered daughter so accurately mimicking a behavior I had seen all too often in the mentally unsound. My concern for Vincent increased.

"And when you said I was in Paris . . . ," I prompted her.

"He said he didn't want to bother you," she told me. "I tried to convince him that you would be glad to hear from him, but he . . ." She frowned, remembering. "He didn't seem to be listening anymore. He didn't say good-bye, he just walked away."

For Marguerite, this was a remarkable observation. Until Vincent's advent, she had hardly seemed to notice anyone outside the family. Thus her grasp of Vincent's mental state was uncanny. Moreover, she painted a wrenching picture. I hated to think that Vincent had come to me and that I had not been there to hold out a hand. I finished dinner quickly and, though it was late, left to go back to Ravoux's. I could not rest without seeing Vincent.

So it was that half an hour later I was rapping on the door of his bedroom. The tiny hall was dark as pitch beyond the glow of my lantern, and I could see only a thin streak of light beneath the crooked door. "Vincent, it's Dr. Gachet. May I come in?"

A moment passed with no reply. Then I heard a chair scrape, and he opened the door. "Yes, Doctor, of course," he said, standing aside. I had interrupted him in writing a letter—the finished pages lay on the splintery table that also held the basin and pitcher for washing. There was only one chair, which he held out for me. "Would you like to sit down, Doctor? I can sit on the bed. Or we could go down to the shed, if you'd prefer."

He sat facing me, hands loosely folded. He seemed composed, showing no interest in why I had taken the unusual step of bursting into his bedroom. Perhaps he was merely indifferent. The single candle on the table left most of the room in shadow; I could make out only the outlines of paintings on the walls and the dim, undefined shapes of his clothes hung on nails. Voices from the café floated up to us in a dull but cheerful clamor.

I took the chair and looked at him carefully for signs of disturbance. He appeared very tired. The lines in his face were etched deeply, and hollows shadowed his cheekbones. "Marguerite said that you had called at the house yesterday. I am sorry I was not there."

He seemed composed. "Yes. Mademoiselle Marguerite was very kind."

"Was there something you wanted?" I began. It was difficult to know how to say what I had in mind. Strangely, Vincent's calm made it more awkward. My hopeful scheme for helping him seemed to have nothing to do with this polite, even wary individual. I pulled from my pocket a small brown bottle. "I have been concerned about you since Saturday. You appeared to be in a very unhappy state. This is a cordial I brew from valerian," I told him. "It is mild, but it often helps my patients feel more serene. You may swallow a spoonful in water as needed." I put it on his table.

"Well, Doctor," he said with a fleeting smile. "You've been able to bottle serenity? That is no small achievement. Thank you."

"No, of course not. It is just an attempt . . ." My voice tailed off.

"I know, Doctor," he said. "Perhaps I frightened you that afternoon."

His suggestion surprised me. It was unusual for Vincent to show any awareness of his effect on other people.

"I frightened myself, if you must know," he explained. "Doctor, I know why you've come. You want to tell me that I will survive this. I'll drink your valerian, and wake up tomorrow and go back to that hillside and the painting will come. And I'll keep on painting, and eventually someone, somewhere will buy another picture. People will begin to understand what I am trying to do. They will grow to appreciate it. They will want me to paint them, perhaps." He looked at me, brows raised, waiting for confirmation.

"Well, of course," I said. "You have withstood these trials in the past." My argument sounded paltry to me, but I raised my hand as if to forestall an objection. "I don't doubt that there are difficulties you have not shared with me. That episode, with my Guillaumin— Perhaps you've had other signs that a spell is drawing near?" I met his gaze and saw an unexpected expression of pity in his eyes.

"Yes," he said. "This is all true. I do desperately fear that another attack is due. I fear that I will do harm. It is a terrible thing not to trust yourself. And surely you can see, Doctor, that if I cannot paint, there is little for me to live for? Should I live for this?" He gestured to the dim garret. "I exist, Doctor, in the margins of other people's lives. Even Theo and Jo sometimes see me as something to dread. At times the painting can make up for that, but can you conceive of what courage I must expend? I force myself to bear the hours when I cannot be painting. There are consolations, I do not deny it. Your friendship has been one of them. So has the birth of my little nephew. Otherwise, I endure."

Silence fell between us. A shout from downstairs was followed by a gust of laughter and the clinking of glasses. That was the world Vincent would never belong to.

"So you see that if I cannot paint—" he began.

"That was today, this week," I broke in. "You cannot know that you will have the same trouble tomorrow."

"True," he said, nodding. "Or the next day. Or the next. How many days would you say I should spend sitting in front of a blank canvas? How will I know that I have really finished?"

I could feel myself curling back into the wooden chair, trying to escape his remorseless logic.

"Or should I stop for a while? Do something else? What else would that be? When painting is the only thing I can stand?"

Again, I had no answer, but he did not seem to expect one. We sat silently in the flickering light. Downstairs they were singing a tune that rose to a near roar and dropped off with apparent comic effect to a mock whisper followed by gales of laughter.

"And besides, Theo has syphilis," Vincent said across the merriment. I didn't hear him clearly at first. He looked at me sharply. "Did you know?"

"I found out yesterday. I don't believe he would have told me, but I saw him at the Gare du Nord. He had fallen . . . He is very ill."

Vincent moved on the bed, turning to straighten the pillow. "His body is ill, and my mind."

"Does Jo know?" I managed to ask. It wasn't the most important question; it was simply the one I was able to utter.

"How can you tell a woman such a thing?" he scoffed. "He believed it was cured. It's only since they married that he knew it had come back. That is why when the baby was ill he was so worried. He thought little Vincent might have it, too. I believe it happens like that sometimes?" He looked at me, inquiring.

"Sometimes," I said.

"But you've seen the baby. At least he seems all right."

"Oh, yes," I said without thinking, "little Vincent Willem is healthy enough." Then I gathered myself together. The difficulty was that I did not know what to say. My vision on the train, the idea that I should stand in for Theo, suddenly seemed ludicrous. How could I have thought it?

Vincent sat on the narrow bed, elbows on his knees and face in his hands. The noise downstairs seemed to have moved into the street. The room had no windows, but farewells floated in through the skylight. His candle was getting low. I had set my lantern on the floor but lifted it now onto his table, where it suddenly brightened the walls. Vincent looked up, tracking this new light source. He still had a smear of dark paint on his eyebrow from the episode in the wheat field.

"And if Theo dies, then where will I be?" he asked.

"Well," I began. "I was thinking. It is not such a vast sum, you know, a hundred and fifty francs a month. More than I can afford by myself, but there are others, surely, who believe—"

"If these people exist, they believe in a man who paints," Vincent cut in, with a mildness that had the effect of a sword. "I have not been able to put the tiniest speck of color onto a canvas for a week." He spread his hands in a rhetorical gesture. "I can't do anything besides paint. I cannot support myself, and I cannot even be sure that I will stay sane. I begin to be something of a problem, don't I? And if I am a problem, even to myself—well." He shook his head. The little burst of energy that had fueled this speech died away.

The words lingered, though. "If I am a problem, even to myself." I found myself sitting in a fashion that mirrored Vincent's, with head bowed and hands slack between my knees. A problem even to myself. Imagine it. You could never escape. The thing that you dreaded, that gave you that leaden feeling, joined to you like a shadow.

We sat slumped for some time, several minutes. I wanted to be able to sit up and reassure Vincent, but I dismissed each source of hope that occurred to me. I suppose, in retrospect, that I could have invented something spurious, perhaps a new cure for hysteria or a medication that would arrest Theo's symptoms, or a buyer in Paris who had seen his work at Tanguy's. None of these stratagems occurred to me at the time, and I doubt that they would have convinced Vincent. I am not a good liar.

"Did you know that Theo was ill before he told you?" Vincent asked, his voice breaking our silence.

"I guessed it," I admitted.

"Will he die soon?"

"I cannot say. It is worrisome that he is so weak. And it seems to be affecting his back. His movements are uneven. But the progress of the disease is mysterious and unpredictable. Periods of poor health are often followed by what looks like recovery. He could survive for years yet."

"As an invalid?"

"Again, I cannot predict."

"He could go mad."

"He could," I had to agree.

"I wish it could have been I," Vincent said, musing. "I am half-mad anyway. And no one will miss me when I am gone. The world can much more easily spare me than him."

"You cannot say that," I protested, but weakly. There was a horrible pragmatism to his reasoning.

"Doctor, let us leave convention aside. Whose life has more value now? Clearly, that of a man who supports a wife, a baby, an elderly mother, and a ne'er-do-well brother. Not that of a man who is incapable in every way."

"No," I said slowly, "I cannot agree. The paintings–"

"But remember, I can no longer paint," he interrupted.

"That is not certain," I said sharply. "And think of your friends, think of your mother, think of little Vincent Willem. Who is to say that your life has no value to him?"

"I cannot go on enduring this life for the sake of an infant," Vincent snapped. "I tell you, from one day to the next I wonder if I will see the sun rise again." He looked across at me. "I suppose I should not say this to a doctor."

"You should not say such things to any friend!" I told him. "If you are threatening to do away with yourself—is that it? Good God! Think of the misery you would inflict!" I stood up and took the half step toward him that brought me across the tiny room. "Imagine for a moment your brother beside your coffin! Imagine his despair, his loneliness!"

"Imagine mine," Vincent countered, looking at the floor. "That's all."

I could not answer right away. I backed into the chair.

"One day after the next, Doctor," he said. "The minutes crawling by. Nothing to look back on but wreckage. Nothing to anticipate but . . . what?" He shrugged. "If Theo dies, how will I live? I cannot in-flict myself on my mother. In fact, I cannot inflict myself on anyone, I know this. At any time I may become violent. Look at what I did to my-self. I know Gauguin claims that I threatened him with a knife. It may be true, I cannot say. Should I take this threat that I am and deposit it somewhere among gentle, kindly people who mean no harm?"

Again, I could not answer, but he did not wait for more than a second before standing up. "Enough, Doctor. I apologize for alarming you. I see that I have. These thoughts should never be shared."

I got to my feet. "No, I cannot agree. What has worried me, Vincent, has been your absence. I would rather see you, distressed as you are, than worry about you being all alone."

"You see, Doctor, that is where you make a mistake. I feel just as lonely when you are here. I am separated now from mankind. I cannot say just why, but it is so. I know that you came to bring me comfort, but there is no comfort on this earth for me."

I picked up my lantern, and the upper half of the room grew brighter. On the wall above Vincent's sagging cot blazed the beautiful canvas of chestnut blossoms he had painted six weeks earlier. I pointed to it. "Surely you were happy when you painted those blossoms?" I asked.

He looked at them and sighed. "If I may say it this way, the flowers were happy. I painted that."

"And you are so sure that you can no longer find that happiness? And put it on canvas?"

"The thing is, Doctor," he responded, picking up my bottle of valerian, "I can no longer afford hope. I am simply too weary." He looked down at the little brown flask. "Thank you for this, I will try it. Quite a change from absinthe."

It was a dismissal. I turned toward the door. But I had to make one last attempt. "Vincent, will you promise me one thing? Will you come to me if these thoughts get too dreadful?"

He smiled wistfully. "All of your years with the mad have not taught you the important point, have they? Once the thoughts get too dread-ful, we are no longer ourselves. I might no longer be Vincent. I will probably become the dreaded madman, and then I *cannot* find you, though I might wish to."

I accepted the rebuke. "I see that. But if at any time— I will tell the children, and Madame Chevalier. I can be here from Paris in two hours."

He did not speak for a few seconds, but the expression of pity had returned to his face. "I cannot make that promise, Dr. Gachet, for I know that you will try to keep me from doing away with myself. But it may be the only hope I have left." I must have looked uncomprehending, since he went on. "The hope that I can at least limit my suffering. This is my greatest comfort. Good night, Doctor."

It took all my concentration to get down the narrow stair. In the back hall behind the café, I encountered Ravoux. "Everything all right up there, Doctor?" he asked me.

"Oh, yes, thank you, Ravoux," I said. "Good night." I escaped out the back door and began my walk home.

I was dimly aware that it was a magnificent night. The stars frosted the sky, and I had the momentary impulse to go back upstairs, bring Vincent down and point upward. "Look! Look at that! Paint that!" I would say. "Isn't it beautiful? Only you can create a beauty to match it!" I could imagine the painting so clearly, with a surface of ultramarine and Prussian blue covering the canvas in flowing strokes, and each yellow star surrounded by a halo of white or lemon yellow. The chestnut trees, cluster after cluster of ribbed, almond-shaped leaves, would be viridian, perhaps, with some umber mixed in. The soft, dusty surface of the road . . .

But he had made himself very clear. No stars, no flowers, no disconsolate elderly doctors would be enough to keep him anchored among us. His pain, he felt, was too great to be borne. And he had given me what amounted to a warning that he might take his own life.

Yet severing oneself from life is not a matter of whim. It often requires an inventiveness and a strength of will that are not available to those in greatest pain. We saw many failed efforts at Bicêtre and at the Salpêtrière: ineptly fashioned nooses, ingestion of the most improbable substances. I remembered that Vincent had already tried to drink lamp oil and had eaten paint. Had those been earnest attempts to die or merely deranged gestures? He seemed earnest now. Was his mind already ranging over his options? There was one he was ignorant of, tucked away in my house, where he refused to come anymore. It chilled me to think that I was in a position to provide the only kind of help Vincent seemed to want now. He had not asked for it. There was no need for him to know that I could supply it. There was no reason for me to think back to the time when I had been asked for such help—and denied it. No reason, though I knew that moment had set the course of my life ever since.

I carried the lantern low at my left side. The circle of light quivered. I held my right hand to my eye to see if it shook, but of course I could not see it in the dark—old, sad doctor that I was. Too fuddled to think clearly. Hands trembling with age, or weakness, or emotion.

I had come to a halt next to a paddock where a farming family kept a pair of plow horses. I heard them rustling in the grass next to me. One nickered, as if to ask who I was. I stepped to the verge and raised the lantern. The long white, whiskered face hovered over the fence, examining me. I held out a hand and felt the beast's warm, moist breath. Life wasn't easy for old César, dragging a wooden plow through the heavy, fertile soil of the nearby fields. I brushed his muzzle with the back of my forefinger, then rubbed the broad, hard space between his eyes. He pressed forward and shoved his head against my chest, rubbing it up and down as if I were a convenient scratching post. I was glad enough, at that moment, to be serving some purpose. But then he ambled away and disappeared into the darkness, cropping a few mouthfuls of grass as he went.

I turned back to the road, trying to brush César's white hairs from my linen coat. When I reached my house, it was as quiet and still as any of the cottages I had passed on the way. I lighted the chamber candle Madame Chevalier had left for me at the bottom of the stairs and climbed up to my bedroom. No light shone from any of the other bedrooms. Although everyone was asleep, I felt the need to be silent. I did not want to be interrupted. I pulled a chair over to the armoire and clambered up onto it, steadying myself against the door. The top shelf held garments I did not use often: a rubberized mackintosh, a coarse muffler knit by Marguerite when she was nine. Behind them lay a flat wooden box that I could just reach with the tips of my fingers. I pulled it forward and carefully dismounted from the chair, holding it beneath my arm.

Twenty years earlier, when I was forty-two, I had served in the National Guard as the Germans swept westward across France toward Paris. We were all issued rifles, each one numbered and registered. I had never thought about weapons before then. I drilled with my rifle, of course, and learned how to load and clean it, but I was a perfectly dreadful shot and grateful never to have to use the gun in battle. I turned it in as required, once the German siege of Paris was lifted. But I still had the revolver.

It was not a government-issued gun. I had come across it on patrol one night, when my unit surprised a small band of looters attempting to break into the cellar of an ironmonger's shop. My commanding officer said I should keep it. "You may yet need a sidearm," he told me. So in my military fervor I did keep it, and furthermore took care of it. It lay in the box, as it had for two decades, with a small pouch of cartridges alongside. They clicked together when I brushed against the pouch.

What was I doing, in my bedroom after midnight, mooning over an outdated weapon? I lifted the gun from the box. My fingers curled naturally around the butt—a revolver is one of those objects whose shape tells you how to use it. It was unloaded. I slipped a cartridge from the pouch and broke open the gun, pressing the cartridge into the barrel. I put my palm under the barrel and raised it until I heard the click as it closed. Then I was sitting on my bed with a loaded gun.

I could take it out into the fields and fire it. I could unload it and put it away.

I could wait to hear about Vincent's suicide attempt. I could wait to know how he did it: poison? A knife? The river?

I could wait to receive the news of an attempt, and rush to find him, wounded, ill, impaired.

I could—someone could—just hand him the gun. As if to say, "Here you are, Monsieur van Gogh, there is no need to prolong your existence, here is an easy way, an efficient way, to ensure that you are a problem no more."

No, I could not do it. I could not put the means of self-destruction into his hands. I felt all the pity in the world for him. But it seemed that to aid him in this would be to concur in his opinion that his existence was worthless. That, of course, was impossible.

I felt some relief as I pried the cartridge from the barrel of the gun and wrapped everything back up. It was so late and I was so tired that I did not replace the box in its hiding place in the armoire, but rather slid it under my bed. I slept well that night.

Fifteen

Both Vincent and Theo seemed convinced that Jo should not know about Theo's illness, and perhaps they were right to try to protect her. The situation had been different with Blanche and me, because I was a doctor. I could not ignore the signs of consumption, yet when she first became ill, we did not discuss her health. Not long after we married, she became subject to coughs, and sometimes she had a fever at the end of the day. I occasionally saw her watching me as I turned away from her to dampen a cloth with cologne to cool her or to pour some cordial into a glass of water to calm her cough. I never quite caught the expression in her eyes, but I thought it was compassion. I understand now that she saw how her illness would end and pitied me.

I was a doctor; caring for this woman, ill with a weak chest, should have been quite routine. Yet it was not. I called in another physician, my friend Sémerie, but we both knew what ailed Blanche and how little we could do about it.

What we did not know—could not know—was the exact form her sickness would take. Blanche was not gravely ill. Sometimes she was quite pale, and sometimes she needed a great deal of rest. At other times she seemed to be perfectly well. As I had seen in the hospitals, consumption could be swift or slow, could appear to vanish then recur, could develop first in the lungs and spread to the bones or vice versa. Somehow Blanche and I agreed, without speaking of it, to act as if the illness did not exist.

It was a good plan. It allowed us a great deal of happiness. Blanche took a lively interest in my work and in my artistic activities as well. We went together to the Salon of 1870, and I was struck by her taste in paintings, which was remarkably advanced for someone who judged by instinct alone. I wrote a series of reviews of the Salon, incorporating her opinions along with my own. As a compliment to her, I signed it "B. de Mézin." Mézin was the name of the town near the Pyrenees where her father's family lived. She was delighted when she held the pamphlet in her hands for the first time.

But Blanche did not get stronger, and once she began coughing blood, we could no longer pretend. In some ways it made life easier, because we could make decisions based on her health without having to invent rationales. I bought the house in Auvers quite simply to get her into the countryside. The air out there was so much cleaner than in Paris that her health improved right away. I continued to travel into town for my practice, staying for two or three nights each week, while Blanche and Marguerite remained in the country. They both loved the garden, and as the summer of 1873 flowed past, I became hopeful. Often the two of them would meet me at the train, and they both seemed to flourish like the blooms on our rosebushes, plumper and pinker each week.

And then, as a culmination of my happiness, my son, Paul, was born that summer. Blanche had been quite well in the previous year or so, and in any event pregnancy often arrests the development of consumption. Blanche feared for Paul, since it is widely believed that tuberculosis runs in families. Because both her mother and her elder brother had died of the disease, she was difficult to reassure. But like his sister, Marguerite, Paul thrived in the healthy atmosphere of Auvers.

As the children flourished, Blanche began to fade. I still wonder what signs I may have missed. Consumption, after all, was such a familiar illness to all of us. Did I overlook a symptom that could have predicted its return: pallor, unusual gaiety, shortness of breath? Was she trying to hide her illness from me, or was she as surprised as I was by what happened on the day Paul fell down the stairs?

Paul walked early, before he was a year old, and he was impossible to restrain. The terraces surrounding the house were a constant danger to the unsteady little fellow, but it was the long flight of stairs outside the front door that tripped him up on that day. The nursemaid whom we had hired to help Madame Chevalier had turned away for a moment only, but that was long enough for the boy to stagger out the door to the top of the steps.

Blanche saw him from the second-story window and called out to the nursemaid, who naturally turned her head toward the house. In that moment, Paul tumbled down the first of the sharp-edged slate steps. Blanche raced down the stairs of the house and flew across the front garden. I heard her from the studio and followed. When I arrived outside, I saw Paul, sobbing, with blood on his pinafore. Marguerite and the nursemaid were sobbing, too. My wife, her face the color of paper, was perfectly still, collapsed on the steps just below the baby. As I darted down the steps to her, Blanche lifted her head, and I saw the brilliant scarlet trickling down her chin, blossoming on her blouse. Her eyes met mine, and I understood instantly. The blood on Paul was not his but hers, coughed up. The baby was angry, and there was a bruise coming up already on his almost hairless head, but he was barely hurt. The real injury lay elsewhere: Blanche's remission was clearly at an end.

Paul was the first to stop crying, and once his stained clothes were removed, his sister was able to dry her tears. The nursemaid was eventually coaxed into believing that she would not be turned out into the street. Blanche and I could not talk about her health until that evening, and there was little to say in any event. The illness had come back. The cavities formed in her lungs had reached some of the larger blood vessels.

She might still have recovered. I had seen patients who lived for years after hemorrhages. Blanche certainly tried. She drank milk from our goat though she hated it. She rested in the afternoon, swallowed doses of this cordial or that as Sémerie prescribed them—she wanted so very much to get well. But she got steadily worse. On some summer days I am still startled by the light falling in a certain way or the scent of the boxwood in the garden—they prompt in me a sharp burst of misery, an echo from those months when Blanche's health deteriorated. We did our best to be cheerful for the children. Marguerite was a bright little girl who loved to make out her letters, so Blanche would draw them over and over on a slate. Soon Marguerite could string the letters together into short words: "Mama, Papa, Paul, *chat, chien.*" Paul seemed to put all of his energies into movement. He still spoke very little but seemed to get exactly what he wanted with gestures and a charming smile. Those hours in the garden spent trying to forget how ill Blanche was were so sweet but so sad.

Her energy faded with the summer sun. By October she tired much more quickly and her cough worsened. The Oise makes winters damp in Auvers. Many tubercular patients seem to improve in the mountains; the dry air is easier to breathe and may arrest the decay of the lungs. I thought of the Alps for Blanche. But she wanted to go south, to Pau, which was at least near her cousins and grandparents.

So Pau it was. We made quite a party, Blanche, Marguerite, Paul, the nursemaid, and I. The children had never been on such a long voyage and Marguerite was enchanted by the train and the landscape flashing by outside the windows. As we traveled farther and farther south, I began to recognize the fellow sufferers among our passengers. Some of them had the telltale pallor, others had the equally characteristic flushed cheeks—it is typical of the disease that two such contradictory appearances should both be symptoms. The consumptives coughed, sometimes with that hopeless, spongy sound that betrays the destruction of the lung tissue. And, if they were accompanied, all of their companions bore the same stricken expression in their eyes.

I had secured a furnished apartment, and I stayed in the little town for a week to see my family settled. I met the doctor who would take care of Blanche and tried to describe my wife's state with detachment, as if she were any other patient. I know I failed miserably, for as we parted he gripped my hand and my shoulder, saying, "I will do everything I can, Gachet, you may be sure of that."

I believe he did. Nevertheless I received a letter from him in March 1875 suggesting that I should come to Pau to bring my wife home. I understood what he did not say: If she wanted to die at home, she must be moved soon.

When I arrived in Pau, I was horrified. Blanche was very weak, and in considerable pain. The disease had progressed to her throat, so she could do little more than whisper. Swallowing so much as a mouthful of water hurt her terribly. I was anxious to get her back to Paris as quickly as possible but even more concerned that she was no longer strong enough to travel. I was angry with the Pau doctor, thinking that he should have summoned me sooner, but he explained that my wife had forbidden it. "She wanted so desperately to get well," he told me. "She did everything I suggested, so eagerly. . . . She thought the air here did her good." He paused, and shrugged. "You know how important it is to keep these patients happy."

I could not blame him. There is no good way to deliver a death sentence. I have often noticed that hope of recovery is among the most powerful medicines we doctors possess, but like every potent dose, it must be administered with care. I will readily admit Blanche was stronger than I in this instance. She persevered without hope for months, protecting me from the truth.

In the end, we sent the nursemaid ahead to Auvers with the children. They were both quiet and frightened, kissing their mother's cheek lightly before leaving for the station. As they walked out into the hall, it was all too easy to imagine them in the black clothes they would soon be wearing. I have always hated seeing children dressed in mourning, and soon they would be my own.

At first I thought I should take Blanche north in slow stages, sleeping in hotels along the way, but it seemed less tiring for her simply to go straight to Auvers. It was a strange kind of traveling sickroom we created, rattling along the tracks the length of France. There is always a sense, when you are caring for the gravely ill, that the world becomes very small. Life goes on outside—we dimly hear voices and footsteps and bells and clattering dishes—but it matters much less than every hard-won breath and every precious heartbeat.

Blanche had not reached that point—yet. This was not a death watch. It was that much stranger thing, a voyage to the death watch. She was awake, and aware of me as I did my best to make her comfortable. She could still smile. Speaking was difficult, though. The Pau doctor had told me that the disease was attacking her larynx. She would not have a voice for much longer.

On our first night in the train, I ate a proper dinner and tried to feed her some soup. She was very thin, and she worked hard to swallow, to please me. Solid food was out of the question. I removed my coat and put on a dressing gown, then helped her to take off her gray traveling suit. She could still manage the tiny buttons down the front, but she had left off wearing stays while she was in Pau. I suppose the free movement of her rib cage might have made it easier for her to breathe. I folded her clothes and helped her clamber between the sheets the porter had put on the folding bed.

"You won't come in with me?" she whispered, clasping my wrist as I tucked the blanket beneath her.

"No, my dear, I'll sleep over there," I said, pointing to my narrow bed. She didn't let my arm go but put out her other hand and clasped mine.

"Paul, I know I'm dying," she said. "This was how my mother died." She paused, and tried to sit up. Sometimes the pressure of diseased matter in her larynx eased if she were more upright. I put my hands under her armpits and lifted her to lean against the pillows. The lamp by the bed was the only light in the train compartment, though out the window the moon was full. It shone on the ranks of pine trees as we sped through a forest, with the contours of the hills rising and falling outside the window.

"I know it will be painful," Blanche continued, renewing her clasp on my hand. Her dark eyes burned large in her thin face. "Will you help me?"

"Of course I will," I promised, puzzled that she should ask. "I will do everything I can. You know that."

"I don't mean laudanum," she whispered, looking up at me. I gazed back, uncomprehending.

"And morphine as well," I said. "If you need it. You may not."

She still looked. She shook her head slightly. Then her breath caught, and she was seized by a spasm of coughing. By now this entailed a wretched procedure of basins and spitting and retching, ending with panting exhaustion. As I busied myself, my mind spun. What could Blanche mean?

She lay back now, propped up with her eyes closed. I had turned off the lamp, thinking that she might sleep, but the train tracks had come around so that the moon now shone directly in the window, casting a broad silver ribbon across the table, floor, and bed. I moved over to the window to lower the blind, but her voice came like a thread: "Don't."

I went back to the bedside and knelt on the floor beside her. "I thought you might sleep now."

"Not yet," she whispered. "The moon is lovely."

"It is," I agreed and held her hand. Her skin was dry and hot beneath my fingertips.

"My mother begged me," she breathed, with her eyes closed. "She begged at the end." My mind was moving slowly, I could tell. I knew I was supposed to understand what she was saying, but I could not. I was aware of my knees on the thin carpet of the train compartment, the stiff linen sheets, the vibration as we rolled over the tracks. Blanche opened her eyes and sat as upright as she could. She glared at me with a passion that seemed alien to her. My wife had always been sweet and placid, but the disease seemed to have burned away that docility. She willed my eyes to meet hers and willed me to understand.

And suddenly, I did. Blanche's mother had wanted help dying.

"And did you?" I blurted out, without thinking. Instantly I would have done anything to take the words back. I did not want to know. I did not want to hear, or see—but she nodded again, fierce and proud, a woman I did not know.

A woman who had hastened her mother's death.

No. A woman who had killed her mother.

I have never been good at hiding my feelings, and that night the moonlight must have revealed my shock, for Blanche took both of my hands in her own and explained like a parent reassuring a child, but with long pauses. "She had only a day or so to live. Perhaps hours. Every breath was a torture. I took from her hours of terrible pain. That was all."

I did not answer. I was horrified.

"You do the same each time you give me laudanum," she went on. "You take away the pain."

"But life itself! To dare!"

This time she shrugged, again a tiny gesture. "What is it then? Life? When it is only agony, why not take it? Is that not the kinder thing?"

"But it's not for us, there's always hope," I babbled. There was no hope in Blanche's case, we both knew. I turned back to her.

She was looking at me with such pity. For a moment it was as if I were the patient waiting for good news, and she the doctor with the death sentence. "There is no hope," she whispered. "There is a little bit of time, and a great deal of pain. That is what the rest of my life consists of." There was no bitterness as she said it, or any effort to convince me, no urging or wheedling. Simply a statement.

"But it is not for us to decide," I said, aware that I was repeating myself. I thought about the assertion again. Did I believe what I was saying? I stood up and stepped to the window. Trees whipped past, quickly enough to make me dizzy. Their tops were silvered, their bodies black. The moon was so bright that the stars all around it were eclipsed. It was a small, cold sun.

"You don't believe in God," came the whisper behind me.

"No," I answered, without turning around. "I don't."

"So you would not be sinning."

"No," I had to agree.

"Then?"

"I swore an oath when I became a doctor. We vow to protect life," I said. I had no idea what I meant.

"When did you ever care for an oath?"

I turned and went back to the bed. "Perhaps this is the only one. Perhaps that is why I feel I must uphold it." I knelt, my arms on the bed and my head cradled on them. I could feel her fingers in my hair, delicate as moths.

She was waiting, but I could not answer. I could not agree to what she wanted, but I could not explain why. All I knew was that when I began to imagine doing what she asked, I felt a wave of revulsion. I could not contemplate it. My mind flinched away.

"All right" came the thread of her voice. "You cannot do it."

I looked up at her, and I could feel tears falling onto my hands. My children have always teased me about how easily I weep—much too easily for a man—but it was not always so. It started that night, in the train, in the moonlight. Since then the tears have always been close to the surface. Her fingers wandered over my face, trying to smooth out the furrow between my eyebrows, wiping one cheek and then the other.

"I should not have asked," she said at length. "Sometimes I forget that you are a doctor."

"If I cannot heal you, what is that worth? What am I then?" Even I could hear the anguish in my question.

"A good man, Paul. A good husband. A good father. Those are the things you are to me. Other things to other people."

She fell asleep with the suddenness of the invalid, and said nothing else for several hours. When she woke, the moon was setting on the other side of the train and we had moved into a rocky, irregular landscape that seemed hostile to life. She asked for water, and lay back on her pillow after drinking. I watched her after that, as she lay propped up contemplating the window without expression. She seemed peaceful.

We never spoke again about what she had asked of me. She remained, as she had always been, affectionate and sweet-tempered. She never got bitter or angry, as some patients do when they are in pain. There was something maternal about her attitude toward me during those last weeks. It was as though our whispered conversation in the moonlit train had revealed a weakness in me, a childlike flaw for which she must make allowances.

She spent a month in Auvers, watching April paint the countryside endless variations on green, and drinking in the sight of the children playing with the ducklings and chicks in the garden. But by early May,

Blanche was ill enough to become frightening to the children, and I wanted her to be closer to Dr. Sémerie, so I moved her to Paris.

In the last days, the illness moved into her pleura, the sacs encasing her lungs. Each breath was a ragged, agonized torture. None of us slept—not the nurse I'd hired, or Dr. Sémerie, who kept watch with us. Certainly Blanche did not sleep. You could see her eyes fall closed and her entire body relax, then the need for oxygen overcame the exhaustion. Willy-nilly the breath would start again, her eyes would open to an expression of hopeless anguish, and the air would rush into what was left of her windpipe, rattling past the clots of bloody sputum, into her wrecked lungs, and then force its way back out. Agony in, agony out. Thousands of times a day.

We gave her laudanum, though it was difficult for her to swallow it. The doses got higher. It did not seem to relieve the pain, it just made dying easier to bear. I worried about the not-too-distant day when the ruin of her throat would make swallowing impossible. How long after that would she survive?

She had been right, on the train. The last two days of her life were merely dreadful pain. There was nothing else. Nothing for any of us, sitting in chairs beside the bed, holding her clawlike hands, brushing her now-brittle hair off her skull of a face. She didn't speak. She could not have spoken, there was nothing left of her voice box. I don't know if she was conscious. I hope she was not. I have hoped that for nearly thirty years.

I did not help her on her way.

Sixteen

ANOTHER DAY PASSED. Nothing happened. I wondered if I had been wrong to rush back to Auvers, yet I could not escape the conviction that my presence there might avert disaster. No news of Vincent reached me at home, so on Saturday, in the heat of midday, I went down to Ravoux's. I found the proprietor taking delivery of a dozen barrels of wine, but he spared a moment to tell me that Vincent had not departed from his routine. "He leaves in the morning, comes home in the evening for his supper," Ravoux said. "He's quiet, but he's always been quiet."

"And he went out this morning as usual?"

"As usual, Doctor, with his box and his canvas and his straw hat. More holes than straw, that hat."

"Thank you, Ravoux. I will just leave a note for him in the shed, if you don't mind."

"Be my guest, Doctor. You know your way."

Despite the commotion just outside in the yard, the shed was silent.

I had not been there in daylight since Theo and Jo's visit, and I was astounded to see the number of paintings that Vincent had finished since then. There was a magnificent sunset and several canvases of ripe wheat beneath dark, damp skies. I was happy to see these—surely they had been painted this week? Yet when I looked at them closely, the paint appeared to be somewhat dry. I reached out to one and touched the bottom corner. I was not wrong. I went from canvas to canvas, peering at their surfaces, touching the edges of the stretchers, sniffing for the odor of fresh linseed oil.

Not one painting had been finished in at least a week. The most recent one, it seemed to me, was a scene of wheat fields. The horizon was high, as if Vincent had placed himself looking uphill. His usual active strokes were quite coarse, the paint almost spooned onto the canvas and arranged in thick ruts. Three crude paths seemed to diverge in front of the viewer, but none appeared to have a destination. Above the fields, the sky shaded from blue to black. The black was the last pigment Vincent had used. It rolled over the sky from the top of the canvas, slashing downward over the blue and closing in on the horizon. Between, there were dozens of black V shapes, as if a flock of huge crows were flying off into the distance. Or perhaps flapping their way toward the viewer? It was dreadfully ominous, and I could not help remembering Vincent's disturbing behavior with the black paint on the palette. Could this have been the last painting he finished before that episode?

Thinned white paint brushed on over the blue sky made a pair of clouds. One of the largest crows was caught up in the cloud, it seemed. Here the white had been applied after the black. A few inches away, the blue dashes of the sky invaded the golden dashes of the wheat, cutting a gash in the horizon. I could imagine Vincent standing with his palette, thinning the white, stroking it onto the blue sky, blending it into a cloud formation, like rain mixed into the air. It was lively, arresting, agitated. It was also dry on the surface.

I stepped back, freeing myself from the spell of the menacing clouds, and looked around the room. The boards laid across barrels that had served as a table were cluttered with Vincent's painting apparatus. Was everything dustier than usual? I could not be sure. The brushes were dry. I picked up a rag and touched a blue spot—it was crusted over. I sniffed, and wondered if the shed usually smelled more sharply of paints and oils. I was desperate to find evidence that the painter had recently used any of his materials.

And I found it. One corner of the table was partially hidden by an empty easel. The surface of the table was clear, but darker than the rest of the unfinished boards. When I stepped closer, I could see that it had been painted over with a dark color. That corner of the room was in shadow, and I admit that my eyes, like those of many an older man, were getting weaker. I had to bend down to see that the paint looked like the mixed black and blue of the sky from the wheat fields canvas. I was puzzled for a moment—why would Vincent paint the table? It occurred to me, then, that he had perhaps brought the canvas home from the fields and set it on the easel. He might then have wanted to darken the sky, and used the table as a makeshift palette.

I braced myself on the table and my finger slipped. The paint was wet. I straightened up and looked at the color on my fingertips. It was thickened, no longer slick. A day or two old. Once again I leaned down and peered at the dark patch on the table, which had an irregular, lighter pattern that I could not quite make out. When it came into focus, I saw that it was writing. Vincent had used the blunt end of his brush to inscribe a message in the wet pigments. He had written, "It is finished."

I felt a jolt as I read it. It was like glimpsing him by the train tracks, but tenfold, a physical blow. "It is finished!" I was as untutored in Scripture as a man could be in Catholic France, yet even I knew the source of those words—they were Jesus' dying statement on the cross.

I stood there, my paint-marked hand held out from my side, looking at the inscription. When I straightened up, I could barely see it. He had been careful in the writing—the letters were evenly sized, evenly spaced, almost childish in their rounded contours. I looked to my left to see if I could find the brush he had used. It would have told me nothing, but I felt compelled to move. I scrabbled through the brushes lying on the table, but none had a telltale cap of black on the end. My mind was racing, racing, but no thought connected to another. Was he dead? Had he killed himself?

I had to find him. I had to speak to him.

It was another hot day, and I dreaded trudging up the hill once again to find Vincent in the glare of the afternoon sun, but I did not think of delaying. Maybe I could no longer help him as a doctor, but I could still be a friend. Surely a friend could help a man in such distress.

These thoughts hastened my step, and it was not long before I saw his figure perched at the top of the rise in that immense field of wheat. I was reminded of the painting that he had covered with a flock of crows, but in fact, there was nothing ominous in sight that afternoon. The heads of grain were glossy and plump as I pushed through them, and the cicadas' buzz drowned out the rustling of my passage through the wheat. Vincent must have heard me coming far in advance, but he did not turn around, even when I stood behind him and greeted him.

"Is it wise for you to be out here, Vincent? Perhaps since you could not paint here last week, you should try a different place. Down by the river, for instance," I suggested, trying to keep my voice light. Though the scene was exactly as it had been a week earlier, Vincent's own appearance was frightening now that I saw him in daylight. He was slumped on his ancient camp stool, but his easel still lay folded beside him. The canvas that lay on top of it was blank except for a frieze of grubby fingerprints along the edges. The primed surface was dingy all over. It looked as if he had been carrying it around all week.

"I don't know, Doctor," Vincent confessed, without changing his position. "I wonder if I have ever been wise." Then he turned around and looked up at me. Beneath the brim of his tattered hat, he was haggard, unshaved, terribly thin, and his eyes were bloodshot.

I bent down to move the easel out of the way and sat where it had been lying. This was not a graceful process; I was far too old to be lowering myself to the ground without something to lean on. I found I had to grasp Vincent's knee, and I ended up with the dirty, blank canvas on my lap. "I see it has not been going well," I said, setting the canvas aside.

"No, Doctor, not well."

"Yet here you are," I said.

"Yes." He paused. "I do not know where else to go."

"Have you been sleeping well?" I asked, an apparent non sequitur.

He shook his head and looked down at his clasped hands. "That is not really possible."

"Why not?"

"I don't know," Vincent replied, sounding surprised. "I lie there. The village is quiet. I cherished that quiet when I first came here. You cannot imagine what a luxury that was to me, after St.-Rémy! All night long there, men cried out or sang or battled their demons or merely snored. In Auvers, peace reigns. Yet I cannot sleep."

"I can take care of that," I told him. "I can give you something to bring on sleep. As your doctor I insist on it."

He did not answer. He merely sighed and lowered his head to his chest. "If I could die by never sleeping again, I would do it. Or, if I could, I would go to sleep forever." He straightened up and looked at me. "An entire night is endless, Doctor. The hours of that silence I so longed for seem to last forever. There is so much that torments me. What is to become of Jo and the baby? What will happen to my canvases? I do not even worry about myself anymore. The entity of Vincent seems entirely . . ." He flicked his hand, as if whisking something away. "Impermanent. Fleeting. I cannot imagine my future. And then, worse than the night is the moment when the sky begins to lighten, for then I understand that I must somehow endure another day."

"Could the day bring nothing worth living for?" I asked, almost whispering.

"What?" he asked, nodding at the blank canvas. "Not that. It will not come back."

"How can you know?"

"It is not that I know. But I can no longer afford to hope." He turned all the way around on his stool now, so that he was facing me squarely. I had to look up at his face, haloed by the tattered straw brim. It was an image that will stay with me forever: the staring eyes, the stubbled, sunken cheeks. "There must have come a time in your life, Doctor, when you had to stop hoping." I instantly thought of Blanche, and the grim voyage home from Pau. "I can see from your face that there was," Vincent continued. "At a certain moment, you understand that the anticipation that had kept you alive has suddenly become a terrible bur-

den. It must be set down. I have not come to this lightly. I have hoped
and hoped for so long now. It has always seemed to me that if I could
only paint, my life, all the difficulties, would be redeemed. I painted,
and trusted that someday my work would be understood." He bent
down and picked up the canvas and held it out to the side, so that we
could both see it and the beautiful landscape beyond. "Painting was my
one escape. I have tried not to pity myself, though my life has been
hard. If I cannot paint, there must be an end to it. There is no reason for
me to draw breath."

He said all of this so simply, without trying to gain my sympathy. I
could not imagine his despair. I knew nothing of his loneliness. But I
had given up hope, and I knew what that meant.

"I wish . . ." My voice trailed off. I could not say just what I wished—
only that things were otherwise, for I understood that I was approaching a terrible juncture.

Neither of us finished the sentence. Vincent lay the blank canvas
facedown on the golden wheat.

I wished that Vincent could paint, of course. I wished for more glorious pictures of the world I knew, pictures that helped me understand
it and that altered the way I saw everything around me. I wished Vincent would paint the wheat fields under the snow—imagine how lovely
they would be! The golden stubble and low gray sky and the patches of
snow that, in Vincent's eyes, would be not white at all but something
else, lavender perhaps, or pink.

I could wish that of the artist. But it was also my friend who sat before me, the very image of desolation. If he had painted a self-portrait
at that moment, it would have been so full of agony that you could do
no more than glance at it. To look longer would have been harrowing.

My mind was boiling. I felt as if the very earth were heaving. I stood
up, once again using Vincent's wiry body as a prop. I felt compelled to
act or at least to move while my thoughts ran wild. I did not want to be
entertaining the idea that overwhelmed me. Somehow a massive rever-
sal had occurred. I had come churning up to the hilltop to prevent Vincent from taking his life, but now, it seemed, I felt he should be free to
do so.

I had entertained such dark thoughts before. There were times, after Blanche died, when nonexistence beckoned me. In those days I understood the melancholiacs I had known at the asylum, drifting barely sentient hour by hour. Eternal rest—for that is what the church promises—takes on a powerful allure. Is death like laudanum? A comfortable, muffled darkness? There have been times when I longed for that. A dose of morphine would so easily have freed me. I could go from pain to no pain, and I found myself deeply tempted.

Yet I had children. It was that simple. I was required to live for my children, and I have not regretted it. Life has brought me many pleasures, many riches. But is there an absolute moral value to living, as opposed to dying? To this day, as my own death naturally approaches, I do not know.

I walked a few steps away from Vincent, then walked back to stand before him. No words came. I strode farther away, some distance down the hill, but my eyes did not even see the green and gold landscape unfurling before me. I clambered back up the hill. No rational thought drove me, and I could formulate no speech. I paused before Vincent, who was still crouched on his stool in his pose of dejection. I opened my mouth to say something, then closed it. I reached out and gripped his shoulder. He did not look up from the ground, but his hand came to cover mine for a moment. Then I walked away. My feet took me down the hill through the wheat field, away from him.

I paced around the countryside of Auvers that afternoon, as Vincent probably had done in his quest for motifs to paint. Sometimes I came across scenes that could have been cut from one of his canvases and nailed to the horizon. How could Vincent contemplate leaving a world that cried out for him to paint it? I was only vaguely aware of the continuing heat and of the sun gliding lower, the shadows thickening.

I did not think of Vincent constantly. My mind wandered, alighting on the strangest things. I wondered whether I would ever receive the Legion of Honor, for example. I thought again about somehow finding a husband for Marguerite. I remembered that the mint was threatening to overwhelm the other herbs in the garden, and needed to be thinned.

Every now and then my mind would tiptoe up to the subject of Vincent and dart away. I thought a great deal about Blanche.

I distinctly remembered a moment, several days before she died, when her breathing grew slow and her pulse very weak. She was next to death at that point. Yet something in her body, or perhaps in her spirit—I will never know which—gathered strength. I was crestfallen when I realized that she had rallied. I caught myself wishing she had died. Surely it is a tiny step from there to easing a departure?

Yet these thoughts repulsed me. There was a barrier that I could not cross. I could not have given Blanche a heroic dose of morphine. Fragile as the thread of life was in her, I could not have cut it. Nor, I realized, could I actively promote Vincent's death.

There it was, Vincent's death. The end of Vincent van Gogh. I kept the thought in my mind for an instant. No more heated discussions about artists. No more wondering what he might say next. No more alarm mixed with admiration. No frustration, wonder, respect. Vincent believed in the power of art, *his* art, to console people for the sorrows inherent in life. Making his beautiful paintings comforted him, and they comforted me. If Vincent killed himself, there would be no more of them.

When. When Vincent killed himself. I vowed to myself, for that moment at least, to try to face the facts as Vincent did. The man had just bid me farewell.

I was tired, so I turned toward home from the top of the plateau, where I had been wandering. Vincent was not asking for my help. Vincent was not asking for *anything* from me. He was simply explaining. Perhaps he was absolving me, too, for it had to be faced: I had not saved him.

I was in the woods at this point, and I had to sit down. There was a fallen tree leaning against a live trunk and I perched against it, bracing myself and trying to catch my breath. I thought of the months he had been in Auvers. I considered the inn, the portraits, the meals, the conversations. They were not insignificant. Vincent had painted many pictures here. He had been pleased with them, and these paintings would not have existed without me. Other paintings probably would have, but not these. I could fairly say that I had done that much at least.

But I had done nothing at all to improve Vincent's mental health. I thought back to my original meeting with Theo, and how confident I had been that I could help Vincent regain his equanimity. My failure was devastating. I had failed Vincent as I had failed Blanche.

When I got home, Madame Chevalier fussed about my trousers and made me drink some lemonade. There were still hours until dinner, so I went into the garden. Nero lay under a bush with his tongue hanging out, and Pekin the pug panted next to him. At the back of the garden is a kind of cave, an abandoned quarry cut into the steep hill rising behind the house. We used it to store garden tools and the animals' feed. I went in to find a wire brush and had to step over several cats lounging against the stone walls to absorb their coolness. The big gray one, Louloutte, followed me out of the cave like a puff of smoke.

I settled onto a low chair, and Louloutte sprang into my lap. I held the brush out with my hand, and she rubbed her head against it, again and again, purring. Then she nudged my hand so that I would brush the other side, running the tines against her cheek. Her eyes were closed and her body perfectly relaxed.

Sometimes the only comfort to be had is physical. You cannot look to a cat for sympathy, and very few are affectionate, but Louloutte's soft weight on my lap, her constant purr, and the rhythmic strokes of the brush provided a simple consolation. Hot as I was, her additional warmth soothed me. At least I was able to make a cat happy.

When she leapt to the ground, I sat with my hands folded over the brush, head tilted back against the chair, and fell asleep. I was wakened moments later by my jaw dropping open, and an insistent nudge on my calf. I looked down and saw Pekin gazing up at me looking heartbroken. He butted my calf again and snorted, then launched himself into my lap to replace the cat.

Pekin was no larger than Louloutte but so muscular that he seemed a bigger burden. He was not content simply to present areas of his body to my brush as Louloutte had—he nudged, he licked, he lifted his chin and howled, his hindquarters wagged his curly tail. His every motion said, "Here I am! Love me!" Even when I finally tipped him onto the ground, he settled next to my ankle, gazing up at me hopefully. Pekin's life was a continuous festival of confident expectation: food, affection, food, affection, surely they would come his way soon and lavishly.

I dozed again, or perhaps I fell into a trance. I imagined Vincent's continued existence: more days up on the hillside, with that blank canvas becoming more grimy every day but never receiving a brushstroke of paint. Vincent getting thinner, more tense, more bizarre. Vincent in the grip of a hysterical fit, rolling, thrashing, shouting, alone in the fields or on the village street. How would I feel, how would Theo feel, watching Vincent suffer all of this? Meanwhile, Theo would be suffering trials of his own: pain, paralysis, even madness. Vincent would have to go back to an asylum; there would be no other choice. I remembered my fantasies about supporting Vincent on my own, or with the help of other artists. Nonsense. There was no money. I could not afford to take him to Dr. Charcot for a private consultation. If—or rather, when—Vincent fell into his pattern of attacks, I could not responsibly prevent his being sent away.

I dwelt for a moment on the idea of Vincent in an asylum, of visiting him, with Theo dead and Johanna back in Holland. Vincent without family in France, in despair. He would have to be watched, perhaps restrained. I pictured Vincent in a straitjacket, shuffling along a dingy stone corridor. His hands would be trapped, his arms crossed over his belly. His eyes alone would be free. That might go on for years. I had seen it often enough at Bicêtre and at the Salpêtrière: Fewer than a third of the patients ever left. Most of them simply stayed, passing the rest of their lives in what was effectively a prison. This stopped me for a moment. Would it not be kinder simply to allow every madman to kill himself? Should they not all be spared that life of imprisonment? But I knew I could not make my considerations more general. I could not think about every case, only about Vincent.

So, then, what if he died? No, I must not mitigate the situation. What if Vincent killed himself? We would all grieve, that was certain. We would regret—oh, *how* we would regret—the loss of his genius.

But would I feel relief for him? Would I be a little bit happy that his misery had ended?

That wasn't what I wanted. I wanted him to get better. I wanted him to pick up that shabby canvas, brush new primer over it, and cover it with paint. I did not want him starving himself to death, believing he was saving the world with his hunger. I did not want him raging around an asylum in the grip of hallucinations. I did not want him throwing himself in front of a train or jumping from a high bridge, and maiming himself yet falling short of death. I knew these decisions were not mine to make. Yet with increasing insistence I thought of the gun in my house.

I tried to brush the animals' fur off my jacket and trousers before I went into the house. Madame Chevalier and Marguerite both cried out when I walked through the kitchen, and Marguerite firmly turned me around and pushed me back outdoors. "Wait here, Papa," she told me and went back for a damp cloth. "How can you even touch those creatures in this heat?" she asked, sponging off the gray and white hairs.

"You know how insistent Pekin can be," I explained.

"You must take these things off," she continued, shaking her head. "You can't come to the table like this. Go up and change, and bring these down. I'll brush them properly after dinner." I nodded and escaped to my bedroom.

Before I changed my clothes, I had to see the gun. I reached under my bed, but my fingers did not meet the box. I lay on my side and peered into the darkness. It was a sleigh bed, closed at head and foot, pushed up against the wall. I had long found that this dark, protected space attracted all kinds of small objects, ranging from marbles to watches to cravats. I did not remember exactly where I had left the gun—toward the head? Toward the foot? I crept along the floor on my belly, groping for a hard corner with my outstretched hand. I swept from foot to head and back again. The box was not there.

I slithered a few inches closer to see if my eyes could penetrate the gloom. A shaft of evening sun raking in from the western window hit the foot of the bed, and a thin line of light glowed beneath the mattress, making the rest of the low space darker. Nevertheless, I could see nothing there at all, not even a film of dust.

I sat back onto my heels, then stood up. Downstairs, Marguerite was placing dinner plates on the table. I moved the chair over to the armoire and climbed up on it, reaching out to feel the top shelf. Just as the dinner bell rang, my fingers brushed a familiar shape. Somehow, the gun had been moved from beneath my bed to its accustomed hiding place.

I changed my clothes quickly and arrived at the dinner table at the same time as Paul. He asked whether I had seen Vincent, and I found myself absolutely unable to discuss my friend. I boldly pretended that I had not. I am normally a wretched liar, but on this occasion I believe I was convincing. Paul spent the rest of the meal speculating on the likelihood of catching an enormous perch that he had spotted by a weir upstream. My mind, of course, was elsewhere.

Who had moved the box? Did they know it contained a gun? Did it still contain the gun? I hadn't opened it—perhaps the weapon was missing! Why had it been moved? Would anyone attach any significance to it? What significance *could* it have?

It would have none, unless it was used.

Naturally as soon as we had finished the meal I made an excuse to return to my room. I climbed once again onto the chair and pulled the box down from the top shelf of the armoire. The gun was inside. So were the cartridges. I pushed the box under the bed again and went back downstairs for coffee.

Later that night, I loaded the little revolver. I slipped it into the pocket of the blue linen coat I had been wearing when Vincent painted me. I left the house quietly, walked to Ravoux's, and tiptoed into the shed. I put the gun on the table, over the spot where Vincent had scratched his cry of despair.

Seventeen

It took me a long time to get home. At every step I considered going back. My strength ebbed and flowed so that I might be able to walk steadily for a dozen paces then find myself unable to drag a foot another inch along the powdery road. When I came to the pasture where the plow horse César lived, I clung to the fence as if a strong tide threatened to suck me away. I was glad it was a dark night, for a villager glancing through his window would have been amazed at the spectacle of Dr. Gachet, panting and sweating as he staggered along the rue Rémy. The stone steps up to the house, when I reached it, rose so steeply that I paused and sat down near the bottom. I remembered that first day when Madame Chevalier had answered the door and I had heard her footsteps along with Vincent's climbing these steps. I put my head in my hands. Would it have been better for Vincent if he had never rung our bell?

I imagined the gun, lying where I had left it. It would still be there. If I were not an old man, heat-stricken and exhausted, I could go back and get it. Yet even as I considered this, I saw again the image of Vincent, wild-eyed in his shabby straw hat. What I had done was the only thing I could do for him.

Eventually I became uncomfortable. The stone steps dug into my legs. My feet ached and stung. The garden around me rustled, full of tiny nocturnal dramas as insects and birds and field mice and cats all went about their business, attempting to kill, or to stay alive through the night. A pair of green eyes glowed momentarily farther up the steps, and I thought I recognized Louloutte's bulk in the starlight, but she had no time for a mere human. She was on the prowl and I was no prey for her—prey only to my own thoughts, regrets, imagination. I rose stiffly to climb the steps into the house. If I bathed my feet in cool water, they might feel better. I could accomplish that much.

When I entered the house, I heard only Madame Chevalier's snores coming from her small chamber on the third floor. Thus when I pushed open the door to my bedroom, I was startled to see a figure sitting on my bed. I nearly lost my grip on the basin of water I had brought from the kitchen, but Marguerite, ever the little housekeeper, leapt up and seized it before it could hit the tile floor. Much of the water had slopped over, so there was a confusing moment of mopping and whispering and setting the basin down in a safe corner before I could ask her why she was still awake.

We were standing in the dark. Marguerite lit the candle on my washstand. When the flame caught, I saw the box that had contained my gun on my bed. The leather pouch of cartridges lay next to it. The box was open, empty. The padded interior had been shaped to cradle the weapon; in the gold, flickering light, there was a dark, gun-shaped cavity in the box.

Marguerite looked up at me, with fear and puzzlement mingled on her face. "What have you done with it, Papa?"

I sat on—no, collapsed into—the mattress beside the box. "How did you know about this?" I asked, touching the goatskin padding. I remembered having the box made back in 1871, for this gun, which I considered my spoils of war. It was the kind of foolish extravagance a younger man indulges in.

Marguerite shook her head slightly with the look of exasperated pity I had occasionally seen on Blanche's face. It was the expression of a woman confronted by a man's folly. "I sweep under your bed, you know. If I didn't . . ." Her voice trailed off. I was supposed to grasp the consequences of not sweeping under a bed.

"But . . . ?" I gestured at the armoire.

"Madame Chevalier and I do not touch your study, but we do turn out the rest of the house in spring and in fall. What did you do with the gun?"

My mind was whirling again. It had been such a long day, so much walking and thinking, so much agitation! What could I tell Marguerite? What did she know, what did she understand? My hands lifted feebly from my lap and dropped again.

Marguerite stood in front of me, holding the candle. Her hand was starting to tremble. "Where . . . what did you do with it?"

"Why are you here?" I countered. "Why not asleep, as usual? What is this to you?"

"Papa, I am *worried*," she suddenly said. Whispered, rather—for this whole exchange took place at half voice. "Paul said Vincent is going mad again. He did not tell you—he spoke with Vincent up on the plateau. He said Vincent looked wild, and was sitting up there *not* painting. And Vincent said he couldn't paint anymore and there was no future for him." She set the candle down on the washstand and raised her hands to her eyes.

I stood and drew her to me. She stood stiffly, her forehead just touching my shoulder. Even so, her tears soaked right through my linen coat and my shirt. She was trying to muffle her sobs.

"Come, let's go downstairs," I whispered. "No need to wake everyone." I picked up the candle and took my daughter's hand and led her to my study. She followed, unresisting, brushing the tears from her cheeks with the back of her hand.

I took a cushion from the stiff settee and placed it in the armchair before guiding Marguerite to sit. I thought about a lamp, but it seemed this conversation might go better with less light.

"So you're fond of Vincent," I said. "And—Paul's tale concerned you?"

"Paul said he was talking . . ." The tears began again. "I can't even . . . Madame Chevalier says it's a sin. . . . You couldn't . . . He wouldn't. . . ." Sobs alternated with words.

What could I say? What was most urgent here? I could not tell. Marguerite's grief? Her affection, whatever it was, for Vincent? His madness, his longing for escape? I knew I could not begin with the gun.

I tried to soothe her, to hush her. She was twenty-one, after all. Paul was still young enough to be callous about Vincent, I supposed. He might see Vincent's madness as a joke. For Marguerite, it was real.

"He *saw* me, Papa. He painted you, you know how it is. Monsieur Vincent really *looked* at me. At *me*." Her eyes welled again.

It was so simple. He had looked at her. He saw her. Did I? I saw a daughter, pretty enough, accomplished enough to be proud of. To me, she was useful to have around, an excellent cook, a formidable housekeeper, but perhaps no more than that. Vincent saw something in her that I had missed.

To this day I do not know what this meant to Marguerite, and I am grateful. Did she imagine that she loved him, that he loved her? Had they formed a bond I failed to perceive?

I took a different tack. "Paul is very young," I said, trying to make my voice reassuring. "I doubt that he understands Vincent's situation. It is sad. You may weep as much as you like for our friend Vincent. When he came here, I thought that I could make him better, happier. It seems now that I was wrong."

"But you are a *doctor*," Marguerite cried. My eyes flew to the door, to check that it was closed. Waking the entire household would be disastrous.

"I am," I agreed. "But illnesses of the mind are stubborn. We do not yet know how to cure many of them. And Vincent's life has been hard. He has used up his resilience, I think."

Marguerite was watching me, still sniffling a bit. I understood so little about her. Did my words mean anything to her? I didn't know. But I went on, hoping to make her understand. "Vincent's brother Theo is very ill. Vincent knows this. Theo pays for Vincent's room and board with Ravoux, and buys his canvases and paints. Nobody buys Vincent's paintings, so he has no way to earn money. If Theo dies, Vincent will be alone. He will have no brother, and no money."

Once again Marguerite's eyes welled. "But Madame van Gogh! And the poor little baby! No father!"

I let her weep for the baby. The baby's case was sad. Vincent's, I thought, was tragic.

Minutes passed. I stood up and patted Marguerite's back. I went to the kitchen and poured a glass of water, then added a few drops of valerian cordial. I brought it back and held it out to her. She took a sip, and then a deep breath.

"But the gun? What about the gun, Papa?"

There it was. The gun. I felt as if Marguerite and I had begun a voyage. Somehow, before morning, I had to help my daughter traverse a terrible landscape, one that Vincent could have painted in his bleakest moments, I thought. But he hadn't—his landscapes were full of sunlight and shadow, or stars or rain or a glowing, haloed moon. And they were always brilliant with color. Not his early paintings of Holland, but his later ones of France were intense and vivid and bright. What I saw ahead of Marguerite and me that night was a prospect of umber and black and stony, bleak emptiness. Vincent's cypress trees would whirl in shades of chalk and charcoal, his rocky hillocks squat frowning in murky, charred brown and gray. There would be no light.

When you are twenty-one, your life *is* hope. That is what it consists of: hope for the future. Everything in you looks ahead to successes and pleasures still to come. To make my daughter forgive my action I had to force her to relinquish hope, at least for that night. She must be made to comprehend the misery and futility Vincent felt. To retain Marguerite's love, I had to introduce her to despair. It was Vincent's art that made this possible—a last gift to me.

"You know Vincent's paintings as well as anyone now," I said. "You have the great good fortune to own one. What does that painting make you feel?"

It was the right question to ask. Marguerite took a breath and looked away from me. Her eyes were fixed, unseeing, and I could tell that she was summoning her portrait to her mind. "I feel that I am pretty," she said. "Elegant, accomplished. That the familiar things around me are beautiful. The walls, the floor—they are ordinary really. But I have spent so much time studying the way Vincent painted them. I run my fingers over the heavy paint of the skirt—gently, very gently. And I feel that I am part of something. None of your other artist friends ever wanted to paint me. And even though I don't understand all of your conversations with Vincent, I know that his painting is something new. And that you believe in it."

"And the landscapes he has painted here: do they make you feel happy?"

"Oh, yes. He sees the beauty all around. And that makes me see it."

"Yes, that is what I think, too," I said. I was sitting at my desk, but that was too far away from my daughter. I moved over to the settee and sat against the tall arm, almost facing her. "So perhaps you can imagine this." She seemed to be following me intently. "Imagine Vincent without that ability. He has not been able to paint for days. He feels . . ." I paused for a moment, searching for words. "Despair, I suppose. Fear. One might even say terror. His spells, my dear Marguerite, are truly horrifying. He fears they will come again. And I think, if our friend Vincent were to paint again, he would have to paint something like this: a bleak, barren landscape, rocky, blighted. Can you see it?"

It was a risk. I did not know if Marguerite could do this. I could see this vision so clearly; while the words came to me, the image appeared as on a canvas in my head.

"Yes, Papa, I think I can. Vincent's colors are always so bright, but perhaps the color would be drained away?"

"Drained. Yes. And the forms . . . You have seen some of his cypress trees?"

"Yes," Marguerite went on. She raised her hands and made a twisting gesture. "Like flames. But also like knots."

"And the branches of the low, stunted shrubs, and the roots climbing out of the ground, all clotted and warped together—"

"And no sky?"

"No. No sky," I agreed. "No—in fact, I think that what Vincent sees is a high horizon, a hill before him without a path, and above him only the clouds of a storm, a heavy, menacing gray."

"Lightning?"

"Perhaps. I have never seen him paint lightning, but his attacks may feel like that . . ."

"Walking toward lightning, then," Marguerite concluded, in a flat voice. She looked at me.

"Through a drab and hostile landscape," I added. "Alone. Vincent feels very much alone." She was quiet. She looked down at her hands in her lap. This, I could see, was a difficult notion to accept. Perhaps, in Marguerite's dreams, she had been part of Vincent's life.

She sighed, then said, "But you have been his friend."

"That is not enough, it seems."

We were both silent for a few minutes.

"And the gun?"

I was suddenly overcome by the magnitude of what I had done. What could I have been thinking? In a flash I could envision the outcome: more tears, grief, regret. Yet it was done. I felt a sudden hollowness.

"I left it in the shed," I told her. My eyes did not meet hers.

"So that he might use it on himself," she stated.

I nodded. "If he chooses. I did not want him to try something else, and fail." I watched her as I said this. I could not explain further.

"Did he ask you? For help?"

"No. He is a brave man. Or perhaps I should say proud. I have not known him to ask for help in anything."

"He did not ask you to do this?"

"No."

She was quiet then. I did not know what she thought. We never spoke about this again. Marguerite has remained the quiet, efficient housekeeper, speaking little, revealing nothing. From time to time, when I pass the open door of her bedroom, I see that a small nosegay of wildflowers has been placed on a table beneath Vincent's portrait of her.

A shrine, in effect. She has not married. She remains affectionate toward me, but sometimes I believe I discern a flavor of disapproval. I will not deny that this pains me.

But that night, she did not move away from my arm. We sat side by side in the quiet room as the candle sputtered and went out. Eventually the darkness outside the window grew thinner, and we went up to bed.

Eighteen

∞

It was hot again the next day. The sun beat down on us like a hammer on an anvil. To my surprise, I had been able to sleep for a few hours, but I felt slow and gritty-eyed all day.

The messenger I had been awaiting and fearing came in the evening, just as the sun finally set. When I heard the bell sound, I knew what had happened, but I waited until Madame Chevalier called me to the door. It was a boy from the inn, who told me that Vincent had shot himself. He had walked back to the inn from the fields and managed to stumble to his room, but Ravoux was worried when he did not come down to supper. He went upstairs and found Vincent lying on his bed. Vincent told the innkeeper what he had done, and asked for me.

I picked up my emergency bag and called for Paul. I sent him sprinting ahead to tell Ravoux that we were on our way, while I hurried at the much slower pace of a sixty-two-year-old man, accompanied by the boy from the inn, who warned me that there was a lot of blood. Vincent could still speak, he said, and Dr. Mazery would meet us there.

I took the stairs as fast as I could and was breathless when I stood in the doorway of Vincent's garret. The room reeked of blood. It is an unmistakable odor, sharp and metallic. The chamber had already been transformed into a sickroom. Vincent's cot had been pulled away from the wall to permit access to both sides. Lamps had been brought up and placed on every surface, a basin of water and reddened towels lay beneath the bed, and a carafe stood on Vincent's table. His paintings and a pair of Japanese prints still hung on the walls but seemed to recede into the gloom, as if abashed at their own beauty and vivacity.

I liked Mazery—he was a burly, bearded man with a simple outlook. He stood up and shook my hand. He did not say anything beyond a few words of greeting, but his frown and the slight shake of his head made his opinion clear: The patient was in a critical state.

Vincent was watching me. He lay almost flat, covered by a tattered blanket. The left half of it was sodden, heavy with his blood. I put down my case and lowered myself into the chair that Mazery had vacated. "I shot myself," he said, in a low voice.

"May I see?" I asked. He nodded, a tiny movement. I pulled back the blanket.

Mazery had already cleaned and bandaged the injury. It was a surprisingly tidy bullet wound: a small, dark circle at the edge of the ribs, surrounded by a larger halo of dark bruising. Blood was still welling from it, but not with the arterial pulses that would have made this a crisis. I reached for my case, but Mazery forestalled me by passing over his stethoscope. Vincent's pulse was regular, and his heartbeat revealed no anomalies. If he had tried to destroy his heart with a bullet, he had failed. I could not get a clear sound from his lungs. Perhaps there was fluid in the thoracic cavity. His breath was slightly shallow, but calm. If the bleeding could be stopped, if no infection set in, if the digestive organs had not been harmed . . . The doctor in me wanted the patient to live: the friend wanted to let him go.

"Are you in any pain?" I asked Vincent, bending over his chest. Listening carefully, I tapped here and there, palpating his organs as I had done the first time I examined him.

"No. A little. Just there, where the bullet went in." His left hand came up slightly, as if to point to it.

"Could you drink some water?" I asked, straightening up. I began to replace the dressing, using fresh lint.

"Why?"

"You might be more comfortable."

"Oh." He seemed to dismiss the thought, and closed his eyes. "Might I smoke?" he asked, without opening them.

"I see no reason why not," I answered, looking at Mazery for confirmation. "Your lungs do not seem to be affected. Let me finish this bandage and I will give you your pipe." It was hard to secure the wrapping: I had to slip my hand beneath Vincent's back to wind it around. I did not want to raise him, lest the bullet should move.

"The bleeding seems to have slowed," I said to Mazery. "Shall we see if there is a clean cover for our patient?" Together we lifted the sodden blanket from him and rolled the bloody section into the middle.

"Paul!" I called down the stairs. "Ask Monsieur Ravoux for a clean blanket, and come up here to sit with Vincent for a moment." His light step sounded on the stair. He looked anxious. Well, it was natural enough. I had not been thinking clearly when I brought him with me; the boy had no experience of such scenes. He held a coarse cotton quilt in his hands, and I took it from him. "Wait just a moment," I told him. "Let me put this over Vincent and make him more comfortable before you go to sit with him."

Mazery had cut off Vincent's shirt but left his trousers. The blood that had soaked into them had dried already to a hard crust, fusing them to his legs. Perhaps we would remove them later. I settled the quilt over him, checking the bandage quickly. It was not yet saturated. "Paul will sit with you for a moment while I confer with Dr. Mazery," I said.

Vincent looked me in the eye. Summoning his energy, he said, "Doctor, if I have failed, I will just have to do it all over again." I stood still for a moment looking down at him. The day before, he had seemed desperate. It had not been hard to believe that he was on the verge of mad-ness. Now he spoke as calmly as if he referred to a mundane project that must be completed to his satisfaction. There was no way to answer him. I went to the door and beckoned Paul to come in.

Mazery and I moved down the narrow hall into an empty bedroom to discuss our patient. We paused for a moment, faces lit by the candle Mazery was holding. There was very little to say. "The heart does not seem to be affected," I offered.

"Nor the lungs, I think. He has not coughed."

"Should he be moved?" I asked.

"To a larger room, with better light, possibly," Mazery said. "Though I don't believe there is one, short of Ravoux's own bedroom."

"No, I suppose not." I looked around at the cracked plaster on the walls nearby.

We were silent. Mazery knew as well as I how powerless we were. I have read since then of remarkable images from inside the body, pro-duced by a kind of camera. Such a camera might have helped us to lo-cate the bullet. I know, too, that most hospitals now perform surgery under circumstances of the most scrupulous hygiene, and that incidence of infection in wounds has been drastically reduced. So perhaps today a patient might survive an invasion of the thoracic cavity. But we were just a pair of provincial doctors in the attic of a village inn. These meth-ods were not available to us. It would have taken a miracle to keep Vin-cent alive.

I was grateful for that. We could, in good conscience, let the man die, as he so plainly wanted to do. "So we will keep him quiet," I suggested, "and hope to control the bleeding?" Mazery nodded. "What do you think about feeding him?" I asked. "A little broth, perhaps?"

"At most. Best not to strain his digestion for a day or two. Is there anything you want to give him, Doctor? A remedy for pain? He seems calm enough."

I shook my head. "I do not believe there is a remedy for this kind of situation," I said.

When we returned to the room, it was silent. Paul was sitting by the bed, looking pinched and pale. Vincent lay gazing at the ceiling. Only the slight movement of his chest gave away that he was still alive. His voice came, though, thready but commanding: "My pipe, Doctor?"

"Of course," I answered. "Wait for me outside," I whispered to Paul, who slipped out of the room like a shadow. "Dr. Mazery, would you like to go home? I will stay with Monsieur van Gogh. Or I may have my son keep watch, if you have no objection. He can alert you quickly if there is any need."

"Certainly, colleague," he said, with a bow of the head. It seemed uncharacteristically courtly, yet appropriate. The presence of death somehow calls for formality.

Vincent and I were now alone. Dark had fallen, and the skylight above his bed reflected the light from the room. "May I put out one of these lamps?" I asked. "They give off so much heat." He lifted a few fingers as if to say, "As you like." His stained jacket, made of the blue cotton twill worn by plumbers, hung on a hook by the table. I had often seen him take his pipe from the breast pocket, so I reached into it. My fingers curled around the pipe's familiar shape. I felt the left-hand pocket, then the right, and retrieved his pouch of tobacco. He smoked a much rougher blend than I did, and as I lit it, the harsh smoke seared my eyes. Squinting, I crossed the room and put the pipe into his mouth. He drew on it, then exhaled. He seemed satisfied.

I snuffed two of the lamps, leaving us with only one source of light aside from the candle next to the bed. I considered opening the skylight but decided that Paul, both younger and taller than I, could accomplish that task. I slid the basin and bloody towels toward the door so they could be taken downstairs. All of these domestic tasks that have busied nurses in sickrooms the world over came easily to me. They were simpler than talking.

What would I have said, anyway? Vincent was already far away. He had his face set on a final horizon. Now that I am old, I sometimes glimpse that horizon myself, and I am not sorry. There is a restfulness to it. What happens here on earth has little significance beside the fact that one will go on alone, to whatever awaits. If, indeed, anything awaits. Jo—or Madame van Gogh Gosschalk, as I should call her—

likes to think that Vincent and Theo are together in Heaven. I fear that Jo's Heaven would be somewhat tame for Vincent, but perhaps it is a place of infinite landscapes and endless sunlight.

I sat in the chair by the bed and looked up at the ceiling to see what might be visible from Vincent's pillow. There was nothing there but the graying plaster and the skylight, now lightly veiled in smoke.

"You should have hung a painting up on the ceiling to look at as you fell asleep," I said. He did not respond, but the corners of his lips curled around the stem of the pipe. I felt strangely relaxed. After the tension of the day, it was restful to sit next to Vincent doing nothing at all. I remembered that Paul was downstairs, waiting to be summoned. I would also need to alert Theo. But I did not move. I just sat there remembering. I thought about the first time I saw him paint, and the time we made the etching. I remembered his antics with the baby and his enthusiasm for the beauty of Auvers. I remembered the ink drawing of the death's-head moth that I had seen on the letter at Jo and Theo's apartment. Nothing escaped Vincent's eye, I thought; he captured beauty wherever he found it. He had reanimated my life with his passion for art.

His genius came at too high a price, it seemed. Why should we expect a man who painted as he did to negotiate life calmly and reasonably? Maybe there was actually no medical diagnosis for a case like Vincent's. Melancholia, epilepsy, hysteria might all be irrelevant. He saw the beauty in the world and he felt the heartbreak. Maybe they were just too much for him in the end.

At any rate, Vincent had finally had his way. He was not in terrible pain. He was weak, certainly. But nothing would be required of him now except patience. I reached over to touch the bandage, slipping my hand beneath the quilt. It was soaked. I glanced back at Vincent, whose eyes were now closed. I could change the bandage, but I did not want to wake him. He would bleed to death over the next day or so. If an internal blood clot formed, it would slow the process. Such a clot might form and then dissolve, or movement might dislodge it. So could the shifting of the bullet. We had little control over the outcome. The best thing a doctor could do for Vincent van Gogh now was to make his final hours as comfortable and as pleasant as possible. This was a task I could accomplish. More, I could put my heart into it.

I stood up, and Vincent's eyes opened. "I must write to Theo," I told him. "Will a letter to Cité Pigalle reach him, or do I need the number of his apartment there?"

Vincent shook his head and closed his eyes. It didn't matter. I would send someone to Paris tomorrow to find him at the gallery. Poor Theo: It would be a terrible shock. In the meantime, I had one more duty to carry out. I summoned Paul from downstairs again, and he helped me change Vincent's bandage. We got a towel from Ravoux and draped it over Vincent's side, beneath the quilt. The innkeeper was terribly anxious and eager to do whatever he could to save his guest. I tried to soothe him, but all that I could find to say was that Vincent was resting.

I looked back from the door, on my way out. Vincent lay still. Paul sat gazing at him. He turned and met my gaze. "Is there anything I should do?" he whispered.

I shook my head. "I'm quite sure he will have a quiet night. Tomorrow will be more difficult, so I must go home and sleep. If there should be any change, if Vincent feels pain, if he starts to bleed more, or to cough, get Monsieur Ravoux to sit here and run like the wind to fetch me. You are here because you have the swiftest feet among us—and because you have been a friend to Vincent," I told Paul. I saw him sit a little bit taller and wished that I could remember, more often, to praise him.

There was none of the customary song in the bar downstairs. Vincent had kept a distance from most of the inhabitants of Auvers, aside from painting a few children and young women. He had probably known none of the men who sat uneasily at the café tables, muttering quietly to each other. But when I stepped into the room to tell Ravoux that I was leaving, everyone fell silent.

"I am going home," I said, making my voice loud enough to carry across the room. "My son, Paul, is upstairs with Monsieur van Gogh. I think Monsieur van Gogh will be comfortable enough tonight, but in the morning his brother must be sent for."

Ravoux was wiping down the tin counter, and his arm halted in its sweep. "What a terrible thing, Doctor. He was a quiet man, never difficult. Will he recover?"

"I don't know," I admitted. "Dr. Mazery and I will do our best, but he is bleeding terribly."

"We'll say a prayer for him," came a voice from the back of the room, followed by murmurs of agreement.

"Yes, do," I said. "I'm sure that will help him."

Ravoux came out from behind the counter and stepped through the door with me into the warm, moonlit night. "But what I want to know, Doctor, is where did he get the gun?"

I tried to look puzzled. "I can't imagine, Ravoux. He barely knows a soul here, besides you and me. It could not have come from us. Perhaps he brought it with him from the South."

"I suppose that must be it," Ravoux said, nodding at my apparent wisdom. "I have heard they're hot-blooded down there. So you really think he'll die?"

"I do," I said, relieved to be honest. "Mazery and I can't do much to save him. And you know how it is, Ravoux, when a man really wants to die."

"Of course. We see it all the time in the old ones, don't we? Just get tired and stop. Not a bad thing, really. But he was so young."

"Yes," I agreed. "That's what makes it hard for the rest of us. I'll be back early in the morning, unless Paul comes for me in the night."

I walked away. The moon was full, and it gave off so much light that my shadow glided before me, a sharp outline with a hole of light in one side, where I held my lantern. I lifted my left hand so that the lantern's light obliterated most of my shadow's torso. That was where Vincent had shot himself, with the gun I had given him.

I dropped my hand to my side, and my shadow resumed a more manlike form. As I walked beneath trees, the shadow merged with the general blackness, leaving my lantern to shine in a golden circle. I was too old to be spending these midnight hours roaming about, but I had to go find the gun. I was certain I knew where it was.

Until I saw Vincent wounded, I hadn't considered the harm that a bullet does to a living body. Torn flesh, broken blood vessels, damaged organs, bruising, scorching, pain. Infection. The possibility of failure, of permanent incapacitation had not crossed my mind as I weighed my responsibility to my friend and patient. I could not help wondering, as I walked, what it meant that he had tried to shoot himself in the heart. Had he held the pistol at his temple and shied away from the destruction that would cause? I found myself attempting to replicate his gesture as he pressed the gun to his chest.

Then I wondered about the preceding moments. Did he walk up and down trying to steady his nerve? Had he strode up the hill this morning with the intention of killing himself? Or did he sit there, trying to paint, willing his hands to pick up the brush, to squeeze paint onto the palette? Did he seize the weapon when the tools of his trade failed him? No, it was not the tools that failed. It was something in himself. Yet I did not believe that his gesture had been a kind of punishment. His suicide was a strange form of kindness to himself. It was as if he had relented, in a way, and no longer held himself to an impossible standard. He allowed himself to be human, and mortal.

My errand this evening was to find the gun, for I feared it could be traced to me. I trusted Marguerite's discretion absolutely, yet I felt this step was urgent. Hence the spectacle of an old man pacing up a hill of wheat in the moonlight. The glossy stalks caught on my clothes as I passed, gleaming silver and black in a braided pattern, dipping and springing back as I passed. I could have been walking chest-high through an ocean.

Sometimes in dreams you cannot do what you know is necessary; your feet will not move, the door will not open. But at other times, everything is easy, and I felt that odd magical power that night. I knew just where to go: I unerringly located Vincent's camp stool and the paint box next to it. I expected to find the gun lying on the wheat nearby, and there it was. I even picked up Vincent's easel. I wanted to erase his presence from the field. This had been an unhappy spot for him. Let him be forgotten by it.

I strode down the hill with my clumsy burden, cresting the waves of grain as if under sail. A breeze had picked up, stroking huge, invisible hands across the field and stirring the topmost branches of the trees. I felt weirdly powerful. I deposited Vincent's painting equipment by the church, where it would be found and brought back to the inn. The gun I intended for the river. I followed the railroad track and threw the gun into the center of a pool where the water was deep and exceedingly murky. It has never come to light.

Nineteen

I WOKE AT DAWN. Without rousing Marguerite or Madame Chevalier, I left my house and returned to the inn, where I found Paul
sprawled on the floor next to Vincent's bed. The room smelled worse
than it had the night before, so I woke Paul up and had him open the
skylight, then sent him home to bed. Soon Ravoux came up the stairs
carrying a bowl of coffee for me, which was very kind. Another Dutch
painter was staying at the inn, a man called Anton Hirschig. I entrusted
him with the letter to Theo, and he left to catch the first train to Paris.
He would be at Boussod and Valadon before ten.

Vincent appeared to sleep through this small commotion. When Dr.
Mazery came, we changed his dressing. The wound still looked clean—
there was no redness and no swelling. The bleeding continued, but at a
slower pace. Mazery had brought some old linens, which we packed
around Vincent's side. I felt for the pulse in one of his wrists, and it was
both slow and weak. Vincent's skin tone was pallid, and the contours of

his face were sharper than ever. I calculated how long it might be before Theo could reach us; there was still plenty of time.

I spent the morning at Vincent's side. When he woke and asked for his pipe, I told him that Theo was coming. I fanned Vincent to keep the flies away, and rested in the chair next to his bed, my mind strangely idle. We heard the village wake and the voices muffled downstairs. Several hours passed. We were sitting this way when Theo arrived.

He had begun his day at the gallery, expecting nothing more taxing than the attempt to sell some paintings and the daily effort to control his ailing body. Yet here he was, in his brother's tiny garret room, dressed in his frock coat and black silk cravat, after several hours of the gravest worry. His eyes were wild, and when he saw Vincent lying with a terrible stillness beneath the pile of covers, he burst into tears. I stood up and led him to the chair. He sank instead to his knees, clasping Vincent's ivory hand to his cheek. I heard Vincent's voice very quietly say, "I did it for all of us." Then he broke into Dutch. As I left the room, I heard the two brothers murmuring to each other in the guttural language of their childhood.

The day went on. I telegraphed my concierge in Paris, canceling all of my appointments for the next few days. I went back to the house to shave properly and inform Madame Chevalier and Marguerite what had happened. Marguerite turned very pale. I assured her that Vincent was not suffering, but she ran upstairs to her room. Madame Chevalier and I exchanged glances, and she promised me that she would take care of the girl. Then I went back to the inn.

Theo appeared to nurse mistaken hope. Around the middle of the afternoon, he came downstairs to find me. I had brought a chair from the café into Vincent's shed and was dozing among the canvases. I stood up, moving the light chair closer to him. He collapsed into it.

"He seems stronger, Doctor, don't you think?" he asked. "It can't have been that grave an injury. His heart was not damaged, I believe?"

"His heart was not damaged," I answered. "But I have seen no sign that he is stronger. Rather the opposite, Monsieur van Gogh. The wound is still bleeding."

"But you have not seen him in the last hour," Theo protested. "You should go up and check on him. Mazery is with him now. He sent me down for something to eat, but of course I cannot eat. I must write a letter to Jo. She is staying with my mother in Holland. This will be a terrible blow for both of them."

"Then let us go into the café," I said, holding out a hand to help him get up. I turned him away from the shed, away from the corner of the table where I had laid a sketch pad across the frightening words Vincent had painted there.

"Come and let Ravoux give you some soup," I suggested. "I will bring you some paper, and you can write your letter to Jo. We will send Paul to mail it when you are finished."

"All right, Doctor," he conceded. "But do check on Vincent. You'll see he is rallying. He is stronger than anyone thinks."

I did check on Vincent, who seemed even more diminished. His skin was now the color of paper, and his form beneath the quilt seemed even flatter, as if his body were simply vanishing. Theo wrote his note with some difficulty, I noticed. His handwriting was inconsistent, letters variable in size and lines climbing up and downhill. I wrote the Dutch address on the outside at his direction, and we did not mention his lack of motor control. Soup had also been a poor idea: it was dribbled around where he had been sitting. I supposed that the nervous strain of Vincent's injury must have been taxing his strength.

Vincent smoked another pipe. Ravoux and I managed to get Theo to drink some tea, and later eat a bit of chicken. He seemed to accept, as the day went on, that Vincent was dying—his face grew ever more stoical, and he spoke of his brother's comfort rather than of his recovery. The temperature in the garret was wretched, but Vincent showed no sign of discomfort. We were all in our shirtsleeves, hair sticking to our faces, but he lay like marble. By evening the wound was still clean and cool. The flow of blood was very slow now, little more than a dark, sticky trickle. His heartbeat was weak, and his breaths were shallow. I turned to Theo as I listened with my stethoscope.

"His heart is very slow, I must tell you," I said. "I am afraid it will not be much longer."

Theo looked up at me. He had loosened his cravat, and he must have rubbed against Vincent's bandage, for there were rusty smears of blood on one of his sleeves. "There was really nothing you could have done, Doctor, was there?"

"Nothing," I said. "No one could have saved him." Theo kept his gaze on my face, perhaps waiting for more. But I had nothing left to say.

When I arrived at the inn just after seven the next morning, Vincent was gone. Theo lay next to him in the bed, his arms wrapped around his brother's body, but he was not asleep. When I stepped into the room, Theo said, "It was a good end. He said, 'I wish I could die like this,' and then he breathed his last."

Grief overwhelmed me in a hot wave. My hands came up to my face, and I found myself crouching next to the bed. Tears poured down my cheeks and my chin, and I watched them spatter the dusty floor. I had known Vincent would die. I had been glad for him. But now that he was gone, I wept.

We knew, all of us who had known Vincent were certain, that we would never have another friend like him. Surely Theo spoke truly when he called his brother "impossible." I had caught glimpses of his stubbornness and unreason. Yet he was generous and brilliant, and he had the rare quality of knowing exactly what he was meant to do in life. His circumstances had not helped him, but he pressed on, following his calling. Perhaps his sense of conviction drew people to him because we all wished for a share of it. Perhaps that made his death that much more of a blow.

As the day unrolled, we were busy. We had to certify the death at the town hall, to notify friends in Paris. Vincent would be buried the next day in the new cemetery up on the hill. I offered to arrange for the grave and to order the coffin, in part to spare Theo the need to leave the inn. The priest refused to loan the church's hearse to convey Vincent's body to his resting place, since his death was a suicide. We were all so stunned with sorrow that we barely perceived the insult. Paul and Hirschig were sent to borrow a hearse from the neighboring village of Méry.

Toward evening the carpenter Levert let us know that the coffin was finished. The heat had abated somewhat, and Theo was lying down in Ravoux's best room. We did not want to transfer Vincent's body until

Theo was awake, and I would not let him be disturbed. I went upstairs, glad of a respite myself, and sat down next to Vincent's bed.

The body had been washed, the bloodied bedding taken away. They had dressed Vincent in his best clothes, a white shirt and a pair of brown trousers. Someone, perhaps Madame Ravoux, had washed and starched the shirt to a brilliant white. Vincent's skin looked waxy next to it. His brow was furrowed, even in death. My hand came up to try to smooth the lines from his face, but I stopped myself.

The skylight was open, and the sounds from downstairs drifted to me as they had on that night when I visited Vincent. Ravoux had insisted that Vincent's body be placed in the café itself, and Paul had the brilliant notion that we hang Vincent's canvases around the walls. I heard hammering, and furniture being moved. Horses clopped past, and someone emptied a bucket into the street. Vincent's room was silent.

I noticed that his table had been tidied, with the papers and pens and bits of charcoal and pencils and notebooks all laid out in rows and stacks. I got up to examine this unfamiliar arrangement, created by hands other than Vincent's. There were several blank sheets of letter paper next to the candlestick, and without thinking I picked them up. I found a cardboard folder to support the paper and examined the charcoal, choosing the largest piece. Then I sat down again, facing the bed, and began to draw Vincent.

I had considered making a sketch of Blanche on her deathbed. I had done so for my young nephew who died in 1873, and his parents were happy to have a last portrayal of him. Blanche, though, was so ravaged by her last days that it would have broken my heart to look at her with that kind of scrutiny. Maybe a deathbed portrait is just an attempt to delay a farewell, to spend a little bit more time with a loved one. Vincent's face was so well known to me, yet this was my last chance to fix it in my memory.

Vincent lay on his back, in three-quarters profile to me. I made a bold line for the contour of his forehead, and drew in the two shallow curves of his eyebrows. Another firm line formed his nose, and already I could see his face taking shape. It was so strange, though, to try to depict Vincent without color. He had seen the world in terms of the full spectrum. On the other hand, perhaps charcoal and paper were the right materials for this task. The room was becoming gloomy as the light faded outside. The brilliant canvases had already been taken downstairs. Vincent's skin was pale as ivory in death—color, for the time being, had vanished.

I used a few thick strokes of the charcoal to indicate the hair at his temple and the top of his head, then made two curved marks for the ear—the damaged ear. It did not look anything like an ear. I quickly made a few horizontal lines to show where the pillow was.

A better artist than I would have been able to convey the lights and shadows on Vincent's face. I used the side of the charcoal to indicate the hollow of his cheek. I rubbed with my thumb, hoping to turn the marks into what was more obviously a shadow.

Vincent had made this all look easy. When he made the etching of me, I remembered his saying that he had already considered my face as a pattern of lights and darks, so that it would be relatively simple to etch onto the plate. And he had done it so simply, so clearly. Now I looked at his closed eyes, and hesitated. I kept telling myself to see simply dark and light, but it was not that simple.

As my charcoal roved over the page, I felt as though I was touching Vincent's skin. I drew a series of parallel lines to indicate the furrows in his forehead. There is a popular notion that the dead are at rest, yet Vincent did not look tranquil. I could not help reaching over to smooth away those creases, but they remained.

I sat still for a moment, hoping to regain control of my emotions, then I leaned forward and put the portrait on the bed, beside Vincent's body. So much for my attempt to dispassionately record the truth. I don't know how long I sat there weeping, though it could not have been long. The light had not changed when I heard a faltering step outside the door. I straightened and began to hunt in my pockets for a handkerchief. I had to give up and wipe my cheek with my cuff, a gesture that took me back to my childhood. I felt Theo's hand on my shoulder. I tried to stand up, but he pressed me back into the chair. Instead he sat on the bed by Vincent's side. He picked up my sketch, and for a moment his eyes filled, too. But he recovered faster than I had from the rush of grief.

"It's for you," I said. "There is nothing else I can do."

He smiled briefly at me, then looked at his brother's body. Vincent's hands had been clasped on his chest. Theo lay his left hand on both of them. "We all did what we could, Doctor. I cannot think what else would have helped him. He had an unfinished letter in his pocket—did you know?" I shook my head. "He said . . ." Theo reached into his trousers pocket and drew out a folded piece of paper. He unfolded it and read, "As for my work, I put my life at stake for it and my reason has almost foundered. Well, that's that." He folded the letter and put it back into his pocket. There did not seem to be anything else to say. He leaned forward and put a hand very gently against Vincent's cheek. Then he stood up. "I have some letters to write. Thank you for making that drawing."

"Do not overtax yourself," I said. "Tomorrow will be harrowing."

He nodded. "I am conserving my strength." I heard his slow, uneven footsteps go down the stairs.

I picked up the drawing, and the charcoal, which had rolled to the floor. Quickly, before I could think about it, I deepened the down-turning line of Vincent's lips and drew the fold running from the edge of his nose. I shaded his lower lip and emphasized his chin. And there it was, Vincent's angular face.

I made a copy of the drawing before giving it to Theo—much as Vincent had copied my portrait for me. We were paired in that way. I have to say that it was not a beautiful image. I have made other pictures—paintings, etchings—that are more pleasant to look at. But this sketch came close to a kind of truth. That was all I was trying for.

We buried Vincent on July 30. His paintings hanging on the walls of Ravoux's café transformed the room. To stand in its center surrounded by such visions was almost blinding. You could tell by the reactions of the handful of men who came for the funeral. Vincent had always felt alone in the world, yet there was his friend the painter Emile Bernard, there was Lucien Pissarro representing his father, Camille; there was even old Père Tanguy, who had closed his shop to pay tribute to Vincent. One by one they stepped over the threshold from the main street, and then they halted in the doorway, astounded. I saw Tanguy studying all of the paintings as if committing them to memory. Some of the men wept, but often they smiled through their tears, for there was joy on the walls. It is easy to forget, especially for those of us who witnessed his last days, that Vincent found delight in what he saw around him, and he brought it to his paintings.

I tried to say that at his grave. We were a small procession following the hearse, no more than a dozen. In addition to those who had come from Paris, there were men from the neighborhood: Ravoux and his son, Levert the carpenter, others who must have seen Vincent roaming the fields.

I wanted so much to pay tribute to Vincent. I wanted to be sure that everyone there understood how faithful he was to his own mission. There was little talking as we trudged up the hill beside the church. Somehow Theo found the strength to follow the coffin and accept condolences without betraying any more weakness than one would ascribe to a grieving man. It was no cooler, though a dry breeze whisked around us. The cemetery is surrounded by wheat fields—we were in the very center of one of Vincent's pictures. "How he would have loved to paint this," Paul murmured as we watched the shifting tones of gold and ocher dancing to the blue horizon.

I told them that. I stood by Vincent's grave and said, "Those of us who knew Vincent van Gogh will always see the world through his eyes. These fields and these skies are his world, but so are the riverbanks of Paris and the hills of Montmartre and the cypresses of the South." I could feel my throat tightening. I looked at the knot of dark-clad men, bare heads bowed in the brilliant sun. I looked at the grave, freshly dug. The rich soil was already drying at the edges in the warm air. I looked down at the simple coffin and thought of my friend Vincent, the painter, the patient I had hoped to save. "He was a great artist," I said, "and he cared deeply about mankind. His art will keep his name alive, I think we all know this." I took out my handkerchief and mopped my eyes. "There is not a man here who will not remember this day and the genius of Vincent van Gogh," I managed to choke out. I suppose those were enough words; they were the only ones I could speak. Theo followed me with similar emotion, then the earth was shoveled back onto the coffin. We had all brought with us some of the flowers that decked the bier at Ravoux's. I had sent Paul out to gather sunflowers that morning: none grow in my gardens, but I knew how much Vincent loved them. Paul had returned with a bouquet that filled his arms. I laid the flowers next to the headstone. I will always see in my mind's eye those heavy yellow blooms nestled against the gray stone. Vincent would have loved to paint them.

Epilogue

∞

WE DID OUR BEST to help Theo pack up Vincent's things. The contents of the garret room would barely have filled a carpet bag, but they were all so worn and battered that Theo did not bother to take them back to Paris. What use could there have been for the faded blue plumber's jacket? I did see Theo carefully wrap Vincent's pipe in a handkerchief and slip it into the pocket of his frock coat. I could imagine this relic taking a place of honor in the Van Gogh flat in Paris.

The paintings and the drawings presented a problem. Theo had hundreds of them already, tucked into every spare corner of his apartment and stacked in Tanguy's attic. He gave many of them to those of us who had known Vincent in Auvers: Ravoux, Levert, and Hirschig were among those who accepted these mementos. He was exceedingly generous to Paul and to me, all but pressing canvases into our hands, but we insisted that he ship most of them back to Paris.

We all wanted very much to find a way to exhibit Vincent's work after his death. How better to commemorate his life? Theo approached several dealers, but none was prepared to take the risk of hanging Vincent's startling canvases. Ultimately he rented a larger flat in his building and persuaded Emile Bernard to select a fraction of Vincent's output to hang on the walls there. Thus he and Jo lived surrounded by Vincent's visions, and those artists and dealers adventurous enough to accept this new view of the world could see the paintings there. A biography was envisioned as well, drawing on the hundreds of letters that Theo had so carefully saved.

Yet before this effort came to fruition, Theo's illness entered its final stage. He wrote to me complaining of dizziness, and also suffered from hallucinations and nightmares. Early in October this calm, loving man attempted to attack Johanna and the baby. Jo's brother notified me, and we managed to find Theo a place in a Parisian nursing home that specialized in cases like his. There was some initial improvement, but soon he was completely irrational and Jo had no choice but to take him to Holland. He died in a Utrecht clinic in January 1891.

Johanna married again, but she has never wavered in her loyalty to her brother-in-law. She has sold some of his paintings and has loaned others to exhibitions. It seems that art lovers, especially in Germany, are gradually coming to understand Vincent's particular genius. I like to think that his most extravagant hopes may someday be fulfilled, and that thoughtful people will find his work both touching and beautiful.

Of course I think every day about the part I played in Vincent's death. I did not understand at the time to what extent the way one dies can color people's memories of the way one lived. I have always remembered Blanche's astounding courage in the face of her dreadful death. She met pain without distress. If I had helped her to die, I would never have seen this strength in her. After her death, I perceived that strength in everything she had done as my wife.

Yet curiously I see a kind of strength and courage in Vincent's suicide—the very opposite of Blanche's stoicism. I have never regretted leaving the gun for him to find. In fact, I sometimes think it was the finest thing I ever did.

Author's Note

IN THE SPRING OF 2005 I was sitting in the art history library at Columbia University, reading a biography of a nineteenth-century French printmaker named Charles Méryon. He was the subject of the thesis I was writing to complete a master's degree in art history. Méryon struggled with madness, and his family had him committed to the insane asylum at Charenton, outside Paris. I was intrigued to read that one of his visitors in 1866 was a doctor named Gachet, a physician who was interested in both art and mental illness. I remembered that Van Gogh had painted a Dr. Gachet. I wondered if Méryon's Gachet was the same as Van Gogh's. He was. I became fascinated by this doctor who befriended artists at a time when art was changing so radically, and who cared for the mentally ill at a time when that field was being redefined as well.

In the course of researching and writing this novel, I grew very fond of Van Gogh. I learned a great deal about the early treatment of madness. (There is a whole subset of Van Gogh scholarship devoted to post-mortem diagnosis. I suspect he suffered from some combination of epilepsy and bipolar disorder, but writers have made cases for third-stage syphilis, schizophrenia, porphyria, and absinthe poisoning among other ailments.) I became familiar with the huge field of Van Gogh studies and thought a lot about suicide, madness, and genius.

The first thing I want to know when I finish reading a historical novel is How much of that was true? To answer that question, I have to say something about the primary sources for Dr. Gachet and Vincent van Gogh. Vincent was well read, trilingual, and a brilliant writer. He was also separated from the people most important to him for much of his life as a painter and thus wrote over nine hundred letters. Within a few years of the Van Gogh brothers' deaths, Johanna van Gogh began the immense project of reading and sorting the correspondence for publication. The first edition, in Dutch and French, was published in 1914–15. An English translation appeared in 1958. In October 2009, the Van Gogh Museum in Amsterdam unveiled its new edition of the correspondence, known as the Van Gogh Letters Project. All of the letters were newly transcribed and translated. They can be read online at http://vangoghletters.org/vg/. Each letter is accompanied by a facsimile, footnotes, and thumbnails of every image Van Gogh refers to, whether his own work or that of painters he admired. The letters that Dr. Gachet reads in *Leaving Van Gogh* are my translations from the French originals. Some of Vincent's dialogue uses or paraphrases ideas from letters that are not explicitly quoted.

Dr. Gachet left a much less distinct trail. His son, Paul, is his principal historian, and Paul's reliability is often questioned. The doctor died in 1909, leaving his house and collection to his children, who remained in Auvers for the rest of their lives. In 1911 Paul married a quiet woman named Emilienne. His nephew Roger Golbéry described an eccentric household in which Marguerite and Emilienne deferred at all times to Paul's wishes. He had little use for the twentieth century, maintaining the Auvers house much as it had been in that summer of 1890. He refused to install central heating or a telephone, and only reluctantly allowed the ground floor of the house to be wired in the 1950s so that he could write at night by electric light.

Paul Gachet's great project was curating his father's collection. One of his principal efforts was a manuscript catalog of Dr. Gachet's most important paintings, drawings, and prints. According to this catalog, the doctor owned twenty-six Van Goghs, twenty-four Cézanne oils, a dozen Pissarros, as well as examples by other artists including Renoir, Monet, and Sisley. Paul Gachet *fils* published many short scholarly works in the 1950s. *Les 70 jours de van Gogh à Auvers* did not appear until 1994. It follows Van Gogh's stay in Auvers, quoting letters and discussing what paintings Vincent produced each day.

Paul Gachet is thus the primary source on his father's life. His goal at all times is to promote the importance of his father to Van Gogh, Cézanne, and the other painters he knew. He refers throughout to "Vincent" as if he had been the painter's peer rather than the seventeen-year-old son of the doctor's household. He also produced a number of artworks that seem aimed at consolidating his claim to special status in the Van Gogh saga: one, for instance, is a painting called *Auvers, from the Spot Where Vincent Committed Suicide.*

Paul Gachet is accurate about many aspects of his father's life. Dr. Gachet did serve at the Salpêtrière in 1855, he did write his thesis on melancholy, and he was Pissarro's family doctor. He did marry Blanche, and she did die in 1875, most likely of tuberculosis. The doctor did serve as a medical officer in the siege of Paris, but there is no record of his ever having possessed a gun. At this writing, we don't know what kind of gun Van Gogh used for his suicide. Nor do we know where he got it, where it vanished to, or the precise location where he shot himself. There has been occasional speculation concerning alternative explanations for his death. Some writers believe Paul Gachet (the son) knew more than he ever told.

Paul Gachet's credibility was severely questioned in the 1950s. He had until then supported his Auvers household and his scholarly pursuits by selling off his father's collection. In 1949, though, he donated the famous Van Gogh *Self-Portrait* to the Louvre along with the second version of *Portrait of Dr. Gachet*. (The first version, with the yellow books, went back to Holland with Johanna after Vincent's death, but Van Gogh had made for the doctor a second, simpler version, which remained in Auvers.) Further important donations followed in 1951 and 1954. By that time the works of Van Gogh, Cézanne, and Dr. Gachet's other painter friends were highly prized.

However, Paul Gachet had not endeared himself to the scholarly community. Although earlier in the century he had loaned works from his collection for museum exhibitions, he ceased doing so. He permitted only limited study of the paintings he owned and prohibited their reproduction. Thus, when previously little-known canvases by Van Gogh and Cézanne appeared in the collection of the French state, some critics were skeptical. Van Gogh's works had been enthusiastically forged for decades, as had Cézanne's. Paul Gachet had been a painter, as had his father, the doctor. Doubt about the authenticity of some of the Gachet holdings was expressed and has periodically resurfaced. In fact, the most current scholarship supports the authenticity of the Van Gogh paintings, though a few small Cézannes have been reattributed.

In 1954 an exhibition entitled "Van Gogh and the Painters of Auvers-sur-Oise" opened at the Orangerie in Paris. Paul Gachet wrote the introduction to the catalog. By this time Van Gogh was a huge figure in the popular imagination. Irving Stone's novel *Lust for Life*, published in 1934, had been an international bestseller. Vincente Minnelli began shooting the film version in 1955 (Dr. Gachet's garden was used as a location). Paul Gachet's stature in the art world had benefited enormously from this development; his spate of publishing in the 1950s seems closely tied to his generous donations. In 1961, the year before he died, Paul Gachet was made a *chevalier* of the Legion of Honor, a distinction that escaped his father.

In 1990, the first version of Van Gogh's *Portrait of Dr. Gachet* (with the yellow books) was auctioned at Christie's. It had been in various private collections since 1890. It fetched $82.5 million, making it the most expensive painting ever sold at the time. The buyer, Ryoei Saito, took the canvas to Japan. Its whereabouts is currently unknown.

The Gachet house in Auvers is open to the public, as is Vincent van

Gogh's attic room at the Auberge Ravoux. The former café downstairs has been restored in the style of the late nineteenth century and is now a pleasant restaurant.

Theo's body was finally brought to the cemetery in Auvers in 1914. The Van Gogh brothers now lie side by side beneath a blanket of ivy. The plateau surrounding the cemetery is still planted with wheat.

Acknowledgments

The writing of this book began several years ago while I was in graduate school, so I thank Lee Adair Lawrence for flattering me into going;
Hilary Ballon and Anne Higonnet for their encouragement; Barbara
Laux and Sue Roy for their company; and my family for their patience
when I kept talking about Walter Benjamin.

As I wrote I had help from early readers and other boosters, notably
Andrea Rounds, Alice van Straalen, Fred Bernstein, F. Paul Driscoll,
Lisa Callahan, and Katherine Fuller.

After writing, selling. I owe gratitude to Lynn Seligman, as well as to
Emma Sweeney for her enthusiasm and editorial acumen, and her colleagues Eva Talmadge and Justine Wenger.

Then publication, with remarkable solicitude and energy. Thanks
to Cindy Spiegel and Julie Grau, first of all. Mike Mezzo and Hana
Landes, Vincent La Scala and Susan M. S. Brown for shaping and

refining the manuscript. Greg Mollica for the lovely cover, Carol Cunningham for the handsome interior, and Sally Marvin for helping introduce *Leaving Van Gogh* to the world.

And none of this would have been possible without Rick, who seemed to take for granted all along that it was a worthwhile enterprise.

ABOUT THE AUTHOR

CAROL WALLACE is the author of numerous books, including *The Official Preppy Handbook*, which she co-authored. *Leaving Van Gogh* is her first historical novel. A graduate of Princeton University, Wallace received an M.A. in art history from Columbia University in 2006. The research for her M.A. thesis provided the foundation for *Leaving Van Gogh*. She lives in New York.

ABOUT THE TYPE

This book was set in Caslon, a typeface first designed in 1722 by William Caslon. Its widespread use by most English printers in the early eighteenth century soon supplanted the Dutch typefaces that had formerly prevailed. The roman is considered a "workhorse" typeface due to its pleasant, open appearance, while the italic is exceedingly decorative.